An Unwelcome Obsession

Ruby Ridgeway

ISBN-13: 9798867917944

To my family

For your endless support

Contents

Her Mother

When the images first made their way online, I was probably the only person looking at her eyes, at the spike of fear balanced there. Besides, it was only natural that I'd flinch at the sight of her curved backside, her breasts angling towards the camera. No one wants to see their daughter like that, but to the rest of the world she was a means to an end that didn't bear thinking about and no number of frantic cease and desist emails had the slightest effect. Even when they took that filth down, it would all pop up again somewhere else.

'You never know, you might be glad of the odd keepsake one day,' her grandmother suggested cheerfully. 'When your body's gone to pot and your boobs are forever getting caught in your waistband.'

'Mum!'

'What? It's true. I wish I'd had the foresight to take some nice photos of myself before I turned to mush. That was your fault,' she said aiming a gnarly finger at me.

But that's the point isn't it, I suppose? That's why these girls do it while they're shiny and new. Pert. Undamaged. Willing.

Not Emily though. It had taken that narcissist months to chip away at her self-esteem, to grind her down until she didn't have the strength to refuse anymore.

'He's never going to stop, is he?' she said. She didn't wail, she didn't yell, she barely whispered. This was who she was now. This was what he'd done to her. 'What am I going to do?'

'We're going to have to kill him,' my mother said. 'Unless anyone's got a better plan.'

251 Days Before the Murder

Her Mother

'There's someone at the door,' David declared, making no attempt to get up and answer it. I swung the kitchen cupboard shut, stretched my neck back and stared at him incredulously.

'I'm under the cat,' he said gripping him tightly and that was the rule in the house. Whoever Ginger was sitting on was relinquished of all responsibilities, domestic, moral or otherwise and so I had little choice but to abandon my half-cooked macaroni, my floury hands suspended emphatically, both for David's benefit and in case it turned out to be the window people trying to convince me there'd never been a better time to buy. Or God forbid, some bloke offering to take a chainsaw to my bushes. An intrusion and an insult in one.

Looking back of course, either option would have been preferable to finding Connor on the doorstep, although at the time it was merely an inconvenience. A surprise at best.

'Hello, Mrs Lawrence,' he beamed, taking in my flustered pretence. 'Sorry. I'm interrupting –'

'Not at all, Connor. How are you?' I grinned, genuinely because at the time I had no reason to think he was a psychopath and honestly, I was relieved I didn't have to buy anything. Or explain why I didn't want to. 'It's been ages. Come in, come in.'

He stepped over the threshold, wiped his feet on the mat and stood there twitching from one to the other. 'Is Emily in?'

His smile was sheepish and the cherry flush creeping up his cheeks stirred me into affection. She was vastly out of his league, but it was sweet that he still had a crush on her after all these years. I actually thought that. I actually thought she could do worse than Connor McGann. I knew his mum, see. That was what did it. I'd known him all his life.

'I'll give her a shout. Emily! There's someone here to see you!'

His eyes darted instinctively towards the thunder of footsteps along the landing. I raised an eyebrow and smiled again, amused by the nerves he was unable to hide behind a charade of shaky confidence. I patted his hand leaving a ghostly trace of myself behind as Emily rounded the banister, her petite silhouette swinging into sight.

'Oh. Hi,' she said, wavering where she stood. She opened her mouth again and closed it like a goldfish in a bowl, too polite to ask what he was doing there. The sides of my own mouth began to ache and slip in the silence that began to feel awkward until Connor reached into his back pocket and pulled out a leather purse.

'You forgot this last night,' he said. Emily took a step forwards. 'You must have dropped it when you were leaving the pub.'

She patted herself down as though she always kept her valuables on her.

'I didn't even realise I'd lost it,' she replied, smiling now and bouncing down the stairs gratefully, her hand stretching out to meet his. Or what he held in his.

'Why doesn't that surprise me?' I exclaimed dramatically. I don't know why. It wasn't like she walked the earth leaving a trail of debris scattered in her wake but I was conscious of the cheese sauce sitting unattended on the hob, a smoky aftertaste no doubt leaching into every mouthful. 'I'll leave you to it. Connor. It was lovely to see you. Say hello to your mum for me.'

'I will, Mrs Lawrence.'

'Clare, please.'

I slipped back into the kitchen, the thought of him already fading like writing on an old note left out in the rain.

'Who was that at the door?' David asked, running his fingers through his grey speckled hair, his legs crossed in the space Ginger had left behind as though I wouldn't notice.

'Connor McGann. He was –'

Emily reared around the doorway, her head tilted, long dark curls sweeping over her face.

'Just popping out for a bit.'

'Alright love. Lunch is nearly ready. Shall I do an extra plate for Connor? You can heat it up later.'

'No.' Her mouth twisted as though the very thought tasted bitter. 'I won't be long. We're just going for a quick walk.'

'Like that? I'd grab a cardi if I were you.'

'K.'

And she was off again, the roll of her gait forcing Connor to step out of her way and into the kitchen, the clatter of her footfall threatening to bring the stairs down.

'David, you remember Connor,' I said mentally running through a spool of fuzzy memories, the pimpled, pudgy chin and overbite in my mind at odds with the shy chiselled smile bearing down on me now.

'Of course.' David's eyes creased with feigned familiarity.

'Linda's son.'

'I know.'

'Linda McGann from my old nursing crew.'

'Yes, yes. I remember,' he cried overzealously, convincing no one. 'How's your mum, Connor?'

'Good, thanks, Mr Lawrence. Still at Brighton General.'

'Still in oncology?' I asked, even though I knew she was.

He shrugged hesitantly. 'I don't know to be honest.'

Of course, he didn't. That much was normal at least.

'Well, give her my love,' I repeated, occupying myself with an intensive rummage through the utensil drawer as much as for the distraction as to find the cheese grater. Connor shifted from one leg to the other again, his gaze drawn towards the drum of feet above his head and I smothered the lull of discomfort that followed by asking him what he was up to instead of basking in the utter banality of the moment. The sheer ordinariness of it. The complete lack of tension and fear, but then who knew how I'd come to value all of that.

'I've got one more year left on a BSc in Business Marketing at King's,' he replied.

'Online or on site?' David jumped in, glad to be back on familiar terrain.

'Bit of both. I've just finished my third-year internship at Microsoft so this is the homerun now. I'm off this week but my line manager invited me back for a month before the course starts. Mum would have liked me to stay on here longer, but I couldn't turn that down. It's a slam dunk career-wise.'

‘Of course. What an opportunity. I’m sure she’s very proud.’ I glanced at the ceiling as though to somehow chivvy my daughter along, to little effect.

‘How’s Olivia getting on? Her results must be due pretty soon,’ Connor said, his interest seemingly harmless. Ha! Harmless.

‘Couple of weeks but we’re hoping for all As and A stars.’ Normally I’d have been deriding the unprecedented predictions and complaining the exam board were giving A levels away, but that was every other year when neither of my daughters were taking them. They really ought to do something to level the playing field in future though. I should write to the Guardian. ‘Then it’s off to Exeter. She won a place on some Art bootcamp so she’ll be starting the course a few weeks early.’

‘That’ll be strange for you both. Quiet.’

‘I don’t know. As soon as one moves out, the other turns up again.’ David jerked his chin upwards, his eyebrows arching towards the still creaking floorboards in Emily’s bedroom. ‘Saving for a deposit supposedly so if that’s the case she might as well stay with us until we kick the bucket. At least there’s a decent chance of that happening within the next few decades.’

A familiar patter on the stairs diverted Connor’s attention and as Emily veered breezily around the doorframe his eyes lit up, the red stain stinging his cheeks once again. Given the length of time she’d taken getting ready, I’d expected a complete make-over but she looked exactly the same, save for an oversized sweatshirt that practically covered her knees.

‘Ready then?’ she asked as though our small talk was holding her up. ‘Come on.’

‘Really lovely to see you both again,’ Connor smiled and I remember thinking that despite the hand they’d been dealt and everything they’d been through, he was a credit to Linda.

‘Come on, let’s go,’ Emily repeated with a sigh that indicated she wanted to get this show of appreciation, or whatever that walk was, over and done with.

‘Nice boy,’ David said as Connor tipped his head and followed our daughter out of the house like a shadow and I believe – although it brings me no pleasure to say it now – that I wholeheartedly agreed with him.

250 Days Before the Murder

Her

It was six thirty-three. I knew this because I'd been challenging the clock for the last thirty-three minutes willing the hands to speed up, willing time to get on with it. At last, I spotted my boss rising to his feet, his chair rolling backwards, his fingers fiddling nimbly with his AirPods, his shirt straining as he reached for his bag.

This was it. This was the moment that I casually stood, my jacket draped across my arm, my backpack hanging off one shoulder. One last glimpse at my phone before I slid it nonchalantly into my back pocket, then… look up, catch his eye, simulate surprise and let our steps fall in line with one another.

Except of course that's not what happened. Only I could drop my mobile and ruin the serendipity of our simultaneous departure with a chalky-white, panic-stricken scramble around on the floor followed by a quick scan of my phone screen for cracks.

'Oh dear,' Raj chuckled with the carefree indifference of a man who took out the extended warranty on everything. 'All ok?'

'Yes, yes.' I sprang up with a manic grin, brandishing my mobile at him and hopped hastily around the desk, clipping my thigh against the corner with a deftly disguised wince.

'Are you leaving?' I cried taking the concept of stating the obvious to a whole new level but he had the good grace to answer with a bob of his head and no break in his stride. I scuttled after him.

'How's the research going?' he asked distractedly, holding the door open for me, his arm stretching across the glass, his gaze resting on our few remaining colleagues as he bid them good night. I slipped out into the street and turned towards him, the low summer sun beating down on my neck, the silky stickiness of the air wrapping itself around me, my top speckling with perspiration.

'Good, good, thanks. Although actually, I was hoping to talk to you about that if you've got a minute.'

Raj's forehead furrowed and he glanced down at the phantom watch on his wrist, his lips parted on the verge of an apologetic rebuff. I pressed on before he had a chance to say no.

'It's just I was thinking… The research is fine and all, but I was hoping to maybe take on a few more responsibilities now that I've been here for a few weeks. I know it's not long, I just wanted to let you know that I'm open to helping out more, maybe with the project managers? I know I've got a lot to learn and I'm – I'm not asking for more money. I'd just really, really like to get as involved as possible and hopefully one day, when there's an opening, I'll be ready to, you know, step in. If, if that's okay?'

Raj nodded his head, his lips stretched into an agreeable smile that came across as a grimace. Maybe catching him on his way home hadn't been the best idea after all, but all the same he said, 'Ambitious, hey? That's what I like to see.'

'I just really like it here.' I rubbed my earlobe self-consciously and swallowed. 'I'd like to get more involved.'

'Okay, well then…' He seemed to be ruminating on a future that included multiple promotions and pay rises for me but then his eyebrows knitted together, his head slanting quizzically. 'Do you know that guy?'

I wheeled around, confused at the turn in conversation, my eyes narrowing towards the car pulling up besides us.

'Emily!' Connor McGann was leaning across the passenger seat, his finger pressed against the window switch, retracting the barrier between us, his tyres grinding against the grit as he slowed to a stop.

'Oh, hey,' I said, a trace of irritation weaving into the vowels.

'I thought that was you.' He propped his hand through the open space and crooked his neck. 'You just finished work?'

'I…' I glanced back at Raj, at the absentminded, good-natured smile he'd assembled, his focus already drifting to thoughts of getting home. 'Just about.'

'Hop in,' Connor cried, ignoring the arch in my voice, his teeth glinting in the sunlight. Thank God, he'd had them fixed at least. 'I'll give you a lift.'

'Oh, don't worry,' I said, batting my hand the way British people do even in the event someone is offering to pull them out of a well.

'Don't be daft. I'm going your way,' he persisted, his shoulders hunching, his nose wrinkling, my desire to refuse based on a fictional conversation with a man who had more pressing places to be. Raj wavered on the spot smiling politely, his body language displaying less restraint.

'Go on,' he urged lightly. 'Grab a lift with your friend. It's fine. We can talk about this tomorrow.'

So I nodded, my teeth clenching behind an enthusiastic grin.

'Great,' I said, thrusting my thumb up towards him like a children's entertainer facing a tough crowd.

Connor popped the lever on the passenger side and I rested only briefly on top of the door as I yanked it open, keen to leave now and cringing as I replayed the thumbs up in my mind. Raj had one hand poised in a wave, the other tapping out a text as he turned away.

Never mind. It was fine. He'd said he was happy to talk about it tomorrow. I'd put the idea in his head, he'd have time to mull it over. This was good. This was fine. I just had to keep my hands under control. Give off a slightly more professional vibe when I next saw him. Whatever, it was over and now the cool air in the car was caressing my neck and sending shivers down my spine.

'That was lucky running into you.' Connor's eyes flicked to the rear-view mirror as he pulled out carefully into the lane of traffic, his hand raised appreciatively towards the driver who let him out, his attention on the road.

Was it lucky or was it a disaster? No, it was fine. I'd said what I wanted to say, albeit badly and with no hint of eloquence, but the ball was in Raj's court now. Besides, either way, it was a win-win for him. I didn't know what I was so worried about. As long as he said yes. Of course he'd say yes. Even if he did think I was an idiot.

Connor twisted around, his seatbelt tightening across his chest as he strained to find the source of our silence etched on my face. I dragged my thoughts back to the present and offered him a non-committal nod of gratitude.

'Yeah. Makes a nice change. I usually get the bus. It takes ages at this time of day. Nice car.'

‘Thanks.’

It was a nice car. It had that new car smell. I ran my fingers over the upholstery and they didn’t stick to anything. ‘Is it your mum’s?’

‘What!?’ He took his eyes off the faltering traffic ahead and spun around to me, his mouth agape.

‘Sorry, sorry,’ I giggled despite myself.

‘*My mum’s?*’

The indignation in his voice made me snort. I shook my head, my fingers splayed to hold back the laughter threatening to burst between them, not a trace of remorse clouding my response.

‘I just meant because you’re a student. Most people our age don’t drive Audis.’

‘Most fifty-two-year-old hospital Matrons don’t either. Bloody cheek. *My mum’s*… She drives a Nissan Micra!’

‘I’m sorry.’ I was clearly not sorry. My face was hurting and I was certain it was red. He rolled his eyes at me, one side of his mouth coiling playfully.

‘I managed to save a bit during my apprenticeship. Bought this and put aside enough for a deposit on a place when I graduate.’

‘Wow, that’s amazing. Well done.’ I dragged my fingers down my cheeks willing them to behave themselves. ‘I could barely keep my head above water with two part-time jobs and the Bank of Mum and Dad financing me. I’m impressed you saved anything.’

‘Well, you’ve got to build towards a future. Be nice to settle down someday. Do all that boring, predictable stuff like getting a house and a family. Anyway…’ He shrugged dismissively and his tongue clicked against the top of his mouth as though he’d already said too much. The car crawled forward, the sun bearing down brazenly below the visor forcing me to squint.

'I don't think that's boring,' I said, taking in his profile. 'It's nice.'

He swallowed, a short smile punctuating his confession. Funny how I'd never really noticed him at school. He was just one of those kids in one of those groups of other kids like him. If our mums hadn't forced us on playdates when we were little, I doubt our paths would have ever even crossed. But there was something different about him now. Something stronger, more confident. More appealing...? Or maybe he'd always been that way and I was the one who'd changed.

'What were you doing in town anyway?' I said with a spark of genuine interest that hadn't been there before.

'Getting a few last-minute necessities before I leave.'

'Don't they have shops in the Big Smoke?'

'Ha. It's all those years I spent in the Boy Scouts. Always prepared, that's me.'

'Mmm. A man in uniform who's always prepared, hey?' I curved my eyebrow suggestively. Connor's eyes met mine and honestly, I only meant it as a joke but heat rose up my cheeks so suddenly, I couldn't even blame the sunshine hammering through the windscreen. I looked away instead and coughed. He laughed and shook his head.

'I'm not off till the weekend, if you fancy getting a drink together sometime this week?' he said. 'If you're not sick of me, that is.'

I pinned my hair back behind my ear and kept my voice light. 'No, you're alright. I'm not sick of you yet. I could probably manage a few more hours in your presence, long as I'm drinking.'

'Oh, is that, right?' he said, flicking the indicator switch and turning into one of the side streets that led to the seafront. 'How are you fixed for time now?'

I drew a breath and twisted a lock of hair around my forefinger casually. 'Guess now's as good a time as any,' I said and he slid the car smoothly into what must have been the only empty parking space left in Brighton.

How lucky was that?

246 Days Before the Murder

Her Sister

Ahh. This was it. This was the life. The evening off. The sun shining. A nice cold beer in my hand. Sweet beats playing. I could have laid out in the garden all evening chilling with my tunes.

'Olive.'

Bugger.

'Olive!'

If I just closed my eyes and pretended to be asleep…

'Olivia!'

That did it. Mum had set off next door's Jack Russell. I tutted and pulled my headphones down past my ears, turning towards the kitchen. 'What?'

'Don't *what* me, madam. Come in here and make yourself useful.'

'Five minutes.'

'Now.'

I groaned and dragged myself up off the sun-lounger, resentfully shuffling through the backdoors and glaring into the darkness, supposedly until my vision adjusted to the light. A thin trickle of sweat dribbled down my back.

'Can you peel the potatoes?' she asked like she was giving me a choice and I groaned again. 'Aww, sweet child. Whatever will I do without you and your sunny disposition when you head off to uni?'

I tutted again and rolled my eyes, but whatever. The rabid mutt over the fence had killed the mood outside anyway. 'What are we having?'

'Quiche, potato salad, green beans and broccoli.'

Gross. I was going to make some comment about the last quiche she'd made but the sound of keys being turned in the front door distracted both of us.

'Hellllloooo! It's meeee,' Emily announced, fairly unnecessarily, the clump of her shoes falling onto the floor accompanying the slam of the door.

'You're home early,' Mum shouted. Again unnecessarily. Emily stuck her head around the doorway, smiled and slunk into the kitchen.

'I got a lift. Again.'

A tall blonde guy I hadn't seen for years slipped in behind her, his hand poised on the brink of a wave, an apologetic grin primed and ready to melt any heart.

'I invited him to stay for dinner. Is that okay?'

'You tell us,' I said and gagged, pointing to the oozing egg shells and flour scattered across the island. 'It's quiche.'

'I love quiche,' said the tall guy. Clark? Kenny? Kevin, that was it. 'But don't worry about me if there's not enough.'

'Of course there's enough, Connor.' Yeah, right. Connor, that was what I thought.

'Can I help with anything?'

'No, you cannot!' My mum had her best hostess voice on. Emily caught my eye and we smirked at each other. 'You two get yourselves a drink and enjoy the sunshine. Olivia and I have got this under control.'

What?

Emily pulled a pained expression and followed it up with a wink as she reached into the fridge, taking out the last two bottles of lager.

'Thanks, Mum,' she simpered and I returned her eyebrow waggle with a scowl and a less than friendly gesture with the vegetable peeler. 'Connor, you remember Olive.'

'Of course!' he smiled. 'You did a wee on our sofa once. My mum still talks about it.'

Laughter tore through Emily with overeager delight and Mum shook her head staging mortification, her bottom lip curled between her front teeth. So not a good look.

'Yes, all right. Move on, people. It's been fifteen years.'

'Sorry,' Connor said, beaming from ear to ear.

'Get att,' I drawled and they both laughed again and headed outside, Connor with a gentle pat of my arm and a semi-repentant grimace. I bared my teeth aiming for amused indifference but probably coming across as a bitch.

'Where's Gran?' Emily surveyed the flowerbeds as though perhaps she'd lined up alongside the rest of the (hideous) garden ornaments, one foot elevated behind her, pissing water from her mouth.

'In front of the telly pretending to be asleep,' Mum shouted as though we were all lost at sea.

'Not now I'm not,' came the wobbly retort from the sitting room. 'Is that a gentleman's voice I can hear?'

Ha, have some of that, Chuckles. Instant karma, but he handled it well, I had to give him that. Quite the charmer and I couldn't have asked for more material to rib Emily with later. I hadn't seen her this smitten since Ginger was a kitten, trying to act all cool and unbothered too. Like, 'yeah, yeah, whatevs' with her cheeks all rosy, giggling like a maniac at everything he said, bless her. Man, I was going to have some fun with this.

'Ohh, you've got a good one here, Milly,' Gran cooed half an hour later, only adding to my enjoyment. The smell of overdone pastry filled the room and the thunk of the baking tin hitting the worktop brought to mind a wrecking ball being swung from a height. 'Come on, handsome. You can sit next to me.'

She shuffled over to the table, a spring in her white bouffant, and tapped the back of the chair next to hers – my chair, I might add.

'Let him sit next to Emily, Gran. That's my seat.'

Not that I'd be needing it the way Mum had me running about while Emily perched on her lazy arse hoofing wine now that she'd finished the beer. I placed a huge mound of beans in front of her and she simulated shock.

'Mum's gone all American sitcom on us,' I explained.

Emily craned her neck to examine the perilous stack of green veg shimmering with melted butter, her mouth gaping, a look of gormless wonder only adding to her allure. 'Is it Thanksgiving or something?'

I strode across the kitchen to get the potato salad and the weight of it bent my thumb beyond comfort.

'Anyone would think she was trying to impress someone…' I said whacking it down between the condiments and a pile of napkins. *Napkins.* 'I told her we only needed half this much.'

'This all looks amazing, Mrs Lawrence.'

'Now, now, Connor. We've been through this. It's Clare.'

'Clare.' Connor doffed an imaginary hat and *Clare* sizzled. She literally bloody sizzled. Whatever this smooth-talker had done, he'd passed the test. My eyes met Emily's and we shook our heads incredulously. I rounded the table and drew my chair out, twisting my torso, my knees primed and ready to finally sit down.

'Olive. Go and call your father, would you?'

Jesus Christ. 'FAAAARRRRTTTHHHHEEERRRR!'

Mum brought the cold hard stare out of storage but refrained from treating Connor to the full blistering family showdown. Not in front of the guest, please.

Dad appeared at the French doors and hovered there, brushing off the dusty remnants of whatever he'd smothered himself with in the shed. 'Are we feeding Americans?' he exclaimed. 'Oh. Quiche.'

We all sighed – all except for Connor who rubbed his hands together in anticipation (of what could only be an ensuing trip to the dentist) and my mum who just glared.

I swung the serving spoon towards Emily and the Ken doll, a lump of potato mayonnaise sticking to it like putty. 'Sorry, rewind. What is this and how don't I know about any of it?'

She shrugged 'You're always down the pub.'

'Er, working, excuse me, but go on.'

'I dunno really. It was just a –'

'It was just really lucky, is what it was,' Connor broke in, placing a hand over Emily's and looking at her, adoration dripping from every pore. She wiggled her head and gave him a withering smile, but her eyes were twinkling.

'We sort of bumped into each other on Saturday night when I was out with Chloe and that lot,' she breathed airily like she'd already lost interest. 'Connor happened to be at the pub with some mates and we got chatting at the bar –'

'Okay. Confession.' He waved his hands repentantly. 'I wasn't actually there with some mates. I'd seen you go in earlier and I followed you. I couldn't help myself, I just wanted to say hello after all these years, see how you were doing.'

'What!'

He smiled sheepishly. 'I know. It probably sounds really creepy now,' he conceded humbly. 'But I just sat there for ages building up the nerve to talk to you and then finally you went to get a round in and that was when I –'

'Pounced?' I raised my eyebrows and fork pointedly.

'Seized the moment, I was going to say,' he cried, dimples at the ready.

'Oh my God. That whole *Emily! I almost didn't recognise you thing…*'

'A complete line. I had time to work on it.' His cheeks were flushed but he was grinning. 'What else was I supposed to do? Let another three years pass before I saw you again?'

'Ahh, well, I think that's romantic,' Mum said, the chunk of broccoli she'd put aside for later framed by her teeth. 'Your father and I would still be staring at each other across the cafeteria if I hadn't done all the leg work.'

'Leg work? Is that what they used to call it?' I made myself laugh at least.

'Olive!'

Oh, whatever. My striking wit was totally wasted on this lot. I couldn't even count on Gran. She'd turned her hearing aid off and there was no point using up any more good one-liners on the rest of them so I diverted my attention back towards the happy couple. 'So what? You finally asked her out...?'

Emily opened her mouth to speak but Connor put his arm around her shoulder and leant forwards, his finger jabbing the space between them.

'Not then. God, no. I was a wreck. But – and this is the best bit – she left her purse behind. I mean I didn't know it was hers but after she left, I happened to see it under the table, looked through it and sure enough it was Emily's so I was like – woah, this has got to be my lucky day, the perfect excuse to see her again.'

'Would have been less lucky for me if I'd cancelled all my cards, of course. He didn't bring it round until the next day.'

'Finally! A lifetime of procrastination has paid off,' Dad intervened, pleased with himself. 'Imagine if you'd done it straight away…'

'Exactly!' Emily cried, vindicated at last. 'Anyway, yesterday, really weirdly, again, Connor was driving down Ship Street just as I came out of the office, which –' she paused for dramatic effect. '– was half an hour later than usual so I shouldn't really have been there either.'

I tinkled my fingers to accompany the atmospheric music I'd conjured to lend an otherwise unremarkable backstory some much needed gravitas.

'Must be fate,' Mum said, this time with some red pepper wedged between her top incisors. I don't know where she got it from. There wasn't any pepper in the meal.

'That's what I told her.' Connor squeezed Milly again.

'I was just glad he had air conditioning in his car,' she said, an underlying bubbliness cutting through the flippancy she was leaning on heavily. Oh, dear God. I returned her unconvincing pretence at nonchalance with total disbelief.

Two hours later she finally closed the door behind him and swivelled slowly around on the balls of her feet.

'Humana humana,' I leered, attempting to brave the top floor now they'd vacated her bedroom and I could get back to binging the final season of Breaking Bad without their sickening sweet nothings interrupting every gang slaying and drug deal.

'Oh, shut up.'

'What? I'd do him.'

'No, you wouldn't.'

'All right, I'd do him if I was straight. Talk about a glow up.'

Emily shook her head, overdoing an eye roll, but I knew her too well.

'What? I'm allowed to say he's hot, aren't I? God knows he didn't use to be.'

'He wasn't that bad.'

Now *that*, I wasn't about to let go. 'Oh, girl. You really are in trouble if you can say that with a straight face.'

Emily swiped my shoulder with the back of her hand and shook her head again. 'It doesn't matter anyway. He's going back to London at the weekend.'

I lowered my arm from the banister. 'So what?'

'Well, you know. Long-distance relationships and all that.'

'Is this London, Australia we're talking about? Or do you mean the one just up the road?'

'It's like an hour and a half away,' she said, taking a sudden interest in the sealant on the radiator cover. 'Besides I'll be busy with work, he'll be busy finishing his degree. I don't want to get in the way. It's an important year for both of us.'

'Oh, for Goodness' sake.' I slowly mounted the stairs, still seeking out her eyes. 'He clearly likes you. You're both single. It's not like you're going to get a better offer round here in the *Gay Capital of the UK.*' I lifted my fist above my head in solidarity with my LGBTQI+ tribe. 'Word.'

'You're such an idiot.' Emily sighed.

I lowered my hand and thumped it against my chest, discretely sneaking away half a step at a time. 'It's not like you've got anything else on, is it? Might as well see where it goes. It's been a while since I've seen you this…'

'What?'

'Slushy. Pathetic. Soppy.'

Emily dipped her head, impervious to any attempt to derail her. 'Great talk, as ever, sis.'

I curtsied. 'Seriously, he seems like a nice guy, you seem happy. See where it goes, I say.'

The corner of Emily's mouth curled reluctantly, the sparkle in her eyes less cautious.

'He is quite hot, isn't he?'

'I would,' I said, my interest dissolving as Walter White and Jesse drew me up to my room.

'No, you wouldn't.'

I turned on the landing, my toe lingering on the top step. 'Nah. But you should. Go for it,' I told her and I'll have to live with that for the rest of my life.

238 Days Before the Murder

Her

The sun glinted off the gleaming glass building opposite, bathing the street in a blanket of gold as the carefree ambience of Saturday afternoon merged into evening.

'This is amazing,' I said, staring down at the bustling scene five stories below. 'You are so lucky to live here.'

'I don't know about lucky,' Connor smiled and tapping his bottle of Sol against mine. 'It's a matter of going for what you want in life, isn't it? Never taking no for an answer. We make our own luck.'

I scanned the skyline, stunning and scattered with architectural icons people on the other side of the planet would recognise, so close I could almost touch them. I leant over the balcony.

'Not bad for a student,' I said, jostling him with my hip and he pulled me towards him, his hand winding around my waist, his lips on the crook of my neck. A shiver ran through me. I took a swig of the chilled lager and feigned nonchalance, which was futile. The second he poked his finger into my side, I spasmed, spluttering, and spat the entire mouthful onto the crowd below.

'Connor!' I squealed, ducking away from the handrail and he threw his head back and laughed.

'You trying to get me evicted?'

I slunk onto my chair again, curling into myself even though there was no way anyone would be able to see me up here. We were in the turret of a castle while everyone else was stuck wading through the moat. I giggled and wiped my chin with the hem of my T-shirt and attempted to regain the upper hand by dripping some lime into my mouth which might have passed for seductive had it not squirted straight into my eye.

'Jesus Christ.'

'You are a right liability, aren't you?' Connor brayed handing me a napkin and despite the fact I seemed to have lost any advantage I had over him back on my home turf, I really didn't care. To hell with playing games. It was too much work trying to keep the smile off my face.

'Thanks again for the necklace,' I said fingering the gold bee resting on my sternum and enjoying the flicker that passed through his eyes as his gaze was drawn to my chest. He reached across for my hand, threading his fingers through mine.

'You're welcome. It's to remind you of me every time you wear it.'

'In that case, I'll never take it off,' I purred only half-joking. He squeezed my hand, loosening his grip and reaching into his back pocket to check his phone for the fiftieth time. His jaw bone clicked and his expression hardened briefly as he switched it off and lay it face down on the table top.

'All okay?' I asked lightly and his irritation turned to confusion and then he smiled again, shrugging reassuringly and leaning back towards me. I veered away glaring playfully. 'That's not some other woman always texting you, is it?'

He took my hand again and kissed it. 'No one's texting me and even if they were, you ought to know you're the only woman for me.' He winked and a thousand butterflies took to flight. I was bloody ridiculous.

'Next time I'll get you a ring,' he teased, stroking his thumb over my finger, his eyes hooded theatrically. 'Show you how serious I am about you if you like.'

I laughed and drained the beer from my bottle. 'I'd rather have the cash,' I said.

'Matching tattoos then. His and hers. Emily and Connor forever.'

'Connoly.'

'Connoly Forever. Let's do it.'

'Maybe next time.'

'I'll hold you to that,' he grinned peeking at his phone again and fist bumping the air. 'Yesss!'

'Good news, I take it.'

'Just a bit of luck on the markets.' Nice for some. 'Why don't you slip into something more uncomfortable and I'll take you out to celebrate.'

And I tittered like a giddy schoolgirl. So uncool. And right in Connor McGann's okay face while drinking Connor McGann's Mexican beer on Connor McGann's swish balcony in Connor McGann's boojee apartment. With Connor McGann from school.

Who would have thought things could turn out so well?

228 Days Before the Murder

Her Mother

The heat was a bit much but then we're never happy, are we? We spend nine months a year lamenting the drizzle that's seeped into our bones and then the sun comes out and we all melt onto the garden furniture. It didn't help matters that my mother had popped round either.

'What's this?' she exclaimed loftily. 'I asked for ginger nuts.' She held up a custard cream as though a plague of rats had each taken a bite out of it.

Ginger's ear twitched at the sound of his name, but he battened down his eyelids, his tail curled around his warm body like a knot, daring anyone to suggest he might like to shove up a little. I shuffled my mum along the rattan sofa instead and squeezed in besides her, tea slopping down the side of my mug onto the glass-topped table as I sought refuge in the shade of next door's untamed bamboo.

'We're out. You finished off the last packet yesterday.'

'You should have said. I'd have brought my own.'

'Live a little, Mum.'

'Custard creams though...'

'Keep your voice down. You'll set off the dog.' I pulled a crumpled tissue out of my pocket and mopped up the beige puddle with a sigh that rattled through me like bagpipes collapsing after a strenuous jig.

'There, there,' my mother said, sweeping crumbs off the indecent camisole top she'd inherited from one of the girls, her crinkled cleavage pink and shiny with a sheen of sunscreen. 'It's not forever. She'll be back. More often than you'd like probably. Anyway, you've still got Milly.'

'I know. Can't help but feel it's the end of an era, that's all.'

My mother, or Bella as she was more commonly known to anyone who wasn't related to her, placed her hand, soft and papery, on mine and patted it. 'Is she packed?'

I raised a wave of derision and allowed it to wash over both of us. 'Who? Olive? I doubt she's even bought half the stuff she needs yet. I've got a good mind to simply clear all of Emily's boxes out of the loft and take them down to Exeter. They're probably full of old bed sheets and mismatching cutlery. There's no point buying more. By the time Number One's saved up enough for her own place, she'll be needing the funds to pay for a nursing home. Hers not mine.'

'Not if things keep going well with Linda's boy, she won't,' Bella blew her cheeks out appreciatively and tapped her thick yellowing nails against the bone china warming her clammy hand. 'He seems to be making something of himself. Nice car, steady job prospects. Tight buns.'

'Mum!'

'Be set for life if she hangs on to him, that's all I'm saying.'

An ancient image of him flitted through my mind. Some birthday party… Was it Emily's eighth? It was fancy dress anyway in the days before Amazon Prime. Nowadays I expect people keep a fire extinguisher on hand at those sorts of things, what with all the cheap polyester tearing around their living rooms. He came as a cowboy, as I recall. Spent the afternoon shooting the other guests which tarnished the mood somewhat, but a certain degree of acting out was only to be expected what with the troubles in his own home. At least they weren't real bullets.

'She's perfectly capable of getting by on her own, Mother. It's not the fifties.'

'I know that, but at least we can be sure this one comes from good stock if it does work out for them both. I'll never forget how kind Linda was throughout my treatment. Always sought me out when I was having my chemo. Brought me an extra biscuit. Now there's a woman who wouldn't try to palm me off with a custard cream.'

I shook my head and inhaled, but there was no point retorting. It would only encourage her and anyway, she was right. Linda was lovely and she'd clearly done a good job of raising Connor on her own. And in those circumstances. It didn't bear thinking about. I'd certainly never seen Emily quite as taken as this. I knew she'd had her adventures at uni, but not with anyone we ever got to meet.

'She'll be missing him, I expect,' Bella continued, swirling the sludge at the bottom of her mug with distain and I knew without being told that a ginger nut would never have disintegrated like that.

'I doubt she's had a chance, they're always texting or Facetiming each other. That's when you talk on the phone with the camera –'

'I know what Facetiming is.' Bella's voice was shrill with indignation and she slapped her mug down on the table startling the cat.

'And she went up last weekend, of course. Did she say, he took her out to some fancy restaurant with a rooftop bar? One of these posh ones on top of a skyscraper. Said she could see all of Westminster up there. Well, she didn't say that. She said *that big building where the prime minister lives*. Honestly, this is what you get for raising a generation on TikTok. TikTok's –'

'I know what TikTok is.'

'It wasn't like that when I was a student nurse, I can tell you. I lived on noodles for three years. Thai Green Curry, that was the best.'

'And you're telling me she's not better off being wined and dined by some lovely, nice-looking thing?'

'As long as she's happy, that's all that counts.'

And she was. She was bright-eyed and motivated. Work was going well. She was putting in the hours and coming home every night with a passionate glow about her, enthusing about the advertising campaigns she was working on, the clients she was still star-struck by, not that she'd ever admit it. She was far too cool and professional for that, attempting to feign nonchalance yet all the while brandishing her promotional freebies and bubbling with the delight of a child let loose amongst walls of Pick 'N' Mix.

And yes, now that her studies were out of the way, I was only too pleased she'd met someone who seemed to be as taken with her as she was with him. More so if the flowers and chocolates that kept appearing were anything to go by. And alright, I'd be lying if I said I wasn't relieved that he was already halfway into a decent career before he'd even finished university. Money might not be everything but it certainly took the edge off everything else.

Besides, it wasn't the fact he had his wits about him financially that made him such an attractive prospect. Anyone could see how smitten he was by her, with his arm forever draped across her shoulders, his fingers never far from hers.

'Bit clingy if you ask me.'

'We won't, don't worry.'

'Still, she could do worse than clingy but rich.'

'Clingy but devoted, Mum. Clingy but besotted with her. Clingy but a very nice boy. Man.' We dipped our heads towards each other and shared a conspiratorial giggle, much to Ginger's disgust.

'He looks after himself too, it has to be said.' Bella sucked her teeth as though perhaps she'd been dribbling and not for want of a custard cream.

'Works out a fair bit, Emily says.'

'It shows. I wonder if he's got a big –'

'Mum!'

'Flat! I was going to say flat. Honestly, anyone would think you were raised by savages.'

'Hmm,' I said. 'Sometimes I wonder myself.'

Of course, in retrospect, it would have been handy if I had been. We might have stood a chance against him then. It might have evened up the fight.

227 Days Before the Murder

Her

My lower jaw gaped painfully and my nose bent with the force of distorting my expression into that of exaggerated horror but still my mascara wand failed to live up to its promise of delivering a dramatic faux-lash look. I squinted at the tube as though perhaps I'd picked up one designed to make *Barely Any Difference*, but it definitely said *Ultra-Volumizing* in shiny silvery writing that rubbed off on my thumb. I sighed and added another layer, willing my eyelashes to instantly plump and lengthen, but they clumped together like a spider had curled up into a ball and died there. At least it was free. No need to mention the whole MagiMasc range was rubbish in their next digital marketing campaign.

I wiped a smudge of lipstick, hoicked my knickers out of my bum cheeks, tugged my hemline down and wrenched the office door handle, wobbling slightly on the heels I should have waited to change into until I'd got to X-bar regardless of how chunky my calves looked in trainers. My face scrunched as the sun, still high in the sky, seared my eyes.

'There you are. I was beginning to wonder if you'd brought a shovel and tunnelled your way out.'

'Connor.' It was a statement of fact more than a greeting and my voice was higher than usual, my eyebrows so arched a child might have stencilled them on with crayons. 'What are you doing here?'

Connor's boyish smile spread across his face as he pushed himself away from the wall, his back angled on the brickwork as though he'd been there a while.

'Surprise!' He stepped forward, closing the gap between us with an embrace. My arms hung awkwardly, strangely resistant and slow to respond, refusing to join in until he pulled back, meeting my eyes with a shroud of confusion. "What's the matter? Are you pissed off? Have I done something wrong?'

'No, no,' I said quickly, brushing off the irritation that prickled the surface of my skin. 'I just wasn't expecting you. We didn't say…' I cocked my head. 'You know it's Olive's leaving do tonight?'

'I know. That's why I came back. I didn't want to let you down.'

My top lip curled exposing the pink of my gums. 'But…'

'I know how down you are about her leaving. I wanted to be here for you. And for her. I mean,' he laughed sheepishly. 'I wanted to show my support. Wish her luck at uni.'

'Oh. It's just that –'

'What? Would you prefer it if I hadn't come?' He drew back, his expression clouding awkwardly.

'Of course not. It's sweet you came,' I said, backtracking. 'It's just I don't think it's going to be… it's not that sort of a night. It's only going to be me, Olive and a few friends you don't know.'

'That's alright. Unless you're embarrassed to be seen with me…' His mouth twisted, his voice wounded, his words edged in uncertainty.

'Oh, Connor.' I took a step forward, my frustration vaporising like wisps of dry ice. 'Of course I'm not embarrassed. I'm just not sure how much fun you'll have. Olive's friends can get rowdy.' I smiled, running my hand down his bicep and he flexed it in the same way I hold my stomach in when someone brushes past me.

'I think I can handle it,' he grinned recovering himself, the trace of hurt outlining his speech only vaguely discernible now. 'But listen, if you don't want me there, I can head back to my mum's. Catch the fight instead. I thought it would be a nice surprise, that's all.'

'It is. It is a nice surprise and don't be silly. Olive'll be chuffed to bits that you made it. The more the merrier. But don't say I didn't warn you. This lot can be ruthless, especially her girlfriend, Flo. She's worse than my sister, if you can believe that.'

I slipped my arm through the crook of his elbow, relief at having someone to lean on in these heels the only consolation for the apprehension that had tainted my spirits, but I shook the worry from my mind. Olive would be okay. There was no point fretting. Besides, there was nothing I could do and it wasn't like it was only going to be the two of us. Or that I'd never see her again. It was just another night out like any other. Why shouldn't Connor come?

The noise erupted as soon as he pushed the door open and I teetered into the artificial gloom, weaving my way amongst the sea of revellers, a blur of flotsam until my eyes adjusted and fell upon a familiar cluster of faces and the purple-tinted hues of my sister's black bob.

'Oh.' That was all Olive needed to say when she looked up from the table, her jaw tightening with a flicker of annoyance she did well to disguise. Well and with uncharacteristic restraint. 'You brought a guest.'

Connor lifted his hands in the mollifying manner I was learning to recognise and beamed disarmingly at the group of young women staring up at him with matching furrows on their foreheads.

'Sorry! I'm gate-crashing,' he shouted, leaning in. 'Hope that's alright. Didn't want to miss the big send-off.'

Olive's lips twitched in the moments before she managed to force them into the semblance of a smile. She bowed back, her arm stretched towards the one remaining chair, her neck straining around reflexively on a non-comital hunt for another. Connor shot off in the direction of a spare seat like a golden retriever chasing a stick while I over-compensated for the slight shift in mood with a round of high-fives that failed to land very well in either sense of the word. Only Olive refused to play along but she'd have left me hanging regardless.

'Sorry we're late,' I cried over the sound of the music that suddenly seemed too loud.

Olive treated me to one of her sidelong glances. 'Yeah, well, technically your bang buddy can't really be late if he wasn't invited.'

I parted my lips, some soothing pretext on the tip of my tongue but sod it, I had nothing and anyway, there was no time for explanations. Connor was making his way back across the room with an ornate wooden chair and the look of a man pretending the weight of it was of no matter to him so I failed to pick up on her meaning and shuffled my own seat to one side as he swung his into the gap.

'Ladies, this is Connor.'

'Hi, Connor,' Olivia's girlfriend drawled, sweeping her sleek mane of curls behind her shoulder before chopping her hand through the air like a bored cabin steward pointing out emergency exits. 'Jo, Tori, Princess Charming, you already know, and I'm Flo. Nice to finally put a face to a name, Connor. We've heard a lot about you.'

'All good, I hope,' Connor displayed his front teeth zealously, still towering eagerly over the back of his chair.

'Oh, God, no. Terrible,' Flo cackled, a seductive sheen of perspiration glinting off her cheekbones, her eyelashes fluttering like the wings of a raven. *That was the look I'd been going for, bloody MagiMasc.* Tori and Jo both threw their heads back and guffawed, their cheeks as ruddy as farmers seeking respite from a storm. We might have arrived late but they'd all clearly got there early.

'Better work on my reputation.' Connor waggled his eyebrows at Flo, the patch of crimson blooming on his neck no doubt down to stifling heat as much as anything. 'Shall I get us a couple of bottles of bubbly? It is a celebration after all.'

'Celebration?' Olive finally spat in a tone that might have seemed less out of place had he just done a huge dump on the carpet. 'You get that I'm leaving, right? This is more of a bereavement party for this lot.'

'Yeah, right,' Tori snorted. 'All the more reason to get off our faces. We're drowning our sorrows.'

Connor made an unsettling clicking noise with the corner of his mouth and stuck out his index finger, his thumb poised on a trigger like the spray-tanned star of an infomercial whose life hadn't gone to plan. Then spinning on his heels, he strode across the sticky floorboards and positioned himself at the bar expectantly. I turned to face Olive and the inevitable music with an apologetic grimace.

'Soz.'

She shrugged. Flo nudged her and rolled her eyes. 'Diva alert.'

'At least he's getting a round in,' I pointed out more defensively than I intended.

'Too bloody right, he is.'

My palms lifted in readiness to join me in a protest, but got no further. There was really nothing I could say.

Olive sliced her finger back and forth through a water ring on the table, her eyes downcast. 'It's just I thought it was going to be you, me and ma homies, that's all. The last send-off together, you know. I mean, he's nice and everything, it just… changes the dynamic a bit and I really wanted –' Her voice trailed off as though it didn't bear thinking about the night that could have been.

'Look, I know. I'm sorry, but there was nothing I could say to stop him coming without sounding like we didn't want him here.'

'We don't want him here.'

'Oh, Olive,' I pleaded, lowering my voice. 'Please, don't make me tell him to leave, it'd be so awkward.'

Flo swung one arm around Olive's shoulder and punched the other lightly until her lips tightened and she muttered, 'Fine.' The words *like I've got a choice* hanging unsaid in the air.

'It's not like I'm never going to see you again anyway. God, I'll be up as soon as you've had a chance to settle in.' I gripped her hand, my own tight smile more beseeching than heart-felt.

'You'd better be,' she growled wryly squeezing my fingers, the veil of confidence she wore like a shield slipping slightly.

My gaze darted towards the bar where Connor stood, his shirt stretching taut across his back as he picked up an ice pail rammed with extra glasses and not one, but two bottles.

'He's on his way back. Look, again. I'm really sorry we've crashed your leaving do but please don't say anything. He'd feel terrible if he thought he'd upset you.'

'As if I would.' Olive shrugged, then like a switch her eyes lit up and she hooted, 'Heyyyy, this is more like it. Let's get this party started.'

Connor placed the champagne on the table with the pride and flourish of a man who'd fermented it himself.

'Ooooh, fancy.' Jo, drained her flute of Prosecco and began refilling it, froth bubbling at the surface, foam spilling down the sides. 'Real champers. Now we've really got something to celebrate.'

Flushed and beaming, Connor peeled off his jacket and I patted the seat beside me, mouthing *Thank you*.

Tori pressed a drink into his hand with a grin. 'Don't go raising the bar too much, mate. I'm supposed to be getting the next round in.'

'Cheers, Connor.' Flo smashed the other bottle against our glasses with a clink and a cascade of bubbles that brought us to our feet.

'A pleasure,' Connor breathed, laughing and licking his fingers. 'Besides, it's probably the last time you'll be drinking champagne for a while, Olive. It'll all be John Smith's and Foster's from now on. Whatever's on offer in the student union.'

‘And what’s this?’ Jo cried. ‘Your student loan we’re drinking, is it?’

Connor tapped the side of his nose, a half-smile he took to be mischievous cleaved into the side of his face.

‘Drugs.’ Tori slammed her fist down on the table. ‘He’s a drug dealer.’

‘Shhhh.’ I scanned the tables around us. ‘He is not a drug dealer. Bloody hell. He just works when he can, like a normal person.’

‘Shame.’ Flo nuzzled into him suggestively and Olive caught my eye. I’d already told her about the insurance pay-out his mum got when his dad died, the place he was going to buy with it, the flash car, the restaurants he took me to, but that was between us. The official line was he’d saved up during his third-year apprenticeship. Everything else was too painful to reduce to drunken small-talk and there was no doubting we were drunk. Both bottles had been drained and stood overturned in the thawing ice.

‘’Nother round?’ Connor scraped his chair back. ‘I’ll get it in.’

‘You got the last one.’ I placed my hand on his arm, restraining him but he bent down to kiss my fingers.

‘Same again?’

The state of the cheer that went up in his wake suggested we’d probably had enough, but as everyone knows, that’s irrelevant when someone else is buying.

‘You can bring him again,’ Flo said and the smug glow that enveloped me loosened my muscles. Even Olive had managed to unstiffen her shoulders and take the stick out of her arse, though I had no doubt she’d put it in a safe place on the off-chance she needed it later.

Connor swaggered back, this time bearing a tray with a bottle of Dom Perignon, six shots of tequila and a manly-looking pint of IPA all of which was met with a roar of approval. Looking back, I'd say that was the tipping point. The moment before good vibes turned bad. Before alcohol infused the ambiance and soured it but that was the moment before we knew the evening had already peaked and we raced along regardless, oblivious to the fact we were now heading downhill.

Connor cleared his throat. 'So,' he said with a heavy-handed dose of near disinterest. 'Is everyone here… you know?'

'What? British?' Olive asked scrutinising the faces around the table. 'I think so.'

Connor coloured slightly. 'No, no. You know what I mean. Is everyone…'

'Able-bodied?'

'I've got bad knees from too much running,' Flo said. 'But other than that, I'm in perfect working order.'

'I'm perfect too.' Jo pressed her hand against her chest coquettishly and Connor shook his head with an airy laugh that almost passed for casual.

'Are you gay, I mean? Are you all gay?'

'Oh my God, he said it. Well done,' Tori teased, lowering her voice to a secretive rasp. 'Yes, we are. All. Raging. Lesbos. Apart from Emily but that's only coz she doesn't know what she's missing. No offence.'

'None taken,' he grinned charmingly. 'In fact, if you ever want to show me what she's missing, I'd be more than happy, you know, to be educated.'

I whacked him on the arm, playfully. 'I am still here, you know!'

'What!' he cried, rubbing his flexed bicep, his face a mask of innocence. 'I'm all for keeping an open mind about these things. You know, if this lot want to demonstrate where I'm going wrong, it would be rude not to let them.'

I laughed and shook my head. 'All right.' As in *all right*, that's enough, not *all right*, let's do it.

'And look, Flo's pretty much your doppelganger. Long as I squint a bit, I can pretend it's you and Olive going for it. That's gotta count for something, right?'

'Eww,' Olive and I said at the same time, our mouths twisting, my discomfort reflected in her eyes.

'You know they're sisters, right?' Jo said, her body language unmistakably defensive, unless you're unpleasantly drunk and/or oblivious that is.

'Course I know they're sisters. That's like, the ultimate red-blooded male fantasy.'

'Yeah.' Tori lowered her drink, her head slanting in distaste. 'I've never really understood the fascination with incest.'

'Believe me,' Connor crowed, all eyebrows and innuendo. 'It's not the incest I'd be in.'

All four women stared at him, the curl of their lips seeped in contempt.

'I don't even know what that means,' Olive replied, her voice flat, her thoughts wilfully composed on her forehead.

'Oh, lighten up, girls.' Connor sunk his pint and slammed it onto the table with a satisfied thunk, the creamy caterpillar basking on his lip no longer amusing. He rolled his hands over, his palms exposed. 'Really?'

Olive squared up to him, then slid her gaze to me, the air between us crackling. I peered at her, my eyes straining for a connection, my heart pounding so hard I had to hold my hand against it. She inhaled and with one slow blink, fixed Connor with a stare.

'You couldn't handle it,' she taunted in a voice only those of us who knew her recognised as dripping in moderation, a note of finality cutting through the charged atmosphere. Flo draped her arm around her, a controlled smile playing on her lips as Tori and Jo fiddled with the rims of their glasses, the expensive condensation sticking to their fingertips like dew.

I felt Connor's arm stiffen, grazing mine, his chin jut forward and a beat passed in silence before he threw his head back with a bark of laughter no less jarring than a plane exploding overhead.

'Let's hope I'm man enough to carry another round of drinks back to the table,' he jeered jovially, his chair screeching as he pushed it back, taking in the empty glasses, the nodding heads, the amiable set of stiff mouths. He turned away and only then did I realise I was holding my breath.

'Don't worry. We'll go after this,' I said.

227 Days Before the Murder

Him

For fuck's sake. What an unbelievable waste of time and money that was and after everything I'd done to make her happy, she was dragging me away like some piece of shit she couldn't wait to scrape off her shoe. Shoes she put on to impress other men before she even knew I was coming, I might add. Shoes I'd probably bought her. Not that she gave a flying fuck and after everything I'd done to make this happen.

It had been fate bumping into her after years of watching her life unfold online but the thing with the purse, that was ingenious. The fact I'd spotted the opportunity to pull it aside as we were chatting at the bar. Slipped my jacket over the top of it while she was distracted with her order, twisting her fingers around the stems of two wine glasses, trying and almost failing to balance the other in between them both. I did offer to help, but she declined. Said she had it but then she was always very capable. Not one of these girls who expected other people to do everything for them. I liked that about her.

And it's not like I'd planned to keep the purse, but let her think I found it under the table anyway. Maybe one day I'd tell her the truth and we'd laugh about it but not right now. It was more romantic this way. Everyone secretly wanted to be saved, capable women as much as anyone.

Only now she was turning against me. Siding with those uptight bitches who'd tried to get between us. Flirting and fluttering their eyelashes, reeling me in and then pretending to take offence just to avoid getting a round in.

I knew their type. Poison, the lot of them. They were the sort of vindictive man-haters that gave dykes a bad name. Emily was better off without them bringing her down, even if she needed some persuasion to see it. And believe me, I would persuade her.

227 Days Before the Murder

Her

We were walking too fast to have a real conversation. Just fractured snippets hissed into the air like sharp gusts of wind and I was fuming. Unable to convey quite how seething with shame and outrage I was in heels that forced me to adopt an unsteady scuttle.

'I just can't understand why you'd say something like that. You don't even know them.' My voice was splintered, my eyes rooted to the speeding contours of the pavement.

'I was only playing along with the joke they started. Jesus Christ.' Connor dug his hands into his pockets, his fingers balled into fists that silenced the clash of loose change jangling against keys.

'You were way out of order back there. Just admit it.'

'I was out of order? So, it's all right for your sister's girlfriend to flirt with me all evening, but the minute I play along – because that's what you're supposed to do in that situation – suddenly I'm some sort of male chauvinist pig. Is that right? They can say whatever they like to me, flash their tits and touch me up, but if I make one jokey comment back, *I'm* the arsehole.'

The defiant come-back I had almost perfected disintegrated behind an image of Flo squashing her boobs seemingly unawares between her arms as she gazed up at him coyly through thick dark lashes. She was a terrible flirt, we all knew it. Encouraged it.

Laughed at the effect she had on men knowing it would come to nothing. We enjoyed watching her wield the power she had over them, every one of the hapless fools convinced they'd be the one to turn her.

My conviction wavered. Connor wasn't the first to be shot down in flames even if he'd only been messing around. I mean, it's not like he was actually suggesting a threesome with Flo and Olive. Not in front of me. I could see where he'd gone wrong. How he'd inadvertently crossed an invisible line he didn't know had been laid, a magic circle scored into the ground designed to keep everyone else out. He was only kidding and Flo had sort of started it.

The resentment that had risen up my throat like bile turned to panic as Connor strode ahead of me, taking the upper hand with him. I wrenched my heels off and ran with them dangling from my finger, my aching feet splaying in relief against the cool concrete, my mind back-peddling, contrite and straining now for some way to smooth everything over. Recast my role in all of this. Reshape the narrative.

'It's just, they get it a lot, you know,' I cried scurrying alongside him breathlessly. 'They've all been teased and mocked or worse, you know. Bullied.'

'What are you saying? That I was bullying them?'

'No, no. Of course not. I'm just saying, they're a bit sensitive about the whole… gay gags thing.'

'I was only carrying on the joke they started,' he repeated. 'For fuck's sake. What are you actually accusing me of here?' He stopped. Turned towards me, his eyes narrowed, nostrils flared, a glint of disgust illuminated in the low sinking sun.

‘Nothing. Nothing.’ I waved my hands, conscious only of quelling the tide of anger directed towards me now. ‘I’m really not. I’m just trying to explain in case –’

‘Unfuckingbelievable. Two and a half fucking hours it took me to get here, half a fucking tank of petrol, not to mention however many bloody rounds back there and this is the gratitude I get.’

‘I didn’t mean –’ I reached out to close the distance between us but he pulled his arm away.

‘Two and a half fucking hours just to get laid into by your fucking oversensitive sister and the rest of her weird fanny-munching mates. Do you think I didn’t have anything better to do than come down here?’

‘I’m –’

‘I was perfectly happy to go home and catch the fight instead, but you insisted. You insisted. *Oh please, Connor. Olive would love you to be there.*’

I wasn’t sure I remembered it like that but it wasn’t the moment to point out that he’d turned up uninvited – unwelcome even. He was pacing back and forth in front of me like a tiger trapped in a cage, agitated and ready to pounce.

‘I turned down three invitations tonight, one of them with the hottest chick at the gym. Jesus Christ. Talk about ingratitude. I only came down here to prove how much I care about you, to show your bloody family that I’m serious about this and look at the thanks I get. I wish I hadn’t bothered.’

‘Connor, I –’

‘How many blokes do you think would have made the effort to come all this way to spend the evening with a bunch of skanks. Let alone allow themselves to be put down like that. It was fucking out of order all of them ganging up on me. Making out I was being sleezy. How dare they? As if I'd want to see any of them up to their business. I'd zip them up in parkas if it was up to me. I was just trying to make them feel comfortable, show them I wasn't fazed by their lifestyle but they went and took it the wrong way. You all did.'

'No, Connor, it wasn't like that. They know you were joking.'

'I *was* fucking joking.'

'I know.'

He shook his head, his pupils constricting, the turn of his mouth steeped in defiance. 'You should have stood up for me back there.'

My throat was tight. I licked my lips. 'I know. I'm sorry.'

'Hung me out to dry. You all did.' The pacing began to slow and he twisted towards me, his shoulders slumped, his chest deflated, betrayal burrowed into his forehead. 'I really didn't expect that of you.'

'I'm sorry,' I whispered meaning it this time, a stab of pain punching the air from my lungs, the blood draining from my legs. He took a step forward, his face angled, contemplating me as a small sad smile slowly spread and he folded his arms around me.

'Let's not do that again,' he said and I didn't know if he meant argue or go out with my sister, but right then, I'd have agreed to either.

219 Days Before the Murder

Her Mother

It wasn't a complete disaster. It wasn't my finest roast either but only David and my mother were in attendance and they both knew better than to reference the petrified vegetables or the chainsaw I'd be needing to slice the beef.

'No parsnips for me,' David said but I ignored him with a withering glare at the dish as I heaped them on, sensing rather than seeing the sympathetic glance my long-suffering guests shared. Not that David was a guest of course – he was simply easy to misplace behind a newspaper or in the shed, tinkering, he said, fixing things he'd picked up at the dump. The dump! It was better than dealing with an affair, I supposed, but how much better, I couldn't say (although the Kenwood food processor he'd found had turned out to be a godsend. It was amazing what people threw away).

'Have you heard from Olivia?' Bella asked using the opportunity to rest her knife on the side of her plate as though the effort of macerating a roast potato had quite taken it out of her.

'Not really. Not since she rang asking for an advance on her allowance three weeks into term. Said the course books had been unexpectedly expensive but she'd forgotten I can see all the charges on her statement so I asked her when did Primark and H&M start selling text books, then? That shut her up for all of five minutes. Then she rang David.'

David looked to be on the verge of justifying why he'd sent her two hundred pounds just like that so I scooped another spoonful of veg onto his plate.

'Emily been down to visit yet?' Bella asked, scalping a carrot with an unnerving squeak that set off a shriek of interference in her hearing aid.

'Down to Exeter? No.' Not since we'd last had this same conversation only days ago. I pushed my chair back, made my way to the utensil drawer and returned with three serrated carving knives which I handed out without explanation. 'She'd be hard pressed to fit it in these days, what with work and her trips to London. I don't think she's been here for the last – four weekends, is it, David?'

'Something like that.'

'She tends to go up on Friday right after she finishes and then heads down first thing Monday morning.'

'Goes straight to the office.'

'Which makes sense.'

'That must cost a fortune.' Bella held her knife aloft incredulously. 'I remember when I lived up there –' *Oh God, here we go.* David's shoulders sagged. '– trying to get in or out at that time cost about three times the price, if not more. I forget –'

'That's the same anywhere, Mum. It's not just because it's London.'

David fixed me with a resentful stare and my tongue clicked as I quickly tried to reel the conversation back on course, but my mother was on a roll.

'Did I tell you about the time I lived in Islington, before I met your father –'

'Yes, you did.'

'You don't even know what I was going to say yet.'

'Did *I* say I thought there was a bit of an atmosphere the day David took Olive up to uni?'

'I expect so.' Bella bristled, examining a hunk of beef with undisguised aversion which I'm pleased to say I rose above.

'I still haven't got the bottom of it. Neither of them has said anything, but I know something was up. Olive wasn't her usual snarly self, which I took to be a hangover at first, but the odd thing was that they hadn't come home together.'

Bella twisted her loaded fork as though it were an interactive exhibit at a museum. 'That's right,' she said dismissively. 'You did tell me.'

'Milly stayed with Connor which I thought at the time was strange, it being their last night on the town or what-have-you.'

'I remember you said.'

'But I thought, well, she'll turn up for breakfast. I'd made waffles.'

'I know, you told me. Waffles, strawberries, whipped cream. I'd have liked an invite.'

'Oh, they were only out of a packet. You didn't miss anything.'

'And did you manage not to burn them?' Bella asked, rudely in my opinion and I'd had quite enough of her behaviour by then, but I was discharged from telling her that by David choking on – what? I don't know. Probably a Brussels sprout by the look of the table afterwards. He's not one for chewing his food.

'Anyway, she didn't turn up until they'd finished packing the car, Connor in tow, of course and there was nothing I could put my finger on. They were all very nice but a mother knows. I mean, since when is Olive nice to anyone? I know the girls are the best of friends these days but you wouldn't know from the way they talk to each other.'

'It's just banter,' David said, still thumping his chest with unnecessary vigour.

'I know, David. That's what I'm saying. There was none of that. They just hugged and said goodbye and see you soon and what-not. And then Milly and Connor headed into town.'

'Well, Olivia was certainly her usual self on the drive. Made me pull in to every other service station to top up on McDonald's. And Burger King. That's right, she wanted to compare the vegan burgers. I mean, vegan burgers? What is the world coming to?'

'David thinks I'm imagining it.'

'Imagining what?' Bella said, despite herself.

'The atmosphere.'

I don't believe it was related but just then her teeth popped out, smashing onto the plate with a clatter like a meteor exploding in space, if that's something they do. Only instead of rocks, the meal I'd spent an hour cooking erupted everywhere – all over her cardigan, David's shirt, the tablecloth I'd only just washed and ironed and I never iron. I don't know what inspired me that time. Boredom probably, what with the house being so quiet.

Anyway, no one felt like eating much after that so I put a wash on and we never did get to the bottom of what was going on.

Honestly. Between my mother and David, I was still finding specks of gravy on the curtains weeks later. They were worse than the children, the pair of them.

218 Days Before the Murder

Her

It was five o'clock and the days were getting shorter, the first hint of the autumn air cooling earlier now. I dumped my handbag on the floor in the hallway, but kept my boots and jacket on.

'It's getting late,' I said. 'I probably ought to start heading to the station.'

'What now? I thought you were staying till the morning.'

I rubbed the chill lingering on my hands under my armpits, unexpectedly startled by a stream of tepid fluid accelerating towards the tip of my nose. I shot up, shielding the horrifying string of snot bridging my fingers and fumbled around my pockets, certain I'd find a Kleenex there, hard and crumpled from when I'd last discarded it. My eyes darted to Connor, but he had his back to me and my status as a 'living goddess' remained untarnished as I wiped my fingers clean on my sleeve.

'I said I might. It's just so much more expensive if I leave in rush hour.'

He steadied himself against a wall and untied his laces, slipped his brogues off, inspected them for dirt and finding none, placed them carefully inside the shoe cabinet. 'I'll pay. Don't I always?'

'I know,' I sighed, resisting the urge to kick my DMs off and put the kettle on for just a few moments longer. 'I feel bad though. We could get to Paris for the price of a train ticket at that time in the morning.'

'Why don't we then?'

'What?' I was already grinding my toecap into my heel, easing my foot out as though the matter had been concluded. Knowing it would be.

'Go to Paris.'

I followed Connor into the kitchen and he turned to me, corkscrew already in hand, a feverish glow about him.

'For your birthday. We could get the Eurostar from St Pancras. It's only up the road. Give me one good reason why not.'

I couldn't. '*Oh la la,*' I said instead like a moron. '*Bidet en suite, monsieur.*'

'I love it when you talk dirty,' he growled taking me into his arms. 'Sorted then. I'll book the tickets for the nineteenth. Your birthday's on Saturday this year, so that's handy.'

'How do you even know that?' I laughed, intoxicated by the smell of him. The oaky, muskiness that made me burrow myself against his chest, inhaling his scent.

'*Est-ce que tu veux un verre de vin, mademoiselle*? It's a *très bon* vintage.' He furnished himself with a wine bottle from the rack, drawing it against the length of his forearm and I was grateful for the visual cue because my GCSE French only extended to finding the station and describing what I liked to do in my free time (windsurfing and tennis, of course). I giggled, pouting and flourishing my hands in what I imagined was a continental manner.

'*Je'*d prefer *un* cup *de* tea, *s'il vous plaît.*'

'*Sacré Cœur! Mais non. Mademoiselle* cannot make me drink alone.'

He clunked the bottle down on the granite workbench, impaled what must have been the one remaining cork this side of the millennium and smoothly twisted it out. I groaned as he reached for the wine glasses draining by the sink, a delighted smirk spreading with every definitive glug of merlot as it sloshed up the sides of the bowl. I hesitated, holding firm for the barest of moments but then, well, sod it. I was staying the night after all. I clasped the stem delicately, my pinky finger extended, swirled the glass and sniffed again, the remnants of mucus rattling unseductively in my nostrils.

'Would *mademoiselle* like anyzing to eat?' he continued in the appalling, yet bizarrely sexy accent he would use on and off for the rest of our relationship.

'*Mon Dieu,* no. *Mademoiselle* is still stuffed from lunch.'

Lunch had been hours ago but I was still recovering from the sticky toffee pudding we'd shared for dessert. I needed to start watching what I ate. All these hot chocolates, cheeky halves and meals out were taking their toll, but it was impossible not to indulge when the weather was so lovely. The atmosphere so charged with life.

The whole weekend had been perfect from the moment Connor had met me at Victoria station and whisked me off to this Japanese-Brazilian fusion place that was always featuring in top London restaurants guides. The portions were tiny and we'd ended up in a burger shack three hours later on the way home, but it was amazing. Unforgettable. Breathtakingly expensive but most definitely

Instagramable and I wasn't normally bothered about that sort of thing.

We'd spent most of the day in bed on Saturday. I'd only left the flat to pop into Waitrose (even though Morrison's was closer) to stock up on enough fresh bread, eggs, orange juice and tortellini to get us through the next twenty-four hours entwined under the duvet streaming European films and cooking shows. Amongst other things.

And then today we'd wandered along the South Bank, the unseasonably bright rays of sun reflecting off the whirls and currents of the Thames as we drank in the last of September's hazy warmth and gazed at the splendour and radiance of the Houses of Parliament (which Mum still claimed I thought was where the PM lived, as though I'd never watched the news in my life).

As the morning turned into afternoon, we'd been marvelling upon the queue coiled like a cat's tail at the feet of the London Eye when we found ourselves outside the aquarium, giddy with nostalgia and daring each other to enter until it no longer seemed whimsical, but rather the most romantic backdrop to a selfie on earth. He'd teased me but finally relented when I refused to go in until we'd walked back to the Tesco Express to buy a cereal packet with a 2-for-1 voucher and it wasn't romantic at all. Not with ten thousand tourists and screaming children snapping at our heels but the penguins were cute. (Not so much the cuddly one he'd bought me in the giftshop afterwards but it was a sweet memento even if it ended up living out the rest of its days at the back of my wardrobe.)

At three o'clock and finally no longer blinking as our eyes adjusted to the light of day, we'd stumbled into a gastropub where the menu sounded like horticulture and the prices reflected the chef's elite ambitions. I'd paid this time – standing firm even though I'd tried and failed to steer him into the pie shop next door which was still exorbitant but at least the thought of adding extra sides to the order didn't bring me out in a cold sweat. It wasn't the first time I'd paid for dinner by any means but it was hard to match Connor's generosity. His pockets were definitely deeper than mine.

'Mind if I check the scores?' he said, heading for the giant sofa in his giant living room.

'Oh no, I knew I should have gone home,' I groaned, only half for effect.

'Just quickly!'

My wine swilled dangerously up the side of the glass as I plonked myself down next to him and our eyes met, wide and fearful both, before crinkling with relief.

'Steady,' he said sternly and I giggled again, my whole hand shaking helplessly as I set it down out of harm's way on the side table. On a coaster.

'Yesss! Come on.' Connor shot forwards and punched the air.

'How can you possibly care so much?'

'Don't be jealouz, *ma petite*.' He leant towards me and waggled his eyebrows the way no French man has ever. 'You are my first love, but zee beautiful game will always be my mistress.'

'And the horses? What are they?'

'Zat, you don't want to know.'

I giggled and reached back for my wine.

'So, talking of Paris.' We weren't but God alone knew I didn't want to discuss the football results. I'd only just managed to get away with not having to watch the match itself. 'Shall I book off the whole of Friday or shall we go in the evening?'

'Book it off, no? I can play hooky from uni for one day. Wouldn't mind getting a quick work out in though before we head off, but I can get up early so we can still leave at around 10.30. That sound okay?'

'I guess so. Let me double-check no one else is already off on the Friday before you book anything though. I mean, it probably doesn't matter if they are. Raj is really nice. I can't see him saying no.'

'Raj is really nice, is he?'

'Really nice,' I taunted in an undertone, working my feet between his back and the cushion. He leaned forward again, pointing the remote closer to the box. Clicking across the icons on the sixty-inch flat screen and pausing ominously on the sports channel. 'We've still got the second half of that Danish film to get through, remember?'

'Swedish.'

'I thought it was Danish.'

'It's Swedish, but what do I know? I must be an idiot, right?'

'Huh?'

He slumped back squashing my feet hard against the back of the sofa. I snatched them out and stretched them over his lap instead, but he folded his arms tightly against his chest rather than touch them. To be fair, I'd been walking all day and they probably stank. I kneaded my soles against his thighs and turned my attention to the subtitles (another sex worker had gone missing in Copenhagen. That made three. It was definitely Danish).

'So, who is this *Raj*?' Connor said as an unsuspecting dog-walker stumbled across a decaying corpse in the undergrowth.

'You know Raj. He's my boss. You've met him, sort of. That day you turned up at –'

'It's just you've mentioned him like half a dozen times this weekend. Should I be worried?'

'Of Raj?' I twisted backwards straining to reach the merlot behind me. 'Um, no.' I chuckled and then felt bad for chuckling. 'He's married for starters, with a kid on the way.'

'So if he wasn't married…' Connor eyed me carefully, looked me up and down. A police dog started barking at a severed arm poking out of the bushes.

'What?' I laughed, tossing my hair back. 'Are you serious? He's like forty or something, like he's old.'

He didn't smile back. 'Yeah? And what about him? Am I supposed to believe this *old geezer* hasn't got the hots for his young ambitious assistant?'

I sat up, pulling my feet into a knot and leaning forward, hyperaware of the turn in the conversation. The taut pitch that had entered my tone. 'I'm not his assistant and no, I told you. He's married. Shanti's pregnant.'

'It's the perfect storm, then, isn't it? His wife's getting fat, probably doesn't want him touching her anymore if she's got any sense and what do you know? All of a sudden he's taking you under his wing, keeping you back late...'

I shook my head, shook the confusion off my face. 'It's really not like that. He's a nice guy –'

‘Right, you said that. Keep talking.’ He stood up sharply and strode into the kitchen, returning a few moments later with his wine glass topped up to the brim, refusing to look at me.

‘I just mean, he’s, you know, like normal. He’s not… Look, can we please stop talking about this?’

He knocked back half of his drink and sat down on the sofa, deliberately keeping to his end. ‘You were the one who brought him up. Keep bringing him up I should say.’

I pressed the heels of my palms against my eyelids until stars flickered in the darkness and the tears balancing there were under control. My hands trembled slightly as I lowered them and I disguised the tremor straining my voice with a cough. ‘Connor, I mean it. There’s nothing going on.’

He said, ‘There’d better not be’ and downed the rest of his wine, sinking back in a smouldering silence that set my pulse on edge. I curled my legs into a ball, arranged my head on the armrest and then I lay there for the rest of the evening, watching the whole scene replay in my head.

216 Days Before the Murder

Her Sister

I balanced the furry bucket hat I'd bought for Flo on my finger and spun it in the air like a circus plate on a stick. It rotated once and fell to the side. Sighing, I sunk my head back onto the pillow, my gaze wandering listlessly towards the patch of mould on the ceiling. FFS, it was definitely growing. That was all I needed. I mean, I knew it was there when I moved in, but now it was spreading through the paintwork like, well, mould, I supposed. Gross. I'd have to take a photo of it as soon as I could be bothered to get up. Date-stamp it in case the bastard landlord tried to keep my deposit. Although, could I really be held accountable for mildewing the surfaces? How much would a person have to sweat to raise that much condensation? Dad would know. I'd text him if I ever got round to recording the evidence. It kind of looked like a face. Or a sheep.

My phone vibrated on my chest and I jumped, anchoring it to my ribcage like I was deploying a defibrillator, if that's something you can do to yourself. With it still buzzing, I prised my hand away and squinted at it, the name lit up on the screen both overdue and unexpected. It took a second or five too long to accept the call.

'Yo.'

Milly's voice was instantly recognisable but different, the frantic edge adorning every word piercing my ear. 'Oh my God. Mum just told me you split up with Flo.'

I sighed, blinked slowly at the mildew. 'Yeah, like weeks ago.'

'Why didn't you tell me??'

I took a breath. Held it in as I spoke. 'When would I have told you? This is like the first time we've spoken in months.'

'It is not!' It bloody was. There abouts.

'Besides I figured you were too busy updating your online presence to see if I was okay.'

'As if.' Christ. Squeal much? The line was practically static with feedback. 'I swear to God, I only found out just now. Mum said she assumed I knew and anyway *I'm never around so it's my fault if she didn't mention it*.'

'Well, she has got a point.'

'Not relevant! And stop changing the subject. What's going on with you guys? I'm gutted. I'm genuinely gutted for you.'

I swallowed. Flung the hat across the room like a frisbee. 'Damn dawg. It ain't no thang.'

'What do you mean? Of course it is. She was like, your first proper girlfriend. You were great together and don't tell me you're fine. You were totally in love with her.'

There was a deep shelf of dirt encrusted under each of my fingernails. Dead skin probably from where I kept scratching my collarbone. Aggravating the eczema that had crept back over the last few days. I tried to flick some of it out with my thumbnail. Ended up pushing it down even further. I held the air in my chest. Looked back at the face on the ceiling. Licked my lips. 'What's that got to do with anything? It was never going to work. She's in Leeds for the next three years, I'm here in the middle of Nowheresville. We're just pre-empting the inevitable while we're still on friendly terms.'

'But that's so horribly sensible and sad.'

'Dude, everyone knows long distance relationships only end in disaster.' I shifted up the bed, rested my head against the wall, nestling the pillow into the crook of my neck until it was bordering on comfortable. 'Sooner or later the pressure starts to build, one of you gets needy, one of you gets resentful. Better to cut ties before things get nasty.'

The line went quiet for long enough to wonder if she was still there. Then, 'Are we still talking about you and Flo here?'

'Who else would we be talking about?'

'Hmmm.'

'Talking of which, how is the creepster?' I said, warming to the change of theme.

'Olive.'

'Too soon?'

'He's fine. Things are fine. Everything's good.'

'Good.' I loaded my *good* with the same depth of sorrow and outrage as I would a response to news of a mass-killing. 'So, when are you coming up to check out my new pad? It's been two months.'

'I know. I'm sorry. Work's been –'

'Work, hey?'

'Yes, work. We've been really busy. One of the team leaders has gone off on maternity leave so I've been promoted –'

'To team leader?'

'No. Jesus, ruin a story, why don't you? One of the project managers got her job so now I'm doing her role.'

'Sweet. That's great news.' I managed to flick some of the dirt out from under my thumbnail and it landed on the duvet cover in a tiny moist lump, languishing there exposed and almost surprised until I brushed it aside. A little piece of myself, forever embedded in the carpet. At least until Mum popped across to hoover.

'Thanks, but you're right,' Milly admitted correctly and not before time. 'I do need to come down. Especially now. I still can't believe you two have split up.'

I dragged my fingers down the side of my mouth. Turned it into a smirk. 'Well, yeah. I am pretty heartbroken now you mention it. I could do with a hug. A shoulder to cry on.'

'Yeah?'

'I could probably hold out until the weekend…'

'This weekend coming?'

It was like I'd asked her to lend me a kidney.

'Let me guess. You're going to London.'

'Don't say it like that,' she said all imploringly. 'You haven't given me much notice.'

I rolled my eyes. 'What about next weekend? That give you time to schedule me into your busy lifestyle? Or do you need to check with the boss first?' We both knew I didn't mean Raj.

'Oh, shut up. I will be up next weekend if only to beat your ass.'

'Promise?'

'I promise.' There followed a silence I couldn't fill. I didn't know what I was getting so choked up about. It was only Emily coming up for a visit. Like she should have done weeks ago whether I was faking an emotional breakdown or not. And I was faking it. I was fine. Absolutely fine. It was just a bit weird, that's all. It took some getting used to but splitting up was definitely the right thing to do. I probably just had a cold coming.

‘Can I text Flo?’ Milly said quietly as though she’d been building herself up to it.

‘Course you can text Flo. I’m not a freak – like your sleazy bellend of a boyfriend.’ Alright, word up – I didn’t add the character assassination but I was sure as hell thinking it especially when she said she had to go because she had *another call coming in*, like, *hello.* I’m sure ‘whoever it is’ can work out how to leave a voice message. Damn, were we ever going to talk when she got here. Two months it had been. If she hadn’t been plastering her life with the greaseball all over Instagram I’d have assumed she was on a covert mission overseas. Not that I didn’t *like* everything she posted. *Like.* Yay!

It was the only contact I had with her some weeks. We’d gone from Snapchatting for hours every day to the odd WhatsApp message and I was lucky to get that most of the time. I scrolled through our thread – the gifs, the voice memos, the stupid back and forths. Ten thousand photos of the cat sleeping in awkward death-defying locations or looking grumpy in seasonal attire. Then lately, nothing. Nearly nothing anyway. I ran my thumb over one of the few recent message exchanges dated two weeks ago. Or more precisely the day Flo and I came to the near mutual conclusion that if we split up before one of us screwed up, we could see where things stood in a couple of years. Because that was what I needed in my life – more friends.

How are you doing? I’d typed. Settling in here nicely but could do with some new blood to party with. When are you coming down? Be good to see you soon xx

K x

K. That's what I got back. My message was clearly a cry for help and that was it. K. We were in the middle of a film, she said three hours after I confronted her about it. It had subtitles.

Did it have a pause function? I replied but apparently not. I didn't get any letters back at all in response to that one, not even F.O.

Ah well, fuck it. I could do another week and a half, long as I knew she was coming. Might even actually feel okay by then. Shifted this bloody cold or whatever it was. And who knew – I gazed back up at the ceiling – maybe the landlord would have done something about the mould by then. As if.

I probably needed to make some real friends though in the meantime. See what my flatmates were up to. Put myself out there. Live a little. Just maybe not today.

I glanced back down at my phone in case I'd missed a text coming through but there were no notifications on the screen – just an idiotic shot of me and Flo sharing chips with a seagull at the end of the pier. I laid my phone back on my chest and shuffled down under the duvet. Whatever. It was already lunchtime. There was no point getting up now. Making friends could wait until tomorrow. Probably ought to show my face at a couple of lectures while I was at it. Finish off that kinetic art sculpture. No point pushing it though. It was bonkers enough Her Highness had deemed to call me. Bonkers she'd been allowed, more like.

I checked my phone again on the off-chance anyone else had been in touch in the last ten seconds, but nothing doing so whatevs. I scrunched up into a ball and shut the world out again. It was better that way.

212 Days Before the Murder

Her

Connor's legs felt snug and warm wrapped around my thighs and I snuggled into him, ran my fingers gently over his chest, the light trace of hair there, damp with sweat. The smell of him all over me. I sighed contentedly, harnessing the duvet above my shoulder and fitting myself back alongside him. He squeezed me.

'Nice weekend?' he murmured, trailing his thumb along the beautiful bee necklace he'd given me.

'The best.'

'Hmm.' He stroked my arm, caressed the goosepimples that instantly sprung up there. 'I wish you didn't have to go back tomorrow.'

'Hmm. Me too.'

'Why don't you pull a sicky? Stay here for a few more days.'

'Hmm. Wish I could.' I nuzzled into the crook of his neck. Let my eyelids droop, my thoughts drift.

I hadn't been exaggerating when I'd told Olive work was busy. The latest MagiMasc promotion was being launched on Tuesday after weeks of negotiations and last-minute changes, but I loved it. God, I loved it. This new role was so much more interesting than what they had me doing before, but I could already see myself working at the next level. Dealing with clients directly, handling my own accounts. Pulling new business in. All right, maybe that was jumping the gun, but in a year or two, definitely. Definitely. Connor craned his head down awkwardly. I raised my eyes, met his.

'What's stopping you then?'

The space between my eyebrows twitched and I stammered, stunned at his ability to read my thoughts, channel my ambitions, until it dawned on me, he was only on about me staying up longer. I laughed.

'Erm. Work. Life. Money.'

'But none of that would be a problem if you lived up here. You could get a new job, save a fortune on travel and see me all the time.'

'Connor!'

He twisted around, his neck bent. 'What? You know it's true.'

'We've only been together a few months. It's too soon. We couldn't do that.'

'How soon is too soon? We've known each other our whole lives.'

I bashed him lightly on the arm and smiled. 'I knew we shouldn't have opened that second bottle.'

'I mean it. Why don't you move in here? It makes total sense. You wouldn't have to pay me anything and it wouldn't take you long to find a new job, there are hundreds of agencies up here. Proper global companies, not like that tinpot outfit you're stuck in now. You'd be working with international household brands, part of things people have actually heard of. You could do whatever you wanted – TV advertising, digital marketing, you name it. You've got enough experience now you could easily get something. Start earning some proper money instead of the paper-round wages that twat's got you on now. And I can support you however long it takes you to get on your feet. The main thing is we'd be together.'

'Connor.' I lifted myself and turned towards him, my cheeks smarting, my heart hammering uncomfortably at his outburst even though I knew he meant well. 'I like that tinpot job.'

'Ahh,' he cried, pulling me closer to him again, folding his arms around me. 'I know you do. I think they're taking the piss, that's all and you're too nice to see it. It's hard for me to sit by and watch you be taken advantage of. You could do so much better. Especially here. The possibilities are endless. And the money… do you even know how much you could be on in London? I know freelancers who earn four hundred, five hundred quid a day.'

'What are you talking about? I'm not even a project manager. Yet. I'm lucky to have a job, let alone one I actually enjoy.'

He sighed and stroked my hair, catching his thumb in a tangle I did well not to yelp at. 'There you go, underestimating yourself again. I'm telling you, baby, if you moved up here, you'd be some project manager's manager before you'd even unpacked.'

I pulled away again, twisting my hair into rope and flicking it over my shoulder. The light from the street lamp outside fell across him, framing the intensity in his face.

'A *senior project manager* and that doesn't change the fact I like working at Optiks. At least for the time being, until I've got enough experience to actually take the next step.'

'Well, all right, I can't force you to see sense, but what if you stayed here anyway? Commuted down to Brighton. You could maybe swing a couple of days working at home every week. People do it the other way round all the time.'

‘It’d cost a fortune.’

‘Not if you didn’t have to pay any rent, it wouldn’t.’

I didn’t have to pay rent at the moment, just a few bills but I had to admit living at home with my parents after three years away wasn’t exactly the dream I’d nurtured since childhood. The lack of privacy, the endless enquiries, the only escape from my mum’s well-meant chatter my bedroom, pink and peeling behind a jumble of teenage relics I never got round to throwing away. The whole house clean and cosy but shabby with pockets of mildew in the bathroom and kitchen cabinets that had seen better days. It wasn’t a fancy apartment overlooking bars and gourmet delis, that was for sure and I did love being in London – the hustle and bustle, the mesh of cultures, the stunning architecture, the beauty of it all. It felt alive. It felt new and unexplored. Not like Brighton where I knew every alley and backstreet, every pub and restaurant. Long as it hadn’t closed down. But still it was madness. I leant forward and kissed Connor’s lips, parted in hopeful anticipation. Pressed my finger against them.

‘Thank you, but it would be a shame to rush things. This is good. This is really, really good.’

He drew a breath, closed his mouth. Turned the corners up tightly. ‘I know,’ he said. ‘I just can’t stand it when you have to go. I’ve never felt like this about anyone before. I love you so much.’

I levelled my eyes to his and smiled. ‘I love you too.’

Wrapping his arms around me again, his heartbeat drummed, strong and steady against mine. ‘I feel like I’m home whenever I’m with you. I’ve never had that. I’ve never known what it’s like to feel completely safe. So completely certain of anything. Mum always means well, but after the fire, after Dad…'

I ran my hands up his side, swaddled him with as much of myself as I could stretch along the length of his body.

"I've always felt on edge, like I need to protect her. Even before the accident – accident or whatever it was – idiocy. My father wasn't a good man…'

'I know,' I whispered softly. I remembered the bruises, the uneasy shadow that seemed to flicker around him, the nervous twitches, the way I'd found his anxiety irritating. Dull. The times I'd refused to come down from my room when he came round with his mum till the visits trailed off and I'd almost forgotten about him. Until years later when he became the boy whose dad had burned the house down with a cigarette, an empty bottle of whisky at his feet. Notorious and yet still instantly forgettable.

The thought of my cavalier disinterest twisted my stomach, weighted my heart with shame. I looked into his eyes. 'You don't have to worry anymore. He's gone and I'm here now. Even if we have to be apart sometimes, I'm always at the end of the phone. I'm always thinking about you. And yes, in a year or so maybe, ask me again. I love being here. You feel like home too, I just don't want to ruin what we've got by moving too fast.'

He buried his face in my hair, inhaled the scent of it. 'I know, baby. I know you're probably right. You can't blame me for wanting you all to myself though.'

I laughed. Hoped my scalp wasn't greasy. Edged slightly away just in case.

'I'll just have to come up with ways to cope without you until Friday,' he continued obliviously.

'Oh, not this Friday,' I said like the thought had popped to mind there and then instead of hovering in the background all weekend like an awkward guest at a party refusing to speak. 'I told Olive I'd go down to Exeter.'

'What?' He bucked upright, incredulous and uncertain he'd heard correctly. 'You've only just seen her.'

I pulled a face. A sort of silly, jovial pout. 'It's been eight weeks.'

'Eight weeks?' He sunk back against the pillows. 'For fuck's sake, let her settle in. She'll be trying to make new friends. She won't want you hanging around cramping her style.'

'She invited me.' I greased my voice with forced lightness. I knew he'd be like this, that was why I'd put it off when I should have told him as soon as I'd spoken to Olive last week. It would have been easier over the phone too. Now I'd left it too late and he was disappointed.

'She's probably just being polite,' he said. 'Besides, it's not that long till Christmas. You'll see her then anyway.'

Christmas? That was like two months away. I laid my head down on his chest, my face unreadable, out of view. 'It's just that she's really upset about breaking up with Flo.'

'Oh, come on. Is that what she told you?' He slid past me roughly, reaching for the glass of water on the bedside cabinet. 'They can't have been very serious if they didn't even make it through the first term. Besides which, she'll be loving being single right now. Hooking up with whoever she wants, no strings attached.

You know what girls are like at university. Always experimenting with their sexuality. She'll be fighting them off.' He chugged the water back and set the glass down on the floor, loosening his grip on me and repositioning himself, his back against the headrest, his eyes slits.

'I don't think –'

'Course she is,' he sneered knowingly. 'Let's hope they're not all curly-haired brunettes though. You've got to admit, that was a bit weird. Her and Flo. I mean, why would you want to date someone who looks that much like your sister?'

I wasn't sure there was more than a passing resemblance between us and only then if you ignored the fact that Flo's hair could have its own modelling career while I always looked like I was wearing mine for a laugh.

'I'll take that as a compliment –' I said and he snorted. '– from both of you, not that I think Olive's got a thing or whatever, for… but she's a bit all over the place after everything that's happened. I mean, you would be, wouldn't you? I just want to make sure she's okay.'

'She's manipulating you.' His voice had a sing-song lilt to it but I could tell he thought the whole 'break up' was an elaborate ruse to get me to shlep all the way over there. It was sad really. I couldn't imagine what it must be like not to have any siblings, not to know that unbreakable bond, that certain knowledge that whatever life threw at you, however many friends came and went, the number of heartbreaks endured, at the end of the day your family would always be there for you, no matter what. It wasn't selfish of her to need me. I needed her too.

'I miss her a bit, that's all.'

'What? You miss her more than you miss me in the week?'

'No, of course not. I miss you the same,' I teased trying to recapture our earlier connection, that smug self-satisfaction.

'Really? The same? After everything we've just talked about. After I opened my heart to you about my dad and that house…'

My smile stiffened at the turn of his tone. I sat up, one leg still draped across his thigh but bunching the covers between us now, my head angled towards him. 'I'm kidding. I miss you more obviously. It's only that… I haven't seen her for a while.'

'But if you go and see her next weekend you won't have seen me for a while. And, it's not just that.' He looked crestfallen. 'I had something planned. Theatre tickets.'

'Oh,' I felt my eyes widen, my jaw go slack. 'For what?'

'It was supposed to be a surprise. You've ruined it now. Fuck it. I'll bin them if you don't want to go.'

That wasn't fair. Of course I wanted to go, I only wished he'd told me earlier so we could have avoided all of this.

I swallowed and my throat clicked when I spoke. 'Is there no way we could change them for the following week?'

'My God, honestly. Sometimes I forget how uncultured you are. No, you can't change them, babe. They're not like, I don't know, vague plans you fixed up with someone you could see anytime. But don't worry about it. They only cost a few hundred quid. They're not quite as hard to come by as gold dust. Close enough but you know, I'm made of money, me, aren't I? You go ahead and do what you like.'

I don't know why but panic was clawing at my throat. A frantic rush of dread that took my breath away, teeming around us like wasps in a swarm. I wasn't equipped for this sort of confrontation and Olive, well Olive had said she was fine.

'Look, I'll… I'll tell her I can't make it.'

'Really?'

'Yeah.'

'Really?' He pulled me into his arms, all sign of the anger that had seeped from him moments before vanquished. Gone. Replaced by tenderness, the affection he drip-fed me. 'I don't want to spoil your plans or anything, I just had the entire thing set out in my mind, you know. I was going to make a whole special night of it all. I've ruined the surprise now.'

'No, no. Honestly, I still don't know where we're going or anything. Forget I know anything about it. I'll come up next weekend.'

'Yeah?' He looked down at me imploringly, his eyes scanning mine.

'Yeah.'

'I love you, baby.' He drew me closer to him, tightened his hold.

'I love you too,' I said stroking the smooth skin on his torso in a voice that didn't quite sound like my own.

212 Days Before the Murder

Him

The trouble with Emily was, she never knew when she was being taken for a ride. She had this naïve trust in people and they could always tell. She was far too nice for her own good. Take that crappy job and all the shit that came with it. Not only did she put up with being everyone's bitch in that pathetic embarrassment of an office, but she was actually grateful to be ordered about, allowed to cling to the lowest rung on the ladder. And it was a pretty ropy ladder at that. Ha. Ropy. I'd have to remember to work that into the conversation next time it came up. She'd like that.

Seriously though, it was like she had Stockholm syndrome or something. Her sister was just as bad, always pretending to be looking out for her when all the time she was trying to bring her down to her own miserable level.

She couldn't stand to see Emily happy, especially not with me. She knew I saw through her crocodile tears. Saw her for exactly what she was – the scheming little cow she'd always been. A calculating liar, always there in the background, niggling away, yap yap yap, bitching about me. Whispering poison into Emily's ear, even when we were kids. Things had been fine until she got in the way and there she was still, doing everything she could to get between us.

Well, let her try. I was onto her. I was onto all of them, the nasty fuckers, but what they didn't know – none of them – was that we were meant to be together, Emily and me. It wasn't a coincidence, running into her that night. It was fate, the universe taking charge of our destinies. What we had was impenetrable. Preordained. That's how strong the connection was between us. How much we loved each other.

They could try all they liked but there was nothing anyone could do to break our bond. And nothing could hurt her anymore, not with me standing by her side – the only person in her life who truly had her best interests at heart.

I had Emily's back now. All those other bastards had better watch theirs.

205 Days Before the Murder

Her Mother

I took my place at the table, the sweet, meaty tones of gravy wafting around me as vapour rose from the jug like a Bisto advert. Only this was no Bisto. The freshly poured jus cascaded down the piped formations of potato purée, pooling spectacularly around the wild boar and thyme sausages, the sautéed broccoli and green beans glistening with garlic butter.

'Oh, David,' my mother gasped, as though he was touching her somewhere he shouldn't and she rather liked it. 'This mash is spot on.'

He beamed, swelling with hollow nonchalance. 'Thanks, Bell. It's just a little something I've been experimenting with.'

I snorted somewhat ungraciously, quickly morphing my expression into one of enthusiastic agreement at the sense of all eyes upon me.

'Go on then, don't keep us in suspense. What have you done differently to it?'

David cocked his eyebrows, a creamy lump of carbohydrate suspended from the serving spoon as though it held healing properties. 'Crème fraîche, would you believe?'

'Crème fraîche?' my mother cooed, simulating the appraisal of a woman who'd heard of it. 'Now there's a thing. I would never have guessed that.'

‘Gives it the lighter texture you’re probably picking up on.’

‘Hmm. I expect it’s healthier too, is it, David?’

‘It is. Boiled the spuds for a good half hour as well. Really made sure all the lumps were out.’

‘I can see that. Have you ever done it this way before, Clare?’

‘Might have,’ I muttered, unable to keep the arch out of my response. ‘I’ve made it so many times over the years, I forget.’

Honestly, I don’t know what they were getting so excited about. It was only mashed potato. David had been ‘getting into’ his cooking as of late and it seemed to necessitate an excessive degree of acknowledgement and explanation. Not that I didn’t appreciate some respite from the kitchen but I couldn’t help but resent his waiting twenty-five years before getting involved. I mean, I’d cooked virtually every meal we’d ever eaten – to very little applause I might add – and then the minute the girls left home (not that Emily had left, I kept forgetting, we saw her so rarely these days), he finally decided to go all Gordon Ramsey on us. Nice for some. It was a good job I didn’t mind waiting three hours for my *pasta al ragù* (spag bol to you and me). Try doing that with two growing girls pulling the weekly shop out of the cupboards if dinner wasn’t on the table at six o’clock on the dot. Crème fraîche? He’d have said it sounded like part of the Dulux range if I’d asked him two months ago.

‘It’ll never live up to the one Clare does with cheese and mustard though.’ David rubbed my forearm as though appeasing a small child, but for the love of God, I could never stay cross at him for long.

'It's delicious, David,' I confirmed benevolently (although I did make a bit of a show of adding extra salt it didn't need. That was unnecessary now I think about it).

'So put me out of my misery, what was the big surprise in the end. Cats?'

Ginger lifted his head and seemed to be assessing the likelihood of his being called upon to provide a judgement on the wild boar, but decided against it, preferring to go back to sleep. I refrained from pointing this out to David of course and instead said, 'Cats isn't on anymore, Mum, but whatever it was supposed to be, it was cancelled and we're still none the wiser.'

'Cancelled?' Bella eyed me sceptically as though, as usual, I couldn't be trusted to have understood.

'Something about the star of the show being ill.'

'I thought they had understudies for that sort of thing.'

'All I know is, it's best not to bring it up – with either of them. Milly gets tetchy if you even mention it and I know Olivia was upset about Emily changing their plans because she hasn't said a word about it. Not one single word.'

'Oh dear.'

'Exactly.'

'I mean, I'm not one to stick my nose into other people's business as you know –'

'Well…'

'But on this occasion, I felt I had no choice.'

'Of course,' my mother said drily and I'm not sure I entirely caught her meaning but thought it best to ignore her, in between mouthfuls of mash. It really was very good.

‘I told Milly that David and I were going to Exeter next weekend and there’d be plenty of room if she wanted a lift.’

‘You’re going to Exeter?’

‘I made it very clear I thought Olive would appreciate her tagging along but all she said was she’d have to ask Connor in case he’d rebooked those mysterious theatre tickets or had something else lined up which sounded very much like a *no*.’

‘But you’re still going down to Exeter...?’

I sighed. ‘Yes, Mum. I take it you’d like to join us.’

She lifted her cutlery into the air with apparent astonishment that I even needed to ask. ‘Well, since you’re offering, yes, I would. I can’t think of anything more pressing than seeing my granddaughter, especially when she’s feeling so down about that lovely girl. She won’t say a word about that either.’

‘I know, bless her.’ I stabbed the end of my fancy sausage and sawed through it with more vigour than was needed, breathing deeply and shaking my head. ‘Honestly, we’ve got one who’s getting a bit too much love and one who’s not getting enough. We can never get it right, can we?’

‘I don’t know about that,’ David murmured suggestively, still high on admiration and not burning the broccoli, but that was me done. One compliment a day for something I should be allowed to take for granted was my absolute limit. But even so, I couldn’t let the comment pass without a rueful grin. There was no harm in keeping him sweet. Who knew, with a little encouragement maybe he’d ‘get into’ the hoovering too. Goodness knew, Emily wasn’t about to do it. Marvellous as it was having her home, she wasn’t one to fret over the housework. Or the piles of cardigans and socks she left in her wake the same way Ginger shed cat hairs.

Still, it was a small price to pay for having her back, even if she was out more than she was in. As long as she still had one foot in the door, I could fool myself into believing she'd be my sweet girl for a little while longer – a few years at least, until I was ready to let her go properly. Besides, Olivia only had another thirty-two months before she graduated so I just needed Emily to hold on until then.

I'd even begun to nurture the faint hope that this thing with Connor might have fizzled out by then too – not that I wished that upon them, not at the time. Not exactly, although perhaps if I'd said those words aloud, perhaps if we'd all aired our slight misgivings, our almost baseless suspicions instead of discounting our doubts as petty jealousies, she'd still be here, the Emily we once knew. The little girl I'd do anything now to hold in my arms again to keep safe. To keep the monsters at bay.

But it was too late for that even then. The monster was already here and he had other plans for our daughter.

202 Days Before the Murder

Her

The microwave pinged a few moments after the pasta started to crackle and I swung the door open with a mild sense of dread, but despite a hint of crust around the edges of the cream sauce, there was no collateral damage to speak of. I slammed the door shut with my elbow and flung the plate down on the workbench, belatedly pressing my fingers into a damp cloth to stem the pulse of heat searing through them. 'Ow.'

'Don't put it on for more than two minutes,' Mum screeched from the living room. 'The plate gets too hot.'

Dad had used the posh crockery and only served up a tiny portion.

'There's more in the pot,' he yelled rendering his grand pretensions futile, but it did look amazing.

'What is it?' I asked joining the cat on the sofa, the tantalising aroma wafting towards him making his nostrils inflate.

'Home-made tagliatelle with wild mushrooms, roasted garlic and truffle cream,' Dad announced, struggling to maintain the slightest degree of modest detachment. Mum clenched her jaw but was otherwise supportive. She'd begun to embrace his latest obsession with cooking now that she'd taken to hiding bourbons in her knicker drawer to stave off the pangs of hunger that would otherwise have felled her in the wait.

‘Homemade tagliatelle? Wowzers.’ It was a little chewy truth be told but that was probably my fault. ‘Mmmm. This is… mmm… this is delicious, Dad. Really good.’ I wiped my thumb across my chin, licked the dribble of cream off it. Resisted drying it on my jumper. Hanging around with Connor really was rubbing off on me.

‘How was work?’ Mum asked seven minutes later when their programme had finished and they remembered I was there.

‘Good. Good. Really good actually. We won that pitch I was helping Chloe prepare for last week.’

‘The washing tablet things? That is good news.’

‘Laundry balls but anyway, guess who’s been promoted to junior project manager…’

That finally got their attention. Even Ginger’s ears pricked up in the flurry of excitement (in a discontented manner).

‘Oh, darling,’ Mum said managing to lean across from the armchair and squish my hand before the opening credits of Bake Off. ‘That’s wonderful.’

‘Wonderful,’ Dad echoed conveying unsurpassed pride without taking his eyes off the telly. A few months ago, he’d have been fast asleep with his mouth hanging open but that was prior to developing opinions on pastry and the best way to cook a tangerine. I scraped the last of the truffle sauce onto my fork and wrapped my tongue around it, playing for time, but this was probably as good a moment as any to have a heart-to-heart. I took a deep breath. Plonked the plate on the floor casually.

‘And also, Connor thinks I should move up to London, you know, into his place.’

That did it. Mum finally remembered she could press pause. My parents' eyes met fleetingly before they turned to me and Mum said, 'Really? Seems a bit soon, doesn't it?' in the same voice she uses when cajoling elderly patients to use the bathroom.

'It makes sense, that's all. We're in and out of each other's houses all the time.'

'Well, you're in and out of his.'

'Exactly, so he was thinking – I was thinking, it makes sense –'

Dad's eyebrows had met in the middle. 'But what about your job?'

I grinned as though I had all the answers. 'I'll commute down. People do it all the time the other way round. The train will be empty, I should think.'

'But it's exorbitant at that time –'

'It's fine, Dad, besides I won't be spending money on rent –'

'You don't spend money on rent here.'

'And I can look for a new job once I'm up there so then the journey won't even be an issue.'

They nearly shot out their seats at that. 'But you love that job!' they shrieked in perfect unison like they'd planned it. Honestly, it would have been funny if my stomach hadn't been churning like a schoolgirl being marched to the headteacher's office. I don't even know why I was worried about telling them. This was good news. I'd finally be out of their hair. They could do whatever it was old people did when their kids finally left home. Jigsaws, bridge mornings, swinging parties…

'I know,' I said, all teeth and jazz hands. 'But it's not the only job in the world.'

‘But you just got promoted…’

‘Which means I’ll be able to get an even better job up in London. They have hundreds of agencies up there and Connor knows someone at his gym who reckons he might be able to sort something out for me. It won’t be hard to find work there. It’s like the advertising capital of the UK. I mean, it is the capital. It’s where everything happens.’

They looked back at each other again, sinking into their respective armchairs, turkey necks sagging in defeat. An almost imperceptible shrug passing between them.

‘It’s just a shame that’s all. We’ve got used to having you back here with us. It’ll be quiet without both you and Olive.’

‘I know, but we’ll be back to visit all the time. And you guys can come up to us. Plus, if we’re seeing each other in the week, he won’t mind so much if I pop down at the weekends or go to Exeter.’

They had that look on their face again, just for a moment. It was a poor choice of words, but it was true. He did get upset sometimes when I tried to see anyone else or make plans without him, but that was only because of everything he’d been through, his insecurities, the lack of trust he had in people who loved him. It wasn’t his fault. Anyone would have been the same growing up in that environment, feeling the way he had, but he was better when he was with me. Slowly but surely, I was helping him work through his pain, put his past behind him and move on. I was fixing him and my being in London would be so much less stressful for the both of us.

It had only been a month since he’d first broached the subject and I’d been adamant at the time that things were moving too quickly, but the more he worked on me, the less plausible my reasons for not going for it seemed and Olive was right, long-distance relationships were hard. There was too much pressure on the time you had together. Every squabble you had felt like make or break. Every disagreement, a crisis. This way we could enjoy each other's company without misinterpreting each other's intentions. Without getting into a row over every petty misunderstanding.

'Well, if you're sure,' Mum said uneasily, pointing the remote at Prue's half-closed eyes, her gormless mouth frozen mid-sentence, the gentle pressure of her thumb against the raised triangle bringing the old dear back to life. Bringing an end to the conversation. At least for the time being.

202 Days Before the Murder

Her Sister

18.53

You already know what I think but do what you like. You always do.

191 Days Before the Murder

Her

I pulled my jumper over my head and yanked my hair free, letting it fall in moist tangles like seaweed, slow drips oozing into the polyester weave. Fresh steam filled the smear I'd cleared in the mirror with the side of my palm, airbrushing me out of my own reflection. 'Kill me,' I sighed.

I eased the door open quietly and padded across the bedroom, but Connor rolled over, his heavy-lidded eyes glowing in the unnatural streak of amber light creeping through the curtains.

'Babe, come back to bed. It's pitch-black outside.'

'I can't. I'll miss my train,' I said swigging back the last of my coffee and setting the mug down on the bedside table.

He groaned, pulling his pillow over his head, his untamed hair matted with the remnants of sleep. 'Miss it then. It's costing you more to go to work than you actually earn.'

'Not quite.'

'Just hand your notice in already. You're going to leave anyway and Adam said that position at his place is practically in the bag.'

I slumped onto the bed and wrestled an uncooperative sock over my damp foot. 'Are you sure he doesn't want to meet me first?'

'He doesn't need to meet you. He trusts my judgement. Unlike some people…'

I paused, already exhausted from simply trying to get out of the house. I really could have done without having to get up at five thirty every day but it seemed a bit rash to give up a job I loved without lining something else up first. 'Let me think about it.'

'Do it today. I'll chase up Adam. Get him to push through the paperwork.'

I slipped back into the bathroom, swung the cabinet open, picked my toothbrush up and scowled at it for a moment, my vision blurry.

'Does that look pink to you?' I said stepping into the doorway and brandishing it under the florescent light.

'What?'

'My toothbrush. I could have sworn it was pink.'

'What are you talking about? It's always been that colour.'

'Really?' I walked over to the window, held it up to the streetlamp. Examined it. I was either going colourblind or mad. It was definitely purple and I didn't like purple.

'Get back into bed.' He reached over, his arms coiling around my thighs and pulled me towards him. 'You're giving that thing more attention than me.'

'I've got to go.' I squealed, forcing myself back up to my feet, a consolidatory kiss primed to brush his forehead, but he jerked his chin up and our lips clashed in a fusion of sour morning breath.

I glanced once more at the toothbrush, the paste dangling dangerously ready to drop and shovelled it in my mouth, striding in the same gulp back towards the bathroom. Shower room really since there was no bath although that made it sound small when in fact it was bigger than our family bathroom at home. At Mum and Dad's house, I should say. I spat in the sink and ran the tap. Took stock of myself one last time in the misty mirror. I looked like I'd applied my make-up with a butter knife but it would have to do.

'Right,' I said heading decisively for the bed. 'I really am off.'

Connor lifted his lips towards me. 'Got your necklace?'

I tugged it out from under my myriad of layers and it swung back and forth as though in flight. He flicked it gently and pulled me towards him. 'Have a good day. Hand your notice in.'

'You too,' I sang, ignoring his advice, if you can call it that. 'Oh.'

He looked up idly as I patted myself down, scanned the floor next to the bedside table.

'Alright?'

'I thought I left my cardholder here when I emptied my pockets last night.'

'Maybe it's in your bag.'

'No, I definitely put it on the side here. I went through my jeans before I stuck them in the laundry basket.' I sunk down onto my hands and knees, squinted into the darkness under the bed, the torch on my phone dispersing shadows like rabbits skittering in surprise. Connor growled as a strobe of light flashed past him, a spark of irritation briefly illuminated as he scrunched his eyes.

'They're not in here. Just go and check in your bag.'

I staggered up, fumbling now, my pulse jittery as I wrenched my dirty jeans out of the laundry basket and rooted through the pockets. I couldn't have lost it. It had my oyster card and the world's most expensive season pass in it.

'Where is it?'

'Go and check your bag.'

‘I didn’t take my bag out yesterday,’ I cried, my exasperation muffled as I scuttled towards the front door, rising panic making my socks slip and skid on the polished floorboards. I grabbed my handbag from the coatrack and waded through it, discarding the tissues and sanitary towels. The forgotten lipstick and an old fluffy tampon that had worked itself out of its wrapper. ‘Oh, wait, I’ve got it!’

‘Told you,’ Connor said appearing in the hallway, the duvet wrapped around him like a Jedi cape, the winter edition. ‘What would you do without me?’

I shook my head, stumbled back towards him. ‘I’m so late now. I’ve gotta run.’

I pecked him on the cheek, but he held the neck of my jumper steady and pulled me back towards him, pressing his lips against my mouth, his eyes open, probing mine.

‘I love you,’ he whispered breathlessly. It was all very intense.

‘I love you too.’

‘Hand your notice in,’ he laughed letting go and I teetered back, deftly grabbing my coat and bag as I righted myself and hobbled out of the apartment with only half a foot in each of my trainers, my bus no doubt on time for once and whizzing past the stop on its convoluted route to the station. My phone pinged in my pocket and I drew it out with only a cursory glance as I stepped into the biting pre-dawn air.

Hand your notice in it said.

165 Days Before the Murder

Her Mother

The heat pumping out from the radiators hit me as soon as we stepped into the house and I sighed, biting back a comment about soaring energy prices and (with only a modicum of resentment) turned down the thermostat before David realised. Having hung my jacket on the end of the banister, I eased my heels off, pins and needles shooting up my legs as blood rushed to fill the crushed capillaries inflating my poor toes.

'Who's hidden my slippers?' Bella cried accusingly as though they had every right to sit pride of place in my shoe cabinet.

Stifling yet another comment, I tossed them on the floor with only a hint of the fragile intolerance that had been building (and occasionally spilling over) since early afternoon.

I had offered to drop her off back at her house around the corner but she wasn't having any of it. She'd been inviting herself over for dinner more and more since David had taken over the cooking. For a woman who liked to brag her enviable figure (wrinkles aside) was down to a strict nun-like diet consisting mainly of tinned sardines, she could certainly put it away when she 'popped in'. Either that or she was combating the rising cost of living by tagging herself onto our monthly outgoings.

‘We’re home,’ I yelled giving David half a chance to run through his intuitive – and not altogether subtle – response to the news I wasn’t alone.

‘How was your lunch?’ he said, dragging his eyes away from a frayed copy of Mary Berry’s Baking Bible and valiantly mustering interest.

‘I had the salmon,’ Bella declared, making her way to her favourite armchair, which as fortune would have it, was also my favourite armchair. ‘It was very overdone.’

‘Really?’ David cocked his head. ‘Was it pan-seared?’

‘Pan-soaked, I should say.’ She adjusted the cushion and settled her thin stockinged legs onto the foot stool, exposing the Ginger coated soles of her slippers. ‘It was swimming in butter.’

‘Hmm.’ David looked to be lost in his own world for a moment. ‘They’d have been better off grilling it in foil and leaving it to steam in its own juices, I’d have thought.’

I perched pointedly on the edge of the sofa, making slightly more of the fact I was unfamiliar with that corner of the sitting room than was perhaps necessary. ‘I had the chicken pie and your daughter is fine, in case you’re interested.’

We’d met her in the shabby little pub around the corner from her office. It was the only way we got to see her these days what with the hours she worked and the long commute. Not to mention the immovable plans that kept her busy every weekend.

‘Sorry, love.’ David slammed Mary Berry shut and turned as if noticing me for the first time. ‘How is she?’

‘Not quite as confident about that new job working out as she was last week.’

'The one Connor was sorting out for her?'

'Connor's friend, yes.'

The curtains swayed and the cat appeared bleary-eyed from behind it, crumpled and stretching in a way that suggested he'd been in that exact spot since we left him there that morning. I patted my lap but he was in no mood for pleasantries.

'I told her not to quit before she had something else lined up.'

'We all told her that, David,' I bristled.

'What's she going to do then?'

I exhaled noisily with a disenchanted shrug. 'She's sent her CV off to a few recruitment agencies. Says it's only a matter of time, but I get the impression she wishes she'd held off before she handed her notice in.'

David sucked his teeth. It wasn't altogether pleasant but I stayed on point. 'So, two more weeks and that's her done down here.'

'And there's no chance she can stay on until she sorts herself out?' he said answering his own question.

'It would be 'too humiliating' apparently. Far better to starve.'

'She'll be all right,' Bella declared, vanquishing all our silly worries. 'There's plenty of work up in London. When I lived in Islington, I was offered something new every other week.'

Even Ginger shuddered and jumped off the windowsill. I rolled my eyes.

'Oh God. Tell David about your crème brûlée, Mother.'

'It was out of a packet.' Outrageous. 'Nothing like as good as yours.'

'Ah, that's very kind of you to say, Bell.'

Jesus wept. I took the cat's cue and followed him into the kitchen. The one good thing about the girls no longer demanding freshly-ironed shirts and lifts to the station at all hours was it was never too early for wine.

139 Days Before the Murder

Her

Jeeessssuuuuusssss. It was five o'clock again. Five o'clock and the chances of hearing back from anyone before they all pretended they'd finished their To Do lists and headed home were diminishing by the minute.

'Why can't anyone get back to me?' I shouted at my phone in a way that immediately made me feel bad as well as fleetingly concerned it wouldn't ring now out of spite.

'Sorry,' I added, probably unnecessarily. I tapped it again in case something had come through in the last few seconds and I'd missed it, but the screensaver was ominously uncluttered. Even the sight of Ginger with one leg in the air and his tongue sticking out couldn't cheer me up.

I'd been officially unemployed for three weeks now and counting and I couldn't help but wish I could take my resignation back. I really missed working at Optiks, missed the buzz, the feeling of being part of something important. I even missed having an hour and a half to myself on the commute to sit and read or do nothing at all except look out the window. Not that I didn't have plenty of time to do that now, but it was different. I was going places then, both literally and figuratively but none of that compared to how much I missed the people. People I thought would miss me too. Liked me at the very least. I mean they must have. They'd thrown me a leaving do even though I'd only been there a few months, which was why I couldn't understand it – what Raj had done.

The thought of it brought a lump to my throat, as painful now as when Josh at the recruitment agency had told me what had happened that morning and now he wasn't taking my calls. The promise of finding me *something amazing*, apparently on hold as well. I scrolled through my emails in case my notifications had failed, pressed refresh and refresh again.

'Shiiiiiiitttttt!!!!'

My phone clattered on the workbench as I turned my attention to the pasta sauce bubbling away on the stove, hob, whatever it was called. It looked as watery as hell and it was spitting everywhere. That would have to be cleaned up before Connor got home. I gave it a wipe with a dishcloth but furious red-hot specks spattered the surface before I'd even thrown it back in the… metal thing the dishcloths go in.

'Fuck itttttt.'

A sharp tinny ping punctured the air and my stomach lurched, my breath suspended in the sickening moment it took to realise it was only Connor letting me know he was nearly home. Which I probably could have worked out from his last message telling me he was on the bus.

I ground my teeth, tears pricking the backs of my eyes. Stirred the pasta sauce again. Tapped my phone, refreshed my inbox, checked the binned emails in case I'd accidentally deleted something important, scrolled back down through everything that had come in that day, double checked all the useless automated junk mail from the recruitment sites I'd uploaded my CV on. If nothing else, there was plenty of work available in care homes in the area. Lots of office administration positions to be had. An offer of an interview from some random bank. Like any of that had anything to do with advertising or project management.

Oh, why hadn't I just waited? Made sure that mystery job Connor's mate kept promising was all sorted, really was in the bag instead of handing in my notice before I'd even had an interview. A proper job description. Especially as there was no job. It had disappeared a week ago along with any more mention of Adam.

'Idiotttt!'

I slammed by finger on the home screen button, shutting Gmail down and instantly a photo of Connor standing in front of the Eiffel Tower last weekend appeared on the memories inlay. I flinched, bringing my hands up to my face in shame, smothering the thought of it but the day played out like an old movie reel against a backdrop of darkness when I closed my eyes.

His face, God, his face, after I told him I'd been there before and I couldn't explain what had possessed me. I'd known he'd be jealous. I could have just kept quiet. Pretended I'd been there as a kid like everyone else on our side of the channel but no, blabbermouth here, Miss Insensitivity couldn't keep her mouth shut. Couldn't let him enjoy the charade. Christ, I cringed at the sound of my words echoing through my head.

'Look, look, over there. It's Notre-Dame. We couldn't see it last time. It was still covered up with scaffolding.'

'Last time?' he'd said, turning towards me, my hair blowing in his face, his hand raised to brush it off, brush his own back, the wind whipping around us, ferrying clouds away as if employed by the tourist board to maintain the pristine views. A horde of tourists and the crisp early winter chill failing to tarnish the blissful exhilaration that had enveloped us the moment we'd pulled into Gare du Nord. Only I could ruin that.

'As in recently? After the fire?'

'Mmm,' I'd smiled, snuggling into him as I realised my mistake. Overcompensating with affection to alleviate any concerns he might have had. 'I came with a friend a couple of years ago.'

'A friend?'

'Just someone I was seeing on and off. No one special.' I'd wrapped my arms around him and lifted my mouth expectantly. 'Not like you.'

'Sorry,' he'd said, pulling away. 'Let me get this straight. You came to the most romantic city in the world with somebody else and then you lied about it and now… now I'm standing at the top of the Eiffel Tower thinking I've never been happier and this is the moment you decide to rub it in my face.'

My cheeks flushed and I'd stuttered, crippled by the rising anger in his voice and the buzz of interest emanating around us. The nudges and surreptitious looks drawn to the commotion.

'I didn't lie about it,' I'd whispered hoarsely, my eyes darting, my thumb imploring on his elbow. 'It just never came up.'

He'd stared at me, his mouth twisted in disgust as he took a step back, wrenching his arm out of my reach.

'Who are you?' he'd spat and there was nothing, nothing I could have said. No words to save me that didn't undermine his feelings, that I could even think to form. I was frozen, incapable of processing whether his outrage was an overreaction, my omission such a betrayal, which of us was even in the wrong, but from the look on his face, it was me. I'd fucked up and he'd barely glanced my way for the next half hour, didn't say one word in the time it had taken us to get back down to earth again and then he'd disappeared.

One moment he was there, his back to me, the set of his shoulders stiff, his resentment unyielding and the next he was gone, his phone ringing resolutely unanswered, the dozen or so frantic text messages I sent ignored.

My passport and almost everything I had with me were back at the hotel and I had no idea where it was, not even the name of it. He'd booked it and followed the online directions and I'd followed him. Followed him everywhere. I only knew it was near an underground station but I hadn't bothered to notice which one. I'd rung him again, rung him every couple of minutes. Paced from one end of the green to the other, each time returning to the foot of the tower as though he'd materialise from behind a bunch of Canadians with an apologetic wave and a keychain. But he hadn't.

It was dark by the time he finally answered his phone and I was cold and angry, ready to lay my own feelings bare but as soon as I saw him, saw the hurt in his eyes masked by guilt and sorrow, I melted. Melted into him, let the violent accusations I'd been fuelled by all afternoon slip away. I was the one who'd screwed everything up. I wasn't quite sure how I could have avoided it other than by actually lying, but I'd spoilt the holiday and any memory we had of it for the rest of all time.

I slowly lowered my hand and turned my phone off. Laid it on the workbench with the screen facing down just as the key turned in the lock and Connor's daily one-liner chimed down the hallway.

'Hi honey, I'm home.'

It was already old by the third time he'd used it, but I wiped my hands down my jogging bottoms and went out to greet him instead of aiming the empty tin of tomatoes at his head.

'Hey.'

'Heeyyy, there she is, my girl. How are you doing?' He stuck his bottom lip out. It was going to be harder to be nice than I'd thought.

'Not too bad.'

He pulled me into a bear hug, swayed me to and fro. I tolerated the effort for a few seconds then stepped back, my face composed to its factory settings.

'Hear anything?' he said the way a doctor might ask if there was anyone you'd like to be there before announcing your leg was going to have to come off. I turned and led him into the kitchen before he saw my expression drop.

'Not yet. I'm guessing it's a no.'

'Oh, well.' He picked up the dishcloth and wiped the spatter I'd missed off the splashback.

'It's just so annoying. The interview went so well.'

It really had and the job was exactly the sort of thing I'd been hoping for. Project manager in a small team working on TV and online advertising campaigns. And the office itself was so cool. Really funky with a free canteen, bar really. You could even help yourself to beer and wine if you worked late, order in pizzas or Chinese. Apparently. That's what the guy who'd interviewed me had said anyway along with *I'm sure you'll fit in really well here. We just need to check your references but, yeah, tell Josh I'll drop him a line first thing in the morning.* And then he'd winked. He'd winked. Everyone knows what that means. I had it. I was so sure we'd even celebrated in the evening. With champagne.

'I know, babe. We've been over this three times already today. The guy sounded like a sleazeball anyway. You're better off not working there.'

'But I really liked it and, it's not just missing out on the job. It's Raj. I just can't understand why he'd do that. To actually go to the trouble of ringing them himself to tell them what a shit employee I was. I mean, how did he even know I'd had an interview at that stage?'

'These people all know each other. They talk.'

'But it was just so malicious. What could I have possibly done to make him sabotage everything for me like that?'

He stirred the pasta sauce and turned the heat down. 'You did kind of shaft him by leaving him in the lurch the way you did. Besides, the guy's an arsehole. That's what arseholes do.'

'But I thought he liked me. He was always so lovely.'

'Oh babe.' Connor returned the spoon to the thing that spoons sit in on the side and squeezed my arm, his lips stretched with pity. 'You're so naïve sometimes, bless you. He did like you – too much, that's the trouble, I told you that. This is all retaliation for not shagging him. Forget about it. Forget about both of them. You can do better.'

There was no point denying it. Besides I wasn't so sure now. I shrieked quietly through clenched teeth, 'I don't know how. As far as Josh is concerned after today, I'm lazy and unreliable. At the very least I've got a terrible reference. He's not going to keep sending me out for interviews now.'

'Forget him too. He's the most slippery bastard of the lot. I did a deep dive on him earlier and you wouldn't believe the sort of shit he's known for. It's all over the forums.'

'What?'

'You don't want to know.'

'What? Tell me.'

"Let's just say, the only way you were getting that job, with or without Raj's intervention, was if you showed him how grateful you were for it.'

I gazed at him aghast. 'No way. He couldn't have done that.'

'On the contrary. He's known for it. Could be you owe your old boss a big thank you for screwing you over before that other tosser did.'

Words failed me and then my eyes stung and my face crumpled. 'Oh God. What's happening? Why is this all so hard?'

Connor stepped towards me again. Took me in his arms, held me where it felt safe.

'Babe. It's just the industry you've chosen to work in. It's full of wankers. I don't know why you're putting yourself through it. The hours are crap, the people are pretentious wankers. Even the money seems okay until you realise you're probably on minimum wage by the time they've made you stay till ten o'clock and work weekends every time they've buggered up a deadline. Believe me, hon, you won't like it. It all seems very glamourous and exciting now but seriously, it'll chew you up and spit you out, that environment. You're too nice for it. You don't even know when people are taking the piss out of you.'

He summed up his verdict with an emphatic cuddle and a smile that was more knowing than supportive. Then he strode to the fridge and paused in front of the cool air, deliberating over the choice of white wine while I busied myself salting the pasta water, my chest hitching. He picked out the Pinot Grigio and swung the door shut, his face instantly softening at the sight of mine.

'Oh, look. I'm sorry. I just don't like to see what it's doing to you. And you're not even working in it yet. Imagine what it's going to be like if you actually get a job.'

'I did have a job!'

'Exactly. And look what happened there. Look, I'm really not trying to make you feel bad. On the contrary, I just want you to consider that there's more than one path in life that you could take. One that maybe isn't so fancy sounding, but offers you regular hours, a bit of reliability. A decent salary. Prospects.'

I drew a breath, willed my voice not to crack as I spoke. Angled my head partially towards him. 'What are you talking about?'

He held his hands up doing his best to look sheepish. 'All right, all right,' he said as though I'd been insisting for hours. 'I didn't want you to think I was interfering, crossing a line or whatever, but did you get any other emails today?'

'I got hundreds of emails today. All of them total rubbish.'

'Maybe one about an interview at a bank…'

I stared at him. He brought out the big guns, the boyish grin. The one he thought was charming.

'Okay. Soooo, I may have filled in a job application for you on their website and sent your CV in. I know it's not the first thing that comes to mind, but think about it. It's a steady job, steady income. You could start immediately.'

'Working in a bank?' My voice was shrill, my disbelief no longer restrained. 'What as, a teller?'

He looked away sharply, shaking his head. 'I knew you'd be like this.'

'But… when have I ever said I wanted to work in a bank?'

'There's nothing wrong with working in a bank.' His eyes narrowed and there was a hard edge to his every word now.

I plucked open the packet of penne and shook too much of it into the boiling water. Harnessed the resentment I'd felt only moments before and veered on the side of reasonable.

'I never said there was, I just don't really want to.'

He slammed a wine glass on the counter. Just one. 'No. You'd rather suck off a bunch of slimy perverts just to get your foot in the door of the advertising industry.'

Jesus. I shook my own head. 'No, I –'

'Do you know how much time it took to sort this all out and now you've got an interview.' He unscrewed the bottle. Filled his glass. 'An actual interview where you don't have to sleep with anyone, unlike anything your fabulous recruiter creep could come up with.'

'Connor, don't get –'

'What? What were you going to say? Don't get what?'

'Nothing.'

'Christ. I should have known better than to try and help you get anywhere.' The glass crashed against his teeth as he sunk his head back, downing most of the wine. 'You know best, right? I'm just an idiot for trying to make you happy. The idiot supporting you while you sit around watching TikTok videos all day.'

As if! I'd done nothing but look for work this last month and I'd have tried harder if he hadn't told me that guy from the gym was about to okay that bloody job that never came to anything, but I couldn't say that. I couldn't say anything. My mouth was dry and my chest tight. The lines of defence swirling around my mind locked inside me.

'Forget about it. Forget I tried to help,' he snarled, filling his glass again.

'I do appreciate it,' I croaked. 'You just caught me by surprise, that's all. I wasn't expecting it. It's – it's really kind of you to have gone to all the trouble.'

He began to mellow, his eyes softening. 'I'm sorry,' he said, taking my hand. 'I probably shouldn't have sprung it on you like that. I just – sometimes it takes someone else to tell you where you're going wrong, to point you in a different direction. One you maybe haven't considered.'

'But a bank though?' I said, forcing air into the question.

'Think about it. What's got safer prospects than a bank?' It didn't seem like the moment to bring up Lehman Brothers. Or Bradford & Bingley. Or, well, multiple economic crashes in recent history. 'And, you're going to love this, I put my number down in the reference section so if they do call to check your credentials, they'll speak to me. I've set up a website and everything. Brilliant, hey? And the best bit is there's a branch down the road from the university. We could go in together every day. I could meet you for lunch.'

I steadied myself against the workbench, pressed my hands down to stop them shaking. Did my best to return his smile.

'And think of the perks. You'll never be turned down for a mortgage. We could take out as many loans as we liked.'

My eyes finally met his. 'Do we need a loan?'

He sighed. 'Oh, look, honey. I know this isn't everything you'd hoped for and I'm not saying you should do it forever. It would just do you good to get back out the house that's all. Start getting back into a routine. Bring some money in maybe, yes? And you know what they say – you're far more likely to get a job if you've already got one.'

Bring some money in. That was what this was all about. His endless well of generosity had run dry and I couldn't really blame him for panicking about how long it would be before I found a job out there. I just wish he hadn't got this one into his head. I mean a bank, but there was nothing I could say without sounding like an ungrateful bitch and he'd only just calmed down. I just… A bank? Like why?

But then why not? It's not like anybody else was banging my door down. His door. God, it sounded awful, but maybe he was right. Maybe I could do it until something better came along. Something more like me and if it made him happy, made him less stressed about money, about me being there, it had to be a good thing, right?

I still wasn't sold on the whole idea but I told him there was no harm going for an interview. To be honest, I'd have said anything right then not to see that look on his face again.

111 Days Before the Murder

Her Sister

Mistletoe and Wine drifted through the floorboards. Mistletoe and fricking Wine for the fiftieth time that day. I closed my eyes and sunk my head back against the pillow, burying any hardwired sense of duty beneath a thin veil of total disinterest.

It didn't even feel like Christmas, despite my mother ensuring those poor Africans knew exactly what time of year it was by blasting out her supermarket playlist at a volume only Gran could miss. No one had even banged on my door demanding if I knew what time it was. By this point normally, Mum had me sticking pigs in blankets on baking sheets and hiding M&S packaging in the recycling bin as if no one would realise she hadn't made all the sides herself, but Dad was properly going for it this year. He'd been preparing the veg since I'd got there last night and we were banned from the kitchen until after lunch which was fine by me. Especially as lunch would probably be at about five o'clock if he said two.

I reached down to stroke Ginger but my hand only grazed the hairy cat-shaped indent left behind when he'd abandoned me at the first whiff of roasting flesh wafting up the stairs. Gross. Just the thought of it turned my stomach. The thought of it and the fact it was stinking up my bedroom.

I groaned and rolled grudgingly off the bed, made my way to the window and pushed it ajar. The streets were quiet and empty, the sky bright and clear, but the air that rushed in through the crack was laced with the stench of cooking fat pouring from every other suburban semi. I gazed across the road, let my eyes linger on the fairy lights tinkling away on Christmas trees in every bay window from one end of the street to the other. Never mind the state of the planet, everyone. We were all going to die soon anyway. Might as well enjoy it while we still could.

I slammed the window shut again in disgust, my eyes drawn reflexively to a movement as a car rounded the corner and drove slowly down the road towards us. Oh, great.

I slunk out of sight and slumped back onto the bed again, my mobile shielding my face defensively as though anyone could see me hiding up here. Or care that I was. The gravel crunched on our driveway but the engine continued to purr for another minute or more, spitting fumes into the atmosphere. My top lip curled and I ground my teeth together, refusing to take my eyes off my phone, even after the succession of doors slamming brought Mum out of the house shrieking with sherry and excitement.

'Olive!' she screamed up the stairs moments later in the misguided belief that not everyone in the neighbourhood had caught the arrival of our star guests. I rolled my eyes and spun onto my stomach.

'Olive. Milly's here.'

Whoop. Milly's here. Better lay out the red carpet. I kept scrolling through the BBC headlines – yes, the headlines – as if I never read the news. There was bugger all happening, unless you counted the fact millions of us were very excited about watching the King give his speech later that afternoon.

A clash of voices and shoes being exchanged for slippers filled the hallway and I stared at an article about how to reduce food waste by making trifle with leftover cabbage or some such crap. There was a final shuffle at the foot of the stairs, a tinkling of laughter and then a click as the sitting room door closed and it all went silent. Well, for a minute anyway.

'Olivia. Get yourself down here. Now.'

For Christ's sake. I threw my phone down and dragged myself off the bed, picked up my phone again – obvs – and sloped out onto the landing.

'Come on,' Mum said in a slightly less aggressive tone, gazing up the stairs at two of me probably. 'It'll be fine when you see her.'

I don't know what she thought she was talking about. I hadn't told her anything about Emily being a total flake and letting me down when I needed her most. I hadn't mentioned how many times she'd promised and then failed to come and see me, invited me across to London only to change her mind at the last minute. I hadn't told her I'd stopped even suggesting we get together after a few months or that we hadn't sent more than a couple of WhatsApp messages to each other since about mid-November. I guess I didn't need to. It was obvious every time she asked me if I'd heard from Milly in a way that indicated she hadn't.

I slunk down the stairs slowly, placing the balls of my feet on each step mindfully, conscious of the spring in the carpet cushioning every –

'Oliiive.'

Alright already.

‘Look who I found skulking away upstairs!’ Mum announced ushering me into the sitting room like a reluctant six-year-old in a nativity play. All eyes turned to me, wide with phoney joy and gladness. Oh God, I’d forgotten his mum was coming too.

‘Good tidings,’ I said with a sweeping glance that covered almost everyone. Emily stood up from the arm of the chair she was perched on like a parrot crouching on the creep’s shoulder.

‘Hey, you.’ She locked her arms around me and held me so tightly I couldn’t lift mine if I’d tried. Which I didn’t especially. When she pulled back, she studied me with the air of a county fair judge appraising a disappointing entry. ‘You’ve lost so much weight.’

‘The heartbreak diet, hey?’ the creep said, looming up behind her. God forbid we share a moment. I stiffened as he stepped between me and my sister and brushed his lips against my cheek. ‘How are you faring up?’

‘Yeah, great, thanks for asking. Living my best life, you know.’

He put his arm around Emily and drew her back to the chair.

‘Come and join us,’ he said gesturing benevolently towards the sofa as though I needed an invitation to sit down in my own house. ‘I don’t know if you remember my mum. She remembers you, of course.’

And we all laughed. Well, I didn’t but I pretended to.

‘How lovely to see you, Olive,’ she said and we greeted each other with one of those horribly awkward hugs that ends in a kiss on the ear because nobody knows how we’re supposed to say hello in this country.

'Milly was just telling us about her new job,' Gran piped up from Mum's favourite armchair. She'd poured her posh voice out of a Bailey's bottle some time earlier and her cheeks were pink and glazed like a honey-baked ham.

'Not so new now, hey, babe? She's been there for a few weeks now.'

Emily nodded with the enthusiasm of a bobblehead blu-tacked to a dashboard.

'What I still don't understand though,' Mum said, pointedly re-adjusting a cushion on the sofa. 'Is what you're supposed to be project managing.'

'I'm not project managing anything. It's a bank. I work in a bank, that's it. I'm a bank teller.'

'I thought you were a project manager.'

'That wasn't really working out, Clare. We thought there was more stability in banking. Better career prospects.'

'But it's not exactly Wall Street, is it? We're not talking one-million-pound bonuses at the end of the year, are we?'

Emily's mouth was beginning to twitch. She drew a breath but didn't seem to be able to get out whatever she wanted to say. I glared at my mum and bashed her lightly on the forearm.

'Why would she be working in Wall Street, Mum? It's in New York.'

'I just mean –'

'What time is Dad pretending lunch is going to be ready?'

'Oh, goodness knows. Have some of those Pringles if you're starving.'

‘Heathen!’ My dad yelled sticking his head through the adjoining doors the moment I shovelled a stack of over-seasoned carbs into my mouth. ‘Lunch is served. I hope you’re all hungry.’

‘Hangry more like,’ I said, nodding towards Mother and I almost could have laughed. At my own joke obviously, but that still counted. I ducked out of her way as she clouted me half-heartedly round the back of my head and when I looked up Emily was standing there, her hand extended for me to grab on to. I smiled, a little bit and for a brief moment, I caught a glimpse of her again.

‘What are we having then? Ohhhh. That’s a big bird,’ Gran exclaimed, shuffling into the dining room, her nails digging into Connor’s braced arm, I’d like to think more than was required.

‘Thought we’d do goose this year,’ Dad announced gleefully dropping it onto the table like a cadaver stiff with rigor mortis. ‘Roasted with a ginger and orange stuffing. And there’s boiled sprouts for the vegetarians.’

I didn’t rise to it.

‘Only kidding.’ He tweaked my cheek and swept his arm towards the table in the style of a weatherman taking credit for sunny spells that afternoon. ‘We have portobello mushroom wellington, enough for anyone to try, if the girls let us.’

I smiled tersely. It was massive but I’d have still preferred not to share with anyone but Emily.

‘Not a nut roast in sight, Linda. I didn’t forget,’ he grinned patting her arm. ‘Instead, we have carrots and parsnips roasted in an agave nectar-glaze. Candied Brussels sprouts coated in spicy bread crumbs, a selection of greens sautéed with garlic, root veg mash and of course, *la pièce de résistance*, roast spuds cooked to perfection in goose fat.'

I groaned. Seriously?

'All except for these,' he whispered, patting the bowl next to me. 'I'd get in there quick, if I were you. You know Milly and roast potatoes.'

That deserved a proper smile.

'Thanks, Dad,' I murmured, just loud enough to hear over the din that erupted on cue like gasps of delight at a fireworks display.

'Actually, Em's not vegetarian anymore,' Connor said taking the seat opposite me so I had to act fast to avoid pulling my cracker with him. The room went silent and somewhere a record probably screeched to a halt. Milly picked up the napkin on her plate and shook it out.

'What? It's not that big a deal. It just wasn't practical having to make two meals every night.'

Mum made a noise like a car backfiring. 'Oh, wasn't it? I wish you'd come to that conclusion back when you still lived here,' she grumbled but everyone laughed and Milly had the presence of mind to look sheepish. Mum caught my eye but I wasn't about to apologise for saving the planet so I helped myself to extra potatoes instead since they were apparently all for me now. It was a hollow victory.

'Easy tiger!' Connor cried, placing his hand over Emily's as she served herself from the other bowl. She sniggered, the colour rising up her neck, instantly dropping the spoon like a hot potato (Hot potato. No? Oh, come on!). I looked across the table at her again and she winced self-consciously.

'I promised myself I'd lose three more pounds before the New Year.'

'From where?!' Gran barked, piling her own plate so high the gravy was going to have to orbit it if the tablecloth were to stand a chance.

'You promised *yourself*?' I said meaningfully.

'Too many pub lunches,' she added taking the tiniest portions of veg as Connor slid a thick slice of dead bird onto her plate. 'King's College is only round the corner from the bank so Connor meets me at lunchtime most days. It's starting to take its toll.'

'You look fine to me,' I said. 'Doesn't she, Dad?'

'Don't get me involved,' he cried, flicking a green bean onto the carpet in his haste to get his hands in the air.

Connor pulled her towards him, kissing the side of her head. 'A couple of pounds and she'll be perfect again.'

'Well, don't go over doing it,' Mum said. 'I think you're perfect now.'

Milly simpered and began cutting her food into teeny-tiny-bite-size morsels and then left most of it under her napkin even though Dad had excelled himself in the kitchen this time. Oh well, her loss. More for the rest of us.

'So, Emily tells us you're moving house, Linda?'

'That's right,' Connor's mum replied, regretting the not-at-all-bite-size chunk of carrot she'd just shoved in her mouth. 'It all seems to be going through okay, but you never know with these things, do you? I'm trying not to get too stressed out about it.'

'Easier said than done.'

'Where are you off to, dear?' Gran said, unaware or unconcerned about the cranberry sauce garnishing the tip of her nose. 'Somewhere local, I hope?'

'Oh, yes. It's only round the corner really. I'm – what do they call it? Downsizing. Connor says I rattle around Downs View.'

'And it costs a fortune to heat for one person, Mum. You'll be much more comfortable in a two-bed flat without the garden to have to worry about.'

Gran puckered her lips like she'd tasted something sharp. 'I thought you loved gardening. You used to bring me in all those lovely apples and pears when I was having my treatment.'

Linda shrugged, her eyes resigned. 'It's gotten too big for me, really. There comes a time when a garden that size starts to get out of hand.'

'And that time was ten years ago.'

'Oh, well. That should leave you with a nice little nest egg. What are you going to do with yourself?' Mum had gone all misty-eyed either at the thought of how she'd spend that sort of money or because of the Pinot Noir Dad had paired with the goose. 'Travel the world? Go on safari? I'd be on the first cruise out of here to somewhere hot.'

'Aren't I allowed to come?' Dad cried indignantly, pretending not to be secretly running through all the wonderful things he could tinker with if let loose in the house on his own for two weeks.

'Oh no, nothing special,' Linda said answering Mum's question and so sparing her from revealing whether Dad was invited or not.

Connor guffawed. 'Thank goodness for that! Please don't go giving my mother ideas! Can you imagine her on a cruise? I wouldn't trust her not to fall overboard. She's hopeless.'

Linda laughed but her hands fluttered as if she didn't know what to do with them. 'Connor's right. I've never been very adventurous. Besides, I'd like to help him out if I can. Put the equity towards his future. His and Emily's, of course.'

I raised my eyebrows. By the looks of the Audi parked on the driveway, Connor didn't need helping out. I craned my neck to avoid his smug reaction and managed to dodge direct eye contact and his inane commentary for the rest of the meal.

'Oof,' Gran cried stripping a last ribbon of goose from its bones. 'Somebody get this feast away from me. I can't stop picking at it. Any more and I'll explode.'

'Me too. David. That was superb, truly.'

There was a general outburst of cheering and groaning which had the unfortunate effect of rousing Dad into a half-seated curtsy which nearly tore the top button off his trousers.

'Shall we have a little break before we move on to the desserts?' he suggested ruefully but thank God. I'd had about eight potatoes, three servings of veg and two slices of pie. Any more and I'd look like I needed to be excused to go and give birth in the shed.

'Right, girls. It's the oldies turn to put their feet up,' Mum wobbled, aiming an overbearing thumb at the kitchen sink with a look that dared anyone to mention she'd had her feet up all morning. 'You know what to do.'

Traditionally washing-up post-Christmas lunch was Emily and my job after we'd stuffed what we could in the dishwasher and it was typically disgusting, but this year I was oddly looking forward to scouring congealed fat and bits of dried carcass off greasy burnt pans. That wasn't to say I didn't run through the usual display of demoralised outrage in case anyone got the idea that this should be a daily occurrence but truth be told, I really didn't mind at all. Not until Connor started stacking plates together and said 'I'll give you a hand,' but luckily Gran squawked, 'You are a guest in this house, young man. Besides I need you to roll me back to my armchair' to which Mum responded, 'It's not actually your armchair' and all of a sudden everyone piled into the sitting room and Milly and I were alone together for the first time in what felt like years.

I clattered across the room wordlessly, my mind weirdly blank, the easy conversation that used to bounce between us effortlessly, now as strained as making small talk with an ex. She scraped the dregs of lunch into the bin and I filled the washing up bowl.

'We should rinse these off first,' she said.

'Okay.' I moved the tap over the small sink, took the plate she handed me. Ran warm water over it. Popped it in the bowl and watched it slide under the bubbles.

'So,' Milly said, picking up the sponge, the both of us facing out on to the garden. 'How are you doing? Really.'

I dropped another plate in the bowl and contemplated her use of *really* as though she'd ever given me the chance to tell her I was okay when I wasn't. As if she ever asked me how I was at all these days. 'Fine. Really. How are you?'

'Fine' she said and we'd have probably carried on like that, taking our passive-aggression out on the gravy but for the fact the next plate I dropped into the water splashed through the surface like a fighter jet crashing into the sea.

'Sorry,' I cried stepping out of her way as she jumped back, her sparkly top drenched, her shriek the first genuine sound I'd heard come out her mouth since she'd got here.

'S'alright,' she said swiping her hand through the bubbles and dousing me in enough scum to put out a small fire.

'Shhh-shhh,' we giggled, doubling over and pressing our fingers to our lips, both of us conscious of not drawing attention to ourselves, of not drawing anyone else back into the kitchen to see what all the fuss was about. We stretched our tops out pointlessly one last time, laughing and letting them drop and cling to us as we took up position once again in the factory line.

'So, what's with the whole natural look, then?' I said peeking at her and away again quickly. 'Not that it doesn't suit you. I'm just not used to seeing you without any make-up at all.'

'Oh, you know. Connor says he prefers me without it. Reckons I give off the wrong impression when I wear too much.'

'Jesus Christ. What have you been doing, slathering yourself in it? I'm talking about a bit of mascara.'

She laughed. 'I know, it's just… God, I thought you'd be all over it. Supporting women's right not to conform to sexualised stereotypes, etc. etc.'

'I'm more for women's right to choose for themselves.' She didn't answer and I couldn't stand the silence now we'd finally started talking. 'Anyway, you look great. You always do.'

'Thanks.' She gave me a sideways glance and a slow smile that faded as she worked her mouth around the words she hadn't asked for weeks. Months really. 'So, have you heard from Flo at all in the last…'

I dropped my eyes towards the dish I was rinsing and handed it to her. 'She's down for a few days. We said we'd meet up, but, not like that, you know. With everyone. You could come. Might make it less weird if you did. It's going to be a bit –'

'Hi there, ladies. How are you getting on in here?'

Oh, for crying out loud.

'Nearly done,' Emily chirped like some bit-part wife in a sit-com.

'Cool,' Connor slid his arms around her waist and rested his chin on her shoulder. My skin crawled as though he'd run his fingernails down the back of my neck. 'We should be getting off soon.'

'Really? But it's only early.'

'Yeah. Mum's tired. We should get her back,' he sighed with a face like a puckered arsehole just as my mum staggered into the kitchen clutching an empty Prosecco bottle.

'You're not off already, are you?'

''Fraid so. We've got the drive back to London tomorrow.' Like he'd said Moscow.

'But we haven't even started Trivial Pursuits yet.'

He smiled at her indulgently like she was rattling a Paw Patrol jigsaw and asking him to play. 'That sounds like fun, but really, it's been a long day. We should get out of your hair.'

There were only so many times Mum could insist that she wanted them in her hair without it getting silly and all Milly did was apologise for having to leave the dishes on the rack to drain instead of drying them and putting them away. And joining everyone in the sitting room for another glass of bubbly – even though she really shouldn't – eating After Dinner Mints and reminiscing about presents gone by, laughing at Dad's tired old jokes and getting nowhere with any of the crappy puzzles that came in the crackers. And then, yes, playing bloody Trivial Pursuits for the billionth Christmas in a row before coming out to the pub with me. To hold my hand and stop it shaking. To make everything feel okay, for a few hours today of all days. But she didn't do any of that. We all just shambled out into the hallway and watched them put their hats and scarves on.

'Well, at least we'll see you at Rachel's at New Year,' Mum said, helping Linda into her coat. 'Linda, you're more than welcome to join us…'

Emily's face fell and Connor arranged his expression to neutral but a look passed between them.

'I don't think we'll be able to make it this year, guys. Sorry,' she said using a whole lot of effort to sound effortless.

'What? But we go every year. You've never missed one. All your cousins are going to be there. Even Ali's flying back from New Zealand.'

'You're not going?' Gran bellowed, turning her hearing aid back on with a screech. 'Did she say she's not going?'

'We can't, Gran. We already made plans with Connor's friends.'

'But everyone's looking forward to meeting you, Connor,' Mum said and Emily let her gaze drift to him hopefully.

'Next time, Clare. We will definitely be there, next time.'

And then they left. It was six o'clock and nobody felt like playing Trivial Pursuits after that so I went upstairs and hung out in my bedroom. Didn't even make it out in the end.

87 Days Before the Murder

Her

The lights glared far too brightly overhead and the décor was stark.

'What do you think?'

'Yes, it's lovely.' I fidgeted uncomfortably on the uber-trendy composite bench and disguised my despair with a wide grin and a requisite scan of the room, the baren superiority of it all. Connor snapped the menu open with grandiose authority, his back erect, his view surely hampered by the discerning way in which he held his head.

'Told you you'd like it,' he said.

'Mmm.'

'Have you decided what you want yet?'

'No, gosh, no.' I skimmed the menu for the fourteenth time. It all sounded amazing, in theory, but God, who wanted to eat any of that stuff? I mean, what the hell was Torched Mackerel Escabeche with Cucumber Tartar and Horseradish Cream anyway? And polenta? Who liked polenta, for Christ's sake? Why did every aspiring chef feel the need to stick it under everything these days? It had all the appeal of a grilled kitchen sponge and the prices were insane. Thirty-two quid for the chicken and whatever miso caramel was. I just fancied a big bowl of pasta from our local Italian but no, we had to come here and marvel at the toddler-sized portions of pan-fried something served with a streak of who-knew-what. 'I can't decide. You.'

'I think,' he said, enunciating every syllable. 'I. Will. Have. The Venison haunch steak.' With truffle polenta, hazelnut puree, oyster mushrooms and chocolate sauce. Del. I. Cious. And only thirty-six smackers.

The waitress sidled up to the table, iPad at the ready and even with Connor's overbearing critic of every wine on the list designed, I imagined, to impress her, I still ended up panic-picking the pearl barley risotto with autumn fruits and spent the next nineteen minutes with half a mind on the conversation and the other dreading what on earth that could possibly be.

'So,' Connor said softly, leaning towards me. 'How was your day?' He stroked the back of my hand suggestively, entwining his fingers around mine. I sighed but I might as well have screamed, the way he stiffened.

'Fine,' I said and even though he must have known I meant it had been awful, that I hated working in the bank and I'd never been so bored or unfulfilled, he accepted my summation and I allowed him to. There was a limit to how many times I could say taking that job had been a mistake and he could accuse me of being ungrateful before it became easier to lie. 'How was yours?'

'Shit, since you're asking. Collins is refusing to give me an extension.'

Another extension, I didn't say. I said, 'Oh no, when's it got to be in then?'

'Monday.'

‘This Monday?’ It came out higher than I’d intended and his fingers tightened on my hand. ‘Well, that’s okay. We can hammer it out over the weekend. I’ve already made loads of notes. I just need to organise them.’

He smirked sceptically. ‘Good job you’ve got a PhD in Business Management. Oh, no, wait…’

My eyes dropped and I shifted self-consciously. I’d been helping him with the first draft of his dissertation for weeks now because he’d been so stressed about it. And no, I didn’t know the first thing about business, but it was putting such a strain on us both I was sure as hell happy to learn if it made him less tense. Less snappy and irritable.

‘Oh, don’t be like that. You know I’m only joking.’ He rubbed my hand but his pupils jerked away dismissively.

‘I know you are,’ I forced a grin and withdrew, my eyebrows bowed jauntily towards the waitress as she approached bearing whatever overpriced bottle of wine Connor had finally settled on and by the time he’d run through the ordeal of swishing it around his mouth like a vintage connoisseur, he was in better spirits.

‘So, you’re up for a little secretarial work this weekend then, are you? I’ll dictate and you type.’

If the last few weeks were anything to go by, I’d be typing, researching, editing and googling ninety per cent of the whole thing while he stormed around the sitting room raging about his professors and the ineptitude of his fellow students – who had already finished the second or third draft of their own dissertations. All while checking the football and cricket scores, the horse-racing, the rugby, the cheese rolling championships in Gloucester if it came to it and getting inexplicably cross or happy about them. Anything to avoid actually doing any work.

'Sure, we've got this. I've actually proof-read the bulk of it already and made notes where it needs more explanation or should be streamlined.'

'Are there no end to your talents?' he asked in a way that didn't sound especially complimentary. 'Well, you've certainly got the outfit right. Slutty undergraduate hoping to sleep her way to a first.'

'What?' My smile slipped and crimson spots impressed upon my cheeks as if by a slap.

'You know half of your cleavage is on display in that top?'

I glanced down horrified, fingers already grappling at my neckline though my breasts were barely showing at all. 'Sorry.'

'You haven't been wearing that all day, have you?' He knew I hadn't. I had to wear a stupid uniform like a school kid. I'd only changed into this because I knew he liked it. I'd been wearing it the night we'd first run into each other at the pub. He'd told me later that he'd fallen in love with me right there and then. 'Suddenly I get why Randy Raj thought you were up for more than a little overtime.'

A bark of laughter indicated he was teasing but I was too taken aback to shake it off in the playful manner he was jockeying for.

'Oh, come on. I'm only joking,' he repeated like a mantra. 'I'm the one who should be offended. Those puppies are meant for my eyes only.'

I hoicked my top up, bunching the V-neck into an optimistic crumple further up my chest.

‘That’s better,’ he said approvingly and sat back to allow the waitress to set our plates in front of us, her eyes lingering on mine long enough to make me glance away.

‘Wow. Better get a shot of this for your Instagram before I demolish it.’ Then grimacing at my dish. ‘What the hell did you order?’

Oh God. It was blackberries. Blackberries in a risotto.

‘It’s not as weird as it looks, honestly,’ the waitress winked, lifting the bottle of wine as if to pour it but Connor placed his hand over the top of my empty glass.

‘She’s had enough,’ he said, returning the wink that had been intended for me.

The waitress stalled, seeking out my eyes again but I shook my head as though it had been my idea all along. She nodded and attended to Connor’s glass instead. ‘Anything else I can get for you, guys?’

But there wasn’t, unless a big bowl of pasta and a high-necked boilersuit were options.

‘What?’ Connor said, querying my expression as she shimmied away. ‘You know how you get when you drink too much. And we’re going to need our wits about us tomorrow if we really plan to tackle this dissertation. Unless you’ve changed your mind...?’

‘Of course not,’ I said quickly, still baffled both by the blackberries and the knowledge that I got *some way* when I drank too much. But actually, I’ve got to admit, the risotto was okay. Not that I’d have it again. Or post a photo of it. Nevertheless, I scraped my plate clean, more out of hunger than delight, and reached for my wineglass before remembering I’d had enough and so veered towards the water jug, winding my fingers around it as though I were cradling a cloud of candyfloss.

'So… I was thinking of going across to Exeter one weekend soon, if you fancy it…? If not, I could go on my own. Get the train.'

Connor's mouth contorted and he looked down sharply at his own plate. 'That'll cost a fortune. It's supposed to be one of the most expensive train services in the country, isn't it? Plus, you'll have to change about twenty times, more if there's rail works. Rather you than me.' He dropped his knife and fork with a clatter, then remembering where he was, pushed them together and dapped his lips with the napkin.

'I know,' I sighed, relieved he wasn't making noises about joining me. There was no way, no way Olive would ever go for that. 'I'll just have to take a good book and hope for the best.'

Connor shook his head. 'The way you jump through hoops for that girl.'

The muscles either side of my neck tensed. 'What do you mean?'

'What do I mean? What's she ever done for you, that's what I mean. Why is it always you running around after her? You at her beck and call.' I didn't run around after her, at all. I hadn't even been to see her, not once since she'd moved away and it wasn't like I could invite her to come visit us. It got Connor's back up if I even mentioned her name and she was just as bad. The thought of putting them in a room together left me cold.

It had been awful enough when Gran and my parents had popped up for the day. His face had fallen the moment I'd told him they were coming and he feigned surprise as if I should have run it past him first. And I knew that I should have, but I'd put it off so many times knowing he'd be funny about it, but they'd persisted – *insisted* – until I'd had to give in and act like there was nothing wrong with them dropping by. Like I wouldn't spend the next few weeks walking on eggshells, dreading him pretending to forget they were coming so I'd have to remind him and watch his face twist with fresh irritation every time.

And of course, he'd been charm itself when they got there. Talked electrical wires and vol au vents with my dad, made my mum endless cups of tea, flirted with Gran just enough to be endearing, but afterwards, after they'd gone, he'd lashed out about the state of the kitchen. The way they'd stacked the dishwasher and let the leftover pasta and garlic bread harden in the serving dishes on the side. How *I'd* left it to spoil instead of covering it in clingfilm, another meal in itself that would have to be dumped in the bin, too far gone for even a dog to eat. Supposing we had a dog.

I'd have eaten it but I couldn't seem to tell him that at the time. And I certainly didn't tell him they'd asked when they could come up again.

'I thought it would be easier to go to her, that's all. Besides, it'll give you a chance to get a few extra workouts in. Or meet up with your uni mates. You haven't seen them for ages.'

'Oh, this is for my benefit, is it?' he aped sarcastically. 'Not so the two of you can go out and get shit faced without me cramping your style.'

'Of course not. I told you, you can come if you like.'

'Oh, please. As if. Your sister hates me.'

‘She doesn’t –’ I began but my voice trailed off without conviction.

‘Oh, don’t worry. It’s not like I take it personally. She hates all men, doesn’t even try to hide it. And she’s jealous of anyone who gets between the pair of you, always has been. She’s never going to think anyone’s good enough for you. There’s no point even trying.’

‘I don’t think that’s –’

‘Oh, come on. What about that time I made that massive effort to come down and celebrate her going to university? She sulked all evening and started a fight for no reason. Don’t tell me I’m making that up.’

‘No, but –’ That wasn’t what had happened and he knew it. Didn’t he? I mean there was more to it than that, but this feud of theirs made any hope of keeping them both in my life next to impossible. It took all my wits to try to diffuse their ongoing resentment. ‘She was just a bit put out about us crashing her leaving do. That was my fault. I should have checked with her.’

‘Asked her permission, you mean?’

‘No. It was all a bit of a –’

‘You see. This is what she wants. To get between us. I can’t believe you’re letting her. I know she’s family but that’s screwed up. I didn’t want to say anything before but really, I can’t stand the way she manipulates you. It’s the mind games I can’t take. Pretending she’s on your side when all the time she’s trying to get you all to herself.’

‘I don’t…’

‘Look. Whatever. I know better than to get between *sisters* –’ He waggled his fingers around the word theatrically as though our so-called relationship were no less ridiculous than claiming to be flower fairies. '– even if it means not being able to defend myself while she fills your head with lies about me because she can't stand to see you happy. She'd rather you were a sad lonely loser like her.'

'Finished with these, guys?' the waitress said, swooping in to take the plates and Connor's face switched back to its default setting. 'Can I get you any desserts?'

'Not for me,' he beamed patting his stomach. 'Babe..?' He squinted across the table, his head slanted sceptically.

'I'm fine, thanks. Just the bill.'

'Just the bill, please,' he repeated as though I hadn't spoken.

'No problem,' she replied, spinning slowly on her heels and sauntering away, hips swinging, plates and glasses balanced on her arm, Connor's eyes no doubt unintentionally fixated on her.

'Let's not fight. Not with you looking so beautiful,' he murmured turning back to me, his eyes hooded, his fingers grazing past my necklace towards the gathered folds of material hiding my cleavage. 'That outfit reminds me of the first night we spent together.' I hadn't worn it the first night we spent together but it wasn't the moment to be pedantic.

'Thank you. You look very handsome too.' I smiled, blushing under his scrutiny as he made a show of mentally undressing me, his lips curled suggestively.

'Nice as it is though, it's going to have to come off as soon as we get home. Very slowly. So slowly you're going to beg me to rip it off and screw you. Hard and deep, the way you like it.'

I tittered awkwardly and pulled my hands out of his grip to make way for the waitress who had returned and was doing an admiral job of pretending not to have heard him, although I couldn't help but feel that it was more for her benefit than mine. Instead, she simulated an interest in a mild fracas at the bar and left the bill on the table, coiling unannounced between a silver dish and a couple of mints.

'Listen,' he said, picking it up and absentmindedly skimming through it. 'I'm just moving some money about at the moment but it's all going to be tied up for a few weeks. You alright to get this?' He glanced up and caught me off guard.

'Er, yes, of course. Sure.' I bent down quickly, pulling my bag up from under the bench, fumbling a little as I delved through it.

'Bloody investments, you know. The higher the return, the harder it is to access it.'

'Sure.' I flicked my purse open, determinedly nonplussed. 'Of course.'

The waitress sidled back over, her smile fixed, the card reader slack in her hand. Connor picked my bankcard up from the table, held it out to her.

'Round it up to a hundred and fifty.' He winked once again, working the lopsided grin he wore for these occasions. My gaze darted to the bill, but I hadn't misread it. The total came to one hundred and twenty-seven pounds and I'd baulked at that. A near twenty per cent gratuity seemed excessive, even for him. My eyes sought out his but he wouldn't meet them. The waitress unfurled the corners of her mouth like she was used to the attention and wasn't particularly impressed. She angled the card machine towards Connor and he tapped it in a way that suggested he was paying for more than a meal. It beeped like a buzzer jarring on a game show.

'You have to put it in or swipe it if it's over a hundred,' she drawled sounding like she'd rehearsed it though she probably had no need, the number of times she must have to remind people.

Connor's face slipped, his arrogance wavering behind a glint of irritation as he turned and stared impatiently, his finger poised, expecting me to announce my PIN in front of the whole restaurant. I hesitated, opening and closing my mouth around the numbers I'd gone to lengths to protect until the waitress remedied the issue, her unfaltering smile brighter than before, her eyes overly casual as she smoothly turned the card reader towards me. Connor's jaw tightened as he sat back roughly and folded his arms.

'That was embarrassing,' he said after she'd bowed her head appreciatively and slipped away from the table.

'No, it wasn't,' I laughed. 'What did she care who paid?'

'It's just a bit dumb me not knowing your PIN code, that's all. What must she have thought? You made me look like a right tit.'

I wavered, struggling to slide the card back into my purse, my hands trembling where I hid them on my lap, out of sight. 'I really don't think she thought anything. It wasn't that big a deal.'

He dragged his coat from the back of his chair, stood up brusquely and stared down at me in disgust. 'You don't think it's a big deal that you don't trust me with your PIN number even though I let you share my flat and everything I own without asking you for a penny?'

'Of course I trust you with my PIN.' I lowered my voice, easing myself along the bench into his earshot. 'It's six one five seven. I don't mind *you* knowing. It was everyone else who was listening in.'

He was tapping something in his phone, making a note of it somewhere probably.

'All right.' He looked up, his jaw still rigid, his eyes still dripping with distain. 'What? What's the matter?'

'Nothing.'

'Are you actually pissed off because I know it now?'

'Of course not. I don't mind at all.' One of my coat loops had frayed loose and the belt snaked down my leg evading the ham-fisted clutches I was making into thin air, comical under different circumstances. Something we'd laugh about at any other time.

'So this is because I asked you to pay for the meal then?'

'No.' I caught my belt firmly and concentrated on tying it, my voice still a low rasp, my step trailing in the wake of his, his words carrying.

'One meal in the last six months. I've asked you to pay for one meal and this is your reaction.'

That wasn't true. I'd paid for loads of meals out. And half the food we cooked at home but I didn't say that. I scuttled through the door he held open for me – ever the gentleman and whispered, 'I'm sorry. It's only – I'm on a bit of a budget. I'd have been just as happy going to Giuseppe's –'

'If you knew that you were going to pay. It's fine if I do.'

The cold night air was sobering, grating against the exposed skin on my neck. Stinging the end of my nose. 'I don't mean that. I was a bit shocked by how much it cost, that's all. And the tip on top.'

'You don't tip?'

'I do. I just –'

‘Hang on then.’ He stopped in his tracks and spun around to face me. ‘Let me get this straight. You’re upset because we had a perfectly lovely meal with excellent service, friendly staff … who deserve a tip, just not from you? Wow. And to think I thought you were a modern woman. Guess all that talk about equal rights and feminism is just that. Talk.’

‘I just wanted some pasta, that’s all,’ I stammered.

‘Long as I paid for it though, right?’ He strode off again towards the tube station. The tube station that would lead us back home. To his home. In this city where I had nowhere else to go. Even if I had the strength to go anywhere but after him. ‘But you can afford train tickets to Exeter, of course. Oh, wait, don’t tell me – that’s different.’

‘No, no. Look, I’m sorry. I don’t know where this has come from. I’m fine with paying. I really, *really* didn’t mind. I’m tired I guess, that’s all. Work’s been crazy. I’m – please. Forget this ever happened. We were having such a good time. Let’s not spoil it,’ I pleaded.

He shook his head, disappointment etched on his face. ‘It’s just hard sometimes when it feels like I’m the only one making the effort in this relationship.’

And even though that would have been – should have been – the perfect moment to tell him I wasn’t happy. That I was scared almost all of the time and I didn’t really know why, I didn’t. I swallowed and apologised and took his hand when he offered it to me like a father forgiving a wayward child and the whole time I was holding it, half of me wanted to stay in that bubble forever and the other half wanted to run.

84 Days Before the Murder

Her Mother

It was the third time I'd rung that evening and I knew I was being a pest but that was a mother's prerogative. We didn't ask for much after sacrificing our bodies, our lives and any hope of financial security for the pleasure of ensuring we were within constant proximity of snacks and water for the next few decades while being blamed for everything from depleted stocks of Shreddies to the onset of global warming.

We didn't really ask for anything in return for imparting the gift of life – not even gratitude – but the least we could expect was a phone call once in a while, wasn't it? Some token acknowledgement that although the heirs to our kingdoms could get themselves home from the station, furnish their cupboards with their own boxes of cereal and presumably find a clean pair of socks without screaming the place down these days, they did still remember us sometimes, perhaps even with fondness although that might be pushing it. I for one, simply wanted my daughter – my first-born – to answer her mobile, preferably before the shepherd's pie was done.

It went to voice mail again and I glared at the phone screen before stabbing the call end button and dialling again. It was the last-ditch attempt (although I had said that before) and this time she picked up, her voice hoarse and muffled as though I'd dragged her from her deathbed.

‘Mum? Hello. Mum? What is it?’

‘Oh. I didn’t wake you, did I?’

‘No,’ she hissed, so quietly I had to turn the volume up and run the risk of cutting her off. ‘We were watching a film.’

‘Oh, dear. I’m not interrupting, I hope? It’s only that I’ve been trying to get hold of you all weekend.’

‘I know,’ she lowered her voice again, if that were even possible. I could hardly make her out. ‘Sorry. I was going to call you back as soon as I had a minute. Was there something important?’

‘No, no. Nothing special. I don’t think we’ve got any news this end.’

‘Okay, well –’

‘Although I did meet up with Sandra for a lovely walk across the Downs on Friday. There were a few black clouds overhead when we set out but luckily the rain held off until the afternoon. Now there’s a thing. You won’t believe how much she’s had to fork out for a new boiler –’

‘Mum,’ Emily interrupted and I’ll grant you a boiler isn’t at the forefront of a young woman’s mind, but two thousand pounds it cost Sandra to fix it. Two thousand pounds when if she’d had it insured with the manufacturers, they’d have replaced the whole thing free of charge. Well, free of charge except for the monthly premiums but still, it was worth considering, even if it wasn’t as interesting as whoever those Kardashian people were currently dating.

‘I need to get back to the film. Connor’s waiting.’

'Right you are. How much is left? Dinner's going to be ready in about half an hour so we'll be done by about eight o'clock.' I'd have to record my programme but at least that meant I could fast-forward the ads. 'Does that tie in with you?'

'Um. Can I try and get back to you tomorrow? Only we'll probably watch something else after this and Connor'll be stuck waiting for me to finish.'

'Oh. Okay, well, why don't you give me a quick bell at lunchtime.'

'I can't do lunchtimes. Connor comes down to meet me.'

'After work then.'

'That might be tricky too. We normally get the bus home together and then we'll probably cook something and eat in front of the telly. It might get a bit late.'

'Well, do you get a tea break at work at all?'

'Um. Yes.' She sounded relieved. 'I should have about ten minutes or so at some point. I'll do my best. If not, I'll get back to you later in the week. That okay?'

It would have to be, I supposed.

'Em?' A deep baritone voice resonated in the background and I'll admit I flared my nostrils more than was appealing, but I held my tongue. I deserve points for that.

'I'll wait to hear from you then,' I said making it sound more like a question than grammar allowed.

'Okay. Speak to you then.'

'Love you,' I went to say but she'd already hung up so it came out as 'Lu-urh' which drew David's attention as he came in to check on how well the mashed potato was browning.

‘That was quick. She alright?’

‘Hmm.’ I put the phone down but I kept my eyes on it for a moment or two longer. ‘She’s watching a film.’

‘Hmm,’ he concluded and after twenty-six years of marriage, that was all he needed to say. He squeezed my shoulder, one side of his face cast downwards in a sympathetic, albeit unflattering frown. ‘I reckon we’ve still got about twenty-five minutes before I have to put the veg on. What say you to a quick game of Scrabble?’

What I said was I’d thrash him and I did, but nice as it was, I couldn’t quite shake the habit of melancholy that had recently come to pass in our house and I knew why, but I couldn’t let myself dwell on it. She had her own life to live now. It wasn’t my place to challenge her choices.

Oh, but if it was, I’d give that girl a good talking to. And take the gamble she’d speak to me even less than she did now.

67 Days Before the Murder

Her

I could hear Connor before I saw him, the low rumble of his seductive laugh, his self-assured timbre, audible behind the purple screen. Jerome and I sprang apart guiltily, adopting an air of impartial interest in the loan application we should have been discussing, instead of dissecting his latest disastrous date, the both of us red and sweaty from giggling behind cupped hands.

'Hi, hon,' I cried breezily, looking up from the paperwork as he rounded the corner and froze, sizing up the scene doubtfully. 'We're just finishing off here. Shall I meet you out front?'

He strode into the small partitioned cubicle and leant across the desk, pulling my necklace out from under my blouse and planting a kiss on my mouth like a dog marking his territory.

'Alright, mate,' Jerome said, ignored until then. Connor jerked his head coolly by way of response and pulled out one of the chairs that were meant for customers.

'I can wait here,' he said, slumping down on it.

Jerome and I turned back towards the form, wooden with nonchalance, our eyes deliberately focused on the print.

'I can probably sign this off now,' Jerome murmured airily. 'If you two want to get off.'

'Great. Thanks.' I beamed brightly at Connor, pushing my chair back as I stood, my coat and bag already reclaimed from inside my drawer, my feet edging around the desk at an unfathomable angle so as to avoid brushing past my friend, work colleague. Acquaintance, if that.

'You looked cosy,' Connor said, leading me out through the foyer past the bored pensioners waiting in line to make their deposits and withdrawals, via the ATMs and out through the tempered glass door into the gloomy light filtering through the mid-February sky. I assumed a quizzical expression, a deliberate jauntiness to my step that could only belong to someone with no secrets to hide.

'What? Back there? Jerome was telling me about his girlfriend, that's all. She seems lovely. Sounds like they make a great couple.'

Connor offered me the crook of his arm and I fed my hand through it, evading his cynical audit with a robust assessment of the fidget poppers and mobile phone covers cheapening every other shop window.

'Like that would stop him.' His voice thickened. 'If he ever lays a finger on you, I will kill him, you know that, don't you?'

'Oh, Connor,' I laughed, slapping his arm playfully with my free hand the way I used to when comments like that didn't chill me to the bone. He gritted his teeth and I felt his eyes boring into my profile, daring me to give myself away.

'In or out?' I sang, sweeping my hand towards the glacial table arrangements outside the pub, the slowing of our pace an opportunity to extract myself from his clasp. He stepped back to hold the door open for me and I strode inside, relieved to be once again within earshot of strangers.

I took up our usual residence in a small booth in the corner, dispensing with the multiple layers of coats and cardigans, piling them high on the padded bench as Connor ordered for us at the bar. I was starving, months of dieting during the cold winter months had taken their toll on my will power but he was already gesturing to the barman, too far into the process to interrupt. I trained my eyes on his back in case he looked around to check before he ordered, but he didn't. Instead, when he did eventually turn, it was with a pint in one hand and a lime soda in the other. I forced a smile, my eyes crinkling with conviction, as he made his way through the airless, murky light towards me.

'Thank you,' I said taking the cold glass and setting it down in a pool of its own dripping condensation. He slid into the booth and at the first sip of beer, his shoulders unclenched. His face relaxed.

'So, when do you think you'll be promoted again?' he asked as though picking up the conversation we'd shelved briefly when he went to the bar.

'Oh. I don't know.' I lifted my glass reluctantly, shrinking at the feel of it against my skin, the icy liquid prickling my chest as I swallowed. 'I doubt any time soon. They've only recently moved me up to loans and mortgages.'

'It's still beneath you though. You should push for another one. What's the point in having a degree if they can't give you a bit more responsibility? And more money, obviously.'

'Well, I know, but I've only been there a few months. They probably think I need more experience before they can move me up again.'

'You just need to push for it. They're lucky to have you and they know it.' He took my hand and squeezed it gently, his thumb rubbing the soft flesh lovingly. I met his gaze, warmed by the faith he had in me.

'Well, with any luck, I won't be there too much longer anyway. I got a call from a recruiter earlier about a small agency looking –'

'Oh, Christ. Not this again.' Connor dropped my hand, sunk his head back and I tensed immediately, kicking myself for pushing it but when he lowered his chin, his expression was dappled in mirth, not the irritation I'd expected.

'Babe, I love you, you know that. You're amazing at many things but how you ever thought you could be a project manager is beyond me. You're the scattiest person I know. You're always losing things, forgetting where you've put stuff. You've got a memory like a sieve and while I may adore everything about you, useless or otherwise, massive companies spending hundreds of thousands of pounds on advertising might not find the whole bird-brained routine quite so cute.'

Bird-brained? I gasped at that. I actually jolted and he grasped my hand again, his bottom lip sticking out in mock petulance, but I pulled away and when he reached forward again and pressed my fingers it was with none of the jest he'd hidden behind before.

'Don't be like that,' he said, the gleeful tone gone, his stare commanding, his grip on my hand an unspoken caution.

'One pie and mash and one soup.'

I started as the barman appeared at our side, rushing to set the plates down obliviously, twin tea towels offering scant protection from the blistering heat searing through them.

‘Mind, they’re hot.’

Connor released me and I sprang back as though wary of nothing more than third-degree burns.

‘Thank you so much.’

‘Can I get you anything else?’ he continued, flicking the towels over his shoulder and resisting the urge to press his throbbing fingers under his armpits.

‘Just take the bread away, mate. We won’t be needing that.’

‘No problem.’

Our joint front vanished as quickly as the wicker bowl of fresh rolls and we stared down at the plates in silence, a silence I could only bear for so long.

‘Thanks for getting this,’ I said lightly.

‘S’alright.’ Connor pulled his knife and fork out of the paper casing, casting the napkin to the side and another sullen cloud of reproach settled over the brutal clatter and shriek of cutlery absorbing the brunt of the atmosphere.

‘Sorry,’ I said for want of any other way to diffuse the tension. ‘I shouldn’t have overreacted.’

He paused, his head still bent towards his plate, waiting for more.

‘And you’re right. I should ask them what I need to do to keep moving up the ladder. They know I’m overqualified, they said as much when they took me on.’

‘It’s what I’m always telling you.’

‘I know. And I appreciate your support. It’s… it’s not so bad there. I could do with a bit more stimulation, that’s all, but it’ll come over time,’ I murmured, all the while quietly formulating an escape.

A retreat from the path I'd wandered onto. The route I knew even as I headed down it, only led to disappointment and regret.

'It's a safe bet,' he concurred, adding substance to what we both must have known was a lie. 'A stable position with a future. You don't seem to realise how lucky you are to have it. Only a few months ago you were unemployed – unemployable practically after what Raj did to you and now, you're rising up the ranks faster than anyone who's ever worked there.'

'Thank you.'

'For the compliment or for getting you the job in the first place?'

'Both, of course.'

He nodded, gracious in his acceptance of credit where credit was due. Then shaking out his napkin, he dabbed the gravy nestling in the folded crevice of his lips before tossing it aside carelessly, an apparently impromptu thought occurring to him.

'Oh. Before you speak to anyone about getting promoted though, I need you to take out another ten thousand pounds.'

'What?'

He picked up his knife and fork again and resumed his demolition of the mash with no more trepidation than if he'd asked me to pass him the ketchup.

'You need to get another loan to cover our expenses for the next few months.'

'But… I've only just taken the last one out.'

'Oh, bless you, I forget how bad you are with money. Seriously though, how far do you think five thousand pounds goes? It barely covers two months' basic living expenses let alone all this lot.' He waved his arm around the pub as if we owned it.

'But I've reached my limit. They gave me the maximum they could last time.'

'Last time you couldn't sign off on your own application.'

The air in my lungs drained, the pieces of the puzzle I'd examined from every angle in bewilderment finally falling into place. My response, when it came, was thin and lacking conviction. 'Jerome needs to authorise it too.'

'Fucking Jerome.' Connor thumped his fist on the table catching the side of his plate, the rattle unnerving. 'Well, go on then. Do whatever you've got to do with *Jerome* to get him to sign off on it. Flirt, flash your tits, whatever it takes bar actually fucking the guy and get it done.'

'I can't.' I shook my head, my voice nothing more than white noise in the backdrop of his grand reveal. 'How would we even pay it back?'

'For Christ's sake, it's not like I don't have the money. It's just tied up, I've told you that. Or what do you want me to do? Pull it out and pay more in penalties than the paltry ten grand I'm asking you for? And then what? Return the car? Give up the flat? We agreed to give the letting agency six months' notice and don't forget your name's on the lease now. Any arrears on that would be as much your debt as mine.'

The blood drained from my face. 'Six months?'

'You can thank Covid for that but what's it matter anyway? We've got to live somewhere.'

But not a high-end apartment in central London. I'd known even as I signed the new contract that it was a mistake but what can you do when somebody's telling you they're ready to take your relationship to the next level even though you're not? There's no saying *thank you but I'd like to carry on living here and see how this goes before deciding whether I'm in it for the long term. No hard feelings*. You scribble on the line because there's no coming back if you don't.

'I don't know why you always act like this is such a big deal. Ten thousand pounds is nothing and it's only for a few months until the deal I'm locked into has matured. Then we can do what you like. Pay the loan off. Reinvest it. Whatever. You decide. We just need to get through to the end of the year. Less than that – five months. As soon as I graduate, I'll be back at Microsoft working my way towards a six-figure salary. I'll be getting more than ten grand in bonuses just for showing up to the office.'

'And is there no other way we can manage until then on my salary? What about the money your mum gave you from the house?'

'Your salary?' He snorted. 'Look, working in a bank has its advantages, but the entry level pay isn't one of them. Not the way we live and as for the proceeds from the house, half of it's tied up in high-interest investments like the rest of our money and the other half's gone. How do you think we pay for all these meals out and fancy shows you like going to? The trip to Paris. The nice car. We're down nearly three thousand pounds a month before we've even left the flat.'

My mouth opened and closed around the words I'd never say. That it wasn't my choice to go to restaurants and cafes every day, that I didn't need the car, the expensive apartment, the eye-popping gym membership, these were all things he demanded, rebutting me if I even suggested tightening our belts with a cry of *money is for spending* or *don't worry about the finances, babe. I've got it.*

But he didn't have it. And whatever he did have was never enough.

My chest tightened and my breath grew shallow at the knowledge that he also had access to my wages. We'd opened a joint bank account a few weeks ago. He said it made more sense to consolidate our earnings, that it would improve our credit history and look better when we applied for a mortgage and so now if I used any of it, I had to explain why and hold my tongue every time the doorbell indicated another Amazon package had arrived with his name on it. Presumably every penny of it had been sucked into the black hole already along with the credit cards we'd maxed out but still, there was one more option and though it pained me to suggest touching the fund I'd been putting aside for a deposit, it was better than the alternative. Besides, it was only temporary, a simple case of moving cash about. For now.

'Let's use my ISA account then.'

He threw his knife and fork down and sighed. 'I've used that already. Borrowed it, if you prefer, if we're still playing at that game – what's mine is yours and what's yours is yours too.'

I swallowed. All those months of saving scrupulously, the years of birthday money I'd put aside, the thousand pounds my gran had given me when I'd graduated and it had gone along with everything else. All of it and the only hope I ever had of seeing any of it again was to hang on until his investments came up for renewal at the end of the year.

‘Look, either you trust me or you don’t. Either I’ve supported you for the last six months and given you everything you’ve ever wanted or I’m robbing you blind. It’s one or the other, right?’

‘I don’t think you’re robbing me. I just don’t know how I’m supposed to get hold of that kind of money’ Without committing fraud.

‘Well, you’d better find a way or come next month we’re screwed.’

There was no need to spell it out. It was pretty obvious I was screwed either way.

66 Days Before the Murder

Her Mother

I'd said *David* twice before he actually looked up.

'You're vibrating.'

His eyes met mine with a flicker of sheer panic as though I'd told him the bomb strapped to his lap was ticking and then he flung himself about the armchair wildly, upsetting the cup he'd balanced on one arm. Of course, I'd known perfectly well that would happen as soon as he set it down there but you have to pick your battles and now there was a dribble of tea on the carpet. Really, I only had myself to blame – not that I told him that.

By the time I'd come back from the kitchen with a rag, he'd managed to find his phone (wedged down the side of the cushion, no doubt) and was chatting away breathlessly the way an exuberant ten-year-old talks about Star Wars so I knew it was one of the girls.

He put his hand over the microphone and mouthed 'Milly' which threw me, I must say. I'd have put money on it being Olive.

I mouthed 'Milly?' with such disbelief, a flash of uncertainty crossed his face and he pulled the phone away from his ear to check the screen, but sure enough it was Emily's distant voice gracing us from her ivory tower.

'Put it on speaker then,' I said ignoring the unreasonable stab of hurt I felt at the sight of her name on David's mobile, though she probably had tried mine first. I may well have left it in my bag again, that would be why.

'Your mother's here,' David announced, far too loudly.

'Oh. Hi, Mum. You okay?'

'Yes, darling. All good here. How are you? How's Connor? How's work?'

David leaned away from me as though I was the one who was about to explode this time but I had no idea when I was going to have the opportunity to speak to her again. I had to get all my social niceties out of the way while I had the chance.

'Good, Mum, everything's fine.' There followed the sort of lingering pause that draws one's eyes towards the phone and I must admit my first thought was that David had gone and cut her off because that was something he'd do, but a fraction of a second later she cleared her throat with a tinny rattle and I relaxed. Which was my first mistake.

'Well, sort of,' she continued in a voice not unlike that of a condemned prisoner delivering a speech at the gallows. 'I mean, everything's okay but I was just saying to Dad…'

David and I shared a look of what I could only describe as grim anticipation. We'd used it before on such occasions as Olive going all about the houses before admitting she'd lost the car keys (£295 to replace), Olive casually mentioning she may have in all likelihood possibly branded a permanent stain onto the worktop with a scolding hot saucepan, Olive creating a dreadful build up to coming out as though we'd care about anything but her happiness (and her not losing the car keys or damaging the surfaces). In fact, now I think of it, we'd shared that look in the static-filled seconds preluding some potentially dire announcement multiple times but never when Milly was part of the equation.

'Yeeeesssss?' we prompted reluctantly, preferring even as we asked, not to know.

'Um, well, it was just I needed to ask you both for a bit of a favour. You can say no of course. I don't want to put you on the spot or anything,' she stammered doing exactly that and it struck me there was a reason I hadn't heard my phone ring. She'd been hoping to talk to her father alone. 'It's just, you know how Connor's money is all tied up in investments and he can't start work until he's finished his course, which is only a few months away but still… we're struggling to make ends meet on my salary, what with all the price hikes recently.'

This was where I'd usually say something about the cost of the weekly shop these days, not to mention gas and electricity. You'd hardly know we were down to half a household, not counting my mother, but I didn't. I managed to hold it in. As all the best TV detectives say it's better to keep schtum and let the suspect fill in the silence. Not that Emily was a suspect, of course – not back then – but it was the same principle with your children. They always hung themselves if you gave them enough rope to do it. Unfortunately, David was less familiar with preferred investigative techniques.

'Things have got pricy,' he blustered, interrupting my incriminating lack of response. 'How are you managing?'

'Well, this is it, Dad. We're not –'

I eased myself down onto the edge of the sofa, close enough to take in whatever Godawful request was coming without unsettling

Ginger, who was already whacking his tail rudely despite refusing to open his eyes.

'– which was why I was hoping I might be able to borrow some money, just until the end of the year when Connor's investments come through.'

'Come through?'

'Are released, I mean. I don't know what you call it. When the term's up and he can access them again.'

'How much are we talking?'

I could almost hear her stealing herself at the other end of the line.

'Ten thousand.'

We both inhaled so sharply anyone would have thought she'd given away the twist in the season finale of Line of Duty. I'm fairly sure my eyes bulged. I know David's did because that was when I made a conscious decision never to pull that expression again.

'And what about Linda? I mean, I hope it's not rude to ask…'

Of course, it's not rude, David, I conveyed silently through the medium of marriage. *For ten thousand pounds we get to ask whatever we like.*

'…but she must be quite flush what with the house sale.'

'She is and she's promised to give almost half of it to Connor. The problem is we need it now.'

I can't tell you the relief I felt at hearing that. Emily clearly took as much notice of Linda's stories as she did of mine. I flapped my hands, spluttering to get the good news out. 'But the sale's gone through. I popped in for a tour of her new flat a few weeks ago. I say tour, it was more of a peek. I mean, I know she said she needed to downsize, but I hope you're not planning on taking my grandkids there whenever you get around to it. There'd be nowhere to put them.' Not that they'd need to stay there with all our empty bedrooms.

David was giving me one of his looks, one of the looks he occasionally borrowed from me I might add, but he was right. I'd stopped thinking of Emily as a criminal when that was exactly what I should have been doing.

'The sale *has* gone through,' she said, a little too hastily I thought but both of my daughters were forever trying to shut me up. 'The money's just taking a while to be signed off by the solicitors.'

Well, I knew nothing about that and I couldn't pretend to but when David didn't object, I assumed it was a thing. I mean, you would, wouldn't you? I wasn't really a policewoman, police person, whatever they were these days.

'Love.' This was as stern as David got but it was indication enough that he wasn't keen to jeopardise our retirement plans just yet. 'We'd like to help you out, but we don't have that sort of cash lying about. We could probably scrape together about six and a half thousand if we borrow what we can from Olive's tuition fund, but we'd have to have it back before she starts the second year. When did you say you needed it until?'

Milly didn't answer straight away and when she did, her words fragmented in her throat, chipped and splintered by harrowing sobs that seemed to erupt from her.

'Thank you, thank you,' she said, wailed really. 'That's so, so kind of you, but I can't pay it back until December.'

David looked as guilt-ridden as I felt but the money simply wasn't there for us to lend her.

'But surely Linda's solicitors will have sorted out whatever this hold up is before then. If we can help you out in the meantime, we'd be happy to…' David's confidence tapered away at the spiked intake of air echoing down the line.

'Sorry, sorry,' Emily cry-laughed. 'I'm sorry, I'm so sorry to ask you this at all. I should be able to manage. I'm an adult.' Which was the sort of thing only a child would say but we all think we're terribly grown up until we get to twenty-five and realise we have absolutely no idea what that's supposed to mean.

'I don't know what to say,' she hiccupped. 'Thank you, thank you for the offer. I want to say yes but I don't want to let you down. I just can't guarantee I can pay you back on time.'

'And what happens if you can't get hold of ten thousand pounds?'

'Connor reckons we'll lose the flat but we'll still be liable for another six-months' rent, we'll have to give up the car, but that's leased so there'll be penalties for that too. We still owe for the rest of this year's council tax, the electricity bill, everything. I thought we were fine, we are fine – on paper. We're pretty well off considering, but we can't touch a penny of it. It's all so ridiculous.'

'I'll lend you ten thousand.'

Both the girls nearly found themselves the recipients of an unexpected windfall the way my mother sneaked up on us like that. Only Ginger remained undisturbed, but deliberately so. I had told her to let herself in to save us the trouble of answering the door whenever she (frequently) turned up, but a short cough or a bit of a clatter in the hallway by way of announcement wouldn't have gone a miss. It took us a moment to recover and by then she'd crowded herself around the phone and was shouting into it as though addressing a buzzer in a deserted office block.

'Can you hear me? I said, I'll lend you the money.'

Emily burst into tears again and I won't detail the extent of her gratitude, or ours quite honestly, shock tactics and heart attacks notwithstanding. Suffice to say, she was relieved and I can't pretend to understand exactly what the issue was with their money, but the fact was, we all knew they had plenty of it and Connor would be working soon, regardless of what happened with the investments and his early inheritance. It all added up to a tidy sum, although I would be having words with Emily about getting themselves into such a pickle. Clearly now wasn't the time though and anyway, I could barely get a word in edgewise. Milly was blabbering ten to the dozen and was no easier to understand than when she'd been sobbing her heart out.

'Please don't tell Connor I've come to you for help. He'd be mortified if he knew. I've told him I'm taking a loan out from the bank.'

'Okay, darl –'

'And please don't mention it to Linda either. She'll feel bad about the money from the house taking so long to come through.'

'Don't worry about that,' Bella said. 'I won't be telling anyone.' And I swear Emily's relief was palpable. 'Just send me your bank details.'

And I was going to say I had them already when Emily said she'd opened a new account – and no, not the joint account that I also had, but another new account, which I now realise Connor knew nothing about so she wasn't completely naïve.

The same couldn't be said for us of course, but that's retrospect for you.

39 Days Before the Murder

Her

The day had turned to night and the flat was dark, the air cooler now, my duvet a cocoon I was loath to shed. I blinked slowly, goading myself to get up. Get up and cook something before Connor got home but my limbs were leaden, weary, my whole body ached. Even my dreams seeped into consciousness mingling with reality, blurring truth with fiction until neither mattered any more. Everything was surreal, my life a show I was watching happen to someone else.

The chill on the soles of my feet as I edged them cautiously onto the floor ruffled my senses, cleared a path through the smog and I sat, my legs poised on the side of the bed like a swimmer awaiting a shot.

I'd felt like this for weeks now. Shattered. Heavy. Undriven even when it came to getting up. My chin sunk to my chest and I closed my eyes again, bright spots sliding across the imprint of light left by the street lamp outside.

It was getting worse not better. What had started as hours spent tossing and turning in the darkness, fretting and fantasizing, choking under the weight of the chains I'd shackled myself within, had turned into days, weeks of all consuming shame followed by panic. Panic and then shame again, no exit route viable for me anymore. Not yet. Not yet and still, I had to get up. Get up and try and shake off whatever the worry had metamorphized into, my immune system running on empty, my every movement an exercise of will.

I was sleeping all day now, shaky and buzzing at night, my ears heightened to any shift in the unsettled stillness besides me, Connor's every quiet breath fingernails scratching down a chalk board.

I'd only been out once in the last few weeks, once and that was to get a sick note from the GP. They'd signed me off at work but I didn't know how much longer I could expect them not to query the length of my absence. How long before I should query it again myself.

The doctor suspected long Covid. That's what he put it down to, even though I'd never tested positive, as impossible as that seemed. I'd check and rechecked, each time fully expecting a clear and comprehensive diagnosis, only to find myself staring at one line on the plastic stick. One line stubbornly refusing to turn into two.

So long Covid it was and I, one of the lucky ones who must have written my symptoms off at the time as those of a cold, if I had any at all. But certainly this – what I was going through now – this was what people were talking about. *The aftereffects*. The brain fog, the confusion, the headaches. Close to collapse and perennially exhausted with no end in sight.

Long Covid was worse than the actual virus itself by the sounds of it. Long Covid was fluctuating and limitless. A trial of endurance. Long Covid was discredited and marginalised, but it was better than any alternative explanation. Alternative explanations required prodding and poking, getting back out of bed and although it didn't explain why I only woke up when I should have been asleep, I didn't need Siri to run through the consequences of dozing all day, anxiety eating away at me all night, a whirlwind of worst-case scenarios tumbling around my mind, quietening only as the sun rose and my eyelids finally drooped. As the door clicked behind the love of my life.

That was unfair. I had to stop doing that. Connor had been really supportive ever since I got ill. Really very patient and loving, running around after me, making me comfortable, bringing me hot drinks and warm soup. Plumping the cushions.

It made me feel even worse about all the dark thoughts I was still having about him. About the money and the way he could be when his mood suddenly snapped, a pendulum always ready to swing, leaving me walking on eggshells no matter how nice he was being. More terrified then, knowing his fury would catch me unawares no matter how prepared I thought I was. No matter how alert I'd been waiting for the façade to come crashing down. On me.

He'd been angry when the loan came through, seething with contempt for the way he imagined I'd got it, his hatred for Jerome – who knew nothing about it – boundless now. Boundless and unconstrained. Uncensored and there was nothing I could say in his favour without admitting I'd turned to my family for help, shifted the dynamic of power he thought he had in their eyes. As if they'd care.

'Why did you get a cashier's cheque?' he'd said eyeing the online statement suspiciously. 'Why not get it paid directly into the account?'

I'd busied myself folding up the blankets in the sitting room, my back to him, my hands occupied. Breezy.

'I don't know, I didn't think about it. They just printed it there and then. It doesn't matter though, does it? The main thing is we should be okay now until your cash is released.'

'Of course.' His tone was velvety and the hairs on the back of my neck stood on end. 'The cash…always got your eyes on the prize, hey, babe?'

I forced a smile, a crack in my voice I intended as a giggle. 'I don't mean that. We need to pay it back, that's all. You know I don't care about your money, Daddy Warbucks.'

'Not as long as I've got it anyway, hey?' He stared at me until the stiff smirk I'd forged with iron will began to slip and I glanced away, jumping as I did at the smack of the laptop slamming shut and the speed with which he rose from the sofa. 'I'm just kidding. Well done for sorting that out.'

He took me into his arms and I was spared from having to smile again, but the tension eased from me making way for mild irritation as he rocked me from side-to-side. Rocked and rocked me, squeezing tighter and then tighter still until the embrace was a stranglehold, my ribs crushed, my breathing laboured, eyes staring wildly, arms trapped. I grunted, writhing, a scream caught in my throat, his lips brushing past my ear, his breath hot and heavy, my skin crawling, recoiling from him.

'If I ever see that prick anywhere near you, I will kill him. I will fuck him up so badly his own mother won't recognise him. And I'll slit your throat too. Nod if you understand.'

I jerked my head and he slowly released his grip on me, allowed me to step back, stumbling from his arms, catching me as I nearly fell.

‘Easy, tiger,’ he grinned, pulling me back towards him, his fingers digging into the curve of my backside as though it belonged to him and then with the sort of slap he often mistakenly took for foreplay, he let me go again.

‘Go and get changed then,’ he’d said. ‘Might as well treat ourselves tonight.’

I pushed myself up from the side of the bed. Pushed the memory down, deep, deep down where it would only surface in the middle of the night, replaying in the montage of moments keeping me awake. Sandwiched in between the look on his face whenever my phone rang, whenever I mentioned popping down to Brighton, visiting Olive in Exeter, the work-do everyone else was going to.

‘Everyone?’ he’d sneer and that would be that.

I shook the look from my mind. It had been weeks since I’d seen it and just as long since I’d wanted to go anywhere or see anyone.

The hallway lit up as I fumbled blindly for the light switch, dragging myself towards the kitchen, bouncing against the wall like a drunk, the fog, thick with sediment, lifting slowly, the air fresher out here. I reached for my phone, charging on the worktop where Connor must have plugged it in before he left, far from me so I could rest, he said, though it must have pained him not to have me respond to every text he sent. Six unread messages, all from him. All an approximation of the same stock phrases – hey, how are you? Just checking in. Text me back when you get this.

I rolled my eyes and sighed. This was better than it had been. This was the Connor I’d fallen in love with, I just wasn’t the girl I’d been back then. I couldn’t remember the last time I’d laughed, really laughed, out loud until my belly hurt and tears ran down my face.

Had I ever laughed like that with him? Maybe. There'd been that one time at the Tate Modern when we'd gone around pretending we got it. Spouting pretentious rubbish about the art work and symbolism like proud parents preening over their child's work on a pre-school display wall. We'd found it hilarious. Nobody else had, not least the curator who'd suggested we might be disturbing the other visitors, but we'd had fun that day. Hadn't we? It hadn't always been like this…

I opened the kitchen cupboard and reached up for a glass, my arm faltering at the sight of the packets and tins lined up in neat rows where the plates and bowls should have been. The mugs and tumblers. Four upturned wine glasses, all gone.

Stepping back, I surveyed the other doors before returning to the open shelves as though I'd imagined it. As though this time, the crockery and glasses would be there, but no, they were in the next one along and the more I stared at the contents of both, the less I could tell whether it had always been that way or if I was losing my mind.

I'd put sugar on the vegetables yesterday and I still didn't understand how. Connor had been so nice about it saying anyone could have made the same mistake, but the jars looked nothing alike. And yet, it was the sort of thing I did all the time now. I was half-asleep, thick with fatigue even when I was awake. Stupid and careless. Ridiculous even. What kind of half-wit keeps misplacing their phone in the fridge? The first few times I only found it when Connor got home and called it for me but now at least, I knew to check there before turning the flat upside down. It would be funny if it wasn't so disconcerting. Distressing if I awarded the implications the weight they probably deserved.

Connor loved to tease me about it. 'You're such a scatterbrain,' he'd say, rubbing his chin against the top of my head affectionately, never far from me. 'I can't believe you worked in project management for as long as you did. If I wasn't convinced your boss fancied you before, I certainly know he did now. Anyone else would have sacked you on day one, you daft klutz.'

And now I couldn't even hold down a basic administrative job. A box ticking role that used as little of my brain as I cared to invest in it – not something I'd considered a perk until now.

My spine cracked as I reached up for the linguine, tight muscles spasming sharply as the pasta shot out of the open packet, spilling all over me and onto the workbench, scattering onto the floor.

'Fuuuu…'

I stood staring down at the mess, unsurprised, until, at the sound of the key turning in the lock, my heart sank and I lurched forward, hurriedly gathering the extent of the meal I'd prepared, awaiting Connor's familiar cry.

'Hi honey, I'm home.' He swung around the doorway. 'Oh, what have you done now?' he laughed, pulling me up to my feet with one hand, the other clasped around my daily health shake. 'Here, take this and go and put your feet up. I'll make dinner.'

My hand shook at the cool weight of the green smoothie, ostensibly packed with the vitamins and minerals I felt drained of.

'Thank you. This looks great, but I might save it until the morning. Might perk me up if I have it first thing. God knows I need something to get me out of bed.'

Connor pinned a loose tangle of hair behind my ear. 'I'd have it now, babe,' he said, concern creasing his forehead. 'It won't be as effective if you leave it. I'll pop out and get you another one tomorrow if you think it does you any good.'

And I kissed him on the cheek gratefully, knowing that as much as I dreaded him coming home, when he was in a good mood, his tenderness and little acts of kindness were the only things that kept me going.

I had to remember that. Without him, I'd have been lost.

39 Days Before the Murder

Him

At first, I started messing around with her for a laugh. A bit of a prank if you like, or perhaps – if I can be forgiven the natural human instinct, to teach her a lesson after whatever stunt she pulled to get Jerome to authorise that loan.

Plus, I was sick of her skulking around every evening like she'd rather be anywhere else and then shooting off to work in the morning as if she couldn't wait to see the back of me, so I thought I'd wake her up a bit when I got home in the evenings. Give her a bit more get up and go, the way she was when we first got together, before she got all moody.

I swapped the coffee around, that's all. No biggie. I put the decaffeinated in the normal jar and vice versa so when she got in from work, she'd fill up on the wrong one and have a bit more to say for herself. And yes, alright, I knew she was always banging on about not sleeping well if she had caffeine after midday, but really, half of that was psychological. Or so I thought. The funny thing was, she really couldn't sleep, couldn't drop off for hours, didn't rest when she did and then the first thing she'd do in the morning was top herself up again to wake up, only of course, the coffee was decaffeinated so no doing.

I'd have swapped it back after a few days, only it was quite funny watching her drag herself into the bank, all knackered like.

Not so keen to jump out of bed and off to see that smirking arsehole. She'd hit the espresso all right when she got there, but that could only keep her going for so long before it started to have the opposite effect. Before she started to get all overwhelmed and agitated. Anxious and worn out, especially if she was already tired. So, she told me she only had one and then by the time it had worked its way out of her system and she got home, I'd wake her up again.

On and on we could have gone like that – nothing shady, just a little less of her at work and more at home, that's all it needed to be, but then she started questioning the coffee, saying she was sure it was a faulty batch, that they'd labelled it wrong. Refusing to drink it even when I made it for her. Getting all sulky and ruining our time together when I persuaded her to go ahead. To get it down her and that's when I had to up the ante, as it were, to keep her ticking over on an even keel, to maintain her equilibrium.

It was only a few sleeping tablets – over the counter, all natural ingredients, crushed up in the new coffee I'd made a show of buying along with a shot of the hazelnut syrup I got to jazz up her latte and mask the taste. Which again was less appreciated than I'd hoped, but that was what I was dealing with these days.

Sure enough, after a week or so of stumbling through the workday on the back of a month of sleepless nights and a dose of EZzz pills in the morning, she was told to go home and take herself to bed until she felt better. Her boss was off to Cancun in a few days and didn't want whatever she had.

It wasn't like it helped me out especially since she was useless while I was out and about and no help at all when I was in, but it did at least get her away from that pervy dickhead who had his eyes on her. And she was still getting paid of course. Win-win. I wouldn't have minded if someone had let me sleep all day instead of having to face the relentless drizzling grey from Monday to Friday.

I didn't do it at the weekend, of course. In fact, the last dose was always on Thursday to give her a chance to shake off the irregular sleep pattern she'd gotten herself into and then bless her, she'd always say by Sunday night she was starting to feel better, but then it was time for her other medicine. Two UWake tablets in a mug of hot chocolate with marshmallows and whipped cream was enough to do it, although it did mean I had to start monitoring everything else she ate. She didn't have the sort of metabolism that could cope with the extra calories, especially as she wasn't getting out and about as much these days. Lucky for her, it wasn't a problem during the week when I could pick up an energising kale and chia seed smoothie on the way home from uni. Those things tasted like shit anyway. It was expected and neither of us had to worry about her getting fat on one of them a day.

The whole operation took some organising and it was a relief when she finally agreed to take something to help her sleep at night so I could fill the EZzz pot up with stimulants and she'd take them herself, no subterfuge necessary. I mean, it was fun, but mad stressful at times. And not being funny, but who wants jelly thighs wrapped around them up at night? I'd have to kick her out of bed if it ever came to that. Everything in moderation, that's what they say, right? Slow and steady wins the race.

24 Days Before the Murder

Her Mother

Their building didn't look as posh as I remembered from the outside but I wasn't quite as in awe of the shininess of it all as last time. I was too busy wondering who on earth was responsible for keeping all that glass clean and how much that cost. It was no wonder they were struggling. David pressed the buzzer again and craned his neck towards the speaker, his eyes trained on the blank screen.

'Maybe she's popped to the chemist…' Bella said, scanning the street with scant regard for all the good it would do her with a cataract in one eye and astigmatism in the other.

'Perhaps, but that doesn't explain why she's not answering her phone,' I said, trying it again.

'She must still be in bed.' David lowered his finger and turned to me questioningly. 'Shouldn't we leave her to sleep? She probably needs it.'

'David.' David looked mildly alarmed but so he should. 'They said she's been off for weeks. Whatever it is she's got, sleep is clearly not helping. We need to get into that apartment and find out what's going on.'

The one good thing about living in a place that size was that at some point someone else was going to have to come or go into it which was exactly what happened right then and if I wasn't in such a hurry, I'd have had a word with the young man who walked straight in leaving the door to soft-close behind him without a care in the world. We could have been burglars for all he knew. It wasn't like they retired, was it? Or maybe they did. I knew very little on the subject and we were in which was the main thing whether he thought we were too old to be up to no good or he just didn't register us at all. Certainly, he didn't hold the lift and I had to thrust myself in as it was shutting and let the doors rebound on my arm. It was rather painful and still we were invisible to him. Blasted Londoners. It gave me no inclination to stay any longer than necessary, that was for sure.

The flat was where we'd left it on the fifth floor but there was no sign of movement from within when we tapped on the front door and shouted through it.

'Maybe we should call Connor after all?' David said, the way a vegetarian might order veal from the deli counter and we gazed at each other, the three of us, stymied before my mother suggested trying Emily again and sure enough, this time when her phone rang, we heard its jittery vibration, echoing and muffled but definitely nearby.

'She must be in then,' Bella deduced, all those hours dedicated to watching re-runs of The Bill on UK Gold finally paying off.

David knocked on the door again, louder this time. 'Emily. Emily! Open up. It's us. Mum and Dad. And your gran.'

The silence that followed was louder than the banging and not for the first time, my heart fluttered and my chest tightened, the air suspended in my lungs, though I wasn't quite sure why.

'Emily!' I cried, my voice unnaturally thin, the jaunty rap of my knuckle against the reinforced grey veneer at odds with the trepidation churning in my stomach, but then I heard it. A scraping inside and the sense of being appraised through the peek hole, the click of the lock and the curious creak of the door as it opened revealing Milly's dishevelled face peering out beneath a matted fringe.

'Good God,' I said or at least someone did.

Milly's eyes were wide, skittish we all agreed when we dissected events later. She poked her head through the doorframe and scanned the length and breadth of hallway like an intelligence officer fearing she'd been compromised. 'What are you doing here?'

No *hello*. No *nice to see you*. She was an absolute mess and after weeks of trying to get hold of her, of being fobbed off by her boyfriend, of finally resorting to turning up at her place of work that very morning only to be told she'd been signed off sick for over a month and we knew nothing about it, I wasn't about to wait for her to invite us in.

'Milly!' I cried, pushing the door back and stepping inside. 'We've been looking everywhere for you.'

She had the look of a startled pigeon about her but that probably had as much to do with the velocity with which David and Bella threw themselves around her as it did with us turning up out of the blue.

'I –'

'We've been calling and calling.'

'Is everything alright?' she croaked gazing at us in bleary wonder as if assessing whether our appearance were merely an unexpected twist in a muddled dream.

‘Everything’s alright with us,’ Bella exclaimed, omitting to mention the shadow that had shown up on her latest scan and the results of her blood test, but that was my mother for you. She was a marvel in a crisis. I’d always thought it was a pity she’d missed out on the War. She’d have been in her element, although she’d have bored us with stories about it forever more so it was for the best. She took Emily by the shoulders and held her at arm’s length. ‘It’s you we’re all worried about.’

Emily blinked slowly, her eyes glossy and lolling. “Me?’

If there were ever a need for tea, it was now and I hadn’t liked to mention it earlier, but I’d been dying for the loo for well over an hour so whatever was wrong was going to have to wait another few minutes. David led Emily into the sitting room while Bella took charge of the kettle and even from the bathroom, I could hear her making a dreadful fuss about nothing being where it was meant to be as though there were unspoken standards of kitchenware formation anyone in their right mind adhered to. But Emily clearly wasn’t in her right mind, that much was apparent and when she looked up as I belatedly made my way over to her, her eyelids were hooded, her skin a sickly sort of pale.

‘You should have told us, love.’ David sat by her side, cradling her, their heads touching. ‘We’d have come up to look after you if we’d known how ill you were.’

‘I know but I didn’t want you to catch whatever this is. Besides, I haven’t been much company. I can’t even get out of bed most days. They reckon it’s long Covid but I dunno… I can’t seem to shake it, whatever it is.’

I plonked myself down on the other side of the sofa and squeezed Emily's waist with one hand, rubbed her thigh with the other. 'And what about Connor? He's all right, is he?'

'He's fine. He's managed to dodge it so far, if it's contagious, and he's been great with me. Really patient.'

'I wish he'd told us. He made it sound like you were sleeping off a heavy night the last few times we called. I was starting to worry you'd become an alcoholic. It was only when we went to the bank –

'

'When did you speak to Connor?'

I caught David's eye and it took all my strength not to say something scathing about him clearly not passing on our messages but then Emily shook her head, confusion or doubt furrowing her forehead.

'Or maybe he did tell me…' she conceded squinting, her gaze drifting off again.

'I couldn't find any biscuits,' my mother sneered accusingly, shunting across the two overfilled mugs she'd smacked hurriedly onto the coffee table, the contents sloshing down the sides and in an instant, Emily leapt to her feet. Debilitating illness or no, she was in and out of the kitchen before we even had time to react, wiping up the spilt tea as though the Russians had been at it.

'Sorry,' she said, either because she'd scared us half to death by overreacting or because she was British and hardwired to apologise even when it wasn't her fault, we never did find out. Instead, the blood drained from her face and her knees buckled just as David stood up, catching her by the elbow and easing her down to the sofa again.

'Oopsy daisy.'

Inhaling deeply, Emily stared intently at the floor, the tea towel still clenched in her fist, too dizzy to notice the look we all shared.

'Right,' I said. 'You're coming home with us – just until you feel better.' I might have told her I had a bag of leeches at the ready the way she flinched.

"But Connor…'

'Now, now, I'm sure Connor's doing his best but he's got his studies and I don't like the thought of you being left alone for so long every day. Besides, he probably needs a bit of a break himself.'

'I can't – I – I… He'll –'

'Settle down.' David placed his hand gently on her arm. 'It's alright.'

'He won't… I can't –'

'Emily.' Bella was standing over us still, the old school matron's voice she used for special occasions indicating she meant business. 'Listen to your mum and dad, dear. All anyone wants is for you to get better and the best place for that right now is back home where we can look after you. Get you in to see Dr Jones. Find out what's really going on, shall we?'

'I'll go and pack you a bag.' I slapped Milly's leg decisively and sprung to my feet. Well, stood at any rate, knees cracking which was only to be expected after all the walking we'd done that day. 'What do you need? Your laptop? Phone? Handbag? You've got plenty of clothes and toiletries back at the house. Will that do you?'

Emily nodded, the voice seeping out of her small and shaky. 'Yes, that should be fine.'

Bella passed her a mug of tea, carefully this time and David held it steady as Milly brought it to her lips, swallowing loudly, tears springing to her eyes.

'There, there.'

The mug found its way back down to the table and David wore track marks into Emily's cardigan as she crumpled against him, her sparrow-like chest juddering while I swept the flat seizing any devices that looked like they'd fit in a bag for life with Bella following in my wake like a ragged leaf stuck to the sole of my shoe.

'How are you planning on getting her home?' she hissed, close enough to smell the Boots meal deal she'd had on the train earlier. 'She's in no fit state…'

'I know that, Mum, but what can we do? David and I'll take one arm each and you can go ahead and open any doors. We'll manage between the three of us.'

'She can barely stand.'

'I'm not asking Connor to give us a lift back to Brighton if that's what you're suggesting.'

I strode over to the coat rack and pulled down Milly's warm winter jacket, the handbag she carried everywhere, a pair of trainers. Her thick scarf in case it got chilly. The last thing she needed was to catch something else.

'Of course not!' My mother sidled up to me, penning me in against the shoe cabinet. 'It's just that… have I told you when I lived in Islington, before I met your father –'

'Oh, for crying out loud.'

'I was with this chap – a cabbie – knew every nook and cranny in London, he did. Every back street. Took me down a few of them, I can tell you.'

'Oh, Mother.'

'Well, I could get him to take us to Victoria. He always said to give him a call next time I was up.'

I elbowed past her and sighed, 'He probably meant back in the 1920s.' I was quite pleased with that one but there was no time to revel in it.

'We're in touch, I'll have you know. On Facebook. He's still an admirer.'

I shuddered and glanced into the sitting room, registering with fresh shock the dark shadows circling my daughter's eyes, the gaunt cleft of her cheekbones. 'Go on then, if you think he'd take us. If not, let's just get an Uber.'

Which seemed to be the thing to say these days, though God alone knew how one went about organising that. No doubt Bella had an app for it.

'Grab Emily's mobile for me, can you?' I said sidestepping around her as she rummaged through her handbag with far more enthusiasm than the situation called for. 'It's charging on the kitchen workbench.'

I was having one last recce around the bedroom when I heard Bella gasp and spun around to find her striding down the hallway, brandishing both their phones at me.

'She's got twenty-three missed calls – five from us, all the rest from the boyfriend. Check yours. I've got two from a number I don't recognise. It's got to be him.'

I pulled mine out of my coat pocket just as his name lit up the screen and Bella and I stared at each other until it stopped ringing. We hadn't broken eye contact before it started again.

'He knows we're here,' I whispered, stepping into the sitting room and catching David's eye, the buzz of the unanswered phone in my shaking hand no less alarming than a swarm of irate bees. His gaze followed mine towards the ceiling, the bookcase, every corner of the room, the absence of cameras no less disturbing than a wall covered in surveillance equipment. As my ringtone finally quietened, David's pocket began to hum but he met Emily's haunted expression with an oblivious smile and ignored it completely.

'Nearly done, are you, love?' he cried jovially throwing a grin my way.

'Nearly,' I sang back, working around my mother who could always be relied on to be standing right in the way.

'Ernie's in Benidorm,' she muttered darkly like a woman scorned. 'But he's sending his grandson who's not far apparently. Said he'd be ten minutes.'

My phone started ringing again.

'Emily, put your shoes on, love. Dad'll help you with your coat.'

David lifted her up gingerly as though any sudden movement might break her, which showed restraint. If it were up to me, I'd have bundled her out of the doorway and dealt with any fractures at A&E.

'I have to let Connor –'

'Don't worry,' I interrupted, smiling. 'He knows.'

Bella handed me Emily's phone. Twenty-five missed calls. 'We need to go, love. The taxi's on its way.'

'I –'

'Pop your arm though here.' David urged gently.

'But –'

'That's it. All done. Let's go.'

He led her out of the sitting room and past me into the communal corridor where Bella was hurrying the lift along with some persuasive hammering that was nothing if not cathartic.

'Shouldn't we –'

'Here we go.'

The lift pinged and we were all four inside of it before the doors had fully opened, the stricken panic in Emily's reflection unavoidable on the mirrored walls, our breath collectively suspended, the thunder of blood rushing past our ears filling the silence until at last we jolted to a halt.

'Oh bugger,' said my mother succinctly summing up the sight of Connor waiting in the foyer. He stood in front of the glass doors, sweat glistening on his harried face, barring our exit.

'What's going on, guys? What have I missed?'

'Connor.' David and I adjusted our grip as Emily froze, tense as a cadaver.

'Em didn't tell me you were coming up.'

'No,' I said. 'We thought we'd drop in. Since we haven't been able to get hold of her on the phone.'

'Maybe your phones aren't working.' He smiled, his tone aimable, his eyes as cold as ice.

David puffed himself up, taking Emily's arm an inch or two higher with him. 'Thought we'd take Milly back home for a few days while she's getting over this bug or whatever it is. Give you a bit of a break.'

Connor stepped forward, his hand stretched out to claim what was his. He smiled again. 'There's no need.' He took hold of her wrist.

'No, but we'd like to,' I said emphatically, the way I deal with difficult patients at work. 'It'll do you both good.'

He pulled her towards him and she stiffened again, her feet peddling backwards.

'I don't think it's a good idea,' he said.

There was a ping and the lift doors slid open behind us, rendering the whole scene immobile as if the curtains were about to close on the first act. And it was the first act, not that we were to know that at the time. It was also that same inconsiderate nincompoop who'd let us in earlier and he strode past us purposefully as one might a group of fundraisers rattling buckets in the High Street.

I clutched Emily's arm tighter and my mother placed her frail hand on Connor's, but he shook it off, grabbed Emily's elbow and dragged her out of my grasp, the clenched smile still fixed in place.

'Now, now, Connor.' David planted his feet firmly either side of our daughter, one fist still wrapped around her upper arm, the other reaching for her waist.

'Taxi for Bella Brown?'

That just about did me in, I can tell you. There I was fixated on Connor while this great strapping lad slipped through the soft-closing doors courtesy of our friend, the self-centred nitwit. And thank goodness for both of them.

‘That’s me.’ My mother lifted a quivering hand, relief smoothing the crinkles from her face. ‘We might need some help taking my granddaughter out to the car if you don’t mind. She’s a bit under the weather. We need to get her home.’

‘She is home.’ Connor had dropped any pretence of affection and gripped onto Emily like a mast in a storm.

‘You know what I mean. Her real home.’ Bella beckoned Ernie’s grandson over with an encouraging wave.

‘Don’t you fucking dare.’ Connor wrenched Emily out of David’s grasp completely and she cried out. Well, we all did, everyone that was except for the grandson who hollered, ‘Oi, mate,’ in a way that suggested this wasn’t his first rodeo.

He placed a palm flat against Connor’s chest with a look that seemed to make him shrivel to half his size despite the bravado and he faltered, his confidence failing.

‘All right, sweetheart?’ our knight in shining polyester boomed tethering Milly’s shoulder and leading her away. ‘Lean on me if you like. I’ve parked on double yellows so excuse the rush.’

Recovering himself, Connor stepped forward indignantly with a half-formed snarl that did him no favours at all and quite chilled me to the bones, but David had found his rhythm by then and pulled himself up to his full height (a good head shorter than Connor but impressive enough).

‘We’ll be in touch when she’s feeling better. Get her to give you a ring, shall we?’

‘I’ll come down with you now,’ Connor snapped.

‘Best not. I expect she’ll be out of it for the next few days or so. Why don’t we let you know when she’s feeling better? You can come down and visit her then. If she’s ready.’

And I must admit if I hadn’t been so hell bent on getting out of there, I’d have liked to have seen what else David had in him. As it was, we piled into the taxi, nerves jangling and got out of there as quickly as we could and then, and only then, did any of us breathe.

23 Days Before the Murder

Her

The Sussex Downs are beautiful all year round, but today the sky was clear, the sun shining and the iridescence reflecting off the sea lent the cliffs a shimmering aura. I drew a breath and tasted salt on the back of my throat, felt the tightness in my chest, the burn in my leg muscles aching after weeks of being laid flat.

'How are you feeling?' Olive said, slowing her stride so I could catch up. She'd made the five-hour train journey back from Exeter that morning and had been hovering over me ever since, forcing me to the shower, to eat, sleep and now out *to blow them minging cobwebs away.*

'Better.'

'Yeah?' I could sense her examining my face but I refused to tear my eyes away from the unsteady footpath ahead. The uneven gravel scattered amongst the mud.

'As in better better or better than before?'

I met her eyes briefly. 'Better better, maybe.'

'That's funny, don't you think?' Her feet fell in step with mine and she pressed her lips together as though to stop herself from saying any more.

'Must be the sea air. I haven't slept so well for ages.'

Olive slowed again, turning to me. 'No?'

‘Honestly, it’s really taken it out of me, this last month or so. I thought I was dying, I really did.’

‘And it turns out, all you needed was a few nights away from Connor.’ It sounded like a joke but she didn’t say it like one.

‘Ha.’ My tone was flat as it punched the air. ‘I’ve finally managed to shake it, whatever it was, that’s all.’

She nodded and we walked in silence for a minute or two, the sunlight bouncing off the glistening waves blinding, the ebb and flow of the tide white noise. And then Olive spoke.

‘I’m sorry,’ she ventured, her voice cracking, her fists clenched. ‘I’ve been so caught up in my own crap, I didn’t really realise what was happening to you.’

‘Don’t worry about it. There was nothing anyone could have done. I had to let it run its course, that’s all.’

‘I don’t mean the bug. If you had a bug…’

My lips parted, but no words came, only the gentle hiss of objections vanishing into the breeze.

‘I’ve been really angry with you, blaming you for not –’ Olive paused. ‘– giving a shit I guess, about me breaking up with…’ She didn’t say Flo’s name. She didn’t have to. I reared, turning to her, my head askance, my arms braced to pull her into a hug.

‘Oh, God, I’m the one that should be sorry. I should have come to see you.’

‘So why didn’t you?’ she whispered refusing to be drawn into my embrace. ‘No judgement. I mean it, why? Why didn’t you come to see me? Why didn’t you even call? Before you got ill.’

‘I did call.’

She cocked her head, rolled her lips between her teeth and hummed doubtfully. I swallowed and softened the scratch in my voice. 'But you're right, I should have called more.'

'So why didn't you?'

My arms dropped back down to my side. 'Olive. I'm apologising. I've said I'm sorry.'

'I know and I'm asking you why you didn't call. Why you didn't come when you knew… you knew… What was so bad that you couldn't –'

'Nothing.'

'I have never needed you more in my life. Why didn't you come?'

'Jesus, Olive. I couldn't, all right. I just couldn't. You don't understand.'

'So, tell me. Please tell me. What is going on with you? Where have you gone? What's he done to you?'

She had that same look of terror, of confusion that I'd seen in my parents' faces, Gran's face, ever since they'd turned up at the flat yesterday. That desperation to help wrangling with frustration. Their silent observations as they tiptoed around me, their subtle insinuations edging towards barbed comments the more Connor texted, rang and drummed his fist against their front door. Their firm determination to let me rest unwavering, growing in confidence in correlation with his irritation and then rage.

He was at the house when we arrived, but so was Lee, Ernie's grandson who'd refused to let us get the train home. Said his grandad would tear strips off him if he ever got word of it and so I'd sat in the backseat wedged between my mum and dad, Gran perched up front delighted to have found someone willing to listen to her stories at last and I'd have slept but for the sickening swirl of acid threatening to rise from my gut and the unnatural palpitations in my neck. The shallow breaths I was certain would cease altogether if my mind strayed at all, if I truly absorbed what was happening. The consequences of what I'd allowed to be done.

But then my eyelids, dull and heavy, drooped and the next thing I knew we were pulling up to the front of the house where Connor was already parked, halfway out of his car, the jut of his jaw visible even in the dusky twilight.

'Shall I run him over?' Lee said but nobody laughed. The bubble had burst and the Merc no longer felt like a chariot. It felt like a trap and one Connor was storming towards, his face neutral, his arms spread in greeting as though we'd arranged this all along.

My heart sunk at the sight of him the way it had a thousand times despite everything he'd done for me over the last few weeks, months, since I'd met him really. I wasn't a fool. I knew there was something off with him, with the balance of control in our relationship and I couldn't explain why it seemed so impossible to express the misgivings that spiralled around my head, day in, day out. Why I clammed up and bit down the retribution on the tip of my tongue. Why I was still a bag of nerves around him even on a good day, as he made me dinner or handed me a bag of new clothes to wear. I didn't know why I couldn't tell him I liked my old clothes, liked wearing a little make-up once in a while. Could get through an evening out with friends without sleeping with one of them.

His love for me was suffocating and right then, I knew I would die if I didn't take a breath of air he hadn't already breathed but I could never tell him that. I didn't know how. I didn't even know if there were words to describe how I felt but in the end it didn't matter. My gran and Lee both swung their doors open and stepped onto the tarmac. God alone knows what Gran thought she was going to do, but Lee got to him first.

'Alright, mate?' he'd said obstructing Connor's path, the spread of his shoulders blocking him from sight. 'You needn't have come down. We've got it all under control here.'

'Appreciate it, mate, but why don't you hop in your cab and fuck off back to where you came from? You're a fucking cabbie. You've got no business being here.'

'He's a friend of the family, Connor. And our guest.' Gran hooked her arm through Lee's and batted her eyelashes as though they'd hit it off at a party. 'Can't have you driving back on an empty stomach.'

'I wouldn't say no to a cuppa if you're putting the kettle on, Bella.'

'Of course.' They rounded the driveway as Mum bundled me into the house closing the door behind us, leaving Dad to stand his ground with the others, the sentry guard of his own house, next doors' dog yapping furiously at them through the fence.

'I'd invite Connor in,' Mum said, the noise outside muffled now, 'only I think what you need is a good night's rest. I know he means well...'

But I didn't object if that's what she was expecting, despite the rising panic. Despite the look in his eyes. I let myself be led up to my childhood room, let my mum pull my top over my head, my jogging bottoms past my ankles, help me into my old Hello Kitty pyjamas and tuck me up in bed.

The intermittent burst of banging and raised voices lasted until the early evening but I closed my ears to it all pretending not to know, pretending not to notice every time my door creaked open and a shaft of light fell across the room. I lay trembling, frozen with unearthly cold, curled up on my side, my thoughts blurring into psychedelic dreams until finally in the silence, I drifted into the abyss.

I didn't stir again until early the next morning when I awoke with a start, my heart pounding in my chest, my lungs tight, the wellbeing posters and fairy lights draped across the walls no longer a comfort. The fluffy cushions and shabby-chic furniture terrifyingly too familiar, evidence of events I couldn't take back. I was not where I was supposed to be.

I checked my phone by the side of the bed. It was 5.17 and I had sixty-four messages.

'Shit.'

I read them all, listened to the voicemails he'd left, the visceral outrage turning to paranoia that I would stay here forever, that my family would turn me against him. Misinterpret his desperation the day before as anger instead of his burning love for me. That they'd distort his bewilderment at my being whisked away just when I needed as much rest and stability as possible. Find darkness in his determination to make me well again, the pills my parents had forgotten proof they weren't equipped to look after me. Not like he could.

I needed him and my place was back in London, in the flat. The flat we shared, both our names on the lease and he'd done nothing, nothing but care for me since I'd been unwell, proved himself time and time again when my own mum and dad hadn't even bothered to come and see me when I was sick. Had only come to the flat once the entire time I'd lived there. They were old, they didn't understand the bond between us. We were destined to be together. It was fate. And I had nothing without him.

My hand sunk onto the duvet, a billowing surge of pastels swallowing my mobile as I massaged the ridge of my nose, my eyelids scrunched tightly, any relief I felt at the distance between us replaced by trepidation and guilt. At the overwhelming knowledge that I was not ready for this. That whatever niggles I had about our relationship were nothing compared to the pit of despair I'd find myself in if I walked away now.

He was right, I had nothing. No money, nowhere of my own. A job I was lucky to have, given the weeks I'd been signed off. And who would take me on anywhere else? I was forgetful and useless, so lacking in innovation and creative ideas I didn't know how I'd managed to pull the wool over everyone's eyes for as long as I had. I couldn't handle anything more complicated than filling in forms, ticking boxes, and I was scarcely able to get that right these days.

I didn't deserve the opportunities I'd been given. Right now, I had a home – an amazing flat in zone one that looked like it was straight out of a magazine– and a man, who cared for me despite all my flaws. Despite his own demons. I needed him. I couldn't do it by myself. I didn't even know who I was anymore without him. He'd given me everything. I was just tired. Run down, but there was no question of me staying here. I wasn't leaving Connor. I didn't know how.

It was too early to call him back but I messaged. Told him not to worry, no one thought badly of him, but they wanted to help, wanted to give him a break. They understood he was only looking out for me but and he was right, they should have told him they were taking me back to Brighton. It was weird not to but I'd had a good night's sleep and was already feeling like I'd turned a corner so I'd be home within a day or so. My fingers shook as I typed the words, Going to try to get a few hours more sleep now. Love you. See you soon xxx

I put silent mode back on, sunk into the pillows, rolled over, closed my eyes and feigned ignorance when the screen lit up the second I put my phone down. When I woke up five hours later, I felt almost normal. A cold cup of tea was curdling on the bedside table with a note from Mum telling me she and Dad would be home from work at six. I tapped my phone, flinching at the eight new messages stacked on the screen, the four voicemail notifications, all telling me to call him and so I did. He answered on the first ring.

'Finally,' he spat.

'Hi.'

'What's going on? Why've you been ignoring me?'

'I haven't, I promise. I just woke up. I've slept for like, sixteen hours or something.'

'Where are you now?' He knew where I was. He had Find my Friends set up on his mobile. He always knew where to find me.

'Still in bed. I called you as soon as I saw your messages. Sorry. I don't even remember half of what happened yesterday, I was so out of it. I sort of vaguely remember everyone turning up at the flat and then getting a cab. Were you there or did I dream that?'

'Oh, I was there.'

'Sorry. I can't remember saying goodbye and sorry about not staying in touch. I must have flaked out as soon as I got here, even without those pills. Think I slept better without them, actually. It's makes me wonder if they were doing me any good –'

'What's that supposed to mean?'

'Nothing. I was just… Where are you?'

'Back home. I had a meeting with Professor Collins that I couldn't get out of. I'll come down and pick you up now.'

'No, wait,' I said before I could stop myself. 'I think I should stay here for one more night. I'm feeling much better, I mean, better than I've felt in ages but I think maybe one more day would do me good.'

'One more day of what? If you need more rest, you can sleep here.'

'I know, it's just that everyone's been worried about me. If I spend some time with them, they'll see I'm over the worst of it. They'll leave us alone once they know I'm all right. They're just trying to help.' I looked towards the door guiltily as though someone might have been listening on the other side.

'Help? They literally abducted you from your sick bed. I'm not leaving you with those nutters. They're psychos. I mean, what the fuck? What were they playing at? And what have they been saying to you? All sorts of shit about me, right?'

'No, no, of course not. I haven't even seen them since we got here. I've been asleep the whole time, I told you.'

‘I’m coming to get you before they start filling your head full of crap about me.’

I eased the duvet off and swung my feet onto the floor, my forehead braced in the palm of my hand until the room stopped spinning. ‘Connor, why would they? They like you. They know how kind you’ve been, looking after me. They appreciate it. Look if I don’t stay a few more days, they’re not going to get off our backs. You know what they’re like. They mean well but –’

‘What do you mean, a few more days? You said one.’

I steadied myself on the bedside table. ‘One day. Let me put their minds at rest and then I’ll come back up.’

‘Oh yeah? Going to ask your fuck-buddy to pick you up, are you? What did you have to do to get him to drive you all the way down to Brighton? Or do you still owe him for that?’

My face looked drained in the full-length mirror opposite, my hair greasy and unbrushed. ‘I didn’t do anything. Gran knows him somehow.’

‘Have you fucked him?’

‘No.’ I didn’t recognise the person staring back at me. ‘I told you, I don’t know him. I just meant I’d get the train up by myself tomorrow to save you the trouble of coming down.’

‘And give them a chance to talk you out of it. Do you think I’m an idiot?’

I pushed myself to my feet. Turned away from my reflection. That grey dishevelled stranger pacing around the worn strip of faded carpet. ‘No. No, of course not. It’s all… everything’s just got a bit…’

'That's your fucking family's fault, overreacting. I knew they were mental.'

'I know. You're right, you're right. I'm going to stay in my room as much as I can, let them feel like they've done their bit and then head up after breakfast or something tomorrow. I'll be as quick as I can.'

'You'd better not make me regret not coming to get you now.'

'I won't, I promise.'

He'd kept me on the phone for fifteen more minutes before I'd managed to get away. Jumped into the shower and stood for an eternity letting the steaming stream of water cascade over me, pummelling my clenched muscles and my aching head until Olivia banged on the door and my heart sank further still.

And now we were here, outside by choice for the first time in so long I might have been walking on the moon, it all felt so strange and unfamiliar. And my sister was still staring at me expecting me to explain something she would never be able to understand.

'He hasn't done anything,' I maintained. 'Except give me a home and look after me. I know he can get a bit intense –'

'Intense, she calls it.'

'But… he means well. He's, he's… had a difficult life. Bad experiences. It's made him paranoid but his heart's in the right place. He just comes on a bit strong sometimes.'

'Strong? He comes on like a complete dick, you mean? He's got you locked up in that flat all day –'

'I'm not locked up.'

'None of us are allowed to visit. You're not allowed to visit us.'

'Of course I am.'

‘So why don’t you then?’

‘I –’

‘He’s abusing you. You’re the only one who can’t see it.’

‘He’s never hit me.’

‘He doesn’t have to. He’s got complete control of your mind. That’s what this is – Coercive control, emotional abuse. It’s a crime, stop underplaying it. He is abusing you and it needs to stop.’

I spun away from her, bending over at the waist, winded, my vision blurred. I couldn’t take this anymore. She stepped forward, refusing to respect the space I craved, rubbed my back.

‘I’m sorry, sis. You know I love you, but I can’t stand to see you going through this. It’s like he’s sapped all the joy out of you.’

Slowly, I levered myself back up, feet pegged to the ground, hands splayed across my thighs to steady me.

'It's not like that. You wouldn’t understand.’

‘I understand you don’t laugh anymore. I understand he’s completely destroyed your self-confidence and your self-esteem. I understand he’s got you working in a bank for some God forsaken reason instead of doing what you love.’

‘There’s nothing wrong with working in a bank.’

‘Apart from the fact they’re evil, no, there’s not, there’s nothing wrong with working in a bank. It’s just not very *you*. Like, what happened to being visionary and creative?’

I took a breath. Bit down the bile burning the sides of my throat. ‘I’m not cut out for it.’

‘You are so! It’s all you ever wanted to do and look, I know you had that one bad experience with your old boss and whatever bullshit he pulled that time, but you can’t let that put you off. And you definitely can't have some dickhole telling you what you should be doing with your life. If he doesn't like your choices, he should bugger off.'

A flash of indignation flared within me, suppressed for so long under shame. 'And then what? What would I do? Where would I live? With you in your grotty student flat? Back here with Mum and Dad breathing down my neck, trying to get me to do what they want instead. Everybody wants me to do something, at least Connor cares for me. He knows that my so-called dream job is a fantasy. I'm not good enough and you lot telling me I should keep wasting my time trying, doesn't help.'

'It's working in a bank that's the waste of time. Time and talent. Your talent.'

'My talent? You don't know me at all. You've got this idea that I'm some sort of arty-career woman with all this energy and ideas, but I'm not anymore. I'm not that person. Even Raj knew that, for all he was an arsehole about it, he saved me the trouble and humiliation of finding out for myself. And instead of pushing and pushing me in the wrong direction, Connor's been there for me, pointing out other paths. Other things I can do that suit me, not the idea of me you all seem to have.'

Olive stared at me, lost for words for once and then she looked up at the sky. At the seagulls squawking overhead.

'I can't tell if you believe all that bollocks or if this is him talking.'

'Oh, Olive. Please stop. I can't do this. I can't cope with all of you at loggerheads. How do you think it makes me feel? This is exactly why I can't see anyone anymore. I can't put Connor in the same room as any of you. You're all as bad as each other and I'm stuck in the middle of it having to make a choice about who I can even speak to. Well, I live with Connor. Like it or lump it, he's my boyfriend and either you stop slagging him off constantly or I can't see you anymore.'

Olive's eyes became slits, her face darkening.

'Look, I don't mean to be harsh, but you don't know him. And I get it, I get why you think he's a bit… But it's okay. It's okay most of the time. When it's just him and me, when we take everything else out of the equation, it's fine. He's not perfect, but neither am I and all he's ever done is try to look after me, to protect me. I'm lucky to have him. You don't know how much.'

She snorted and looked back at me shaking her head. And then she sighed. 'I just need you to know, that I am here for you. If you ever want to talk… if you ever feel…'

I put my hand on her arm. 'All I need is for you to believe me when I tell you, he's not the person you think he is. He's got my best interests at heart.'

Her voice cracked and her eyes were downcast but she agreed. Agreed to stop interfering. Agreed to give him another chance. Agreed to help me make it easier for all of us by patching up their fragmented relationship, by letting go of the aggressive image she had of him when all it did was make the situation worse, make him more paranoid. Make him call and text me more, behave in a way that maybe frightened me a little bit, that certainly stressed me out. It wasn't all my family's fault but anyone would get anxious and irate, would hit out at the ones who cared about them the most.

'I'm sorry,' Olive said continuing up the path. 'I didn't mean to upset you.'

'I know.' I linked my arm through hers as we finished the ascent, relieved to be on flatter terrain now, the sea far below, the rumble of traffic louder, a sure sign we were heading home.

'Speak of the devil.' Olive lowered her voice and my heart lurched, my hand intuitively reaching for my phone to check for a missed call or message telling me Connor was on his way but my pocket was empty, my mobile charging back at the house.

'Up ahead.' Olive's gaze lingered on the couple sauntering towards us, pushing a Bugaboo. The glamourous Asian woman cooing into the pram, the tall, dark-skinned man, an arrogant new father smug with pride.

'Emily!' His face lit up at the sight of me. 'I thought it was you. Shanti, this is Emily, the rising star who abandoned us at the end of the summer. I told you about her.'

'Oh!' The woman replied with a broad smile and clearly no recall, seizing the opportunity to stroke her finger down her world's soft plump cheek.

'The one who ditched us for the shiny lights of London.' Raj beamed at us both and his wife grinned again blowing air though her lips.

'Sorry, baby-brain,' she laughed.

'Talking of which, this is Sunni. Sunni, Emily and sorry, I've forgotten your sister's name. I know we've met once or twice –' He held out his hand towards Olive whose eyebrows had taken on a stance.

'Are you for real?' she said in a way that suggested she'd been watching too much daytime reality TV. Raj faltered and Sunni's eyes shot open, his lips puckered into the shape of a wail.

'Olive,' I said restraining her with a firm touch. She stuck her index finger in the air, affronted and rotated her hand, her neck weaving determinedly.

'You know we know, right?'

Shanti and Raj squinted at each other, blood draining from his cheeks, colour rising in hers.

'Leave it,' I said to Olive. 'Please. Let's just go.'

'No, sorry, what?' Shanti's voice was as sharp as cut glass, not a trace of amicable dizziness remaining. 'What's going on?'

'I don't –' Raj stuttered.

'Your husband's a dickhead,' Olive said hands on her hips now. 'He fucked up my sister's career out of pure spite because she had a better opportunity.'

'Whaa…'

'I mean, who does that? Who goes out of their way to contact a person's prospective employer only to lie to him about them? That shit was cold.' I didn't know where she'd picked up the attitude, all I knew was I was going to die if I didn't get away from the lot of them soon. Raj turned from his wife towards Olive and back to me again.

'I swear to God, I have no idea what she's talking about. I'd never do anything…' he gasped.

And then I realised, stupidly, far too late that he hadn't done anything. Only three other people in the world knew about that interview and only two of them wanted me to get the job. And for once no amount of lying to myself could explain that away.

23 Days Before the Murder

Her Sister

Her phone was ringing as we let ourselves into the house.

I said, 'Don't answer that,' stretching my arm across the threshold in front of her and I was not messing about. She was white as a sheet, like, properly pale and not because she was ill. That was bollocks. Anyone could see she was frightened. Anyone who knew her. 'Let it go to answerphone but don't listen to it. Delete it straight away.'

She pushed past me. 'I need to speak to him some time. There has to be –'

'Oh, don't. Don't you dare say explanation. I'll tell you the explanation, all right. He's a manipulative controlling narcissist.'

She pulled her coat off and draped it over the banister. Tore her shoes off as if they hurt.

'Oh, Olive, please stop. This isn't helping. You're making it worse.'

'Making it worse?' I bellowed, tossing my boots across the hallway and leaving a muddy mark on the wall I would never acknowledge. 'How am *I* making it worse? He's the one who's clearly screwing with you.'

The phone beeped with a new message as I followed her into the kitchen and I rolled my eyes. 'Delete it.'

She snatched it off the worktop before I could see how many notifications she had. Hundreds probably.

'When are you going to tell him?'

'Tell him what?' she said, grinding her teeth.

'That you know what he did. That you're leaving him.'

She bit her lip and stared down at the phone.

'You are leaving him now, right? I mean, you can't think there's any way back from what he did.'

'We don't know what he did. Or why.'

'We know he's an arsehole. We know you could do so much better.'

'I told you. He's just insecure.'

'We're all insecure. We don't go around taking it out on everyone else. There's a limit to how much of someone else's shit you have to take responsibility for and I know I said I'd support your decisions but I can't stand by and let him do this to you anymore. There's something wrong with him.'

'There must be a good reason –'

'Oh my God.' I stood in front of her, refusing to let her walk away. 'What is it? What do you see in him? What's he got over you?'

She sank down onto a kitchen chair, buried her face in her hands, hair spilling between her fingers onto the table. When she looked up, her eyes were red, wide and desperate.

'My money,' she croaked. 'Gran's money, all right?'

I lowered myself down next to her. 'I don't understand.'

She took a haggard breath. 'I lent him a few thousand pounds. I can't end things now. I only need to hang on until the end of the year and then we'll see but I need that money back. I can't start all over again with nothing. And it's not even mine, all of it. Gran lent me some. I have to get it back.'

'Gran's old. She doesn't give a shit about a few thousand pounds.'

'Ten thousand pounds.'

'Sheeshhhh.'

She ran her hand through her hair again, scraping her scalp.

'And you can't get it back?'

Emily lifted her shoulders, defeated and I shrugged.

'Well, fuck it. If that's all it takes to get rid of him, it'll be ten thousand pounds well spent.'

'I'm tied into the lease on the flat as well. I've got loans and credit card debt I need to pay off. All the money in my ISA account's gone.'

Christ almighty. I mean, I knew they weren't living on Pot Noodles but that was a pretty hefty whack to have got through in the space of what, six or seven months? Guess the price of petrol really had gone through the roof.

'Well, look,' I said feeling slightly out of my depth. TBH, I could have done with Mum or Dad being there, really or Gran but she was at chemo, not that Emily knew that. The olds had told me not to mention it what with all this going on so she was stuck with me. Me and all my financial acumen. 'Let's just find out, let's find out how bad it is. What exactly we're dealing with here. You can't stay in that flat.'

'But –'

'Emily. Just find out.'

So she got on the blower to the estate agents and that was a blast.

'Put it on speaker,' I said in time to catch the nasally woman at the end of the line saying, 'I'm sorry but that's not the name we have on our system.'

Emily looked at me like I might know something about it.

'But my name's definitely on the lease,' she contended. 'I signed some papers. How else would I even know who we let the flat through?'

'I've only got the one name on here.'

'Which'll be my boyfriend, Connor McGann. He was the original tenant and now we both live there.'

'Ok. But as I said your name's not on the lease so I'm unable to confirm or deny any details about it, unless you're ringing to settle the debt.'

'Debt?'

'The outstanding rent but I should warn you, there's nothing we can do about the eviction date. We've got new tenants moving in in two weeks' time. It'll just clear any bad credit your boyfriend – *the current tenant,* sorry – will accrue if we need to use the deposit for damage.'

'What?'

'So would you like to settle the balance with us today?'

I slammed the call end button and we stared at each other.

'What the flippin' pancakes?'

'We're getting evicted,' she muttered looking back down at the phone screen. 'When… how… what's he done with all the money I gave him? That was for the rent, bills. Where's it gone? And when was he going to tell me? Two weeks. We're being evicted in two weeks' time.'

'*He's* being evicted in two weeks. Less than two weeks. You're not even on the lease. But since you are about to become homeless, now's probably as good a time as any to call it a day.'

'I definitely signed something.'

'Emily. This is a win. Maybe the loans are fake too.'

'No, they're real and in my name, along with the overdraft.' She rubbed her eyes, dragged her fingers down her chin. 'I don't understand what he's spent it all on.'

'Maybe he's got another life somewhere, a wife and kids…'

'How? He's always with me.'

But he wasn't. She had a few hours off when she went to work – when she finally fell asleep after tossing and turning all night, more like lately.

'I'm not being funny but what does he do all day? Like if I go to more than three lectures I'm done for the week'.

'His course is more –'

'No, it's not. My flatmate's doing Business Management. He barely leaves his room other than to take a dump and mess up the kitchen. Half of it's online, like everything else these days.'

'He goes to the gym, he goes to the library –'

'No one goes to the library. What is this? 1986? He's up to something but you know what? Who gives a shit? Cut your losses and run. Come live in my grotty student flat if you like. You'll be in a box under a bridge in two weeks' time anyway.' I meant she'd be living in it but the thought of her winding up in a box wasn't as farfetched as it might have been before Connor McGann popped back into her life.

'Oh my God,' she wailed sinking her head back into her hands. 'I don't understand what's going on? It's… it's… I feel like I'm going mad. Am I? None of this makes sense.'

The fear and panic in her eyes when she looked at me was more haunting than anything I'd ever imagined when I thought of her trapped within that relationship. I clasped her hands between mine and held them there, steady, ready to be the rock she needed.

'It's not you. It's him. He's done this. I don't know how, but he's done this. And we – Mum, Dad, Gran, me – we are going to get you out. Do you understand? It's over.'

And I've got to be honest, I had no fricking clue what I was talking about because the person I should have been telling was her boyfriend. He was the one who was going to need convincing. And locking up.

23 Days Before the Murder

Him

I knew the minute they walked out the door with her that they wouldn't give her back, that they'd get into her head with their nasty small-town mentality and their ugly lies. Especially the sister with her obsessive jealous streak, always twisting everything, interfering and poking her nose into shit that had nothing to do with her.

That's why I had to get Em away from them in the first place and now they'd got their claws back into her again and I was going to have to redo all the work I'd put into sorting her out the first time round.

And none of this would have happened if she'd listened to me and chilled the fuck out instead of constantly questioning why she felt so tired, distracting me and putting me off my game. If she hadn't been so fucking needy, I wouldn't have made so many mistakes. Picked so many losers. She killed my winning streak with her incessant whining, with that crap hole family of hers up in my business and now she's surprised – she's surprised we're in the shit, that we're going to lose the flat, as though I didn't have it all under control. I'd been all set to put a ton down on Ruby Red coming in at fifteen to one that afternoon, that very afternoon when the old fuckwits broke in and kidnapped her, distracting me. Fifteen to one. Enough to get us out the black hole her not working had sunk us into. I mean I'd made sure she'd still be getting paid whether she turned up or not, but she wasn't going to get promoted lazing around on her arse all day.

Small price to pay for getting her away from that slimeball and all those other tossers sniffing around her or so I thought. Now I had the original cunts to deal with and no home, thanks to them getting all up in my face. They were going to pay for this. They all would, even Emily.

If she thought I'd suck it all up and take her back she was mistaken. She was coming back all right, but on my terms. She owed me an apology. Hell, she owed me more than that. They all did and by the time I was done, I'd make them wish they'd never even had a daughter. I'd sure as hell make sure they never saw their daughter again.

21 Days Before the Murder

Her

The doorbell made me jump even though I'd been expecting it all morning. Even though my heart had sunk at the crunch of gravel spitting in the driveway as his tyres ground over them, as his heels crushed the jagged pebbles leading to the front path. Dad opened the door.

'Connor,' he said, his voice tempered with resolve and I pictured him stepping back to let Connor enter, his teeth clenched, his middle-aged paunch sucked in, chest puffed out.

'She in?'

'Go through to the kitchen.'

The door swung inwards slowly and Mum and I glanced at each other one last time before his shadow fell across the floor and his solid frame filled the space that suddenly seemed small and suffocating. He opened his mouth to greet her as she rose from the table but no words came and she nodded at him, unsmiling.

'We'll be in the sitting room if you need us,' she said, squeezing my shoulder and beckoning my father with a slight snap of her neck.

He waited until the double doors clicked behind them before leaning towards me hesitantly, his cool lips catching my cheekbone as I flinched from his touch. He dragged a chair out and sunk down on it, his hands clasped in front of him on the table, his head bowed down towards them.

‘So,’ he said.

‘Hmmm.’ My mouth folded uncharitably, my own hands buried under my armpits so as not to shake. So that he couldn’t reach for them.

‘That’s it then, is it? You’ve made up your mind.’

I wound my tongue around the swirling rebukes failing to fully form in my mind.

‘Without talking to me,’ he continued, still staring down. ‘Without hearing my side.’

‘There are no sides, Connor,’ I said finally. ‘There’s just the truth and the truth is you lied to me. I’m not on the lease and you haven’t paid the rent on the flat for months.’

‘That’s their mistake. I can’t be held responsible for their balls ups. You signed the contract. You know as much about what happened at their end after that as I do.’

‘And the rent?’

‘Paid. All of it. It’s all bollocks. Some administrative error they’re not going to admit to.’

‘But they must have been in touch. They must have warned you we were going to be evicted. You must have known.’

‘Of course I bloody knew. I’ve been trying to get it sorted without worrying you. And this is what I get for being considerate. Maybe if you hadn’t been so ill you could have –’

‘I’m not ill anymore.’

‘Good. You sort it out then. Give me a break from shouldering all the stress and burden of looking after you. Do you think it’s been easy trying to do all this by myself while you’ve been lying in bed all day?’

I wanted to challenge him about those weeks of confinement, the debilitating fog that had made me a prisoner of my own home – his home, but I couldn't bring myself to face the only plausible explanation for my feeling fine again, for feeling strong enough to walk away.

'What happened to the money I gave you?' I said instead.

'The ten thousand pounds you borrowed illegally, you mean? The fraudulent loan you and your boyfriend could go down for if the authorities ever got wind of it?'

'I borrowed it from Gran.'

'What?' he sneered disbelievingly.

'I didn't get the money from the bank. Gran lent it to me.'

'No, she didn't.'

I stared at him and he swallowed, scratched the stubble on his chin. 'So, you don't want it back then. I told you my investments are going to mature soon, but if you don't want to hang around...'

'I don't believe you.'

'This is bullshit. This isn't you talking. This is them, getting in your head.'

Specks of saliva stung my cheek and I shrank away instinctively wiping them away with the back of my hand, my breath snagging in my chest, my heart hammering. Dad hovered pointedly by the door, his concerned expression framed in the glass inlay, his fingers resting questioningly on the handle but I shook my head. I needed to be the one to do this.

'I don't think we should see each other anymore. I don't think we're good for each other.'

Connor's jawbone rotated in tiny circles and his nostrils flared. 'This isn't you. This is them.'

'I'm sorry,' I countered firmly.

He prised my hand from the table, grasping it with his own. 'Please. You can't leave me like this. I know I've made a few mistakes – we both have – but I'll try harder. I'll be better. I'll sort out the mix up with the flat and we can go home or bugger it, bugger them, we'll go somewhere new. Somewhere bigger. Make a fresh start of it, just you and me, away from everyone else. It'll be just like it used to be again. You'll see.' He reached for my necklace to reassure himself, to remind me I was his, but his fingers grazed the nook where it used to be and faltered in the dead space, his eyes creasing in confusion as they met mine.

The air between us crackled and my every muscle was taut, my nerves so stretched that when his phone buzzed, the shock racked my body and left me reeling. He grabbed it.

'What the hell?' His chair squeaked on the kitchen floor as he leapt to his feet, pushing it backwards, the legs teetering at a fraught angle but not before I glimpsed the CCTV image of Olivia entering the apartment. His apartment. 'What is this? What's going on?'

'So, it's true then?' I hadn't wanted to believe it, but there was no denying it now. 'There are cameras hidden everywhere?'

'Get your sister the fuck out of my flat.' The escalation in his voice was too much for my mum and dad. They burst in from the sitting room, trembling both, colour high on their cheeks.

'She's getting Emily's things,' my dad growled, squaring up to Connor as Mum made her way directly to my side. Pressed her arms around my shoulders where I sat. 'And then she'll be out of there. They both will. For good.'

Connor's eyes glittered. 'I'm calling the police.'

'She's only taking the stuff that belongs to Emily. She's got every right –'

But Connor had already stormed out the house, wrenching his jacket off the chair and patting down his pockets in search of his car keys, his phone tucked under his chin, his voice raised as he alerted the operator. The car door slammed and his tyres spun on the gravel, spattering as he reversed but the weight of his presence grew heavier instead of lighter as the engine roar faded in the distance.

'Call Olive,' Mum cried. 'Tell her to grab what she can and get out before the police get there. God knows what that boy's telling them right now.'

But she was wrong. Connor wasn't a boy – he was a man and he was coming after Olive now. He was coming after all of us.

21 Days Before the Murder

Her Sister

It smelt of old trainers, that was the most memorable thing about it. The sort of unavoidable prickly stench that invades you like fumes at a petrol station. The paintwork had seen better days and the chair had the arse-flattening properties of a park bench but with none of the views.

I leaned back nonplussed and ignored the four stained walls pressing in on me, stared down the plain-clothed coppers trying to intimidate me across the chipped Formica desk. One of them leant forward and pressed a button on a video recorder. A red light came on. I recognised this bit from the telly only it didn't usually make me barf a little into my mouth, but whatevs. That's how they wanted you to feel. That's how they got you even when you hadn't done anything.

'This interview is being recorded and may be given in evidence if your case is brought to trial,' The white one began like a casting agent reading the world's lamest script. 'We are in an interview room at Islington Police Station. The date is 25th February, 2023 and the time by my watch is 15.07. I am Detective Constable Jake Pinkton. The other police officer present is Detective Constable Amir Kudus.' Detective Constable Jake Pinkton finally looked up at me. 'Please state your full name and date of birth.'

My pulse quickened but I sighed as though I had other places to be. 'Olivia Sophie Lawrence, fifteenth of the fifth, two thousand and four.'

'Do you agree that there are no other persons present?'

I scanned the cramped room deliberately, stalling for time, composing the mask I'd need to get through this phoney sham. This total set up. 'Yeah.'

Kudus inhaled but that was the most I got by way of a reaction from either of them. Pinkton blinked wearily and went on. 'Before the start of this interview, I must remind you that you are entitled to free and independent legal advice either in person or by telephone at any stage. Do you wish to speak to a legal advisor now or have one present during the interview?'

I rolled my eyes. This was such a waste of time. I'd already explained that nothing dodgy had been going on. Just let me go already. Legal advisor? For what? 'No.'

'For the record, please state your reasons for not wishing to speak to a legal representative.'

This guy could not have been any more disinterested. My neck moved independently as a rush of outrage swept through me and I had to press my hand against the table to hold the sass in.

'Because I haven't got time to sit around all day waiting for you to appoint one. I just want to get this over with. I haven't done anything.'

Pinkton ran his tongue over his teeth, presumably to dislodge a shard of the shawarma he was breathing out of his pores.

'In that case…' He clicked the top of his pen three times and took a deep breath. 'Olivia Sophie Lawrence, you have been arrested under suspicion of burglary. *Y*ou do not have to say anything. But it may harm your defence if you do not mention when questioned something which you later rely on in court. Anything you do say may be given in evidence. Do you understand?'

'Yes, I understand.' I slumped back in the chair but all I heard was *court*. My heart pounded in my chest. I gritted my teeth, levelled the weird brittle tremor buggering with my voice and shrugged. 'What I don't understand is why I'm here.'

DC Kudus finally made his debut just as I was beginning to think he'd only been drafted in to make up the numbers. 'You're here because according to the officers who brought you in, you were apprehended while trespassing within the private residence of Mr Connor McGann.'

'Trespassing?' I shot up defensively, bruising my spine on the back of the chair with only a slight grimace. 'For the fiftieth time, we had a key.'

'Which according to Mr McGann,' Kudus continued, not even attempting to get into character, 'was stolen from his possession when he was lured to a meeting with his ex-partner, Emily Lawrence, who used to reside at the address where you were arrested.' He leafed through the pile of papers stacked in a splayed brown folder. The hand had to come up for that one.

'No, my *sister,* Emily Lawrence, gave me a key *before* she lured him to a meeting.'

Pinkton glanced up from the notes he'd been making in his black pad and clicked his pen again. 'And does your sister currently reside at that address?'

‘Sort of. That is, she did but she’s in the process of moving out. I was in the process of moving her out.’

‘And does she have any documentation which would allow you to enter the residence on her behalf, such as a lease or bills in her name?’

The room was starting to feel smaller. The air was stifling. I swallowed. ‘Well, no, but that’s because… he… Connor. He… Look, all I know is she lived there up until a few days ago.’

Pinkton’s eyes were stony. Not because he hated me, I don’t think. More like he wished he’d put the kettle on before he came in here.

‘But she doesn’t now and I would be correct in stating that you did not have permission from Mr McGann to enter and remove items from his property with the intention of permanently depriving him of them.’

‘I wasn’t permanently depriving him of anything.’ My voice was squeaky now. I thumped my fist against my chest and cleared my throat. ‘It’s all Emily’s stuff.’

‘And so when we check the contents of the boxes found in your possession, it’s safe to assume we won’t recover any items belonging to Mr McGann.’

‘It’s safe to assume right, Miss Marple.’ I froze at my own burst of insolence, but in my defence, this was all well out of order. I blinked and Pinkton eyebrow twitched like it wasn’t the worst thing he’d ever been called but even so, I bit down on the smooth flesh inside my mouth in case I had anything else to add.

‘Including a gold necklace valued at approximately twelve hundred pounds?’

Jeez. 'The gold necklace with a bee on it?' No wonder the creep was always checking she still had it on. I grinned, entirely exonerated and suppressed a *ha!* 'That's Emily's.'

DC Kudus sat up at that – to adjust his buttocks, it transpired. 'According to Mr McGann, it was returned to him some time ago and has been in his possession ever since along with a number of other items of value which appear to be missing.'

If this wasn't the crappiest interrogation on earth, I'd swear they'd rehearsed it. I sighed again, my expression lethargic, my leg jiggling uncontrollably under the table. Keep it up, this was almost over.

'That's BS but whatever man, let him keep it all, the freaking weirdo. And he wonders why she left him.'

'So you agree that Emily Lawrence no longer lives with Mr McGann,' Pinkton repeated, the bright light above us bouncing off his thinning hairline.

'Yes, I agree. That's why I was getting her things.'

'To be clear, you knowingly entered the residence and removed items from Mr McGann's home –'

I opened and closed my mouth again in quick succession.

'– without his permission.'

'I...'

'In other words, you admit burgling Mr McGann's apartment, as defined by the law.'

'No. I'm not admitting to anything. How can it be burglary if my sister asked me to do it.'

'Your sister, Emily Lawrence, who, by your own admission, no longer lives there and does not have permission to enter without Mr McGann's explicit agreement.'

'No, no. No, it's not like that. He's the one you should be talking to. He's the psychopath. He's been drugging her and God knows what else.'

Pinkton tapped his pen on the desk. 'And you've got proof of this, have you?'

'Well, no. It's probably too late now but it's obvious. She was bedridden for weeks and as soon as she left him, she made a miraculous recovery.'

He nodded non-committedly, his mouth turned down at the corners.

'And she's reported this, has she?'

'Not yet. She won't. She's scared of him. You would be too if you knew him.'

'Only without any proof of wrongdoing on his part, you need to be careful who you repeat these allegations to or you could be looking at malicious slander on top of the burglary charge.'

'Jesus Christ. So, he can do whatever he wants but I'm the one who gets done for some bogus offence. This is cracked up, you know that, no?' I scratched the patch of dry skin that had flared up on my collarbone.

'Unfortunately, whether you meant to or not, you have broken the law.'

'But what about him? What if he's been abusing my sister all along?' My skin felt sticky now, inflamed and raw.

'Unless your sister is prepared to make a statement reporting the abuse, our hands are tied. Besides which, there's no guarantee that any such investigation would affect the outcome of your own case, should Mr McGann choose to press charges.'

I drew my hands together and sank back into the chair, mainly to stop myself from falling off it. Not that these clowns had to know that. 'Are you serious? This is a joke, right? Don't tell me. Some TV crew's going to roll in here any minute and tell me I've been pranked.'

Pinkton flicked back through his notes until he found the bit he'd been looking for and underlined it. Three times. 'Extenuating circumstances aside, at the time of your arrest, your accomplice, Lee Davies was waiting for you outside in his car, is that correct?'

'My accomplice? Come on. Is that what this is all about? My *accomplice* parking on double yellow lines?' My voice was getting shrill again. I glanced down at my fingers and quickly balled them into fists to hide the dry blood trapped beneath the nails.

'As you are no doubt aware,' Pinkton said, still staring down at the crumpled pages of his book. 'Mr Davies is well-known to the police.'

What? Well-known to the... Oh, Gran.

'And as you may also know,' Kudus broke in, warming to the theme. 'There's been a recent spate of burglaries in the area.'

'What?! That's not – that's nothing...'

Pinkton leant forward, his elbows pinned to the desk, pen oscillating between his stumpy fingers. 'To be clear, you are not currently being held on suspicion of any further incidents but it is my duty to warn you that your fingerprints will be tested against any outstanding offences.'

'What the…? Do it. Test them.' It wasn't like I had a choice anyway. They already had them. Plus, plus, I hadn't done anything. 'I've got nothing to hide. Wait, is this the bit where I say I need a lawyer?'

Pinkton squeezed his eyes together and opened them with the look of a man filling in a tax return. 'If you require legal representation, we can stop the interview at any time and arrange that for you free of charge, assuming you don't already have a lawyer.'

'Of course I don't have a lawyer. I don't even have a Nectar card.'

'In that case, this interview is terminated at 15.21 to be resumed once a legal advisor has been appointed to your case. In the meantime, you will be escorted to a cell until he or she arrives. You will then have an opportunity to talk through your options before we continue questioning you further.'

Oh my God. 'Fine.' *Oh my God, oh my God, oh my God.*

They both pushed back their chairs and stood, DC Kudus with an apathetic nod towards the door I took to mean I was supposed to follow them out, which was easier said than done given the fact all the blood had drained out of my legs (probably due to the medieval torture chair although I could hardly be blamed if they had to give it a hose down after I left).

I assumed an air of casual nonchalance as Pinkton handed me over to a guy in uniform who guided me down a twisting corridor which eventually led to the reinforced door that clanked behind me and then and only then did I have a little wobble. Just a little one, but hell. I hadn't eaten since breakfast and besides which Lee Davies, *my accomplice*, was *well-known to the police*. Yayy. Fuck me.

I collapsed onto the bed, not caring who had lain on it before, staring at the ceiling, the grey walls streaked with – well, I didn't know what the walls were streaked with. It was probably best not to think about it. The stench of sweat and adrenalin permeated the air, sharp, acidic and weirdly ticklish. I pressed my hand over my chest and felt my breath catch as my heart vibrated erratically through the thick weave of the last jumper I'd probably get to wear for the next few years. It was all going to be orange jumpsuits from now on and I looked terrible in orange. *Known to the police*. Oh my God.

This was all ludicrous. A complete bloody farce. Any Year 10 Psychology student could tell you this was textbook nut job behaviour. Having me arrested. Me? For *stealing* Emily's toothbrush and knickers, just because she didn't want him anymore. Just because he could. Just because, technically it was completely illegal, imbecilic though it was. Shit. I was screwed. I was so screwed.

There had to be a way out of this. Surely, I wouldn't go down for a first offence, not in the circumstances. What if I held my hands up and pleaded guilty to a lesser crime. What would a lesser crime even be? Littering? Christ, I needed to speak to someone who knew what I was up against. Who could get me out of this. Burglary. *Burglary?* And with a known criminal. Jesus wept.

My throat tightened and I brought my knees up to my chin, wrapped my arms around them and curled into myself, rocking, my whole life suspended in the hands of a vindictive lunatic. Tears balanced in the corners of my eyes for an hour or more before the little window on the door slid open with a screech that set my teeth on edge and Miss Marple stuck his head through the gap before he opened the door.

'On your feet, Olivia. It's your lucky day. Mr McGann has decided not to press charges.'

'So, what?' I'd have leapt up but I didn't trust myself not to keel onto the floor. 'I can go home now? This is over?'

'Assuming your fingerprints don't tie you to any of our wider investigations, yeah.'

He jerked his thumb towards the corridor and I finally allowed myself to react. To ease myself up from the pee-resistant mattress, my legs stiff and achy, more like I was being released from a Zumba class than an inquisition. I mustered an air of confidence and swaggered, cocky with redemption, out of the cell.

'Oh, and Miss Lawrence.' My stomach roiled and I swear my heart stopped right there and then. 'In future. you might consider getting a Nectar card. It's free and you get rewards every time you use it. They soon add up.'

'Oh, thank you. Thank you, I will, Officer.' Jesus Christ, sarky wanker. But whatever, man. I was free.

14 Days Before the Murder

Her

The hazy morning light creeping under my curtains leaked through my eyelids like bleach, the dull ache corrosive. I drew my wrist across my eyes, exhausted from the effort of trying to sleep, relieved the charade was over for another night and yet reluctant to begin a new day. I turned my head, my breathing shallow, and reached for my mobile, thumb shaking as I finally gave myself permission to turn it on. It beeped with the resonance of thirty-nine messages.

I closed my eyes again, arms wrapped above the duvet as if in prayer, steeling myself to face the barrage of pleas and excuses trickling into threats, knowing I should ignore them but unable to move on until I'd opened every one, the weight of the phone on my chest crushing like a foot pressing down on me.

Facial recognition failed as it so often did these days and I entered my pin manually, trembling before I'd read a single word, knowing already the contents of every line. I clicked on the WhatsApp icon, scrolled up, vision still blurry, to the first unread message under Connor's profile picture. Of the two of us.

12.13

Im sorry. How many more times do u want me to say it. Whatever it is u think ive done im sorry. Just call me and we can sort this out

12.15

I know your up. Please call me. Im sorry. I love u

12.24

If ur awake call me. U cant leave me like this. We r destined to be together and u know it

12.57

Emily. Please. U cant do this to us. I know u love me and I love u. Don't let your familky come between us. They'll say anything to keep us apart. They just want u to move back in with them. Please dont listen to them.its all lies. Call me before they poison everything we have together. U know im telling u the truth

Missed voice call at 13.13

Missed voice call at 13.14

13.15

Why wont u answer the phone?? I need to talk to you

Missed voice call at 13.21

13.22

Pick up

13.47

Please call me as soon as u see this. I can't do this without u. I love u. I don't understand what happened. We were fine until your family turned u against me. This is all them. Theydont care if ur happy.they just want to hurt me and keep u to themselves.

13.49

If i kill myself it will be ur fault

13.51

U r being completely selfish. This is my life too. I have a right to talk to u before u make this decision for both of us

13.56

I will press charges against ur sister after all if thats the only way to get ur attnetion. U can explain its all ur fault when she gets banged up. Call me back

14.37

Call me as soon as you see this

14.53

Why are u doing this? Uve already cost me my flat nad my car. Everything wa s fine until I met u. if i get kicked out of uni too it will e ur fault. Call me back before its too late to fix everything

15.06

Em. We have to talk. we belong togwther

Missed voice call at 15.37

15.38

I know ur awake. I can see the light on.

Missed voice call at 15.40

15.41

Come down and talk to me. This isnt fair. We love each other

15.43

Stop being a bitch and answer me.

15.51

Uve got to –

I swiped off the screen unable to read anymore, checked the time and turned my phone off. Sunk my head back against the pillows and stared at the ceiling, the hollow vibrations heaving in my chest absorbed by the mattress. It was quarter past six. Early still but not too early to get up. Throwing the bedclothes off, I planted my feet on the carpet and walked across the room as though wading upstream, wrapping my mum's ancient dressing gown around myself, the belt knotted at the waist, the arms a little on the short side.

Six hours stretched endlessly before my meeting with Raj but it would probably take that long to transform the wreck I avoided in the hallway mirror into anything resembling the girl who walked out of his office less than five months before. It was certainly beyond my dried-up tube of Magimasc's limited capabilities. A trowel and a bucket of cement would struggle to disguise the sunken shadows surrounding my eyes. The scars shielded within them.

The kettle boiled and the coffee dissolved in the mug as it always did, murky and dark until the milky whirlpool settled, a tiny bubble floating on the surface, gone with the first tentative, scalding sip. Ginger wound around my ankles, miaowing hopefully, his first and only thought at the sight of me, food, which was at least preferable to the abject horror I seemed to raise in everyone else.

'Come on then, grumbles.' I split open a sachet of Sheba and bent down, gagging at the stench as his purring deepened and he kissed me on the end of my nose with his own. The room spun and I steadied myself on the floor, Ginger's affection turning to genuine concern – that I wasn't going to feed him after all rather than for my wellbeing in all likelihood, but still he nudged me until I was well enough composed to slide the gruesome sheet of reconstituted meat and jelly into his bowl and then that was us done pretty much until teatime.

Mum and Dad appeared briefly about an hour later, clashing cups of tea and scraping burnt toast (Mum) and when they left, the house had that empty feel of something unlived in. I shifted through the rack of clothes hanging in my wardrobe, the flimsy summer dresses and unravelling cardigans that hadn't made the cut when I'd packed my most flattering or professional outfits for the move up to London, all of which lay in tatters now, piled on some landfill site. Shredded and stuffed in the black bag Olive had found ready and waiting in the hallway. His hallway. Every piece of clothing I'd owned before I met him reduced to rags.

He'd cut up my clothes before. The tops that showed off too much cleavage, the skirts that rode up my thighs. The blouses that seemed to be made in my size instead of that of a twenty-stone sumo wrestler.

I'd come home from a rare night out with some work colleagues back when I entertained ideas of making friends at the bank but he was furious that I'd worn a dress that hugged my figure, that I looked half-decent in and so when I got back, I found everything he found offensive scattered in pieces across the bed. And I'd said nothing, neither of us had and the next day he'd turned up with four bags bursting with more appropriate outfits and I knew well enough by then to behave as though all my Christmases had come at once. But even those baggy, high-necked sackcloths had paid the ultimate price for my betrayal this time.

I settled on a pair of high-waisted trousers that made me look bloated but had cost too much to give away and a tatty shirt I could hide under the jumper Mum was saving for a special occasion. I'd have asked if it was okay to borrow it but I didn't like to interrupt her at work. Besides, I knew she'd say yes. They said yes to everything these days. Anything to make me happy. To make me stay. To keep me from contemplating going back to Connor the way a moth won't give up on a flame until its wings are too burnt to reach it.

They didn't have to worry about that. I was done and there was no going back. I was already broken and the hold he had over me, reduced to ash at my gran's insistence that the ten thousand pounds I'd borrowed was of no use to her.

'The cancer's back,' she'd announced gleefully as though this solved everything. 'I'll be sorry not to leave it to you and your sister, of course, but if that's all it costs to get rid of him, then I'll trot off to the underworld with a spring in my step.'

The ground beneath my feet had tilted. The air had been sucked out the room.

'Now, don't look at me like that,' she'd continued. 'There's still the house. I've already put it into your names – yours and Olive's, to do what you will. Live in it, sell it, I don't mind as long as that dildo doesn't get his hands on it.'

'No, Gran, don't say that.' My eyes had filled with tears. 'You'll be fine. You'll beat it. You always do.'

She'd taken my hand in hers, creased like parchment paper, the veins visible beneath translucent skin.

'Not this time, my love.' She'd smiled comfortingly when it should have been me consoling her but instead, I crumpled on her frail shoulder and wept.

'Please don't leave,' I'd sobbed and she'd patted my back.

'There, there. It'll be alright, you'll see.'

And now I was dressing hesitantly for a sort of unofficial interview with my old boss again. An opportunity to pick up from where I left off with a man who didn't hold grudges or want me to prove myself in bed before I proved myself at work. Who genuinely seemed to think that I was an asset to his team. *Capable, hard-working and full of fresh ideas*. Those were his words when I'd approached him, head hung low, not daring to meet his eyes, a week after Olive had accosted him.

'And I'd have said as much if I had ever been asked to provide a reference for you.'

I'd smiled the way people are supposed to but I know that it didn't quite reach my eyes. It never did these days, but still he'd suggested meeting up today to discuss a potential role, more complicated than the one I had before, better paid and it was all I could do not to back away there and then. Not to admit I had nothing of the talent and enthusiasm he remembered. That he'd mistakenly seen in me. But I'd been too lost for words, any words. Too overwhelmed to respond with anything more than a nod and a croak he took to mean yes when he opened his appointment calendar and suggested an early lunch at twelve o'clock today.

We met in a café. Part of a chain Connor and I used to go to near the bank.

'Pass the ketchup, would you, babe?' he'd said the last time we'd been there, nodding towards the sticky bottle that was really no closer to me than him but I'd put my fork down, reached over and slid it across the table. He'd glared at me as he took it and my eyes widened, lingering on his before they dropped down to my plate.

'Why did you pull a face at me?' he'd hissed leaning towards me.

'What?' I looked at him again, my confusion genuine.

'When I asked you to pass me the ketchup, you pulled a face.'

'No, I didn't.' I hadn't. I knew better than that. 'My waistband dug into me when I stretched forwards, that's all. I might have winced a bit. I wasn't pulling a face at you, I promise.'

He'd eyed me suspiciously and a layer of tension had settled over the meal.

I pressed my eyelids, careful not to smudge my make-up, and when I opened them, Raj was hovering on the other side of the table, assessing me the way a Royal Engineer might examine a grenade – alert and ready to leap away if it started ticking.

'Hiya,' he ventured hesitantly. 'All okay?'

I glanced at my phone as another WhatsApp notification lit up the screen and buried a scream under a stiff smile.

'Hi Raj. Good, good, thanks. How are you?'

He'd dragged a chair out, relieved, and settled down, piling his coat on the corner seat and emptying his pockets onto the steel surface between us.

'There we go. Right, have you ordered?' he asked distractedly, seeking out the waitress with an upturned chin. I put my phone on Silent, turned it over and ignored the tiny shafts of light radiating all around it for the next forty-seven minutes.

It was decided, I would start back at Optiks next Monday, on a higher salary with more responsibility and no, Raj didn't want to hear any excuses. I couldn't have forgotten that much in the few months I'd been away and even though his faith in me was misguided, I began to sit up as he spoke, my muscles unclenching, the darkness inside my head lifting.

'So, I don't know if you remember that pitch you worked on with Chloe, the laundry balls? Not very exciting, I know.'

‘Of course I remember. We won it.’

‘Yep, well, thanks in no small part to your idea about the –’ He spun his finger in the air and tapered off.

‘Thing with the –’ I spun my own, nodding.

‘Exactly. Well, that was what I was going to put you back on. We’re supposed to be rolling out another online promotion at the end of the month, but we’ve had a few issues with the freelancer I drafted in. Be good if you could take over, what with your having prior experience of the brand and I know you and Chloe make a good team.’

The sandwich Raj had insisted on buying got stuck in my throat and I coughed, water springing to my eyes, the look of a deranged lunatic about me.

‘I mean, if that’s alright?’ he added hurriedly as I swigged back my smoothie and spluttered again, this time in a different colour. I shook the underside of my hand at him and grinned apologetically through a steady stream of tears.

‘Yes, yes. Sorry. Went down the wrong way.’ I thumped my chest, gasped and sat up again, tittering self-consciously at Raj’s face, suspended in concern or if he had any sense, regret.

‘Alrighty then, are we good? Got any more questions? About the position, I mean. Chloe will get you up to speed about where they are with the project.’

I smiled again and shook my head, sandwich discarded under a napkin. ‘I don’t think so.’

‘Great.’ He pushed his chair back and began to fill his pockets with the loose change, wallet and phone scattered across the table.

Then slinging his coat over his arm, he said, 'Sorry to dash off. I've got at meeting at one, but… I'll see you on Monday. Right?'

'Right.' And I stuck my thumb up before I could reign it in. 'And thanks again. For giving me another chance.'

'Thank *you*, Emily. It'll be good to have you back.'

And with that he swept out of the café, coat draped over his shoulders, one arm already in the sleeve. I observed his journey past the window with an unseeing gaze, nervous excitement threatening to bubble over in a way I'd never expected to feel again. I was back on track. Within a few weeks it would seem like I'd never been gone and I'd be able to put this last eight months or so behind me. I settled back in the seat, smiling to myself and my eyes drifted across the street towards the hordes of busy shoppers, the dawdling school kids, the office workers grabbing lunch, all of them in constant motion. All except for one.

Connor's lips were curled into a snarl, his eyes dark slits, hands pushed deep inside his jacket, legs planted firmly apart. I reeled back with the force of a closed-fist, a wave of nausea doubling me over like a punch to the gut and just like that, I was back to square one. At least that's how it felt. What I didn't know was it was far worse than that.

10 Days Before the Murder

Her Mother

The oncology ward was every bit as underwhelming as it had been during the last two rounds of chemo. Top brass was clearly hoping patients would be too grateful to complain if their treatment was successful or too dead if it wasn't. Either way, it was apparent that the dying didn't merit even a bunch of fresh flowers, though we should have counted our blessings that the weak grey tea and basic range biscuits hadn't been slashed from the budget.

'Doesn't look like she's in today,' Bella stage-whispered scanning the staff nurses and it didn't. I'd had a good look around when we arrived, half-relieved not to have to confront Linda, half-disappointed not to be able to give her a piece of my mind.

'Keeping a low-profile, I expect. As well she should. What kind of mother must she be to raise a child like that?'

'The apple doesn't fall far from the tree, isn't that what they say?' Bella fidgeted knowingly with the intravenous tube attached to her swollen artery, the bruise around it already blooming.

'Certainly not in this case.' I picked up a Woman's Own from the coffee table and leafed through it absent-mindedly but my mother wasn't ready to let the subject drop.

'Imagine if that father of his had stuck around. He might well have turned out even worse.'

‘You make it sound like Roger went out for a packet of cigarettes and never came back. The man burnt himself to smithereens.’

‘Yes, well. I suppose that didn’t help the boy’s state of mind. Not that that’s any excuse. What he needed was some firm discipline, then maybe we wouldn’t be in this mess.’

I sighed and pursed my lips. ‘Hmm, well, that’s not exactly Linda’s strong point, is it?’

Bella tucked her chin in towards her chest and raised her eyebrows, which did absolutely nothing for her. I continued anyway.

‘I’ll bet she’s wishing she hadn’t sold up that big house of hers now. Not only has the you-know-what blown through the equity but she’s stuck with him under her roof again. And I told you there wasn’t room to swing a cat in that place.’

‘Good. They deserve each other. It’s just a pity it’s so nearby. Sorry, am I boring you?’

Talk of swinging cats had reminded me to chase David to check that Ginger had turned up. It wasn’t like him to stay out all night and he certainly wasn’t one to give breakfast a miss. I tapped out a quick text, remembering only after I’d sent it to ask after Emily too. The phone binged almost immediately.

11.03

No sign yet. He’s probably tucked himself up in a wardrobe or bucket somewhere. He’ll turn up.

He did do that. I replied with a rolling eyes emoji and added, Any other news?

11.05

Just more of the usual. No more photos, but plenty of angry texts. Her phones out of battery again so I told her to leave it off for a bit. Finally persuaded her to go back to bed too.

That was good at least. She needed as much rest as she could get. I was sure she wasn't sleeping well again. The dark shadows under her eyes were back but that wasn't surprising. She was a nervous wreck. Worse since Connor had shown up outside the café yesterday. David had had to leave work to go and get her and the coward had scarpered as soon as he'd arrived. Didn't stop him from sending Emily photos of her with Raj though, laughing and smiling as if that was a crime. As if she had anything to be ashamed of. It was nothing but a spineless attempt to intimidate her. Absolutely pathetic, that's what it was. A grown man throwing his toys out the pram. What was more worrying was that he'd obviously been checking her emails in order to know where to find her.

'Change your passwords to everything,' David had said. 'Your Gmail, your bank accounts, anything he might be able to access. And make it something he'll never guess.'

I said change it to **** YOU. That way if he ever did work it out, he'd know we were on to him but I didn't know what she chose in the end. Ginger1! I should think if it wasn't before. That was the trouble with passwords. No matter what everyone said, it didn't pay to be too clever or you ended up forgetting them all. I turned my phone off and returned it to my handbag.

'Just checking on your granddaughter, Mother.'

‘He’s not shown up at the house again, has he?’

‘I don’t think so. He’s reverted to texting.’

Bella shook her head irritably. ‘I told her she should call the police. Make some kind of report.’

‘I know, we’ve all told her but you know what she’s like. Burying her head in the sand, hoping it’ll all go away.’ I shrugged. Took a swig of painfully cold water from the tiny ribbed plastic cup that came out of the dispenser. I’d need at least four to even touch the sides. You’d think I’d have been used to the desiccating heat after working in hospitals for over half my life. If I hadn’t been in such a rush that morning, I’d have looked harder for my stainless-steel bottle but Emily was forever using it and not putting it back. Emily or Olive. They were as bad as each other. The beaker made an unpleasant cracking noise as it crumpled under the force of my last sip and the blue-rinsed octogenarian next to us turned expectantly. I lowered my voice. ‘Besides, I think she’s had enough of the police after everything they put Olivia through last week.’

‘Oh, those charges were never going to stick,’ Bella tutted.

‘Not under normal circumstances, no, maybe not. But then she wouldn’t normally be arrested in the company of a *known criminal*.’ I stared at my mother pointedly, tapping her arm with the magazine but she made a noise like a flyswat travelling at speed and pushed the pages away.

‘Oh, that. It was nothing. A six-month suspended sentence for fencing stolen goods when he was a youngster, that’s all. I suspect Ernie might still dabble in a bit of money laundering here or there. A taxi company would be a good front for that. Keep it in the family. You could drive around in circles all day…’

‘Or take a bunch of unsuspecting strangers all the way down to Brighton. Twice.’

‘Oh, yes. Clever.’

‘I didn’t mean it as a compliment.’

Bella tutted, readjusting her bony buttocks fruitlessly. ‘Well, we’re not exactly dealing with The Krays, are we? Give the boy some credit for his ingenuity. Besides it might not hurt to know someone who knows someone, if you get my drift.’

I knew exactly what she meant and I wasn’t inclined to disagree, which was unlike me. Being around my mother always brought out my resting teenager, but on this occasion, there was comfort in her madness and I almost said as much except that her attention had shifted beyond my shoulder.

‘Uh-oh, incoming.’

Well, I didn’t need to turn around to guess what that meant. I stiffened and held my breath waiting for the all clear.

‘It’s alright. She’s gone into the back – oh no, there she is again. Talking to the receptionist. Keep looking at me like we’re deep in conversation.’

‘We are deep in conversation.’

Bella’s eyes flitted behind me. ‘I think she’s pretending not to see us.’

‘Good.’

‘Oh dear. That’s torn it.’

‘What?’

‘We made eye contact.’

‘Oh, Mum.’

'It's not my fault. We both looked up at the same time. Anyway, don't worry about it, she's trying to look busy. I expect she'll come up with a reason to rush out in a minute. Oh no, wait. Bugger. She's coming over. Try to look normal.'

'I am normal.'

My mother yelped in surprise as though running into Linda at work were as astonishing as bumping into her on the banks of the Nile. I glanced up, equally startled, though marginally less dramatic, while Linda merely shuffled awkwardly between us with the sort of expression one might normally see outside a headmaster's office. She squashed her clipboard tightly against her breasts, her face strained, words failing to form on her cracked lips and for a moment, I was certain she was going to vomit. I was on my feet, supporting her elbow before I knew it.

'Sit down, Linda. You look like you're about to pass out.'

'Oh no, I'm fine.' But she allowed me to twist her towards the chair, settling for a second or two before she leapt up again, one hand fluttering, the other still clamped to the clipboard. 'I just wanted to say…' Her eyes filled with tears.

'There, there. It's alright.' Bella reached up and patted her arm, the sticky tape holding her canula in place straining.

'I'm so sorry, for everything that's happened. Emily's such a wonderful girl. I know Connor can be hard to live with sometimes. I hope he didn't…' Linda trailed off and there was nothing we could add because mark my words, whatever she'd been about to say, he had.

'I'm sorry he's taken their break up so badly,' I said because I was.

'Yes. He is struggling. He really does love her.'

To say we fell into an uncomfortable silence at that point would be like suggesting sending close to two hundred texts a day was a bit much, which we didn't mention either. Perhaps we should have done. It was hard to tell how much Linda knew about the situation but any resentment I'd harboured towards her had vanished the moment she'd almost fainted and frankly she had quite enough on her plate, what with Connor holed up in that tiny flat with her now. I don't imagine he was any more charming to be around with all this going on.

'Is he studying at all?' I said, mainly because I couldn't bring myself to ask after his welfare. 'His finals must be coming up soon. Will he go back to London, do you think? Go back to uni?'

I was hopeful but a shadow passed across her eyes.

'I don't think so. Go back to London, I mean, not with only a few months left on the course. He'll keep commuting up for the moment. Save a bit of money. Hopefully once he's back working at Microsoft and earning again, he'll be able to rent something, assuming he gets the grades.'

That seemed unlikely given that most of his time seemed to be dedicated to stalking Emily. Perhaps if he put as much effort into his dissertation as he did his WhatsApp messages, he might be able to turn it around but it seemed unkind to add to Linda's woes so I made a sympathetic trumpeting sort of noise she could interpret as she chose. My mother was less subtle.

'Do you think he should get some kind of help? Psychiatric care or something?'

‘Psychotherapy, I think you mean, Mum.’ I knew she didn’t but as I said, Linda seemed particularly vulnerable and it wasn’t really the place or time to bring up the obvious fact her son was as nutty as a packet of trail mix but half as pleasant. Not even half. I quite liked trail mix. Except for the coconut.

‘I have tried to bring up counselling, but…’ Her face collapsed again, her mouth wobbling and both Bella and I found ourselves cooing like a couple of street pigeons. Well, woodpigeons. Things hadn’t got that bad yet.

‘I’m sure he’ll get over it soon,’ I said even though I was sure of no such thing.

‘I hope so,’ she returned, gazing back at me gratefully. I rubbed her arm and pulled a tight upside-down smile and she nodded, lifting the clipboard.

‘I’d better get on,’ she said apologetically.

‘Of course.’

‘And I’m so sorry again. For the way Connor has behaved, and – ’ She looked down at Bella and steeped a sob. ‘And that you’re back again. It’s back.’

My mother blinked slowly and smiled, her head cocked, running her thumb along Linda’s arm one last time before she turned tail and practically raced out of the door.

‘Bitter pills may have blessed effects,’ Bella murmured sagely and to this day I don’t know if she was talking about her pain killers or the way everything played out in the end.

8 Days Before the Murder

Him

That fucking family of hers. I swear, if I ever got a minute on my own with any one of them. They'd done this to us. Especially the dyke. I could have had that ugly bitch banged up for what she did, but were they grateful? Of course not. Well, screw them. I could change my mind and press charges any time I liked. What she did was illegal. It was only out of respect for Emily that she wasn't in prison already. But she had been arrested and cautioned. There'd be a record of that if she ever tried anything again. If they ever tried to pin anything else on me. It'll all look like tit for tat. Revenge for calling her out after she broke in.

The thought of her rifling through my stuff still made me sick. Made me want to put both of my hands around her neck and squeeze. Keep squeezing until her eyes bulged and the breath went out of her. Till she crumpled down onto the dirt where she belonged.

This was her fault but Emily wasn't blameless. She was weak. Easily led. She let them poison her against me. Let them get inside her head. My whole life had been fucked since she started all of this. The slot machines wouldn't pay out. Every horse I picked trailed in miles behind the others. One even broke its leg at the third fence and wound up with a bullet in its skull.

It was like she'd put a curse on everything around her. Everything I touched turned to shit. Every bet I made sunk more and more of my funds until I'd had to borrow more from people who weren't going to be happy to hear I wouldn't be able to pay it back. I'd already sold everything I had trying to bail us out of the debt she'd got us in, including that necklace she tried to steal back. Everything Mum had as well that should have been mine to rely on when the old hag finally carked it. And now it was all gone and Emily, the selfish sanctimonious bitch, was still swanning about expecting me to beg her to come back.

Well, she could go screw herself. I'd get her back all right but only when she was so wrecked, she'd be the one crawling back to me on her knees because no one else would want her, the dirty lying whore. I'd wipe the smile off that scheming face. Teach her not to fuck with me. By the time I was done, no other man would want to touch her with a barge pole, not even that sketchy scumbag who couldn't wait to get her back under him in that crappy agency.

No need to ask what she'd had to do to make that happen. Be interesting to know what his little wife thought about it all though… That would show them all who was boss. A couple of photos of the two of them sneaking around behind her back would do it. We'd see who was laughing then. Not Emily, that was for sure. If I had my way, she'd never laugh again. Not unless I told her to.

7 Days Before the Murder

Her

The bus was packed with the usual early morning crowd, some I even recognised from the months I'd taken it to and from the office – on the days Connor didn't surprise me by picking me up before and after work. Taking me out to dinner on the way home. To a pub, to the beach, the evenings spent away from my family stretching into nights, until the move up to London took me away altogether.

I could see it now. See it clearly and yet at the time it had all been such a whirlwind. I'd thought myself the one holding all the cards, the one in control. I'd been smug and I'd thought I deserved it. Now I spent every minute of every hour of every day trying to convince myself that I didn't. That I didn't deserve him. Didn't deserve what was happening.

But it was hard not to blame myself. I'd allowed him to breeze back into my life, been swept away by his lifestyle, the promise of nice meals in fancy restaurants, exotic holidays, expensive clothes, my friends' envy. And now I didn't even see my friends any more.

I lurched suddenly, shrinking back from the window as a blonde-haired cyclist sped past on the inside lane and left me reeling, dizzy with an ice-cold fear that twisted my stomach, knocked the wind out of me. The woman to my right turned first towards me, then away quickly, shuffling an inch or two closer to the edge of the seat while I stilled my breathing, the thump of the blood pounding in my ears.

The bus pulled up to the stop and I did it again. Tracked the jumbled queue instinctively, my pupils dilated, skittering across the sea of faces, the panic lodged in my throat a lump that hurt every time I swallowed.

Perhaps I should have let Dad bring me in today, he'd offered. More than offered, he'd practically begged but I insisted that we couldn't let Connor win. I couldn't let him break me and so now the hairs on the back of my neck were prickling with the sour expectation that I wasn't alone. That my every move was under scrutiny, was being recorded, ready to twist and distort. Ready to use against me.

He was everywhere all the time. At the supermarket, on the pier. Parked across the road in his mum's Nissan Micra for hours at a time, only disappearing when my dad, who'd taken the rest of the week off work to be with me, stepped onto the front path, the crunch of the gravel drowned out by the rev of his engine.

And we'd reported it, finally I'd reported it but there was little they could do the police said, at this stage. I only had to hope it got worse so they could intervene, do more than have a word with him, even though he'd been in the back garden and I knew that with absolute certainty. He'd sent me photos of my bedroom window, a vague smudge in the background that could only have been me. But there was nothing to say when it had been taken. Nothing to prove that his being everywhere I turned wasn't a coincidence.

'Start keeping a diary,' they'd said. 'Record any incidents where he shows up uninvited or contacts you, anything at all that makes you feel uncomfortable, but try not to worry. We often see this sort of behaviour after break ups and most of the time it peters out. They find someone new, start another relationship. These things have a way of sorting themselves out but make a note of everything he does anyway just in case.'

'Just in case of what?' Dad had said, his teeth grinding.

The police officer taking my statement had smiled diplomatically the way he'd been trained to. 'I know it's hard but try not to catastrophise. Often situations like these seem worse than they actually are. Give it a few weeks and if this lad's still bothering you, come back and let us know, but like I say – take notes in the meantime.'

I had a book full of notes. I could fill a library. Break the internet with screenshots of his messages alone. And Ginger was still missing.

'Cats have a way of turning up,' PC Riley had explained patiently. 'Honestly, if we ploughed our resources into finding lost pets, we'd be in the red within a week. He'll be back as soon as he gets hungry, I expect. And if he's really got himself into a pickle, he'll end up at a shelter or the vets. That's what usually happens. Long as he's been chipped, he'll be returned to you. In the meantime,' In the meantime again, 'try not to interpret every little thing as some sort of malevolent act orchestrated by this ex or you'll end up driving yourselves mad. Most times, they get bored and move on within a few weeks.'

My phone screen lit up with another notification and my heart stopped but it was only Dad.

8.43

All okay?

I replied with a thumbs up and two kisses, then added, Nearly there. No news. xx

A split second later it pinged again and I jumped, startled even though I'd know to expect a reply.

Good luck today xx he'd said and I wasn't sure if he meant at work or simply surviving. The phone felt hot in my hand, hotter than normal even, the charge already half-drained. I should have turned it off to save the battery but I needed to know it was at hand at all times. That I could get hold of anyone I needed in seconds. I glanced at Connor's muted WhatsApp feed, but no new messages had appeared since last night. Maybe the constable was right. Maybe he was getting bored. Getting over me. Despite everything I knew about Connor, a spark of hope bloomed inside me. A ripple of relief.

I pressed the bell as the bus neared my stop and stepped carefully around my neighbour, sweeping past the bag she was clasping on her lap, the feet she tucked under the seat. The sun was bright and the sky clear, the warm buzz of anticipation at being back in Ship Street irrepressible.

Chloe's eyes widened as I opened the door and made my way across the office. She leapt up and hurtled across in bare feet, tripping over the heels already abandoned under the desk and threw her arms around me with a repressed scream. 'I'm so glad you're back.'

She'd messaged me in the week to say as much, her first text since October even though I'd thought we were close. I expect she thought so at the time too. I'd filled her in very briefly when she asked why I was back, said I'd explain more when I saw her, but it was probably obvious from the way my clothes hung off me, the sharp angles of my back, the gaunt set of my cheekbones which she studied, failing to mask her shock as she pulled away.

Raj was on his way over, a broad smile and confident swagger suggesting we were all going to pretend everything was fine, even though I'd told him what was going on. Warned him Connor might not take my going back to Optiks well. Might turn up and cause trouble. But Raj wasn't put off by something he couldn't really imagine and I was thankful he had no intention of tiptoeing around me. I preferred it that way.

He clapped his hand on my arm and it hurt more than it should have done, but I stood taller as Chloe skipped back to her desk with an excitable grin, kicking her shoes under it as she went.

'Glad you made it,' Raj beamed. 'It's all pretty much the way you left it. Few new bodies maybe but you know almost everyone here.' I scanned the office, the upturned faces staring expectantly, some smiling and mouthing hello, others already buried in their work again. Or their breakfast burritos.

'Think this is even the same laptop you had last time. IT still need to set up a new log in and email for the internal network but you can access everything else. Think it's the same password as you had last time. They said it won't take too long but I've sent the initial brief you'll be working on and the office contact list to your Gmail account in case you want to reach out to anyone. Chloe's heading it up though. She's got all the info you'll need. I've put you on your old desk opposite her.'

She teamed a silent shriek of joy with a head bobble and jazz hands that I couldn't help but smile at.

'Any questions, just ask her. We've got a meeting scheduled for eleven – it's in your calendar. That give you enough time to catch up, do you think?'

I nodded. 'Should do,' I said more confidently than I felt, taking my coat off and hanging it on the back of my chair, plugging my phone into its charger and lining my purse up next to the pen-tidy. The pen-tidy I'd bought in Rymans when I first started there. Before.

Raj stuck his thumbs up and I couldn't help but think he'd caught that from me which filled me with warmth too. I adjusted the seat and watched him head back to his office, breathed deeply and lifted the lid on my laptop, the weight and size of it familiar and comforting.

'Any more trouble from the psycho?' Chloe hissed and I shook my head. 'You free for lunch?'

'Sure.'

'Fill me in on the goss then, yeah?'

I nodded again, my blood pumping faster at the reminder that even though I had the same computer, the same desk, the same pen-tidy, nothing was the same. Everything had changed. Everything had a memory of Connor attached to it, a stain that would never go away.

I pressed the heels of my hands into my eye sockets until luminescent squiggles floated into infinity. Then I sighed, pulled myself together, logged onto my laptop and opened my Gmail account. Clicked on the attachments Raj had sent through, pages and pages of projections, graphs and diagrams, tables and the brief.

Pages and pages of writing that meant nothing to me. It was gobbledygook.

'Senseless, irrelevant tripe,' Connor whispered, the cool trace of his breath on my neck, a chill trickling down my spine. I inhaled, steadied my fingers against the keyboard. Concentrated and tried again – reading and re-reading the same paragraphs, deciphering the same lines and circles, the colours that blurred into one, but even before I'd got started, I couldn't shake the feeling that I'd failed. I should have been celebrating being back but instead Connor's voice kept chipping away at me. Day in and day out. Night after night.

'You'll never be good enough and there's no shame in that. You're just not up to it. You can't even keep track of your toothbrush. How many times have you insisted it's changed colour overnight, when the truth is you're just a little bit ditzy. In a nice way of course, but let's face it, you can't even remember where you put your keys half of the time. How you think you'll be able to manage whole projects is beyond me. You'll screw something up one of these days and that'll be somebody's business on the line. It's one thing being empty-headed in your own home, but at work? There's going to be consequences. Expensive consequences. You need to get out now before you really fuck something up.'

I closed my eyes, but he was still there. Inside my head. Would he be pleased that I was back where I started, still close to the bottom and destined to make a fool of myself? Or worse.

He never liked me working here. Found it demeaning that I'd settled for such a small operation when he was headed for Microsoft and the huge inflated salary that would come with it. Not that I had a hope of doing better if I kept pointlessly pursuing this line of work. Chasing after dreams that didn't have a hope of coming true.

I was kidding everyone, including myself. Hoping no one would notice I didn't have a clue until I'd caught up. If I ever could.

'You up to speed then?' Chloe asked removing a gnawed highlighter from her pink champagne lips and I jumped, spinning back to my laptop and clicking on the screensaver, the Ecoballz brief replacing the sweeping shoreline once again.

'No, sorry. I'm still reading through it all.'

'No worries. I need to chase Mo for those mock-ups anyway. Just let me know when you've finished.'

'Will do.'

I squinted at the blurry lines, forcing myself to concentrate. Easier said than done with everyone's phones pinging constantly, the chime of messages coming through all at once like some weird concerto.

And then I glanced up under the heat of their surveillance. Contorted mouths hanging half-open, devices pressed to their chests or suspended in front of them, their necks bent gleefully peering at their screens. Surreptitiously peeking back at me and then at each other. Raj was rising slowly from his seat in the back room, horrified and reluctant. The blood drained from my face, my arms, my legs, the density of the atmosphere grounding me to the chair, my eyes darting from one colleague to another. Chloe lowered her Samsung and leant across the desk towards me, her lips parted, words failing as my own phone began to ring. I grabbed it.

'Delete it. Delete it for everyone,' Olive shrieked.

Adrenalin was rushing through my body, my jangling nerves loosening my grip. 'What? What's going on?'

'He's posted a picture of you from your WhatsApp account. You need to delete it. Now.'

'God –'

'Now, Emily.'

Chloe grabbed my mobile from me, her fingers moving deftly, her forehead rutted as I choked on the toxic jolt rising up my throat, my palms pressed against my face, dread immobilising me.

'There.' Chloe held her arm out, her neck snapping left and right daring anyone to react. 'Wait. You should probably change your password.'

'I already did,' I whispered.

'He must know it.'

'Just delete the whole app,' Olive cried, her voice tinny and desperate. Too distant. 'Before he does it again.'

'Oh, God' I breathed. 'What was it? What did he put up?'

Chloe bit her lip and sank back down, pushing my phone across the desk. Behind her the account managers were nudging each other and laughing.

'One of you. Naked. Just the top half,' she added hurriedly.

Raj was heading towards me, a look of uncomfortable concern making his face grim.

'Everything okay?' he asked, unable to meet my eyes. I still hadn't lowered my hands and the tears I'd been holding back spilt over, soaking my fingers.

'I'm sorry,' I gasped.

'Raj –' Chloe broke in.

'It's okay. I know, I know.' He dragged his chin down and pressed the sides of his throat anxiously. Every single pair of eyes in the office was drawn to us. 'Have you deleted it? WhatsApp, I mean.'

I nodded. 'Chloe…'

Chloe bobbed her head vigorously with a thin smile designed to instil comfort where there was none. My screen lit up again with another incoming call. Thirteen texts message notifications from different names on my contact list. Fourteen. Fifteen.

'What do you want to do?' Raj murmured bending down next to me, his hands resting on the side of the desk.

'Send her home, Raj,' Olive shouted from nearly two hundred miles away and he glanced up, confused. I picked up my phone. Spoke hoarsely into it.

'I'll call you back.'

A pause. 'K.'

Immediately, it started ringing again. It was my dad. Oh God. My Dad.

'Sorry,' I croaked over the ringtone.

Raj shook his head. 'Don't be silly.' He looked around the room, registering the jubilant, curious gawking, glared and rapped his fist efficiently. 'How 'bout you head home now? Do what you need to do and let's start afresh tomorrow.'

A pain like a knife slicing through me took my breath away and I groaned. Raj's features were carefully arranged to convey reassurance but when his fingers brushed past me, he recoiled sharply as though it stung. As though I was contaminated. He blushed. 'Want anyone to come with you? Chloe could –'

‘No, no.’ I’d already grabbed my bag and shoved my phone and purse into it. Dragged the coat off the back of my chair. ‘I’ll be fine.’

I sprung up with one last snatched glance at them both and shot out of the office, my legs shaking and threatening to give way beneath me, convinced as I stepped onto the pavement outside that Connor would be there staring at me from across the street, but he wasn’t. In his place were dozens of strangers milling around leering and whispering. I was certain they all knew. They had to. Everyone had seen me naked and the worst part was, whatever photo he’d shared wasn’t the only one he had of me. He’d taken hundreds, far more explicit than that. And videos.

The ground gave way beneath me and I staggered, clutched the wall and threw up against it, my head spinning, my heart pounding in my chest. And as the whole world caved in on me, I fell back into an empty doorway and cried so hard and for so long I didn’t know if I’d ever be able to stop.

5 Days Before the Murder

Her Sister

It was like walking into a funeral parlour. Everything was very still and quiet.

'Hellooo,' I called out from the hallway but nobody answered. Flo was waiting outside on the doorstep looking worried but I beckoned to her to come inside.

'Are you sure this is okay?' she said, stepping onto the mat and wiping her shoes.

'Of course.'

'I don't want to get in the way.'

'Don't be daft. They'll be pleased to see you.' I hung my coat on the end of the banister and took hers, stuck it over the top of mine and grabbed it as it slid to the floor, three times. 'For Christ's sake.'

I bunched up the pink padded folds and slung it behind the post, white beads of sweat breaking though my hairline. Flo smirked, shaking her head as though some things never changed.

'Still got it,' I crowed and she nodded, teeth showing, eyes dancing as she leant forwards and kissed me on the mouth. My lips burnt.

'Hell yeah, you do.'

I pulled back and stared at her, at the perfect porcelain skin, the endless eyelashes, those plump lips I never thought I'd feel again.

I had the arsehole to thank for that ironically, not that I ever would. Flo had rung me as soon as he'd sent her the photo of Emily in the buff five days before and I'd brought her up to speed with everything. How they'd broken up, how he'd been stalking her, how when Emily went to the police to report the photos he'd been spreading online, they'd asked her if she'd had any issues with her own phone recently. With the battery getting too hot and running down quickly. With any glitching or apps working slower than usual.

And then one of the detectives had picked it up like it was contagious and scrolled along until she found an app with an innocuous icon of a squiggly line. Then she'd held the mobile up with the tips of two fingers and announced, 'See this here? It's spyware that's been installed on your phone, giving whoever's monitoring it complete access to everything on it, including your location, which explains how he always knows where you are and is still able to access your email and social media accounts even after you've changed the passwords.'

And when Milly had burst into tears and asked her how long it had been there, she'd said, 'Hard to say. Could be he's been keeping tabs on you since before you split up, but he'd only need to know your telephone number to install it so he could have done it at any time. We'll need to download the contents of your phone to form a case against him anyway. I suggest you wipe everything on it once you get it back. Then get yourself a new number and only give it out to only a few trusted people.'

So that was where me and Flo were and when we'd exhausted a vilified exchange of anecdotes about Connor and *that* night at the X-bar, we just kept on talking. It was like we'd never split up and she was the one who suggested meeting up over the Easter break. She, who'd met me at the station the second my train pulled in. She, who'd kissed me at the bottom of the stairs in my hallway like there was never a time when she'd said we shouldn't do that anymore.

My heart soared and I had to do my best to quash my spirits. Get the urge to whoop under control, one, because I'd look like a twat and two, because I was about to see Emily for the first time since Connor had entered Phase 2 of his attempt to annihilate any sense of self-worth from her.

I smiled and pulled Flo by the hand towards the kitchen, opening the door and peering around cautiously before entering.

'We're here.'

'Come through, love,' Mum screeched. 'We're in the front room.'

And there they all were, hidden in virtual darkness and crowded around Emily like they were forming a line of defence. Or maybe an attack by the look on Dad's face. My parents stood up when we walked in.

'Flo. It's so wonderful to see you.' Mum squeezed her with a bear hug which was totally embarrassing and OTT but Flo did a top job of seeming not to mind. Even so.

'Get off her, Mum.'

'It's just so nice to see you both,' Mum squawked pulling back, her hand still clutching Flo's. Dad let go of me and rubbed her shoulder with a satisfied nod.

'Oh, my!' Gran cried, creaking to her swollen feet. 'You look so much like Milly, I had to do a double-take then.'

Which couldn't have been further from the truth. Emily looked awful. Just awful. Like really, really bad.

'Don't get up, Gran,' I said, helping her back down into Mum's armchair and pecking her on the cheek. Flo followed suit but wasn't released quite as quickly which gave me a second or two to compose myself before squishing down beside Emily on the sofa.

'How you doing?'

'So-so,' she said, tears springing to her eyes. Her chin wobbled and I put my arms around her and rocked a bit. The cushion sprung up as Flo flopped down on the other side and kissed her temple, her hand snaking round Emily's thigh.

'What a tosser,' she murmured and a sound like a whale surfacing racked through Milly and she started crying for real, snot and everything. Mum passed her the box of tissues on the coffee table.

'I'll put the kettle on,' she said because torturing the bastard who'd done this was out of the question so tea would have to do instead.

'And I'll get the biscuits,' Dad added jumping on any excuse to leave. 'I'd offer you some lavender cake but someone seems to have finished it.' He threw an accusatory glare Gran's way and her mouth gaped in practiced denial.

I rubbed Emily's back. 'Have you spoken to the old bill again?'

She shook her head, refusing to take her eyes off the crumpled tissue in her fist. 'Not since Wednesday. My liaison officer's coming over in a bit though. I'll find out if there's been any progress then.'

'Did you manage to get it all taken down from Instagram and Facebook?'

She nodded, a jagged breath catching in her throat.

'What about Snapchat? Is there anything they can do about the screenshots going around?'

She shook her head, paling. Gran grimaced, exposing her pink NHS gums. 'She's deleted all her social media, haven't you, love? But someone –' She apostrophised the air, 'keeps setting up fake accounts under her name. We've told everyone not to accept friend requests or follow her but he's still posting things.'

'Things?' Flo asked kindly and my stomach flipped. Emily sagged.

'Photos,' she whispered. 'And clips.'

We both inhaled loudly. I'd told Flo about the videos, but somehow it sounded worse coming from her. Mum shuffled in with a tray and pushed the tissues along the table with the corner of it, sloshing tea onto the plate of biscuits.

'Careful, love,' Dad yapped, almost as protective of them as he was his first-born child. 'Macaroon anyone? It's a new recipe. They've sunk in the middle but they taste alright. Not my finest effort though.'

I took one to be polite even though I hated almonds – that's how bad things were. That's how much everyone was creeping round each other. Well, almost everyone. Mum sank down into Dad's chair and studied the faded photograph of us all on the side of her mug.

'What I don't understand,' she said quietly, 'is why you let him take them?'

Dad blanched, looking away from Emily. He put the plate down and paced in front of the bay window, pausing only to draw the curtain back a crack. To peer through it as though the front bushes were of more interest than the details of his daughter's unsavoury habits.

'Everybody takes them, Mum,' I exclaimed, indignant for Emily's sake. 'Everybody films themselves having sex. It's just something you do these days.' I avoided looking at Flo who was avoiding looking at me. Or anyone else in the room. 'Even I've been sent more dick pics than the whole of your generation put together. At least I hope so,' I shuddered. 'Not that you guys should start –'

'But don't you ever worry what would happen if… well, this. If this exact thing happened?'

Milly sobbed again.

'Clare. This isn't helping.' Dad dropped the curtain and turned back to us. 'What we should be focusing on is finding out what else he's done with… whatever he's got and how to get it all taken down.'

'There are facial recognition searches you can do,' Flo suggested. 'They might not catch everything out there but they're pretty good.'

'Facial what?'

'You run a search of any images featuring Emily. If he's posted any more photos or videos of her anywhere, they're likely to show up.'

'Oh God.'

I scooted up closer to Emily, squeezed her knee. 'And then we can get them taken down.'

'But what's to stop him putting them back up again?' Mum asked, getting high-pitched and agitated.

'The police,' I said, much as the thought of having anything to do with them made me nauseous. Much as they'd done bugger all about it up till now. 'You just have to keep reporting everything he does no matter how many times they mug you off. There'll be evidence they can use against him now. This isn't just stalking. This is online… something. Revenge porn. This is traceable. He's fucked up.' Mum blinked at me pointedly. '*Screwed* up. God.'

Emily rested her nose on her knuckles and the air whistled when she breathed, her voice muffled and craggy. 'I just don't know if I can face it.'

'You have to, Emily. He's not going to stop otherwise. He could go to prison for this. He should go to prison. And it's not just you. We all know he's done something to Ginger.' My own voice caught at that. At the missing lump on the windowsill. At the absence of teeny feet sticking out from under the curtain. Everyone looked down sharply and shook their heads disbelievingly, like there could be any other explanation. Milly juddered again and Flo put her arm around her.

'Oli's right. He's not going to go away and this could just be the start of it. He could be dangerous for all we know.'

But I'd always known he was dangerous. I'd known it every time he'd narrowed his eyes at me or held me too tightly when he said hello. I'd known it with every poison-laced word that dripped from that supercilious sneer of his.

‘Well, the police are on it now,’ Dad said, back in practical mode and forcing another macaroon on me. ‘What time are they coming?’

‘Any minute now.’

Flo leant forward, caught my eye. ‘I should probably leave you to it for a bit,’ she said. ‘Let you…’ She rubbed Milly’s back and pushed herself up from the sofa with a cute little sad wave. I followed her out.

‘Meet you later?’ I said sounding like a total loser but she smiled and kissed me on the lips again.

‘Yeah. Snap me.’

I swung the door open and standing on the step, her finger stretching towards the bell, was a blonde woman with dark roots and a look of quizzical surprise.

‘Oh. Emily…’

‘No,’ I sighed, rolling my eyes and ushering Flo past her. ‘Come in.’

It didn’t bode well if that was the level of genius supposedly dealing with Milly’s case. She took her shoes off without being asked and I lead her down the hallway.

‘Cup of tea?’ I said because despite everything the rozzers had put me through a few weeks ago, I wasn’t who they thought I was. Would a burglar have said ‘how d’you take it?’ No, I didn’t think so.

I saw her through to the front room and rushed to the kitchen to put the kettle on as quickly as possible, barely dipping the teabag in the boiling water before charging back to join the others. DS Smarty-Pants smiled gratefully and eyed the mug with only a flicker of unease that suggested it wasn't the worst thing she'd ever seen in her line of work, but it wasn't far off. Either way, she made no attempt to drink it. Which was rude, I thought, but only to be expected.

'The problem we have in these sorts of cases,' she continued candidly, perching on the edge of an armchair. Gran turned her hearing aid on and we all glared at her before turning our attention back to the detective. 'Is proving it's your ex uploading these intimate images of you.'

'Of course, it's him. Who else would do it? No one else even has photos like that of her.' I spun round to Milly. Well, banged into her. The sofa lacked wiggle room with a family of four squashed on it. 'Do they?'

'Unfortunately,' the DS interjected meaningfully and Milly winced. 'They do now,'

'What's that supposed to mean?'

'It means that once photos and videos are online, they tend to stay in circulation which makes it increasingly difficult to prove who's posted what, let alone get them taken down completely.'

I leant forward. 'But can't you trace that sort of thing?'

'We might get lucky but I'd expect someone with Connor's IT knowledge to be using a Virtual Private Network to cover his tracks. If that's the case, it'll be almost impossible to trace any of his online activity.'

Even Gran knew how to use a VPN to hide our identity when we were up to no good online. Not that streaming illegal downloads of the latest movie releases was in quite the same league as blowing up someone's life.

‘But what about the first photo?’ Milly whispered. ‘The one he posted on WhatsApp?’

The detective’s mouth contorted. ‘It was posted from your account, Emily. Suspecting he did it and proving it are two very different matters. The spyware we found on your phone would explain how he could have gone about it, but we still need evidence to show it was Connor who actually uploaded it. In the unlikely event he didn’t disguise his IP address, we might be able to trace it to one of his devices, but we’ll need to get a warrant for that. And in order to get a warrant, we’ll need to build a stronger case.’

‘So that’s it?’ I said. ‘You’re not going to do anything about it? He can just go on spreading this shit around and you’re not even going to clean it up, let alone stop him? You haven’t even mentioned the fact he keeps turning up at the house and everywhere else she goes. Can’t Milly get some sort of Stalking Protection Order?’ Yet more proof if anyone needed it, that I read the news.

The detective nodded in a way I was beginning to recognise meant no. ‘It’s quite hard to build a case against stalking, so what we’ve done is issue Connor with a harassment order which means if he tries to contact Emily again or harass her in any way, he’ll be getting another visit from our officers.’

‘A visit?’ I sneered.

‘In the meantime –’ I felt Emily flinch beside me but the copper rambled on regardless, ‘we’ll gather as much information about it as we can and keep investigating the image-based sexual abuse. It generally takes about seven to eight months to form a strong enough case to put in front of a judge. I know that sounds like a lifetime but the problem we’ll have, even if we can find evidence that he put the content up in the first place, is proving that he did so with the intent to cause harm.'

'What's that supposed to mean?' I said, my lip curling. The detective crossed her ankles and her arms defensively like she'd already anticipated our response.

'It means, that while it's an offence to share non-consensual pornographic images, we have to be able to prove he did so with the intent of causing embarrassment or distress.'

'What?' I was the only one reacting. It was clear that the others were already resigned to the facts. The detective looked straight at me and nodded again like she couldn't believe what she was saying either.

'It's only illegal to share these types of images if he was motivated by revenge or a desire to hurt Emily.'

'Of course he did it to hurt her.'

'And that's what we have to prove. We have to be able to discredit any suggestion that he was oblivious to her feelings, that he didn't realise she'd care –'

'But that's ridiculous.' I shot to the front of the sofa cushion, my palms raised incredulously. Emily put her hand on my arm and I lowered it back down on her leg, but only to make her feel better. This was bat shit crazy. 'No, I'm sorry. That's bollocks. Who wouldn't be distressed or embarrassed if someone sent naked pictures of them to everyone on their contacts list? Who would want strangers jerking themselves off to footage of them going at it?'

Emily and Mum shrank back as if I'd slapped them and Dad turned away again, fingers tapping the armrest, his foot bouncing on the floor. Only Gran looked to be enjoying herself like this was all part of some amateur theatre performance and any minute she might be called upon to join in.

'I understand it's incredibly frustrating. It's a loophole in the current Online Safety Bill that we're hoping will be amended before too long.'

'But that's still too long for my sister, right?' The detective conceded, inclining her head.

'Well, what about the rest of it? The stalking? The endless bombardment of texts and phone calls?'

'As I said, the harassment order against him will hopefully put him off, but in the event he continues, we'll have evidence that he was aware his actions amounted to harassment which we can use if it ever goes to court.'

'If?'

She cleared her throat and engaged with the scum forming on the surface of her tea. 'To manage your expectations, very few harassment cases make it that far – about five percent – and only one percent result in a conviction, but I'm confident we have the makings of a good case against Connor.'

My head started to swim as much because nobody else appeared to be outraged by this information. Gran was pursing her lips like her teeth were about to pop out and Mum and Dad were both sat there looking grey and tiny and old like they'd aged about fifty years in the last few weeks. And Emily… Emily was rung out. Like properly done in. Like if there'd been a cliff nearby, we'd have all been sitting on her right now, holding her back.

'And what if you don't?' I squealed on behalf of everyone. 'What if this is one of the ninety-five percent of cases that don't make it to court? Or if it does, what if he goes to jail and comes out even angrier at Emily than he is now? What if this is just the start of it? What if it escalates? You read about this sort of thing every day. He's not going to give up until he's completely destroyed her, I know it. I can feel it. No matter what we do, he's always one step ahead of us. No matter how bad it gets, he can always come up with a way to make it worse.'

'That's enough, Olivia,' my dad snapped and I turned slowly towards the three petrified faces staring back at me in horror. And Gran who was clearly anaesthetised to all of this by a weekly dose of Death in Paradise. 'We all need to calm down and let DS Lowes do her job.'

But even DS Lowes didn't seem confident she could stop him. Short of attaching Connor McGann's feet to an anchor and tipping him overboard into the Channel, there wasn't much anyone seemed to be able to do. Not legally anyway.

3 Days Before the Murder

Her

The kettle clicked and the burble of boiling water in the background was replaced by the clink of a spoon.

'Does anyone take sugar?' Flo called from the kitchen.

'Does anyone take sugar?' Olive tore her eyes from the laptop and turned indignantly. 'How long have you known me?'

'I meant Mills, obvs.'

I swallowed, still focused on the screen, on the rows and rows of naked women and partially-dressed girls, some pouting, lips bloated, breasts turgid, their legs spread in sharp focus while others, pale and doughy, stared keenly into the lens of a smartphone, their performances blurry and amateur. A sickening few on their knees, the rest with thick-veined penises already rammed inside them, every thumbnail accompanied by a tagline promising to make good on the worst kind of fantasy. For a price.

My thoughts were spooling wildly but I couldn't stop scrolling through the pages, numb to the images of *hardcore anal*, *wet pussies* and *donkey dicks*, the grannies, the step-moms and babysitters, intent only on unearthing the images of me.

'No sugar for her,' Olive replied when I didn't. Then sizing me up, 'or maybe one for shock. Make that two.'

Flo crashed a couple of mugs down onto the dining room table. 'Got any coasters?'

‘On the sideboard.’

Flo rattled around behind us, the rustling and clanking stretching my nerves.

‘They’re not here.’

‘Try the top drawer.’

For crying out loud.

‘Ta-dahh. They were in the cupboard. Nice Toby Jugs by the way.’

Olive grabbed the hand Flo draped briefly on her shoulder. ‘Thanks. They’re collectible. Apparently.’

Oh, shut up. What was wrong with them? How could they be so blasé?

Olivia bent her head to the side and kissed Flo’s crushed fingers, masking my lack of acknowledgement either of her girlfriend or the coasters she’d chucked down. The only thing I knew how to do anymore was scan and click, click and scan. Flo swept back into the kitchen and returned with her own tea, dragged another seat around the table and squeezed in next to me.

‘Anything?’

I shook my head.

‘Maybe you’ve found them all now.’

I sneered dismissively. ‘There’re millions of these sites. I’ve barely touched the surface.’

‘You can’t look through all of them,’ Olive said. ‘I mean, Jesus Christ, you’ll drive yourself mad. Besides if there was any more stuff out there, it would have shown up when you searched for the images.’

'We only checked for the photos and videos we know about. God knows what else he's put up there.'

'But that's what the facial recognition app's for.' Olive rubbed my back but I stiffened, refusing to be comforted, refusing to let up.

'That was rubbish. Half the pictures it brought up weren't even of me. For Christ's sake, Flo was in two of them and I know there are more photos of me online, like normal photos. I might have wiped all my social media accounts, but I'm still tagged on other people's posts and hardly any of those showed up.'

'Why don't we concentrate on getting the ones we know about taken down.'

I spun around to Flo, cutting away from the barrage of filth, my eyes boring into her.

'What do you think we've been doing? We must have sent five hundred emails over the last few days. The websites don't do anything. Or they say they're going to look into it. It could take weeks to get it all taken down and in the meantime –' In the meantime, ' – other perverts, sickos I don't even know, are sharing it all and reposting it on other forums.'

'Hey,' Olive said, her voice firm, her hand still soft on the nape of my neck. 'It's not Flo's fault.' And at that a sob juddered through me and I buried my face in my hands. Flo pressed her head against mine and pulled me towards her.

'Shhh, shhhh. It's alright. It's all going to be alright.'

But it wasn't. It was never going to be alright again. This was going to follow me around for the rest of my life. It was going to infiltrate every job I ever applied for, every success, every relationship. My children were going to be able to Google my name in twenty years' time and find photos of me clutching my breasts, one hand inching towards a cropped patch of pubic hair, my skin prickling with shame as Connor barked orders at me, my eyes skittering with discomfort, embarrassed enough to be exposing myself to a man who'd seen it all before, let alone the world. Let alone my own father.

God, what had I done? The tears racked through me but I pushed them down again. Pushed the damp knotted coils of hair back from my forehead, took a haggard breath and ran my finger down the trackpad. Clicked onto the next page, over and over, fanatically swiping, my lips twisting even though my instinctive reaction towards the grotesque images had tapered into acceptance. The sight of semen dribbling down vulvas virtually unremarkable after forty-eight hours spent scrolling past them.

Another text pinged though on my old phone. Olive grabbed it.

'Don't look,' she said, but not before a grimace flashed across her face.

'Not him?' I asked coolly, my voice somehow even.

'Unknown number.'

They were all unknown numbers, all the messages pouring in threatening to rape me, kill me, follow me home and slice my tits off, they were all from strangers. Or acquaintances. Neighbours. Friends disguising themselves. How would I know? They could have been from anyone. My details were out there somewhere, being shared around and although I'd got a new phone and handed the number out selectively, I'd kept the old one to gather evidence to use against Connor if and when this went to court. When.

But he'd gone quiet. That is to say, ever since he'd hacked into my WhatsApp and moved this up a notch, he'd been careful. Had told the police his phone had been stolen before the first photo even came out and as ludicrous as that was, they couldn't prove he was lying. Couldn't say for sure who'd bombarded me with hundreds of menacing messages in the days running up to his great reveal. Not unless they managed to link the so-called stolen mobile's GPS signals to his movements, but all that required time. Time and luck and now I didn't know who was calling me and hanging up. Who was fantasising about chopping me into pieces. And I had no idea if whoever was doing it knew where I lived.

Whoever else was doing it. I wasn't stupid. I knew Connor had to be responsible for at least some of the threats, his communications hidden behind foreign VPNs and burner phones that would never be linked back to him.

But on the other hand, I hadn't seen him for six days in a row now and the only sighting of him in that time was when Gran bumped into him at the community centre. Bumped into him, she said but in reality, he'd stood outside the window watching her Chair-obics class. A bunch of old biddies perching on the hard plastic chairs that were normally piled up against the wall, twirling their ankles and stretching their arms over their heads. He hadn't taken his eyes off her for the full ten minutes or so it had taken him to drain his protein shake, his muscles bulging from a recent session in the gym, his interest in her no longer charming.

'He'll have to try harder than that to intimidate me,' she'd said and I didn't query why in that case, she hadn't confronted him, seen him off or at least reported him to the front desk. What did I expect her to do? What could anybody do? There was no law against working out in the same building as my grandmother. No harassment order stipulating he couldn't happen to live in the same few square miles as me.

And maybe it had been a coincidence. Granted I hadn't left the house since Monday but he hadn't been hanging around outside, only to drive off as soon as Olive or my parents hurtled out of the front door brandishing a camera.

Maybe that PC was right. Maybe he had got bored and moved on and these latest posts and messages were all out of his hands now, had taken on a life of their own. Or maybe the police had scared him off. Maybe this had all got out of hand, had gone further than he'd ever meant it to and he'd backed off altogether now.

A small spark of unreasonable hope flickered inside me, but I stamped it out. He might have made mistakes, taken things too far, but none of that would explain the matter of Ginger's disappearance. A cold shiver ran down my spine. A fresh twist of pain. Mum and Gran were still out putting Missing posters up on lampposts, refusing to accept the only plausible explanation. The uncanny timing. The fact psychopaths always seem to have a trial run before working their way up to mutilation and murder.

Flo cocked her head. 'What time's everyone else getting back?'

'Dunno. Why?' Olive said, leaning back and straining her neck to talk across me.

'No reason.' Flo looked around, her ear angled, her forehead knitted. 'I just thought I heard…'

We all froze, my hands paralysed above the keyboard, Flo and Olive's eyes locked into each other behind me. In the distance, next door's dog was barking furiously. And then the key turned in the door and Mum's voice carried down the hallway.

'We're back,' she said in a way that would normally illicit some degree of sarcasm, if not from me then definitely from Olive, but instead we all sank back against the dining chairs, slack with relief.

'In here,' Olive yelled so close to my eardrum it caused that whole side of my face to spasm.

'How are you getting on? Oh.' Mum drew to an abrupt halt behind me, her distaste lacing the air.

'Still going,' Flo said, the gravity of her insinuations too heavy to miss. 'Kettle's just boiled.'

I felt them all looking at each other, the silence telling, their breathing laboured.

'Anyone need a top up?' Mum chirped deliberately, heading into the kitchen.

'I'll have a cup,' Gran said, sidling up behind me. 'Goodness. That's enough to put you off your garibaldis.'

I couldn't concentrate with everyone here, hovering over me and interrupting. It only magnified the sordidness of the situation, brought me back into the room instead of on some other plane, another dimension where explicit content of this sort was normal. I slammed the laptop shut and shifted around, my neck twisting towards the floral scent of Gran's perfume.

'How did you get on?'

She shrugged, flapped the few remaining posters in her hand. 'I think it's safe to say we ran out of lampposts. I take it nobody called.'

I shook my head, not trusting myself to speak and Flo rubbed my back again, slid her hand across to Olive and gave her shoulder a quick squeeze. I pushed my seat back, embroiled instantly in a deferential crush of limbs and chair legs, a self-conscious foxtrot as the three of us disentangled ourselves from the other's space.

'More tea, Olivia? Flo?' Mum shouted busying herself to avoid dwelling on the quiet at her feet, the lack of obstacles forever threatening to trip her up, the insistent meowing that always had the ring of an accusation. The torment over what had happened to the grumpy old thing spiralling into darkness.

'No, thanks. Think me and Flo'll head into town.' Olive glanced at Flo for affirmation. 'I need to pick up a few bits.'

'Right you are.' Mum didn't correct her grammar or ask me if I wanted anything. I was on the automatic tea-refill list. Someone must have brought me one every fifteen minutes for the last week. I don't know if they thought it was medicinal or they needed to feel like they were helping in some way but there was a limit to how much more of it I'd be able to take.

'You alright if we head out?' Olive said taking my elbow, the sincerity in her concern too much to bear.

'Of course. You don't have to ask me.'

She and Flo exchanged a look again and I bit back the urge to tell them all to stop treating me like I was an invalid. Like I couldn't be trusted to make it through the day without them needling me for information and updates, their very presence a constant reminder of why we were all there.

'K,' she said with none of her usual narkiness. 'Let us know if anything…'

She tapered off and scratched her head, the end of her sentence too obvious to bother airing. I jerked in response, formed a tight-lipped smile she'd have been hard pressed to catch and she beckoned Flo with a tilt towards the door. Gran stepped into the gap they'd left behind, the top of her springy white hair grazing my chin, her tiny arms surprisingly strong as they gathered me into their fold and held me there, wordlessly.

I could have stayed in her embrace forever, breathing her in. Memorising the very essence of her, the sensation of her sagging skin pressing against mine, the bird-like brittleness of her bones the only indication she wasn't well. That she wasn't going to make it this time. I closed my eyes and allowed her to absorb some of the anguish choking me, the shadows circling like a pack of starving hyenas but as I clung to her, a scream erupted from the hallway.

'Oh my God!' Olive yelled. 'Guys! Guys, look!'

And there darting through her legs, bedraggled and scrawny, was Ginger, his back arched, fur standing on end. His pupils so dilated his eyes were entirely black.

'Oh my God!' we all shrieked in varying degrees of excitement, startling him further. 'Ginger? Oh my God, Ginger. Where have you been?'

Mum swept him into her arms and burrowed her face into his matted coat, his dirty nails clawing at her neckline. 'Oh, Grumbles. What's happened to you?'

He scrambled to the floor leaving behind a red gash my mum was too preoccupied to notice. Olive rattled the packet of biscuits that had sat undisturbed on the windowsill for over a week but he dashed under the table and hid there, refusing to venture out until at last, he took a tentative step towards the fresh saucer of tuna and cheese he normally had to beg for. He wolfed it down as though he hadn't eaten for days and finally, water dribbling down his chin, he allowed us to stroke him.

'He's traumatised, bless him,' Mum said, her legs stretched in front of her on the kitchen floor, gently tracing the skeletal topography of his back.

'I reckon he's been in someone's shed this whole time,' Gran said.

'That'd make sense.' Olive offered her hand to Flo and groaned as she pulled her to her feet. 'I mean, whatever, he's back, right? I didn't expect that.'

'I don't think any of us expected to see him again,' Mum said and then looked away sharply as everyone else turned their gaze to me.

'Yeah. Yep. Good. I mean, that's one less thing, right?' I said. 'Like, I mean, if he didn't hurt Ginger, that's good news, no?'

'It's great news. It's – it's –'

'It means maybe things aren't as bad as we thought they were,' Flo said. 'I mean, they're still bad, I'm not going to lie, but maybe he's not…'

'As bad as we thought he was.' Olive nodded eagerly. 'This is a win for us.'

'Yep,' I said, my voice clipped, determined. 'This is really, really positive.'

We all grinned, convincing ourselves that it was over. That our minds had taken us to dark places when in reality, the cat's disappearance was down to his insatiable curiosity. Was completely unrelated to everything else that had been going on. Things that maybe Connor wasn't even a part of anymore.

'Look, we've really got to go,' Olive said, glancing over to Flo for back up, 'but, you know, call me if anything else –'

'Nothing else is going to happen,' I said meaning it this time. 'Go. Have a nice time. Everything's fine.'

Connor had nothing to do with whatever had happened to Ginger. He wasn't a psychopath, he was a narcissist. A horrible, petty, mean dipshit who'd taken his resentment and revenge too far but I wasn't about to let him ruin my life. Not over some photos and a few nasty messages. I wasn't in danger. I was unlucky, that's all. He was going to go down for everything he'd done and when he did, I'd be standing in the courtroom, my head held high, laughing as they dragged him away.

'I'm going to lie down for a bit,' I said at the soft click of the front door, stroking Ginger one last time before I stood, because I could, because he was there and not stuffed into three different bin bags.

'Okay, love.'

I ruffled Mum's hair and ran my fingers down Gran's arm, a spring in my step I knew was ridiculous to entertain. Things might not have been as shit as I thought they were, but they were still pretty shit, no two ways about it.

But he hadn't murdered the cat. I was allowed to cling to that if only for a few hours. I trotted up the stairs, spun around the post onto the landing and pushed my bedroom door open. The smell hit me immediately. The musky oaky-ness that made my stomach turn, my skin crawl. I paused in the doorway, shock rendering me immobile, my eyes wide and focused on the plush toy resting against my pillow. The stuffed penguin Connor had insisted on buying at the aquarium which I'd jammed into the back of my wardrobe, forgotten, even before any reminder of that day had turned sour.

The next thing I knew, I was on the other side of the room screaming, my fingers delving into the seams, ripping its soft stomach wide open, the stuffing scattered across the carpet. Mum and Gran either side of me, terrified and bewildered, aghast, their efforts to calm me no match for my hysteria until at last, spent, I sank down onto the bed, the empty casing drooping on my thigh, their arms around me, their questions flying at me all at once.

'He's been in here,' I said so quietly they had to lean in to hear me.

'What?'

'He's been in my room. While we were all here.'

'No.' Mum whipped around violently as though he might still be standing there in the shadows. Gran's back braced.

'We've got to call the police.'

'What for?' I said. 'They never do anything.'

But my mum called them anyway, her voice quavering, her fingers wrapped tightly around the handle of her largest kitchen knife as she and Gran burst into every other room, fists twisted around each other's cardigans, cursing my dad for not being there. For taking on extra shifts to avoid spending time with me. To avoid looking me in the eye.

'No sign,' Mum said. 'They'll be here any minute.'

We lined up on the edge of my bed, our faith that someone was coming to save us probably misguided.

'I should have known it wasn't over.'

'They'll be able to get him for this.'

'That's what they always say. That's what they said about the stalking, then he started posting pictures, then the videos went up. Then the cat.' I shook my head, confusion muddling the facts. The cat was back, but… 'He's trying to destroy me. Those photos…' I hung my head.

'You never know, you might be glad of the odd keepsake one day,' Gran said, squeezing my leg and nudging me. 'When your body's gone to pot and your boobs are forever getting caught in your waistband.'

'Mum!'

'What? It's true. I wish I'd had the foresight to take some nice pictures of myself before I turned to mush. That was your fault,' she said aiming a gnarly finger at my Mum.

'He's never going to stop, is he?' I whispered. It wasn't a question. 'What am I going to do?'

'We're going to have to kill him,' Gran said. 'Unless anyone's got a better plan.'

3 Days Before the Murder

Him

For Christ's sake. My idiot mother, that useless fucking moron. She let the cat out. Said she'd heard strange noises coming from my room, like she had any right to be snooping around, listening at doorways. I had to tell her I'd found it wandering around outside and locked it up for safekeeping while I organised taking it to a shelter. Stupid numpty believed me, of course, but then she would. Didn't seem to recognise it but that wasn't surprising. She had all the brain power of a cabbage.

Ten days it had been in that cupboard. It defied belief she hadn't got wind of it before, the mangy animal wouldn't shut up. I'd practically had to play music twenty-four seven just to cover up the sound of its screeching, the disgusting fleabag. I should have battered it to death when I had the chance, but it was too late for that. All my plans for a grand finale had been laid to waste. I was going to have to find another way to get to Emily, but that would be entertaining in itself. All hope of a memorable climax wasn't lost. Far from it.

Wonder how long it took her to realise how easy it was for me to get into her house. It had probably never occurred to her that I might have taken a copy of the key months ago. Couldn't have or she'd have changed the locks, the paranoid bitch. No more breaking in for me though, but I couldn't have her thinking that just because the stinking cat might turn up alive, she was out of danger.

Shame though. It had been fun, moving things around. Finishing off the leftovers in the fridge, helping myself to tea and cake. Had to hand it to old Dave. His culinary skills had really come on – more so than Clare's anyway, but that wasn't hard. That inept old bag couldn't boil a frankfurter. Maybe I should just sit back and let her do her precious kid in without any intervention on my part. Kill Emily off with a bout of listeria. Dysentery probably, given the state of that house. If she didn't die of heart failure first.

God, to overhear her freaking out about those dumb pictures. What did she think? That anyone was going to want to touch her with a body like that? She was convinced I'd leaked her phone number. As if. I wasn't about to share the pleasure of taunting her with anyone else. How else could I control exactly what she was thinking all of the time, how many texts she got from deranged perverts, how bad the threats were? The degree to which it was doing her head it. And now I had her looking at hardcore porn. Christ, she could have done that when we lived together. How many times had I suggested she open her mind to a bit of experimentation, a roleplay or two? But the sanctimonious prude had refused to take the bait, pretended I was only joking and now look at her. Bet she hadn't seen minges like that since Clare squirted her out of her roomy old tuna taco.

I bet she was secretly getting off on all the men jerking off to her now too, not that she'd ever admit it, but I knew, I'd always known there was a dirty little slut inside of her begging to be let out.

Well, she'd better not be enjoying it too much, that wasn't the point. She needed to know who held the power in our relationship, who controlled who. Thinking she could walk away from me? Not on my watch, babe.

She wasn't quite there yet. She still had a few lessons to learn about respect, but she would. She'd come around and then we'd see who was calling the shots. We'd see who was in charge and if she didn't come round to my way of thinking, I could hardly be blamed for what might happen. I certainly wasn't about to let her walk away from everything we had, that was for sure.

2 Days Before the Murder

Her

The house was crawling with workmen and engineers, wires and cables strewn across the patio and driveway, hanging half-tethered from the brickwork while inside, plaster dust permeated the air, the incessant drilling, the jovial banter that set my teeth on edge forcing us out into the garden. Next door's Jack Russell was scrambling at the fence, its nails grating against it, the penetrating pitch of its constant yapping enough to make me want to scream. To join Ginger under the sofa where he'd hidden at the first sight of burly men in high-visibility jackets heading up the path. Mum decanted her tea tray and passed the mugs around the table.

'Sorry it took so long. I had to make one for all the workmen. There are a lot of them. I hope they're not planning on leaving it all looking like that.'

'I'm sure they'll clean it up,' Gran said. 'You should be pleased. The place needed a hoover.'

Mum pulled off a deadly sidelong glance but refrained from adding comment. We had a visitor after all. DS Lowes took the tea but refused the offer of one of Dad's macaroons and he cleared his throat, appraising the untouched plate with concern. I clenched my jaw and looped my hands between my legs to curb the instinct I suddenly had to lash out and send the ruddy things flying across the lawn.

‘So can we get him for breaking in?’ I said instead. The detective inhaled, gripping her mug handle and rotating it.

‘We’ll have to see what comes back on the forensics report. Hopefully there’ll be some usable prints in amongst the rest of yours and with any luck we’ll be able to catch Connor on camera in the vicinity. We’ve asked your neighbours to check any doorbell or CCTV footage they might have. There’s nothing covering the immediate area but there might be some further up the street. Even if we can’t prove he entered the house, he’s not allowed within a square mile of you so if nothing else, we’ll have him for that.’

‘But he moved the penguin. He’s been through my stuff, loads of times probably. Things have been going missing for a while, being swapped around. We all thought it was Gran.’ Gran blinked rapidly, her head bobbling but Mum shot down any protest with a look that suggested it wouldn’t have been the first time she’d raided the cupboards or borrowed her best frying pan without asking. Gran sank back heavily against the waterproof cushion, air wheezing from the seams, her arms folded. I lifted my eyebrows and grimaced at her, then carried on. ‘It can’t be that hard to prove he put that bloody thing on my bed. None of us did it.’

‘I know, but we still have to physically place him here at the time leading up to the discovery.’

‘Well, have you spoken to him?’ Gran said, perking up. ‘Has he got an alibi?’

‘Says he was at home alone.’

‘There you go then.’

DS Lowes squinted and bared her teeth. ‘It’s not uncommon for people not to be able to prove where they were at any given time, but we still have to put him here, in the house. We're pressing for a warrant to check the GPS on his phone but I doubt he'd be so stupid as to take it with him. He seems savvy enough to leave it behind, at least the one he's got registered under his name. And if he did do it –' We all shot forward, outrage bubbling over but she stilled us with a gesture of acknowledgement. '– I suspect he came by foot. We know his mother took the car to work that day and other than her trip to and from the hospital, there's no record of the licence plate showing up anywhere else.'

Gran leant forward, taking a biscuit and examining it before putting it down again. 'How about all the cameras en route from Linda's place to here. There must be hundreds of houses on the way. Some of them are bound to have filmed him going past. And there's a garage, the BP station. I'm sure it's got CCTV up in the forecourt which must cover the pavement outside, not to mention the cars that would have driven past him. Lots of them are fitted with dashcams these days. He must have got here somehow. Someone will have caught him.'

DS Lowes scratched the underside of her chin and smiled in what Gran would later describe as a patronising manner. 'You're probably right, Bella, but in these sorts of cases where there's been no actual violence or damage, any investigations we carry out are limited by time and our budget. We're thinly stretched at the best of times.'

'You mean we're not a priority,' Mum snapped.

Lowes folded her lips apologetically. 'I will do everything I can to pin this on him, but I have to be honest with you. We need more evidence, more actual physical evidence that he was here, that he's still harassing you, that he posted all the explicit images of you online –' Dad sat up, his back erect and looked away. 'And that he did it intending to cause harm.' Both Gran and Mum took a sharp intake of breath at that, ready to let rip but Lowes put her hand up, fingers splayed, palm exposed. 'I know. I'm just reminding you what we're up against. Without concrete evidence linking him directly to any of these acts, we don't have enough for a warrant to search his residence and any devices he might be using.'

'But, that's ridiculous,' I said finding my voice at last, reedy and pitched against the boring and hammering in the background. 'He did all of that. We know he did. You've seen all the messages he sent me. You know my phone was hacked. It's not me doing any of it, is it?'

'I know, but as far as the CPS is concerned, all we have is a jilted lover who contacted you multiple times following the breakdown of your relationship but has apparently since stopped, we have the police record of your sister illegally entering Connor's apartment –'

'To get my stuff back!'

Lowes sloped her forehead meaningfully. 'Followed by accusations by you of stalking and coercive control, which I have no doubt are true, but the timing could be interpreted as retaliation for getting Olivia arrested.'

'My God,' Dad muttered under his breath, seizing a macaroon and lobbing it at a woodpigeon. Even Mum looked startled and she hated woodpigeons. Couldn't forgive them for polishing off the seed whenever she tried to fix the bald patches in the grass but she drew the line at culling the wildlife in front of guests.

‘You’ve got the texts. You’ve got the photos, the videos,’ Dad said, his confidence shaking as he hit the last word.

‘They’ve only got the earlier texts,’ Gran announced triumphantly before Lowes could explain. ‘Don’t forget he says his phone was stolen and someone else has been doing all that since then.’

‘This is farcical.’ Dad pushed his chair back and stood, fingers pressed against the glass-topped table, their tips flattened and violet.

‘You’re right, you’re right,’ Lowes said placatingly, her smile grim. ‘That’s not to say we won’t get him, just that right now we need a stronger case to prove he’s behind all of it. But who knows, maybe he’s overplayed his hand with the break in. Just because he’s been able to cover his tracks so far, technology-wise, maybe he’s slipped up this time. Of course, he has been to your house multiple times so if we do find his finger prints on anything, it’ll have to be on something that wasn’t present on any of his previous visits or it won’t get past the judge.’

‘So,’ Dad continued, red in the face. ‘We can’t prove he broke into the house without CCTV footage – which you’re not going to track down because of money –’

‘A lack of resources, yes, I’m afraid so.’

‘We can’t prove he sent hundreds of vile messages and threats to Emily’s phone because he says it was stolen, which is absolute rubbish, and we can’t prove he posted the sex tapes and photographs because he’s using a VPN to disguise his IP address. Is that right? Have I missed anything? Are there any other ways he’s able to get away with destroying our lives that I’ve missed out?’

Mum pressed her hand against Dad's shoulder and guided him down towards the seat, patting him on the back as he lowered himself reluctantly, his mouth a thin line, his spine straight.

'He's also giving out her number to the scum who look at that stuff,' she continued passively, 'though I'll guarantee he's behind some of those threats to do God knows what to her. He's just hiding his identity. I might not be a police officer, but even I can deduce that.'

'I'm sorry. I assure you that we're doing all we can.'

'And you'll forgive us,' Gran said, 'if we don't agree.'

Lowes looked down at her mug, made as if to lift it but changed her mind, tilting it towards herself. 'The good news is, you're all doing exactly what you should be. Keeping notes of any incidents, changing the locks, installing alarms and CCTV.' She waved her hand towards the two men fitting cameras to the back wall and nodded. 'We will get him. He'll slip up. They always do.'

'And if he doesn't?'

She didn't answer, not directly. She looked straight at me. 'I hope you know you're doing really well with all of this,' she said. 'You should be proud of yourself. A lot of people wouldn't be able to take it on. I just need you to hang in there and I promise you, I promise you, I will keep pushing this until we get the breakthrough we need.'

Her face crinkled suddenly as an overpowering stench wafted across the garden. I buried my nostrils between a web of fingers.

'Sorry to interrupt.' One of the workmen was striding towards us, his arm stretched in front of his barrelled torso, a decomposing fox dangling from two fingers, his pinkie distended as though the matted tail was a bone china teacup. Next door's dog lost it completely and started barking and smashing himself against the fence so hard the boards were splintering. 'Found this down the side of the house. What do you want me to do with it?'

'Urghh.' Mum covered her face with her jumper and nudged Dad frantically. 'David.'

Dad rose reluctantly to his feet, one hand back on the table, the other playing for time on the top of his chair. 'I'll – I'll get a bag for it. I suppose…'

We all turned to DS Lowes but her eyes widened above her cupped hand and she shrugged. 'I don't know, sorry, that's not something they…'

'Of course they don't.' Dad pushed his chair back, took the fox from the workman with a look of disgust and disappeared into the shed with it, appearing moments later with a refuse bag he took great pains to shake out as loudly as possible. Then after several failed attempts at stuffing the corpse inside, he finally managed to get it in, tie a triple knot and stride off pointedly in the direction of the bin to the tune of the dog yapping and jumping alongside him all the way down the length of next door's garden.

'Sorry about that,' Mum murmured, lowering her jumper but not daring to open more than the side of her mouth.

'Not at all,' DS Lowes said. 'Look, I know this is hard, but try to stay strong. I'll let you know if we get any leads on the forensics. In the meantime –' I rolled my eyes. 'Keep your cameras on. If he comes back, we'll have him for breaching the restraining order and that might be enough to get a warrant to search his place and gather the evidence we need to get him off the streets.'

We all started to stand, but she batted her hand. 'Don't worry. I'll see myself out.' She slid out from behind the table and adjusted her jacket, brushing herself down as though attempting to wipe the stench of fox out of her clothes. Then with a tight professional smile she headed off, returning Dad's curt nod with her own as he stepped out of the French doors, flapping water off his hands the way a dog shakes itself dry.

'Well, that was a waste of time,' he said, flopping back onto his seat. 'What do we actually pay these numskulls for? Not enough evidence? Oh, for Christ's sake. Who's done that to the fence?' He was up again and pawing over the split wooden board as though someone had scratched his Ferrari.

'Leave it, David. Come and sit down.'

'I need to sort this out. No one else is going to do it, are they?'

Mum fixed him with a cold stare and crossed her arms. I patted the chair besides me. 'It can wait until tomorrow, Dad. Please just come and sit down with us.'

He dragged himself away from the fence and slumped down again and we stayed there going over and over the same old complaints and theories for the next hour or so until the home security people called us inside to run through the basics and explain how to download the app onto our phones.

'It is very clever,' Mum said after they'd left but no one answered. We were all too busy staring at the live stream, the empty dining room, the empty kitchen, the empty hallway, the empty garden.

'Oh, for goodness' sake,' Dad yelled, leaping up from his armchair. Ginger flew off his lap with a hiss and rocketed back to his safe spot under the sofa. Mum tutted. ‘That bloody dog’s coming through the fence.’

He stormed out and we all huddled together instinctively following the events on our phone screens, watching him marching out of the back doors, an eighteen-rated sound track accompanying the video footage of the dog running rings around him, barking and darting back and forth, stealing bites from something under the bushes.

‘That’ll be the macaroon your dad threw over there earlier, I expect,’ Mum said.

‘Or the woodpigeon.’

Gran winked and nudged me. ‘Wouldn’t trust my teeth on either of them.’

‘Aww. Don’t be mean,’ I said lightly. ‘He’s trying.’

‘He is very trying,’ she and Mum said in unison and for a moment we all lost ourselves in laughter. In normality. In the hope that we’d built an impenetrable wall around ourselves.

Gran wiped a tear from her eye. ‘What’s happening now?’

‘Ermm.’ Dad was on his knees, crouching over the dog. ‘I don’t – it… looks… like… he’s…’

‘Oh, God. He hasn’t hurt it, has he?’

We scrambled up and raced towards the back garden, our feet slipping and sliding across the wooden floors, Gran trailing behind.

‘Dad!’

‘Somebody call a vet.’

I sprinted over to him bent over in the faded light and skidded to a halt. ‘What’s happened? What have you done?’

The dog was lying on its side, convulsing and foaming at the mouth.

'Call a vet. Get Mike and Janet over here.'

'But –'

'Now.'

I spun around, smacking into Mum.

'David?' She stared over my shoulder at him, horrified and I turned back. The dog was lying still now, stiff like a Victorian exhibit in a museum. I sank down onto my knees, the damp grass soaking through my jeans, almost but not quite touching its small head, its bared teeth. Gran's bracelets jangled as she slid her arm through Mum's and rested her weight against her. 'It wasn't one of your biscuits that did this, is it?'

Dad glared at her. 'It found something under the hyacinth. Some kind of meat. Don't let the cat out until we're sure we've picked it all up.'

'Some kind of meat?' Mum said. 'It must have been laced with something. Look at that thing. It's been poisoned.'

'Well,' Gran said. 'Guess we can safely say, we've got proof someone's been trying to hurt Ginger after all. Let them try to palm us off with excuses now.'

I looked up at her and then down to the body on the ground, the adrenalin draining from me replaced by dread, but the others began to nod, very subtly but their eyes sparkled with relief. Excitement they tried to hide with moral outrage, but Gran was right. This had to be it. This had to be the stroke of luck, DS Lowes needed. The slip up that would send the rest of Connor's dominoes crashing to the ground.

And it was all caught on camera this time.

The Day Before the Murder

Her Mum

The sun was beating down above and I wished I hadn't worn my kagool but you never can tell how the day's going to turn out. I hadn't put the washing out either which was yet another indication that I needed to get my wits about me. We only had one chance to complete our mission or we'd risk raising suspicion. One chance and it had to be now. Bella had seen Connor arrive at the gym just as she was leaving that ridiculous class of hers. Honestly, Chair-obics. Who comes up with these things? She got more exercise sprinting over to our house uninvited every time she guessed the oven timer was about to ping.

'Remind me again why we couldn't bring the car,' David grumbled, undoing the top button on his shirt and letting his jacket flap open.

'Because we want it to look like we're in if he decides to pay a visit to the house. I'm not happy about leaving Emily alone, anything could happen. We all know what he's capable of.' I turned on my heels. Bella was hoicking up the enormous handbag she'd insisted on bringing even though it was far too fancy for her outfit and kept sliding down her shoulder. 'Are you managing, Mother? Let me know if you need to stop.'

'Don't worry about me. I could outrun both of you.' That might have been true once but these last few months hadn't been kind to her. I slackened my pace and the tempo of our heels clicking on the pavement slowed.

'I can't believe we're having to do this, I really can't. If this was a teledrama, I'd have turned off ages ago,' I said.

'It does seem very Channel Five,' Bella agreed and she would know. She'd watch anything.

David wrenched off his jacket and folded it over his forearm and I thought better of pointing out the long strip of sweat on the back of his shirt and the patches staining his underarms. He'd only insist on going back to change and time was of the essence.

'I still don't understand why they haven't banged that maniac up already,' he said repeating himself, but then we all were. It was all we talked about these days. 'What more do they want? Blood on his hands? It'll be on theirs if they don't do something about him soon.'

'It's like the detective said, David. There's lots of compelling evidence against him but it's all circumstantial.'

'But what does that mean, *circumstantial*? Anyone would be a fool not to realise who's behind all of this. It's common sense.'

'But there's nothing actually linking him to any of the individual crimes other than Emily and while we know he's the only one with an axe to grind against her, there's still no irrefutable proof it isn't someone else or that he's definitely doing it all.'

'There was a dead dog in our garden. What more do they want? They've got CCTV of the ruddy mutt in its death throes.'

And David looking less than athletic chasing after the thing which he wasn't best pleased about but there's no law against letting yourself go. Fortunately, or he'd be sent down long before they ever locked up the lunatic.

‘I don’t think anyone’s disputing Rusty was poisoned, David.’ He was Rusty now in deference, instead of *that damn dog*. It didn’t seem right speaking ill of the dead. ‘But we’ve gone through all the footage from that afternoon and Connor’s not on it.’

Bella wagged a finger. If she’d had a monocle, she’d have been milking it for all it was worth. ‘I think he left whatever it ate there the day before – at the same time as he broke in. For some reason, he brought the cat back and left the murder weapon in plain sight for Ginger to find. He must have wanted us to see what he could do. Classic power move.’

The building on the left looked familiar, but I doublechecked the address. All these places looked the same, but I was wrong to doubt myself. *Confidence, Clare*, I thought sternly, pointing to the main entrance and heading towards it with, I must admit, a degree of trepidation. I pressed the buzzer and David held the door open for us when it clicked. What had my mother been saying about the cat? Oh, yes.

I shouted in her good ear, ‘He must not have been banking on the poor thing being too traumatised to go out.’

I’d had to get the emergency litter tray out of the garage. Hopefully that was just a stage. It only felt like yesterday that I was changing the girls’ nappies and I’d be doing my mother’s soon enough. I could do without having to clean up after the cat as well.

‘And it would explain the fox.’ Bella’s voice was echoey in the large, faceless hallway, and breathless though she refused to slow down. ‘The pathologist will be able to tell us, but I’d estimate, with the heat and humidity over those two days and the state of decomposition, it probably died a good twenty-four hours before we found it.'

'They're not going to conduct an autopsy on a fox, Mother. They don't even have the budget to investigate real crimes. We're small fry as far as they're concerned. This is nothing but a domestic. If we want to send Connor down for any of this, it's going to be up to us to find the evidence.'

Which was why we were at that very moment hauling ourselves up the stairs to Linda's first floor flat, not because the lift wasn't working – it was far too nice a complex for that – but because I remembered it had a camera we were hoping to avoid. Of course, it transpired there was one on the stairwell as well but it was too late to turn back by that point. We were halfway up and fully committed to our task.

'Pop your jacket back on, love,' I said to David as we staggered down the corridor but I had no time to explain before Linda popped her head out and waved at us from the doorway.

Her smile wasn't altogether comfortable and she said, 'Well, this is a lovely surprise,' even though I'd told her we were coming, albeit only fifteen minutes before. 'Come in, come in.'

She saw us straight through to the living room without insisting we take our shoes off. I expect she felt we might think it a bit of a liberty given the circumstances, but I wouldn't have minded. There'd have been less of a trace of us, though I don't suppose it mattered, what with Linda being a witness and all.

The living space was small, but pleasant enough, sparsely furnished and decorated floor to ceiling in Laura Ashley. Not an IKEA storage box to be seen. I managed to catch David's eye and indicate towards his armpits but he did nothing about it other than rearrange his jacket on the back of a chair and produce a silver block of macaroons from his pocket.

'Oh, for Goodness' sake, David,' I said. 'What have you brought those for?'

'What?' He was perfectly affronted as though we hadn't agreed we'd bring the box of marzipan fruits that nobody wanted. 'This is the first lot that came out perfectly. I thought we could have one with a cup of tea.'

'I don't mean to be rude, love, but I did tell you what I'd do if I ever saw another macaroon again.'

'Well,' David blustered as if I was being unreasonable by withdrawing my services as the resident Guinea pig after five failed batches in so many days. 'They're for Linda really.'

'Linda's allergic to nuts, David. You know this.' He was going to pretend this was complete news to him despite banging on about it at Christmas but Linda kindly interrupted and said it was the thought that counted. David apologised and laid them down on the coffee table, their foil fortress unscathed so as to prevent even a fleck of almond making its way into the air. Even my mother didn't make a move towards them.

'Sorry for landing ourselves on you without much warning,' I said, sticking to the script. 'We just wanted to make sure you knew there were no hard feelings.'

'Oh,' Linda said, blushing and seemingly lost for words.

'Connor not in?' Bella asked in a hammy stage voice that would give us away if she wasn't careful.

'No, he's popped out for a bit. Did you want to speak to him?'

'No, no. It's you we've come to see,' I said regretting not having formulated more of a backstory to our sudden intrusion and Linda shuffled in the awkward silence and said, 'I'll put the kettle on then, shall I?' Which put Plan A back on track.

Bella and I followed her into the kitchen, which was harder than it sounds given the size of it.

'Alright to use your facilities?' David shouted already halfway down the hall.

'Of course. First on the left.' But I'd already told him he needed to head for the second on the right.

'Lovely place you've got here,' Bella said, squeezing up against me and bowing as Linda reached past apologetically, cracking the cupboard door open as far as she could without hitting her and sliding out a box of Asda's own brand tea, which surprised me. I'd always taken her for a Twinings sort of advocate, but it seemed hard times were hitting us all.

'Thank you. It's small but we manage.' The water boiled and she busied herself with the teabags, but her hands shook and she sprinkled sugar all over the worktop, despite me saying none of us wanted any. 'Was there something in particular you wanted to talk about?'

Bella and I looked at each other. 'We just wanted to check in,' I said lightly.

'See how you were doing.'

'I should be asking you that, Bella. How are you feeling about this latest round of treatment? Any side-effects?'

'Oh, just the usual. Nausea, bloating, headaches. My nails have gone black and I look like a bald eagle up top but there's nothing to speak of.' She tapped her wig with an immaculately painted fingernail and laughed self-depreciatingly. Linda's mouth crumpled sympathetically and she rubbed Bella's arm before twisting away to reach for the mugs. I nudged my mother and bulged my eyeballs at her. We needed more time.

'Have I shown you my new head of hair?' she said hurriedly, fiddling with her sprightly white curls and slipping the netting off. Her scalp was a raw patchwork of dried scabs and tufts of light down. She looked like a plucked chicken and I almost slipped out of character. It was the first time she'd let me see her without her war paint, as it were and she no longer looked invincible. She was frail and vulnerable, a bent daffodil, dry and browning in the last days of spring. I nearly forgot why we were there. I snapped to my senses just as Linda was suggesting an antiseptic cream for her head.

'I've got some in my bedroom,' she said, lowering her mug and the clink as it made contact with the granite worktop made me jump.

'Don't worry,' I shrieked, startling us all. 'I've got some at home. You should have told me, Mum. I didn't realise you were suffering.'

But of course, I knew she was suffering. She was in constant discomfort, if not pain, but she wasn't one to complain. And she certainly wasn't one to let anyone see her looking less than well turned-out. I knew what a sacrifice exposing herself like this was and took her hand. Which was a mistake.

Linda had picked up two mugs and swanned into the living room before I had another chance to distract her. There was a direct view of the hallway from there and no way David would be able to slip out of Connor's room unnoticed, but I needn't have worried. He was sitting in an armchair without a care in the world, looking to all intents and purposes like he'd just woken up from a nap.

I glared at him questioningly and he made some sort of rotating gesture which could have been anything, but apparently meant Connor had fixed a locked bolt to his door so he was unable to get in and investigate. I wasn't best pleased and it certainly made for an awkward twenty minutes of chit-chat, but if we couldn't uncover any incriminating evidence against him in his room, we had no choice but to rinse Linda for clues, without her realising, of course.

'Did you hear, our cat turned up?' I said like I was commenting on the weather.

She jolted. 'I didn't know he was missing.'

'Yes, nearly a fortnight but then he turned up a few days ago looking like he'd been dragged out of a drain hole.'

'Maybe he was,' she said, downing her tea.

'I think I will have some sugar,' Bella said with only a few mouthfuls to go and Linda made to rise, but my mother bolted past, taking her handbag with her. 'Don't worry. I'll get it, dear.'

Linda shifted uncomfortably, not quite knowing what to do with herself, but Bella bustled into the kitchen while I picked up on my cue and launched into an animated version of Ginger's homecoming at a volume designed to drown out the banging of cupboard doors and sliding of drawers. I'd only just got to the part about David struggling to get near the dog when she interrupted and shouted, 'Are you okay in there, Bella? Do you need some help finding it?'

My mother appeared in the doorway, empty-handed. 'Just looking for a biscuit,' she chirped, 'but not to worry. We should probably get going now. Leave you to it.' She stared at me pointedly and strode towards the front door.

'Oh.' Linda scrambled to her feet as David and I rose simultaneously and followed suit, the both of us only just remembering to grab his jacket from the back of the chair.

'Well, this has been lovely,' I said hurriedly planting a kiss on Linda's cheek and chivvying David into the corridor. 'You must come to us next time.'

'Yes –' she said sounding distinctly spooked, her hand on the doorlatch as if she didn't know what else to do with it. "Well, thank you for coming.'

Bella beckoned to me urgently and even David was charging towards the stairwell like a hamster on a wheel. I turned, waving one last time before I swung out of view and joined the others on the landing above where we huddled, motionless until we heard the lift ping and open, followed by a series of loud, clumping footsteps and finally the muffled bang of Linda's front door. Made you wonder what the point of going to the gym was if the psychopath wasn't going to bother using stairs.

We put our fingers to our lips and crept down all two flights of steps, only daring to make any noise once we were out on the pavement.

'That was close,' Bella gasped, her eyes twinkling. 'Lucky I saw him heading back.'

'I'll say.'

'Wonder if Linda will tell him we popped in.'

'Probably. Did you pick up the macaroons?'

David patted himself down. 'No. Oh, that's annoying.'

‘Well, we’re not going back for them now.’

‘No,’ he said, surprisingly agreeably. I’d been braced for a fight but he was strangely jovial. ‘Let’s get out of here. I feel like I need to hose myself down after that.’

Judging by the state of his back that wasn’t a bad idea and despite enjoying a nice cup of tea, the whole afternoon had been a complete waste of time. We hadn’t gathered any useful intel, David had failed to even get into the bedroom, let alone discover a stash of burner phones or a scrapbook of chilling snap shots of Emily with her eyes scratched out and quite what Bella had expected to uncover in the kitchen was anyone’s guess.

But at least we hadn’t been caught in the act. I must say, as much as I fantasised about running him over in the car, the thought of facing him in the flesh sent a shiver down my spine. He was a man who wouldn’t stop until he got what he wanted, but what he didn’t realise was, neither would we.

The Day Before the Murder

Him

Those pathetic freaks. What were they hoping to achieve by snooping through my stuff behind my back? What were they even looking for? A half-empty packet of rat poison? As if I'd be stupid enough to leave it lying around. Still, it was a good job I'd taken the precaution of putting a lock on my door, although I've got to admit, that was just to keep the old lady out. Didn't occur to me the out-laws would be dropping by too.

My idiot mother tried to deny it at first, but their mugs were still warm on the worktop. She hadn't even had a chance to wash them out and I watched the three of them exit the main doors down below, giggling with excitement, the wankers.

Must have made their day playing cops and robbers. Only I was no robber. I could break into their house, all right, but the last thing I wanted was to steal anything. No, I had other plans now. I was sick of trying to reason with their bitch kid. She'd had her chance, but instead of apologising and begging me to take her back she'd reported me again, this time for what happened to the mangy dog next door as if they weren't all secretly pleased about it.

If anyone should have been pissed off, it was me. That burger was meant for their beloved moggy and now I had the police breathing down my neck again, threatening to get a warrant to trace all my online activity. As if I wouldn't know how to cover my tracks. I told them to go ahead, but if they had anything concrete against me, I'd have been downstairs in a cell by then. But they didn't. I was better than them.

If they had any sort of case against me at all, they might have been able to force my VPN provider to hand over my usage and connection logs. Then they'd have plenty to use against me and not just regarding the porn I'd made available online. They'd find all sorts of searches related to chloroform and sulphuric acid too. How to make a body disappear. Everything they needed to get me put away but they had nothing. A handful of outlandish suspicions they had no way of proving. No way of connecting me to anything I'd done.

It had been fun while it lasted but I was bored now. That slag had screwed me over, I was neck-deep in debt with loan sharks blowing up my mobile and hanging around outside, I'd been kicked out of King's for coming to blows with that loser, Collins, who was only going to fail me anyway and so now Microsoft had washed their hands of me too.

I had nothing to look forward to except what I was going to do to get even with the slut who'd done this to me. I hadn't decided whether I was going to maim her so badly I'd never have to see her smug smile again, inflict so-called life-changing injuries on her as it were, or just get it over with in one go. I was leaning towards both.

The way I saw it, I could throw a cup of acid at her, do a few years, less for holding my hands up to it straight away and for good behaviour. Then after following her journey through countless operations, her agony every time they stitched another skin graft onto her ugly face – once she'd come to terms with her hideous injuries and started getting cocky about surviving, that was when I'd finish it. Slowly and with attention to detail, burning the sight of her begging me to stop into my memory to replay wherever I was and whenever I wanted.

Or maybe I'd just get it over and done with right now. Quick and efficient. Maybe take the rest of those interfering, judgemental fuckers out too. They deserved it, although it'd probably be worse for them to find the body, or if I made it disappear, they'd go to their graves never knowing what had happened to their precious little girl.

I didn't know. There was a lot to consider. It all sounded pretty good. One thing was for sure though, the way they were honing in on me. Whatever I decided, I had to act on it soon or I might not get the opportunity again for years.

The Day of the Murder

Her Mum

Hours had passed and I lay in my bed with the curtains closed, torturing myself with the images that were never far from my mind. Emily's lifeless body, limp and mutilated in a pool of her own blood, her disembowelled torso sprawled like a blanket across her grandmother's cold corpse.

I repeated the version of events I'd dissected hundreds, if not thousands of times, namely that at the time of her death, my daughter had four injunction orders out against the man who killed her. The third emergency call she'd made that day recorded the murder and what with that and the forensic evidence left at the scene, the police were able to piece together the timeline – how Connor had broken through the backdoor while David and I were at work, how my mother, slight and racked with cancer, had tried to protect Emily, had thrown herself in front of her at the first sign of a struggle.

She'd died first. One stab wound to the neck, not an instant death. She'd have been alive long enough to witness the attack on Milly. Heard the screams as the knife entered her body twenty-six times, from behind mainly as she cowered over Bella's frail frame, shielding her from any further blows. To no avail.

My poor mother. I didn't know why I kept dragging her into it but that was what I saw every time I closed my eyes – that or a variation of it. Sometimes he stabbed Emily, sometimes he slit her throat, sometimes he strangled her against the wall. Sometimes she was alone and other times, one of us was caught in the crossfire like countless other murders that had gone before, months or years after the threat of harm had been reported. After harassment warning notices and restraining orders had been placed – pointlessly – the efforts of the police futile within a system that did little to protect the safety of victims until the crime was worthy of investigation – murder being, in the most part, hard to ignore.

Things had got worse since the incident with the dog, which was a shame because honestly, if he'd left it at that, I wouldn't really have minded. It was a horrible creature truth be told but of course, it didn't deserve to die, nice though it was to be able to sit in the garden now without being heckled.

Unfortunately, since then the madman seemed to have thrown all caution to the wind. Whereas before he'd been covering his tracks and harassing Emily from the shadows as it were, now he was fully exposed, reckless even.

He'd reverted to turning up at the house at all hours, taking photographs and staring at the windows with complete disregard for the CCTV cameras zooming in on him, their lights flashing. The good news was that now the police had everything they needed to prosecute him for breaking the harassment orders, but he didn't care. No matter how many times they cautioned him, he continued to flaunt their instructions to stay away.

A court case against him was inevitable now we had the incontrovertible evidence we needed to prove he was knowingly stalking Emily. He'd serve time – not enough – but they would get him for that if nothing else, but instead of making us feel better, his reckless behaviour and lack of constraint was even more sinister than when he'd been hiding behind fake social media accounts and unknown numbers, abusing her from afar. Now, he was destabilised, disinhibited and deranged. And he was out wandering the streets without the slightest concern for his own future, which only made me fear for Emily's all the more.

It was enough to keep me awake at night, every night. We'd all lost weight. We lived in constant dread of his next dastardly move. Emily still hadn't been able to face going back to the office, both David and I had used up our annual leave ensuring she was barely alone in the house and Olive was back from Exeter more time than she was there. Thank goodness for online learning, that was all I could say, but university wasn't just about that. It was about the experience, dipping your toes into the shallows of adulthood and God knew what else if Olive had her way, but he was ruining it for her. He was ruining all of us, not just Emily although, ultimately, she was paying the greatest price for me letting him into our lives.

Maybe if I hadn't insisted on the kids getting to know each other all those years ago, just so that I could decompress with a friend and colleague sometimes. Share a laugh and a gossip over a glass of wine with a grown up once in a while. And by doing so I'd invited a vampire over the threshold. A parasite who would bleed us all dry. On and on until he took things so far, even the law couldn't protect him.

But until then I had to contend with my stomach lurching every time the telephone rang. Every time the doorbell went which was exactly what it did just then and true to form, a wave of nausea flooded over me.

I leapt to my feet and staggered down the stairs gripping the banister, my head woozy with exhaustion, stale air trapped on my lungs until I was able to breathe again.

'Who's there?' I called to the blurry silhouette in the obscured glass, my fingers tensed on the door chain.

'It's Detective Lowes. Could you open the door?' Her voice was familiar but there was something restrained about it. Something that made my blood run cold.

I released the chain, unlocked the Chubb lock, both bolts and the latch and drew the door handle slowly inwards. DS Lowes turned, unsmiling and I knew, I just knew that this was the moment she was about to tell me something terrible had happened. That whatever she was here for, life would never be the same again.

The Day of the Murder

Her

I heard the bell but didn't make a move to answer the door. I stayed in bed, the lights off, the curtains closed, curled in the foetal position, head bowed under my duvet, rigid and consumed by the stench of my own sweat and fear. I was a statue carved from flesh and bone, but inside terror gripped my chest, squeezed my heart and swirled in my empty stomach. I'd thought things would get better once Connor had been dealt with but I was no less anxious than before.

The door cracked open and the sunlight drenching my bedroom crept into my cocoon, but I ignored it.

'Emily,' Mum hissed padding over and shaking my shoulder gently. 'Emily, the police are here. Something's happened. Put this on quickly and come downstairs.' The weight of her old dressing gown pressed lightly upon my thigh and I opened my eyes, the blood draining from my limbs. She peeled the cover off my head and stroked my face.

'Come on,' she said. 'You can do it. I've got you.'

By the time we got back downstairs, DS Lowes had taken a seat in the living room but she stood up as soon as we walked in.

'Can I get you anything?' Mum said out of habit and I longed for the detective to say yes, to delay the next link in the chain of events, but she shook her head and spread her hand towards the sofa.

‘Please,’ she said. ‘Take a seat, both of you. Is anyone else in?’

‘David’s at work and Olive’s out somewhere. Wait –’ Mum’s face paled and her nails dug into my arm. ‘It’s not… nothing’s –’

‘No, no. They’re both fine.’ Lowes held her palm up reassuringly, then with a streak of uncertainty that clouded her eyes, she added, ‘At least as far as we know. I’m here about Connor McGann.’

I flinched at the sound of his name and kept my eyes scrunched shut tightly as though expecting a punch. When I opened them, the detective was staring at me.

‘As you may already know,’ she said, ‘he was found in a state of collapse not far from his residence at around seven am this morning.’

She studied us, our lack of emotion, drawing out the tension like a thespian in a scene. When neither of us spoke, she filled the silence.

‘He was pronounced dead in the ambulance on the way to the hospital.’

My head snapped back.

‘Dead?’ Mum clutched my hand in both of hers. ‘As in… dead?’

‘Yes, as in dead. No longer with us.’

I felt Mum’s eyes seeking out mine but I stared straight ahead, my skin burning, white noise rushing in my ears.

‘And was he…?’ Her voice trailed off as DS Lowes took a pen and notepad from her bag.

‘We won’t know until we’ve had the results of the post-mortem but for the moment, it is being treated as a suspicious death. I’m here as a courtesy because of our ongoing relationship but the

Homicide Investigation Team will also want to speak to anyone who had a reason to wish him harm.'

'I doubt they've got the manpower,' Mum cried, dragging my hand onto her lap and rubbing it. 'It'll be quicker to talk to anyone who didn't want to see him dead.'

'Mum.' I came round at last and pressed my free hand on top of hers, shutting her down.

'I know this has probably come as a shock to you both,' Lowes said as if that was the last thing she thought. 'But we'll need you to come in and make statements regarding your whereabouts over the course of the twelve hours or so proceeding Mr McGann's death.'

'Oh, it's Mr McGann now, is it?' Mum said and DS Lowes opened up her notepad and clicked her pen against the first fresh page. Mum rose to her feet. 'I must say, you're quite spoiling this. We should be celebrating. He's dead. That is what you said, isn't it? The madman who has been making our lives a misery is dead?'

Lowes nodded, crossing and uncrossing her ankles, careful not to give away her own feelings regarding the latest developments in her ever-evolving case. Mum strode across the room.

'I need to call David. He'll be thrilled.'

'I'd rather you waited until after you've answered some questions, if you don't mind. It's just a formality, I'm sure.' Her eyes darted between us both the way my mum's did when she was trying to catch me and Olive out in a lie. This wasn't the same detective we'd met before. This one didn't have us pegged for victims.

'You're not under arrest, of course, but it would be useful to eliminate you from our inquiries. So, let's start with a brief outline of your movements between, say, yesterday morning and the early hours of today?' She framed her sentence like a question, when we all knew it was a demand.

The room suddenly seemed to be closing in on me. My head was spinning, my breath catching in my throat, her focus on me triggering an overwhelming surge of guilt even though I had nothing to feel guilty about. Connor deserved to die a hundred times for what he did to me.

'Emily?'

'She was here at home with Olivia and Florence all evening. She hasn't left the house in days.'

'And you, Clare? Can you account for your whereabouts last night and this morning?'

'We had tickets for a show. The Theatre Royal. We booked it months ago, before all of this and the girls insisted we go, but we spent the whole time looking over our shoulders. Hated every minute of it. Now, if it had been tonight, I might have enjoyed it. That's bad timing for you.'

DS Lowes glanced up. 'We, as in…'

'David and I.'

She looked back at me, her head slanted, her eyes delving beyond the thin shell sheltering my reactions. I shifted under her scrutiny, my cheeks hot, temples throbbing. She nodded casually. 'So Emily and Olivia were alone then. We'll be able to check that on your CCTV footage, of course.'

'Yes, check away. They've got a concrete alibi. Or a virtual one. Would it be virtual?'

'Actually,' I paused, my knuckle worrying the corner of my mouth as I considered the best way to phrase what I was about to say. 'Olive and Flo went out.' Mum looked at me strangely. 'Flo came over for a bit and then they left for a few hours. I said it was okay.'

Mum spun around as though I'd said we'd held an orgy with fifty or so of our closest friends. But it was the opposite.

'So, you were here in the house on your own all evening?' she gasped.

'It was fine, Mum.'

'No wonder you haven't got out of bed all day. Honestly, your sister.' She tutted, taking a cushion and plumping it on her lap.

'It isn't her job to babysit me, Mum. Besides they were here before you and Dad got back. We just didn't mention it because we knew you'd get mad.'

'I'm not mad I'm just… Well. I don't suppose it matters now, does it? We don't have to worry about that anymore. I do wish I could tell someone.' She fidgeted impatiently like a child waiting to open a present on Christmas Day.

'This will only take a few more minutes, Clare. I just need to double check – you're saying you were home alone all evening, Emily, but Olivia and Florence went out for a bit.'

I coughed. 'Yes.'

'At approximately what time?'

'Um, not long after Mum and Dad. Six thirtyish? Seven? It'll be on the CCTV.'

'And did you see what time they got home?'

'Maybe ten? I'd have to check.'

'The CCTV, yes, you said.' She held my gaze until I broke away from her surveillance.

'What does yesterday have to do with anything if he died this morning?' Mum interrupted, rupturing the tension that had been building in the air.

DS Lowes spoke carefully. 'Until we know the cause of death or how long he'd been lying there, we have to explore every avenue. His mother didn't hear him come in last night or leave this morning. It's possible he wasn't discovered for some time.'

My stomach heaved. An image of him lying on the cold hard ground flashed through my mind. Mum's hand went to her chest.

'Oh, dear, Linda. I should probably give her a ring, see if she's okay.'

'As I said, we're nearly done here.' Lowes paused allowing the pressure to build, her eyes concentrating on mine. It was as if she could see right through me. Read the thoughts I'd swallowed a million times, the longing I'd been consumed by, the desire to see Connor dead, but now he actually was, my nerves were failing me. The adrenalin I'd been living off for weeks dwindling to dregs.

'So other than yourselves, can you think of anyone who might have had a grudge against Mr McGann? Perhaps from before your separation?'

'I...'

'Have you tried everyone he's ever had contact with? The man was a narcissistic bullying leech. You could probably throw a stone and hit someone with good reason to kill him.' Mum narrowed her eyes and gripped the cushion on her lap. 'I hope you don't think any of us had anything to do with his death.'

'As I said, the murder squad will be looking into the movements of anyone who had reason to cause him harm,' she said not answering the question. 'And we will need to access your home security cameras.'

'You think he was here?' Mum sat up, instinctively panicked.

'We don't know what happened as of yet, but please keep in mind that while I sympathise with everything that's happened, we can easily get a warrant if you refuse to cooperate with the investigation.'

'Who said anything about not cooperating? I wish we could take credit for this, but none of us have anything to hide.'

DS Lowes looked at me again, her pen poised. 'Is that right, Emily? Now would be the time to say, that's all.'

I focused on the sharp cracks that resonated around the back of my eyes whenever I blinked. She continued to stare at me, a half-smile of encouragement distorting her mouth.

'It was me.' Gran appeared in the room as if out of nowhere, smashing the tension with an elegant flick of her fingers. 'I did it and that's all I'm going to say. Don't ask me how it happened. I'm not telling you a thing about it or it'll ruin my plea. I'll be going for manslaughter by diminished responsibility.' She tapped the side of her head. 'Because of the dementia and all the pain relief I'm on.'

'Mum! What are you doing?'

Gran strode over to DS Lowes, her wrists pressed against each other, her arms stretched out. 'I get very confused sometimes. Can't be held accountable for my actions but I did it. Take me in and let's get this whole damn witch hunt over with.'

Detective Lowes looked Bella up and down sceptically, her mouth hanging open as she tried to form a response. As she took in my grandmother's diminished height, the wasted muscles and loose skin, the yellowish tint of her pallor.

'I put something in one of those ghastly protein shakes he was always drinking at the gym. Yesterday, when we went to his flat. Linda will tell you – I was in the kitchen alone for several minutes, but that's all I'm going to say.'

Mum and I froze, our spines straight, our hands clasped unconsciously mid-air, jaws agape, our hearts in our throats. DS Lowes angled away from us dubiously. Gran took a step towards her, lifting her arms in compliance, awaiting the handcuffs that would snap us all back to attention.

'Or did I stab him? Or hit him over the head? I can't remember, it's the drugs. Take me in and let's see what my lawyer has to say about it.'

'Gran, what are you doing?' I said finally finding my voice as Mum and I leapt to our feet, our fingers still tangled around one another's.

'It's alright, dear.' Gran smiled at me lovingly, warmth radiating across the room, her eyes sparkling. 'This is just the way it's got to be. I couldn't let him hurt you anymore.'

'Mum –' My mum launched towards Gran but DS Lowes stepped in between them, blocking any contact like a referee in a fight.

'Go on, ask Linda,' Gran urged, her neck stretching proudly in defiance of the uncertainty registered on the detective's face. 'I had every opportunity and I'd do it again.'

'Bella Brown,' Lowes said warily, stepping forward. 'I'm arresting you on suspicion of the murder of Connor McGann. You do not have to say anything –'

'Mother, for Goodness' sake.'

' – but it may harm your defence if you do not mention when questioned something which you later rely on in court.' The caution continued but the sound of her voice was a blur, the words raining down on us, gunfire.

'This is ridiculous.' Mum flapped her hands as though to persuade the pair of them to stop all this silliness and calm down. 'You can see she's not capable of murdering anyone, let alone a deranged lunatic twice her size.'

Gran grinned proudly. 'Aren't I? You'd be amazed what I can achieve when I set my mind to it. Besides, what would you have done if you only had a few months to live?'

Mum's face folded with hesitant understanding, the realisation that this was happening settling in, her body slumping.

'Do send Linda my apologies for taking advantage of her hospitality but I'm not sorry for putting an end to all of this,' Gran said and with that, DS Lowes led her away.

The Day After the Murder

Her Sister

The room had two squeaky brown sofas facing each other but it smelt the same as the one in Islington. Old trainers and B.O. There was no table or video recorder this time. It was the sort of place where they brought you a cup of tea and the news that your family had been wiped out in a pile up on the A27. Whatever was happening right then, they were keeping it on the downlow.

I couldn't help but notice I was still contained though, despite the lack of locks on the door. But this wasn't an official interview, that was for sure. It had the feel of a parent-teacher conference about it. The space was nondescript, the paintwork bland and the poster on the pinboard suggested that if I saw something odd, I should report it. Well, this was odd alright. No one had told me what the hell I was doing there yet. Surely, they had everything they needed – a dead psychopath and an angry granny with at least ten thousand reasons to kill him and nothing to lose admitting she'd done it. Sounded to me like they should take the win and let the rest of us get back to plotting her escape from jail.

The door clicked shut and D.S. Lowes offered me a seat opposite the one she was taking. The geezer she'd introduced me to outside, squished down next to her awkwardly on the sofa like it was three sizes too small for him. He unbuttoned his jacket and dislodged the bunch of paperwork mashed under his armpit, his little piggy eyes set on finding somewhere to dump it. Good luck in here, mate. I folded my arms across my chest in case he was planning on giving it to me, but in the end, he balanced it on his massive man-spread. Lowes moulded herself against the armrest as far from his thigh as his unhealthy lifestyle would allow, an invisible shield of anti-douchebag repellent radiating off her. We made eye-contact and looked away just as quickly. Nuff said.

'So, Olivia, or do you prefer Olive?'

'I'd prefer sir.'

'Right. Sir it is.' Like we were buddies. I glanced over at Lowes, but she refused to meet my eyes this time.

'First of all, I'd like to thank you for coming in to help with our enquiries. I've invited DS Lowes to join us today because our investigations so far suggest that Connor McGann's death may well be connected to the harassment charges filed against him.'

No shit, Sherlock. 'Not sure I'll be much help. You lot know everything there is to know about the luno.'

DS Richard Hardy leant forward and Lowes bent back, curving her spine around the top of the sofa. Only subtly like I wouldn't notice but I saw everything. After last time, I knew to be on guard around these shady jokers.

'We were more interested in your movements within the timescale in question.'

'Right, but why? You know, like, if my gran's confessed –' I pulled at my neckline and scratched my collarbone. '– I don't really understand why I'm here at all.'

'We just need to tie up a few loose ends. Make sure we haven't missed anything.'

I inhaled impatiently, the stagnant air whistling through my nose. 'Go on then.' Bust a move.

'According to your witness statement, you were home from approximately two fifteen in the afternoon until quarter to seven on the evening before last.'

I shrugged. 'That's what I said.'

'You also stated that your girlfriend, Florence Parker, arrived at your house at six thirty, just before your parents left for the theatre.'

'I am correct.'

Hardy peered down at his notes like he was stewing on some sketchy detail. When he looked up, he had a cleft in his forehead from where he'd been furrowing it. 'When she arrived, Florence was wearing a distinctive pink puffer jacket and a large furry hat.'

What! This guy. 'You've making it sound like some massive Russian bearskin thing. It was a bucket hat. Like, it was normal-sized.'

'A normal-sized hat,' DS Hardy repeated, producing a pen from inside his jacket and writing something down. My lips rounded in protest at his absurd attention to detail but he stabbed a full stop on the page and carried on. 'At which point, after an interval of approximately fifteen minutes mainly spent upstairs where there are no cameras, you both went out leaving Emily alone in the house until your return at ten thirteen, the exact time of which you can be certain of because you were conscious of getting back before your parents noted your absence.'

'Yup. Like I said.'

He stared straight at me. 'Were you conscious of the time because you were worried about your parents finding out you'd gone out or because you knew you might be asked?'

I glanced at Lowes but she let the pause drag, waiting for me to answer.

'How would I know I might be asked?'

'Did you realise you might be called upon to explain your movements on the night in question?'

'What? Wait, I looked at the time because I wanted to make sure we were back before ten thirty coz my old dear had made me promise I wouldn't leave Emily on her own.'

Hardy shuffled through the paperwork again, scanning some document and finally nodding to himself like he had everything he needed. I jammed my hands under my legs to keep them from straying towards the raw patch under my T-shirt. 'Can you tell us again where you and Florence went after you left the house?'

'Me and Florence went to the park –' I said in the hoity-toity tone my mum always used whenever some clown was trying to sell her faster wi-fi connection, '– where we partook in the consumption of several bottles of cider.'

Lowes swung her knee, swapping her legs over and creepy Uncle Dick looked confused, his voice cagey like he was feeling his way through the next question. 'You didn't want to go to a pub where there might have been other people who could have backed up this account?'

'What? No. Why would I have – how would I have known I'd need anyone to back up anything? We went to the park because it was a nice evening and it was cheap. If I'd known it was going to be important, I'd have flashed a few of the ten million cameras on the way just to make sure we had a nice solid alibi.'

Hardy gave me an exaggerated doubletake. Like worst acting ever. Even Lowe's impartial expression faltered.

'You seem very aware of the cameras,' he exclaimed.

'Isn't everyone?'

His eyebrows arched. 'Some more than others, it seems. We will be checking the footage, of course.'

'Good. Finally, something positive might come out of having my civil rights exploited.' I threw myself against the back of the sofa. Fidgeted like I had an itch on my shoulder blade. Forced myself to stop. This was all getting a bit déjà vu-y.

He pulled a regrettable sad face. 'Unfortunately, as you may be aware, given your apparently extensive knowledge of closed-circuit systems, coverage in the area surrounding the park and indeed the roads leading to Connor McGann's house is patchy to say the least.'

I rubbed my back against the pleather cover again. 'I'm not sure what you're getting at.'

'Just that we're unable to corroborate your version of events at this time, that's all.' He stared across the room unblinkingly, waiting for me to say something. When I didn't, he looked down at his notes again. 'You also stated that you didn't take your phones with you so there's no GPS trail proving where you were either. Why was that again?'

What was this? They had my grandmother in custody. What did they need to keep investigating all of it for? I had things to do, for God's sake. Places to be. 'Because the thought of Connor McGann stabbing us all to death has turned my mum into a paranoid freak so now that she's worked out how to use Find my Kid on her iPhone, she uses it to track us down every ten minutes. If I'd taken it with me, she'd have known.'

'And would she have known Florence hadn't taken hers?'

I shot forward, vague waves of PTSD washing over me. The feeling I wasn't in control. 'Yes, I told you. She was freaking out. She made Flo share her location with her in case anything happened to me. What could she say? No? Have you met my mother?'

DS Hardy rubbed his chin. 'Mmm. It's very convenient though, wouldn't you say, that neither of you can prove where you were. Or you weren't?'

'It's very inconvenient, I'd say.' I slapped my hand on the armrest, harder than I meant to and Lowes jumped like I'd massively startled her. I brazened it out. 'Look, sorry, I don't understand. My gran's already confessed to killing him, right? Much as I wish she wasn't banged up for it, I don't really get why I'm here.'

Seemed I'd woken Lowes up. She finally spoke. 'We're having trouble piecing together your grandmother's story, Olive.' Use the suspect's first name, establish rapport. 'She seems unsure of certain events. Such as the time and place of the offence. The method she used to kill Mr McGann. How she was able to do it.'

Good old Gran. If anyone was going to pull off an insanity plea it was her. Guess it wasn't that much of a leap.

'Well, like she said, she's been losing it a bit lately. The woman's nearly eighty and the meds they've got her on are like, cartel-style quality. Before they cut it with baking powder and talc and all that shit.'

'Is that right?' Hardy asked, overeager and interested.

'I'd imagine. Jeez. I mean, we've all got Netflix, right?' I pressed my tongue to the roof of my mouth and looked at my nails. Dry blood stained the tips down to my cuticles. I pulled at my top again to cover my chest. I didn't even remember scratching it up. 'So, what's your theory then, if you don't think she did it? That my five-foot girlfriend and I waited until it was dark, lured Connor down into a dark alley, did him in and then made it back before anyone noticed. Oh my days. That's a bit of an ask, isn't it? Like me, maybe, I could understand. Emily's my sister and all, but Flo? We've only just got back together. Be a bit much for a third date, don't you think? A bottle of Bulmers and a spot of murder in the first?' It wasn't our third date but I didn't know what the acceptable etiquette was regards to all of that. Dinner beforehand, maybe? Manslaughter after a musical? Who knew?

Hardy budged forward with a squeak, nodding like we were in agreement. 'We did think that. It takes a lot to actually kill someone, to watch them die.'

'I thought he died in the ambulance?'

'Bit much for an outsider, like you say,' he continued like I hadn't spoken. 'Maybe she was happier staying at home.'

He bobbed encouragingly again and looked to Lowes for confirmation. This role playing was bloody terrible. I nearly said something but it would have only dragged it out.

'That would make more sense,' he continued in the style of a Cbeebies presenter. 'Murder's a crime of passion. It's usually personal. I think you're right. I don't think your girlfriend would have done it. Not actually pulled the trigger, as it were. The stakes weren't high enough. Now Emily on the other hand… Emily had good reason to want him dead.'

This was genuinely very impressive police work. It was like watching Law and Order in a dodgy accent, but I refused to accommodate him with a reply.

'So –' Like the pieces were all falling into place, '– if Florence didn't participate in the murder, maybe she stayed behind. Let you and Emily see to the rest.'

I narrowed my eyes. 'Not that I'm trying to land my girlfriend anywhere near this thing but you have looked at the home security footage of that night. You can see Milly's still in the house when we leave, right?'

'We can see someone who looks very much like Emily in the house and you and someone who looks very much like your girlfriend leave, yes.'

'Oh, come on now. Be serious. What is this?'

'It was a nice evening, by your own definition. So nice, according to your statement, you went to the park rather than stay indoors.'

I spread my hands waiting for the question.

'So, what was the purpose of Florence wearing a thick winter coat and an unusually large hat?'

'Man, why d'you got to keep dissing the hat? It's a nice hat. I gave it to her. It's what you do. If someone gives you a hat, you wear it. Even if it's fricking massive or whatever.' Wankers. Now I was going to feel bad about that hat for, like, ever. And it was a nice hat. It wasn't my fault I had to wait until spring to give it to her after our break. Making me feel bad. There was nothing wrong with it.

There was a knock at the door and someone poked their head through. What now? DC Hardy dragged himself up from the flat cushion like a fisherman hauling in a whale and rolled out the room to speak to them. DC Lowes swiped her hair from her eyes and licked her lips like she was about to say something, but a swollen finger beckoned her into the corridor before she had a chance. I could feel a damp puddle collecting under my thighs, the heat in the airless room weighing down on me, dormant like it hadn't been ruffled by a breeze since these four walls were built around it.

It was starting to rattle me, being there. *Was* rattling me. The leading questions. The fake camaraderie. I'd been here before and despite getting away with a slapped wrist the last time, this was murder. They weren't going to let it go so easily. I couldn't count on being left out of their overzealous theories, even with Gran happily taking the rap for it all.

I didn't even understand why she was. Why she'd confessed right away. Hadn't even waited to see what evidence they had, but whatever, this was obviously what she wanted. Her last gift to us all, our fears and worries locked away in a lead box and tied up nicely with a bow. Her swan song if you like.

Hardy opened the door again, his sweaty forehead glistening. He pointed a finger at me. 'Don't leave the country,' he said and jiggled off again.

Lowes walked back in with a smile. 'You're free to go.'

I stared at her warily, rising slowly to my feet. 'What was that all about?'

She opened the door and I slipped out into the blue laminate-floored hallway.

‘Seems your grandmother was telling the truth,’ she said in a way that suggested she shouldn’t be saying anything. ‘The cause of death has come back.’

I turned to her expectantly and she glanced back down the empty corridor. ‘Respiratory failure due to an acute overdose of morphine. Her very first explanation before she started rattling off every possible means of death ever recorded. Nice move by the way, let her know – not that anyone’s convinced, but it’s creative. Keeping DS Hardy on his toes, that’s for sure.’

I stopped dead. ‘So how do you know it was definitely her and not one of us?’

She studied me. ‘It’s like she said. She had the motive, the means and the opportunity. It’s not a closed case but according to the pathologist, the drugs would have entered his system no more than ten minutes before he collapsed, probably as he was heading for the gym some time before seven am. We’ll be checking the bins between his house and the community centre but the post-mortem shows the only things in his stomach were the undigested remains of a protein shake and a nut-based biscuit. The working theory is that Bella mixed crushed morphine tablets into the carton when she was alone in the kitchen and he drank it unknowingly the next morning. Do me a favour though and keep the news to your immediate circle until they’ve had a chance to charge your grandmother formally. Her legal advisor’s on the way. If he’s got any sense, he’ll play the cancer card. Push for the charges to be dropped in light of that fact that she’s not likely to live long enough to make it worthwhile pursuing a prosecution.’

I scrambled down the corridor, struggling to keep up with her, a mad rush of questions busting up my throat like vomit. 'Should you be telling me all of this?'

'The cause of death will be common knowledge within the hour. The rest of it's common sense.' She bustled through the reception and held the main door open for me. 'Besides,' she added like an afterthought, 'when my colleagues searched McGann's room, they found a number of items indicating he was planning a final fatal attack against your sister. I'm glad that didn't happen.' She smiled again. 'Send my regards to your family, won't you? And be sure to pass on everything I said.'

I opened my mouth to thank her but she'd already turned her back and gone.

2 Days After the Murder

Her Mum

Anyone would have thought we were celebrating the Coronation or some sort of Jubilee, the amount of bunting the girls had draped over the house. The table was practically sagging under the weight of hummus and the atmosphere was one of carefree joyfulness. Emily bounced into the kitchen clutching an empty plastic container and a cardboard sleeve which she proceeded to happily shove alongside the rest of the three for two packaging.

‘Steady on, love. You’ve got to rinse that pot out and squash it all up. Honestly, you kids. The recycling bins are going to unionise if you manage to ram anything else into them.’

‘Okay, Mum,’ she sang doing nothing about it and dashing out again.

‘Quick,’ Olive squealed. ‘They’re coming.’

All three of the girls, my two and Flo, lined up at the window vying for a view of the car pulling into the driveway followed by a spate of muttering which was presumably the sound of David helping my mother up the path. I stood behind the sea of shoulders and hair, straining for a peek with varying degrees of success. They were all taller than me but it was enough to hear their squawks of delight and know that everything was as it should be again.

And I should have anticipated being bowled over as they abruptly spun around and thundered to the front door. That was on me, but a thousand thoughtless post-adolescents could have run through me right then and nothing would have spoilt my mood. Really, you don't know what you've got until you almost lose it.

I heard David shout, 'We're back,' through the battalion cry that greeted them and within a moment or two, Emily and Olive were escorting Bella into the kitchen like the doddery old dear I suddenly realised she was.

'Here she is,' I bellowed only just allowing myself to believe it when I took her into my arms.

'Come on then, Gran. Tell us everything.'

'What happened?'

'How did you manage to get off?'

'Did you really do it?

'Why did they let you go?'

'How did you get away with it?'

'Are you alright?'

'How did you kill him, Gran?'

'My goodness, girls. This isn't Guantanamo Bay, is it? Can't a hardened criminal get a decent cuppa before you bring out the waterboards? It seems so long since I had an English breakfast tea with normal milk, I can hardly remember what it tastes like. It's all UHT inside. Clare…' She fixed her rheumy blue eyes on me. 'Tell me you bought ginger nuts.'

'We did better than that, Gran.' Olive hooked her arm through her elbow and led her into the dining room.

'Oh, my.'

Flo tottered through with a pile of plates and Emily turned and treated me to a thumbs up and an enormous toothy grin. I'd forgotten what she looked like with light in her eyes and I must say, I was quite choked up at the sight of her. It was as though the burden of existing had been lifted and now she could live again.

David put his arms around my shoulders and pulled me towards him and for a second there, we simply stared at each other.

'Let me put the kettle on,' I said, rubbing his love handles affectionately and breaking away. 'Don't want to get beaten up in the yard.'

'Don't drop the soap in the showers, whatever you do,' David said because he could always be relied upon to take a joke too far but I feigned amusement anyway and set about making the tea.

Considering the girls had earned enough Nectar points to qualify for a free shop next time we popped into Sainsbury's, they'd made light work of the lunch spread. I'd only been gone five minutes and already the quiches and stuffed piquante peppers had gone. My mother was masticating on a vegetable samosa and refusing to elaborate on the details of her grisly crime. Her incarceration and release on the other hand, were apparently fair game should anyone wish to know how she outsmarted the long arm of the law.

'I kept smiling sweetly and changing my story. It isn't hard to make people think you're cuckoo at my age. I spend most of my time trying to convince everyone that I'm not. All anybody sees when they look at us senior citizens is a bunch of demented old biddies and all they hear is half-baked nonsense every time we speak.'

'And all they smell is wee,' David said and I must admit I did laugh that time, not because it was true – always – or even funny but because I was happy and sometimes that's all it takes.

‘Anyway, they realised there was no point attempting to convict me. I mean, officially I’ve been released on bail pending a trial. Not a flight risk they said but the fact is, if they put me in front of a jury, I’ll only play the dementia card, if I even live long enough to get to court. Which I must say is a pity. I’d rather like to have been prosecuted. It looks jolly fun on the telly and I’d have quite happily represented myself. Now, that would have been quite a finale. Everyone would have remembered me then,’ she said, which brought the mood down somewhat, but I said, ‘Mother, you will always be remembered, no matter what.’

And before we knew it everyone was dabbing napkins against their eye ducts, trying desperately not to smear their mascara. All except for David who didn’t wear make-up and had taken advantage of the diversion in order to steal the last remaining Scotch egg. I didn’t know why. He’d only complain later that the ones he made from scratch were better.

‘Listen, Gran.’ Olivia lowered her voice. ‘I know you don’t want to talk about it but we all think you’re amazing. I hope you don’t ever, ever feel, like, well…’

‘Guilty for doing what you did.’ Flo topped my mother’s plate up with onion bhajis for want of a damehood and Emily rested her head against her shoulder, at peace.

Bella smiled enigmatically, wiping greasy pastry flakes into Milly’s long curls and said, ‘Don’t worry, I won’t. I’ve only ever done what’s for the best.’

And I think that was the moment that it actually sunk in, that he was dead. Connor McGann, the sociopath who wanted to destroy my daughter and take us all down with her, was gone and half of me was euphoric and the other half expected to feel at least a tiny bit contrite, but that was euphoric too. Perhaps the wickedness of Bella's actions would hit home after the initial relief had worn off, when this all stopped feeling like one of those horrible dreams that you're gradually able to control as you awaken. Perhaps in years to come the shame of this murder would taint our family history, but for now it didn't seem sinful at all. It felt like justice had been done and there was no one to miss him but Linda. Now for that I did feel bad. It would certainly make bumping into her in the supermarket awkward. I would be online shopping for the foreseeable, that was for sure.

And then as if I'd summoned her, there was a rap at the door and we all looked at each other, plates wilting limply, a selection of bite-sized snacks dangling en route to our mouths. David shot through to the sitting room and looked out of the window.

'Good God,' he said. 'It's her. Linda. What do we do?'

It took a woman of substance to speak and when she did my mother said, 'Let her in, Clare. It has to happen sometime, but maybe let's not show off all of this.'

There was a collective stampede as everyone brushed themselves down, checking each other's teeth for debris and scattering to different rooms, the door to this one closed firmly behind us. I found myself in the hallway and I must say, I stood there for a moment gathering my courage and everything else I needed to get through this next eventuality.

Another rap vibrated through the varnished wood and this time I opened it.

‘Linda,’ I croaked remorsefully, with absolutely no pretence. The very sight of her there on my doorstep, every bit as broken and brave as I would have been in her shoes, had brought all my latent emotions to the surface. The sociopath was her son after all. ‘Won’t you come in?’

She remained where she was, her bag wedged against her side, hands gripping it like the side of a lifeboat. ‘I wanted to speak to your mother. Is she here?’

I stepped back and ushered her in with a tight nod. Goodness knows where I found the strength. Any faith I had in my knees had vapourised the moment Linda had knocked on the door. A distinct clamour of flower pots and bikes being shunted around resonated from the side passage, which I guessed correctly was David and the girls bailing on us and I wasn’t displeased about it. There was only one person Linda needed to see.

Bella attempted to stand when we walked in to the sitting room but Linda shook her head, the nurse in her overriding any other instincts she might have had upon seeing my mother. And then she surprised me by bowing down and giving Bella a hug. When she drew back her eyes were watering but she held firm. Stoic. I wasn’t sure I could find it in myself to forgive so freely.

She took a deep breath and a step back, lowering herself down shakily onto the sofa and perched on the edge of the cushion, the bag still gripped in her hands like a shield. A lifeline she clung to with embedded nails and white knuckles, tension rippling beneath her blue veins.

The silence I thought would go on forever was finally shattered when she said, ‘Why did you do it?’ Her words a whisper on a breeze. I had to sink down onto David's armchair before my legs gave way beneath me. Clutching the armrest, I steadied my breathing and strained forward to hear her. We were all civilised here, after all.

'I'm dying,' Bella said. 'Anyone would have done the same.'

'Not anyone.'

'Well, I just did what was right.' She was brazen. 'The only person to blame in any of this was your son and he got what he deserved so…'

'But why confess?'

Bella sighed, her head wobbling like she wasn't entirely sure herself. 'I didn't know who I was protecting, to be honest. Not at first.'

I whirled around towards her, my eyes on stalks, everything I'd known to be true until that moment, a lie. Bella lent forward and laid her hand on Linda's. The poor woman looked down and blinked slowly, composing herself for what was to come while Bella launched into a sermon with the same inappropriate enthusiasm she used to dissect her weekly dose of Midsomer Murders.

'I knew it wasn't anyone Connor owed money to. They'd have stabbed him or shot him. And there'd have been no trace of the body.' She seemed very confident about this. 'So then I thought that Flo and Milly had pulled the old switcheroo. Left Flo sitting in the house with the CCTV for an alibi while Emily and Olive saw to business, but I couldn't quite reconcile Emily's state of mind with that and Olivia is terrible at performing arts. She gets that from you, Clare.'

She glanced over, her eyebrows raised and I'd have objected but for the fact I was finding this all rather hard to take in. She tapped Linda's bag.

'Then I thought for sure that it had been David with those blasted macaroons because he was very persistent with them despite being well aware you had an allergy, Linda. I was certain he was counting on the fact that Clare and I were so sick of them by then, there'd be no chance we'd have any, leaving a fool-proof trap for Connor. We all know almond masks the taste of arsenic, but then I realised – David's so precious about his cooking he wouldn't waste it on someone who was about to die. Besides, he's just not that clever. He might bake a nice Victoria Sponge but he's no master criminal.' She lowered her voice. 'And I don't mean any offence, Clare.'

I hadn't taken any. It wasn't something I thought he aspired to be. She patted my hand. 'He's grown on me since he turned his hand to cooking.'

'Thank you, Mum. I'm sure he'll be pleased to hear it's only taken thirty-odd years.' I shook my head. I was allowing myself to get distracted when I should have been focusing on every word. I had the horrible feeling of having the world pulled out from under my feet and I was half-expecting my mother to point the finger at me next.

Instead she said, 'So that brought me back to me and my own connections to the underworld but of course, if that was the case, they'd have never found a body, as I said. Furthermore, I'd have known if I'd orchestrated it all. I'm not actually demented.'

I'd never thought she was, but I was beginning to question my own sanity. I took an intake of air which came out sounding like a seal on heat and I should know. We'd had a ghastly encounter with one on a day trip to Eastbourne not long before. Bella swivelled towards me with a touch of the Hercule Poirot.

'Honestly, Clare. Don't tell me you actually thought I'd done it.'

'Why wouldn't I?' I gasped. 'You told me you had, Mother! Besides, what were you doing in Linda's kitchen all that time?'

'Looking for biscuits like I said.'

'Oh, for Goodness' sake. It's been days, Mum. If you aren't a homicidal maniac, don't you think you could have told me?'

'I'm sorry, dear. I love you very much but I still shiver at the memory of those nativity plays performances. One year she even forgot the baby's name.' My mother looked at Linda in a way that felt very much like a betrayal and a flashback of my teacher hissing *Jesus* from stage right rocked me. I was sure he said it with more emphasis than necessary. A child picks up on these things.

'I knew perfectly well that you'd overreact,' Bella continued kindly. 'You are prone to and I didn't want you telling the police what really happened.'

'I don't know what happened!'

Bella lifted her hand as though that was only to be expected. 'In your defence, I wasn't a hundred percent sure myself until the results of the post-mortem came back. As soon as that fat detective said it was a fatal overdose of Oramorph, I thought, oh that'll be Linda, up to her old tricks again.'

That was it. That was me done. It was like I'd turned the telly on halfway through the climax to a series I hadn't seen or even heard of. It could have been Danish for all I understood.

'How did you know how I'd done it?' Linda said, finally meeting Bella's eyes. 'The first thing you told the police was that you'd put it in the protein shake.'

'Well, that's what I'd do. Great minds.' Bella tapped her temple and winked.

'But why tell them you did it? That's what I don't understand.'

My mother took her hand again. 'Linda, you have always been very kind to me. I will never forget those Viennese Swirls you used to bring me on my darkest days.' Oh, Viennese Swirls. How was I ever supposed to compete with that? 'I've only got a few months left to make everything square in this world and I feel like I've achieved that now. I won't even make it to court, if they even bother with all that. Justice has been done. No point in everyone wasting their time with an investigation or some long drawn-out trial.'

'I don't know what to say.'

'You don't have to say anything. I hope you never do. Same goes for you, Clare. Not even to David and the girls. Let them think I'm the woman they wish I was.'

I tutted. As if I'd risk repeating any of this. I'd be the one locked up. In an asylum. Any more surprises and I'd be checking myself in.

'Well, thank you,' Linda said quietly.

'Thank *you*,' Bella replied. 'It can't have been easy.'

'What –' I said, my mind finally clearing. "What made you do it, if you don't mind me asking?'

Linda sighed, her eyes clouding over and I realised I was holding my breath.

'I was putting his washing away just before he put a lock on his door and I found it all hidden in one of his drawers. This stuff he shouldn't have had – duct tape, rope, those plastic clips they use for handcuffs. A bottle of acid and I knew, just like I knew as soon as I found the cat in his room – sorry, yes. I probably should have mentioned that but, well, I hadn't realised it was yours until you said and then, well, none of the parenting books tell you how to deal with that, do they?'

I knew it! The poor thing had never been the same. He was still hiding under the sofa. I'd have killed the lunatic all over again just for that if I had the chance.

'I was too late you see. I tried to protect him from his father, but the damage was already done. Years and years of living with a monster – it can't not have an effect, can it? Or maybe it's genetics, maybe there was nothing I could have done. All I knew was he wasn't going to stop, not until something bad happened, just like his father would never have stopped until I was dead. Until we all were and I don't have any regrets about that but it's not the same, is it? As your son.'

I hoped that was hypothetical. I was quite lost for words. Roger too? It was getting to be a habit but of course it made perfect sense. Only my mother could have worked it out right from the start, but then she always did and invariably spoilt it for the rest of us. I was glad in a way that she hadn't told me.

'It wasn't his fault, you see. None of this was. It was mine. I should have been stronger all those years ago, walked away the first time his father hit me, but I didn't, I stayed and brought Connor into it too. My beautiful boy, he never stood a chance. And I thought he'd got away with it, that he'd managed to survive that man, to overcome his natural predisposition but then little things started creeping in and each time I convinced myself that I'd be able to smooth it all over and make it okay – the gambling, the debts. Maybe if I'd let him face the consequences sooner, he wouldn't have felt so entitled, maybe it wouldn't have all spilt over into something else, but in the end, he was just like his father – undermining me and making me think I was going mad. I thought I deserved it because I was weak but then I saw how he was doing it to Emily and she's such a wonderful girl. The thought of him hurting her, I just couldn't…' she shuddered and looked up. 'He wasn't going to stop. It was never going to stop so I had to do something myself.'

'Where did you get the morphine?'

She batted her hand. 'Oh, people are always returning unused medication to the oncology ward. They're supposed to take it to a pharmacy but I suppose they want to see a familiar face one last time, someone who knows what they went through. A connection to their loved one after they've passed. It only took 200 milligrams mixed into one of those ready-made milkshake things.'

Bella nodded, taking some sort of pleasure in her unnerving homicidal insights.

'He drank one every morning before he went to the gym. Obsessively, one might say. And I meant to confess straight away, but when the policeman came round, I was in so much shock… I shouldn't have been but I kept thinking all morning that maybe he hadn't drunk it, that he'd noticed the taste and thrown it away and part of me hoped – much as I wanted to end it for him, for all of us – that I'd failed, that I had one more day with him.'

Her eyes glistened and I got up and sat beside her, my arm around her shoulders, my thigh pressed against her leg. I couldn't fathom the torment she'd faced every day, watching the life she'd created distort, spreading darkness instead of light. Endlessly waiting for the moment a knock on the door brought the news she'd been dreading – not that it was over, but that her son had done something so unspeakable it was all anyone would speak of again. I couldn't imagine the battle she'd gone through making the decision she had, seeing it through, knowing she had no choice but my heart went out to her for it.

'I wanted to protect him but he was gone, my little boy, gone long ago. I failed him and I just needed a couple of days to grieve, to really come to terms with everything before I handed myself in. But then they rang me to say you'd already confessed.'

She looked up as startled, no doubt, as she'd felt when she'd first heard. My mother smiled.

'That was the easy part, you handled the worst and you mustn't feel guilty, not ever. You did the right thing. For everyone, including Connor. Life's fragile but it can also be painful and sometimes it's kinder not to drag it out. I should know.'

And with that we formed a huddle and wept for a while.

91 Days After the Murder

Her

The sky was cloudless but for a few thin wisps of vapour gathering on the hazy horizon. Seagulls soared, dipping and diving into the rippling ocean, scattering dappled light, their cries carrying on the warm breeze as an ancient Spitfire puttered in the distance. I threaded my arm through Mum's and our steps fell into line, our feet beating a slow rhythm against the coarse dry grass.

'Alright?' I said.

She patted my hand. 'I'm alright. How are you holding up?'

I pressed my lips together in the semblance of a smile, my head askance. 'Oh, you know.'

Olive swivelled towards us and pointed up at the plane above. ''Do you think that's her? Keeping an eye on us.'

Dad followed her gaze, shielding his eyes against the glare of sunlight glinting off the metal.

'Could be,' he laughed. 'She was never going to make it as an angel.'

I squeezed Mum's arm and her eyes crinkled. 'Well, she'd be pleased to hear that, at least.'

We waved at the plane as it neared, our cries muffled by the roar of the engine and then as if on cue, it flew high above us forming a perfect somersault.

'Definitely her,' Olive said and we all grinned, picking up the pace along the cliff path once again until we reached a weather-worn bench.

'This do?' Dad said, looking back at Mum for confirmation.

'This is perfect.'

We sat for a while in silence looking out to sea, our breathing indistinguishable from the ebb and flow of the waves surging down below, our faces turned towards the sun.

'Nice to be back, Olive?' I said eventually, opening my eyes.

'I know, right? Long time, no see.'

'Think we've seen more of you these last few months than we ever did when you lived here,' Mum said, nudging her knee and Olive twisted her mouth into a half-smile of resignation.

'Hopefully next year won't be quite so hectic.'

'Hectic?' Dad snorted. 'That's one way to put it.'

A few beats passed and all thoughts remained unsaid, all feelings contained, but our minds intertwined wordlessly.

Gran was right when she said she wouldn't go down for murder, although she picked a hell of a way to get away with it. At first, she started sleeping more, upping the meds, then within a few weeks of Connor's death, she was half the size she'd been and the doctors admitted there was nothing more they could do other than try to make her comfortable. They never succeeded. Mum took personal leave to look after her and provide the full-time palliative care she needed and, in the end, she died in her own home with the four of us at her side. She was the strongest woman I knew.

I sat at the cliff's summit soundlessly tracking the gradual drift of a tanker sailing out to sea, a billow of dark smoke rising from it, blurring the boundary between the Earth and the sky. The celestial sphere. I pictured the twinkle in my grandmother's eyes before she closed them for the last time. I could feel her but I knew she wasn't there, not then nor now, but still she was by my side.

Dad was getting antsy, his foot tapping on the mud speckled ground, his thigh chafing against my bare leg.

'Is it too early for a baguette?' he said, lugging the picnic bag onto his lap. 'We've got camembert, rocket and cranberry or goat's cheese, tomato and grilled peppers. Or one of each, I've done plenty.'

'Thank you, David.'

He passed them down the row to a flurry of exclamations, first appreciative and then irritated at the amount of clingfilm he'd used to wrap them, then appreciative again. Rapturous even.

'Do you know,' Mum ruminated, her eyes fixed on the distance, a chunk of white crust distorting her cheek. 'We were listening to Tom Jones on the radio on the way over here and I've just realised something. That song, Delilah, it's –'

'A sing-along about an innocent woman being slaughtered in her own home,' Olive said.

Mum swallowed her mouthful. 'Hmm. It's quite taken the edge off it for me, I must say. I'm not sure how I feel about it now.'

'Outraged, Mum, that's how we feel about it. It's a popular song trivialising a women's murder.' Her finger was up in the air. Some things were getting back to normal at least.

'Does it though?'

'Put it like this,' Olive said, wiping a drizzle of oil off her chin. 'If everyone stuck their arms in the air and went *how awful, somebody find the sick bastard who did this* then great, good work, Tom, but instead we're all supposed to sing *Why, Delilah? Why you do this to him?* It's pure victim shaming and it's endemic.'

'Haaa.' My mum exhaled like a horse and her shoulders collapsed. 'Feels like every day something's taken away from us.'

'I know, right. First it was poor old Jimmy Saville and now this. And they call it progress.'

My sister rolled her eyes and I shook my head and laughed. This was what I had to put up with for the next three months until she went back to university – Olive and her opinions, but I couldn't have asked for more. I'd never take her for granted again. I'd never take any of them for granted. Life was slowly, agonisingly sometimes, getting back on track. With Gran's house now passed on to Olive and me, we'd somehow grown up and regressed at the same time but we were becoming more like the people we'd once been before.

It had been hard in the immediate aftermath of the murder. I'd felt stunned upon hearing the news, euphoric once it had sunk in and then terrified again as though it was all yet another elaborate ruse designed to trick me, that as soon as I let my guard down, he'd attack. His being dead didn't stop him lurking around every corner or whispering in my ear, it didn't stop the graphic images of me circulating online. Talking of which, Olive deals with all of that now, the internet searches, the cease and desist emails. Which helps. And I'm learning to come to terms with everything, to live with it all.

I didn't go back to Optiks for a month after I walked out that day. Couldn't face it, the humiliation, the embarrassment. Knowing

I'd never be respected there again, that every sly look that passed between colleagues, the slightest smirk in their tone would send me plummeting back to the moment Connor went public, made me the local celebrity I would always be. If I chose to let it define me. If I couldn't move on.

I was sweating and shaky the morning I started back again, exhausted from sleep deprivation and drained by unrelenting panic, expecting a wry reception but when I stepped into the office, everyone was walking around in swimsuits. And I mean everyone. The skinny account managers with their puny chests and tiny pink nipples, Babs, who'd been fighting a losing battle with doughnuts for years. Raj, Chloe. Everyone. There was a sea of stretchmarks and insecurities spread out as far as the eye could see and I was mortified, I'm not going to lie.

I knew they were trying to be kind, to normalise what had happened to me, to readdress the balance of power in my favour, but no one wants to be confronted by that on a Monday morning and I said – I told them there was no need, that it was alright, but even then, they insisted on seeing their stand through in Bermuda shorts and beachwear, rolls of soft flesh bulging over their chairs, prickly rashes blazing against their pasty skin. And five minutes before a client meeting, when Raj said they should put their clothes on again, everybody refused. In the end, even the clients stripped off in solidarity with victims of online image abuse and I was the odd one out for being fully dressed.

It was one of the weirdest things that had ever happened to me, but then after about an hour it wasn't weird anymore. I'm not sure how legal it was but I can say this – that was the first time I'd looked anyone in the eye for months and that was the day I decided to join a charity dedicated to helping victims of stalking. I work as a volunteer there, sharing my story and helping other people who've been through the same thing as me. Men and women. No one's immune from harassment or abuse – any type of abuse. But there is help out there and things we can do to protect ourselves. There are red flags and signs that are obvious in hindsight, but there's also manipulation, coercive control, fear, bullying, blackmail and so the one thing there shouldn't be is shame.

Anyone who experiences any form of abuse is a victim - or survivor as some people prefer to call themselves. Either way, they're not at fault. The pricks who offend and the laws that protect them are. The rest of us, we're just skin and bone and matter and half the time we're a hot mess, but regardless of what anyone says, we're okay. We know we are. I know I am. Or at least I hope I will be one day.

'Is it time?' my mum said and we nodded, scrunching the clingfilm into balls and squashing it into our pockets. Olive and I stood up, arms linked around Mum as Dad delved into the bag again, emptying it of crisp packets and slices of lemon drizzle. Then he pulled out a small cardboard package and quickly brushed a few crumbs off the top. Mum shook her head, an appalled micro-expression flitting across her face, but she rearranged her features and took a deep breath, taking the box in her hands.

'Right,' she said. 'Does anyone want to say a few words?'

But there were none, not really, none that could sum up how we felt about my gran, none that could fully define who she was and so Mum lifted the lid and held her arms out in front of her.

‘Are we sure we’re allowed to do this here?’ Dad said, last minute concern overdue and irrelevant.

‘I’m pretty sure we aren’t,’ my mum said.

‘Let’s do it then,’ he smiled and she tipped the box upside down, shaking the ashes into the air which swirled, sucking them along its current and scattering what we once held so dear across the sea. We watched the cloud of silvery dust drift away like a swarm of butterflies and Mum shook the ashes one final time, letting the last of them flutter on the breeze.

And as the Spitfire climbed high in the sky above us, the pain of our raw, unhealed wounds lifted and we let go of it all.

Printed in Great Britain
by Amazon

35705567R00216